INCLUDES BONUS STORY OF
Little Shoes and Mistletoe BY SALLY LAITY

My Valentine

Tracie Peterson

THORNDIKE PRESS
A part of Gale, Cengage Learning

GALE
CENGAGE Learning·

Farmington Hills, Mich • San Francisco • New York • Waterville, Main
Meriden, Conn • Mason, Ohio • Chicago

GALE
CENGAGE Learning·

Thorndike Press, a part of Gale, Cengage Learning.

Thorndike Press® Large Print Christian Fiction.
The text of this Large Print edition is unabridged.
Other aspects of the book may vary from the original edition.
Set in 16 pt. Plantin.

LIBRARY OF CONGRESS CATALOGING-IN-PUBLICATION DATA

Names: Peterson, Tracie, author. | Laity, Sally. Little shoes and mistletoe.
Title: My valentine / Tracie Peterson.
Description: Large print edition. | Waterville, Maine : Thorndike Press, 2017. | Series: Thorndike Press large print Christian fiction | "Also includes bonus story of Little shoes and mistletoe by Sally Laity."
Identifiers: LCCN 2016047384 | ISBN 9781410496270 (hardback) | ISBN 1410496279 (hardcover)
Subjects: LCSH: Large type books. | BISAC: FICTION / Christian / Romance. | FICTION / Christian / Historical. | GSAFD: Love stories. | Christian fiction.
Classification: LCC PS3566.E7717 M9 2017 | DDC 813/.54—dc23
LC record available at https://lccn.loc.gov/2016047384

Published in 2017 by arrangement with Barbour Publishing, Inc.

Printed in the United States of America
1 2 3 4 5 6 7 21 20 19 18 17

My Valentine

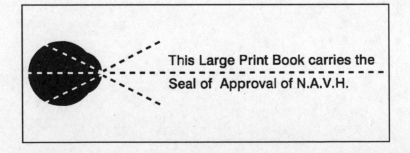

This Large Print Book carries the Seal of Approval of N.A.V.H.

MY VALENTINE

CHAPTER 1

January, 1835

Hear, O Israel: The LORD our God
is one LORD.
DEUTERONOMY 6:4

Darlene Lewy hurried to pull on warm woolen petticoats. It was a frosty January morning and living so close to the harbor waters of New York City, the Lewy house always seemed to be in a state of perpetual cold. Shivering and slipping a dark blue work dress over her head, Darlene could hear her father in his ritual of morning prayers.

"Shema Israel, Adonai eloheinu Adonai echad," he recited the Hebrew in his heavy German accent.

Darlene embraced the words to her heart. *"Hear, O Israel: The Lord our God is one Lord."* She smiled. For all of her years on earth she had awakened each morning to the sound of her father's faithful prayers.

Humming to herself, Darlene sat down at her dressing table. Taking up a hairbrush she gave her thick, curly tresses a much-needed brushing, then quickly braided and pinned it into a snug, neat bun on the top of her head. She eyed herself critically in the mirror for any escaping hairs. Dark brown eyes stared back at her from beneath shapely black brows. She was no great beauty, at least not in the eyes of New York's very snobbish social circle. But then again, she wouldn't have been welcomed in that circle, even if she had been ravishingly beautiful and wealthy to boot. No, the upper crust of New York would never have taken Darlene Lewy into its numbers, because Darlene was a Jewess.

Deciding she made a presentable picture, Darlene hurriedly made her bed and went to the kitchen to stoke up the fire and prepare breakfast. Her kitchen was a sorry little affair, but it served them well. Had her mother lived, perhaps they would have had a nicer house, instead of sharing the three-story building with her father's tailoring shop and sewing rooms. But, had her mother and little brother survived child-birth, fifteen years earlier, Darlene had little

8

doubt they'd still be living in Germany instead of America.

"Neshomeleh," Abraham Lewy said, coming into the room.

Darlene could not remember a time when he had not greeted her with the precious endearment, "my little soul." "Good morning, *Tateh,* did you sleep well?" She gave him a kiss on his leathery cheek and pulled out a chair for him to sit on.

"It is well with me, and you?"

Darlene laughed. "I'm chilled to the bone, but not to worry. I've stoked up the fire and no doubt by the time we get downstairs to the shop, Hayyim will have the stove fires blazing and ready for the day." Hayyim, her father's assistant, was a local boy of seventeen who had pleaded to learn the tailoring business. And, since Abraham had no sons to carry on his tradition of exquisitely crafted suits, he had quickly taken Hayyim under his wing. Darlene knew that the fact Hayyim's father and mother had died in a recent cholera epidemic had much to do with her father's decision, but in truth, she saw it as an answer to prayer. Her father wasn't getting any younger, and of late he seemed quite frail and sickly.

Darlene brought porridge and bread to the table and waited while her father recited

9

the blessing for bread before dishing up their portions.

"Baruch ata Adonai eloheinu melech ha-olem ha-motzi lechem min ha-Aretz." "Praise be Thou, O Lord our God, King of the universe, who brings forth bread from the earth." Abraham pulled off a chunk of bread while Darlene spooned cereal into their bowls.

"There will be little time for rest today. Our appointments are many and the work most extensive," he told her.

"I'll take care of all of the bookwork," she answered as if he didn't already know this. "I've also got Mr. Mitchell's waistcoat buttons to finish putting on. Is he coming today?"

"No, he'll come tomorrow. I told him we must have a week to finish and a week we will have."

Darlene smiled. "Eat, Tateh." The Yiddish word had never been replaced by Papa as she heard many of her neighboring friends call their fathers.

Abraham gave his attention to the food, while Darlene watched him for any telltale signs of sickness. The winter had been hard on her father and even though he'd stayed indoors except for trips to the synagogue on *Shabbes,* "Sabbath" as her American

10

friends would say, Darlene worried that the grippe or cholera or some other hideous disease would take him from her.

"You should hire another boy to help you with the work. There's no reason why you should work yourself into the ground," Darlene chided. She had taken on the role of worrier since her mother's death and even though she was only five at the time, Abraham said she filled the role quite adequately.

"*Oyb Gott vilt* — if God wills," Abraham answered and continued eating. It was his standard response to subjects he didn't wish to continue discussing.

Darlene gave the hint of an unsatisfied snort before clearing her dishes to the sink and returning for her father's. He was a stubborn man, but she loved him more dearly than life itself. She tried not to notice that his hair was now completely white, as was his beard and eyebrows. She tried, too, not to see that his coat hung a little looser around his shoulders and that his complexion had grown sallow. Time was taking its toll on Abraham Lewy.

With breakfast behind them, Darlene hurried to tidy the kitchen. Her father had already gone downstairs to begin his workday and she didn't wish to lag behind and

11

leave him alone. For reasons entirely beyond her understanding, Darlene felt compelled to watch over her father with a jealous regard. Maybe it was just concern over his winter illnesses. Maybe it was the tiniest flicker of fear down deep inside which made her question what might happen if her father died. She had no one else. Even Bubbe, her father's mother, had passed on years ago. If Abraham were to die as well, there would be no one for Darlene to turn to.

Changing her kitchen apron for the one she wore in the shop, Darlene made her way down the rickety wooden stairs. She would not allow her mind to wander into areas of morbidity. She would also say nothing to her father. He would only begin suggesting the names of local men who might make good husbands and Darlene refused to hear anything about such nonsense. She would never leave her beloved Tateh.

"Good morning," Hayyim said with a nod as Darlene passed by.

"Good morning." Her words were rather curt given the fact that her mind was still on the distasteful idea of marriage. Hayyim, three years her junior, was very much taken with her, and looked at her with such longing that it made Darlene uncomfortable.

He was a child as far as she was concerned and his feelings were nothing more than a crush. She could only pray that God would forbid such a union.

She was nearly to the front counter when the door bells jingled merrily and two men entered the shop. Their warm breath puffed out against the accompanying cold air and Darlene couldn't help but shiver from the draft.

Dennison Blackwell, followed by his son, Pierce, entered Lewy & Company, stomping their feet at the door. A light snow had started to fall and the evidence left itself on the doormat.

Abraham stepped forward to greet them. "Welcome," he said, his w's sounding like v's. "It is fit only for sitting by the fire, no?"

"Indeed you are right," Dennison Blackwell said, shaking off little flakes of snow from his coat lapel. "It's only just now begun to snow, but the air is cold enough to freeze you to the carriage seats."

"And your driver?" Abraham said, looking past Pierce and out the window. "Would he not want to sit in the kitchen and warm up by the stove?"

"That's kind of you, but we won't be terribly long and Jimson doesn't mind the cold. He's from the north and actually embraces this weather."

Abraham smiled. "Then God did have a purpose for such things."

Dennison laughed. "Yes, I suppose He did at that."

Darlene watched the exchange with little interest. What had captured her attention, however, was the tall, broad-shouldered form of the younger Mr. Blackwell. She stole glances at him from over the ledger counter and nearly blushed to her toes when he looked up and met her stare with a wink and a smile.

"Oy," she muttered under her breath and hurried to lower her eyes back to her work.

"It seems," Dennison was saying, "that both Pierce and I will be required to attend the annual Valentine's ball."

"Ah, this is the auction where bachelors are sold to their dates, no?" Abraham said in a lowered voice that suggested the entire affair was a bit risque. "Such doings!"

"True enough. Pierce has been abroad for some time and now finds that his wardrobe could use a bit of updating. We'll start with a suit for the ball and he can come back later to arrange for other things."

Pierce smiled. "My father highly praises your work. I was going to journey to London and have my suits made there, but perhaps

14

I won't have to travel so far after all."

"Certainly you won't," Abraham said with complete confidence. "We do much better work here. You will be more than happy, I think."

Taking their outer coats, Abraham motioned them into the back room where he and Hayyim would take measurements and suggest materials. Darlene couldn't help but watch the trio as they passed through the curtained doorway. Pierce Blackwell's dark eyes had penetrated her strong facade of indifference and it shook her to the very core of her existence. How could one man affect her in that way? Especially one Gentile man.

She busied herself with the ledger, but her curiosity was getting the better of her. Not knowing what they were talking about was most maddening. If she dusted the shelves near the back room entrance, perhaps she would be able to overhear their conversation. Taking up a dusting rag, she moved methodically through the small room.

"I suppose the easiest way to explain it," Dennison Blackwell said, "is that we, too, serve one God, but one God with three very distinctive portions."

Darlene's hand stopped dusting. *What in the world is going on?*

Dennison continued. "We Christians believe in one God, just as you of the Jewish faith believe. However, we believe from scripture that God has made Himself available to His children in three different ways. He is God our judge, God our Savior, and God our spiritual leader and consolation. Thus we say, God the Father, the Son, and the Holy Spirit. It's like an apple. You have the core of the fruit where the seeds lay in wait. Next you have the sweet meat of the fruit itself and finally the tough, durable skin which covers over all. One apple, yet three parts."

Darlene nearly dropped her cloth. What kind of *meshugge* "crazy" talk was this? God and apples? Did the Gentiles worship fruit or was that all that existed between their ears for brains? The very idea of comparing God to an apple outraged her. She dusted furiously at the door's edge without seeing her work. Instead, she concentrated on the curtain which separated her from the men.

"Hold up your arm, Mr. Blackwell," her father said authoritatively.

"Please, call me Pierce. My father says you two have become good friends. I'd be honored to consider you the same."

"The honor is mine. Your father is a good man."

Silence seemed to hold the room captive for several minutes and Darlene found herself breathing a sigh of relief. *Good,* she thought, *Tateh won't allow for such blasphemy to continue in his shop.* She was about to turn away when her father's voice caused her to stop.

"So the misunderstanding is that we Jews believe you have taken other gods, while you are telling this old man that there is but one God and you serve Him alone?"

"Correct," Dennison answered and Darlene felt a strange sinking in her heart.

"I remember when I came to America, Reb Lemuel, our rabbi in the old country admonished me to remember the Word of God in Deuteronomy." Abraham began to recite, " 'And it shall be, when the Lord thy God shall have brought thee into the land which he sware unto thy fathers, to Abraham, to Isaac, and to Jacob, to give thee great and goodly cities, which thou buildedst not, and houses full of all good things, which thou filledst not, and wells digged, which though diggedst not, vineyards and olive trees, which though plantedst not; when thou shalt have eaten and be full; then beware lest thou forget the Lord, which brought thee forth out of the land of Egypt, from the house of bondage. Thou shalt fear the Lord thy God, and serve him, and shalt swear by his name. Ye shall not go after other gods, the gods of the people which are round about you.' "

Good for Tateh, Darlene thought as Abraham's recitation ended. He would never fail to tell the truth before man and God.

"There. That should do for you," Abraham said. Darlene could hear the rattling of items and longed to know what was happening. Her father continued, "Perhaps the scriptures speak not of New York City, but the heart of the matter is still intact, no?"

"I agree," Dennison replied. "And were our God a different one from yours, I would be inclined to agree. But honestly, Abraham, we serve the same God."

Darlene was nearly knocked to the ground by Pierce Blackwell's solid frame coming through the curtain. Gasping, she was stunned by his firm hold on her arm and the look of amusement in his eyes.

"Weren't we talking loud enough for you?" He grinned broadly and released her to stand on her own.

"Shhh," she insisted with a finger to her lips. She moved quickly from the curtain, irritated with both herself for getting caught, and Mr. Pierce Blackwell for doing the catching.

Pierce followed her back to the ledger counter. "I'm certain they would include you in the conversation if you but asked. Would you like to know more about what they were discussing?"

"Leave me be," she said and turned her attention to a column of numbers. She would try for the fourth time to figure out why the column didn't add up to match the one on the opposite page.

Pierce would not leave her be however. In fact, he made it his particular duty to keep at her for an answer. "I'm serious. My father and your father have been discussing the Christian faith for some time now. They contrast the differences between Jews and Christians and reason together the similarities. I'd be happy to enlighten you . . ."

"I won't hear such blasphemy!" Darlene interrupted. "I won't be *meshummad* to my people."

"Meshummad?"

"A traitor," she replied harshly. "Now, please leave me alone. I have work to do and you mustn't interrupt me again or I shall never find my mistake."

Pierce glanced down at the column of figures. "It's there in the third column. You have a six and it should be an eight."

She looked up at him with wonder written in her expression. His stern expression was softened by a gentle smile. "I don't believe you." She quickly added the numbers and realized he was right. "How did you do that? There are more than fifteen numbers there. How can you just look down at my paper and instantly see that?"

Pierce shrugged. "I've always been able to do that. I guess I'm just good with figures."

"I suppose that would be an understatement," she said, still not allowing herself to really believe him. She tore a piece of brown paper from its roll and jotted down a row of numbers. "Do it again."

Pierce looked at the paper for only a moment. "Three hundred twenty-four."

Darlene turned the paper back around and used a stubby pencil to add up the column. "Three hundred twenty-four," she muttered. She looked up at him with real admiration, momentarily forgetting that she disagreed with his theology. "I must say, that is most impressive."

Pierce gave a tight, brief bow. "So does that mean you aren't mad at me anymore?"

Darlene slammed the book shut. "I'm not mad. Now if you'll excuse me, I have work to do." She hurried across the room and made a pretense of rerolling a bolt of discarded remnant cloth.

"Well, if we can't discuss religion," Pierce said, following her doggedly across the shop, "perhaps we could speak of something else."

"There is nothing to discuss." She finished with the bolt and took up her sewing basket. "I have work to do."

"That's the third time you've said that," he mused.

She glared at him. "It's true."

"I suppose it is, but does it preclude us having a simple conversation?"

He was so totally insistent that Darlene knew there'd be no dealing with him other than to stop running and allow the discussion. She sat down to her worktable and took up needle and thread. "So talk."

Pierce leaned against the wall and crossed his arms casually. He watched her for several moments, making Darlene stick herself twice with the needle. When he said nothing, she finally began the conversation the only way she could think of. "So you are going to the annual Valentine's Ball?"

Pierce grinned. "Yes. My aunt Eugenia insists I attend. It's for charity and she always manages to purchase my ticket, so I end up with the young woman she desires I keep company with."

21

Darlene shook her head. "Why not just skip the dance and invite the woman to dinner at your house?"

"My reaction exactly." Pierce laughed. "I told my aunt that fancy dress balls were of no interest to me, but she insists I owe society a debt and that this is one way to repay it."

"Sounds like a lot of nonsense to me."

"Valentine's Day or the dance?"

"Both." Darlene's reply was short and to the point. She picked up a black waistcoat and placed a button against the chalk mark her father had made.

"Have you no interest in dancing or in receiving valentines from your many admirers?"

"I suppose I don't. I'm not very familiar with either one." She stitched the button to the coat and deliberately refused to look up. She was afraid of what Pierce's expression might say. Would he disbelieve her, or worse, pity her?

"Valentine's Day can be a great deal of fun. You can set up amusing limericks and post them to a friend, or you can pen something more intimate and romantic and send it to your true love."

"Oy!" At Pierce's mention of true love, Darlene had managed to ram the needle beneath her fingernail. Instantly, she put her finger in her mouth and sucked hard to dispel the pain. Tears welled in her eyes, but still she refused to lift her face.

"Are you all right?" Pierce asked.

"Yes. Yes. I'm fine." She prayed he'd drop the subject or that his father would conclude his business in the back room and both Mr. Blackwells would leave the premises. She studied her finger for a moment then took up her sewing again.

"So, do you have a true love?" he asked.

Darlene barely avoided pricking her finger again. Resigning herself to the path of least pain, she put her sewing down and shook her head. "No. I have no suitors and I've never sent valentines. I don't find myself in the circle of those who dance at fancy parties either for charity or reasons of romantic inclinations."

"Have you never received a valentine?"

Pierce asked the question in such a serious tone that Darlene had to look up. He seemed very concerned by this matter, almost as though he'd asked if she'd never had decent food to eat.

"No, we don't celebrate such nonsense. Now, if you'll please excuse me . . ." She fell silent at the sound of her father's voice.

Dennison and Abraham came through the

curtain. "I can have both suits ready in time for the ball. You will be pleased, I think, Pierce." Her father beamed a smile first at Pierce and then at her.

"I'm certain I will be, sir." He turned to Darlene once again. "It was a pleasure, Miss Lewy. I've enjoyed our conversation."

Darlene nodded and feeling her face grow flushed, she hurried to lower her gaze back to her work. *Oy, but this day has been a trying one already!*

CHAPTER 2

For there is no difference between the
Jew and the Greek: for the same Lord
over all is rich unto all that call upon him.
ROMANS 10:12

Pierce finished doing up the buttons of his
satin waistcoat and went to the mirror. He
studied the reverse reflection of his cravat
as he tied it neatly into place, then gave
himself a quick once-over to make certain
nothing was left undone. His gleaming dark
eyes only served to remind him of another
pair of eyes. Just as dark and far more
beautiful behind ebony lashes, Darlene
Lewy's eyes were burned into his mind. She
had stimulated his thoughts all day, and now
as the hearth fires burned brightly for dinner, Pierce had still been unable to put the
feisty woman from his mind.

He took up a fine blue frock coat and
pulled it on. He adjusted the sleeves and

collar, all the while wondering if Darlene would help to sew his new Valentine's suit. It was silly, he knew, to ponder such useless matters, but the lovely girl would not leave his mind, and for the first time in his twenty-six years, Pierce was rather besotted.

Hearing the chimes announce the hour, Pierce made his way to the drawing room where he knew he'd find the rest of his family. Constance, his fifteen-year-old sister, sat rigidly proper in her powder blue silk, while Aunt Eugenia's ever-critical gaze roamed over her from head to toe in order to point out some flaw. Dennison stood bored and indifferent at the window.

"Good evening," Pierce said, coming into the room. He walked to his aunt Eugenia and placed an expected kiss upon each of her heavily powdered cheeks. Then turning to his sister, he winked and stroked her cheek with his hand. "I see we're all very much gathered together."

Dennison turned and nodded with a smile. "There must be a foot of snow out there already."

Pierce shrugged and took a seat on the couch opposite Eugenia. "It's a part of winters in New York. I suppose by now we should just expect it, eh?"

"It makes paying one's obligatory visits

very difficult," Eugenia declared. At forty-four she was a woman of proper elegance and grace. Her dark brown hair showed only a hint of gray and was swept up into a high arrangement that made her appear a bit taller than her petite frame could actually boast.

"Perhaps New York society will endure your absence for one day," Pierce suggested with a smile. This made Constance suppress a giggle, but not before Eugenia delivered a scowl of displeasure at her niece.

"Young people today do not understand the obligations of being in the privileged classes. There are rules, both written and unwritten, which simply must be adhered to. It is the responsibility of your elders," she said, looking directly at Constance, "to ensure that your behavior is acceptable and proper."

Pierce rolled his eyes. Aunt Eugenia was stuffy enough for them all. Let her adhere to society's demands and leave the rest of them alone. Changing the subject, Pierce beamed a smile at his sister and asked, "And how did you fill your afternoon, Miss Constance?"

"I wrote thank-you letters," she said with a hint of boredom.

Constance was a delicate young woman.

She was just starting to bloom into womanhood with her tiny figure taking on some more girlish curves. Her dark brown curls had been childishly tied up with a bow, but nevertheless, Pierce saw the makings of great beauty.

"Well, if the lake freezes over properly, we'll go ice skating tomorrow, how about that?" Pierce offered.

Constance's face lit up with excitement, but it was quickly squelched by Eugenia's overbearing declaration. "Certainly not! Constance has been a bit pale of late. I won't have her out there in the elements, only to catch her death."

Pierce looked to his father, the only one really capable of overriding Eugenia. Dennison smiled tolerantly at his sister. "Eugenia, the girl cannot live locked away behind these walls. If she is pale, perhaps it is because her face never sees the light of day. I say let her go and have a good time. Pierce will take proper care of her."

Constance jumped up and threw her arms around her father's neck. "Oh, thank you, Papa!"

"Well, that's settled then," Pierce said with a nod to his aunt. He was growing ever weary of her mettlesome ways and the only reason he continued to endure them was that she hadn't actually caused any real harm. Not yet.

"Dinner is served," remarked a stately butler from the entry door.

"Thank you, Marcus," Eugenia declared.

Dennison came to her side and offered his arm. With a look of cool reserve, Eugenia allowed him to assist her, leaving Pierce to bring Constance.

"Oh, thank you ever so much, Pierce," Constance said, squeezing his arm. "You are a lifesaver. I should have completely perished if I'd had to spend even one more day in this house."

Pierce chuckled. "Well, we couldn't have that."

"What did you do today?" Constance asked innocently. "Did you meet anyone new? Did you have a great argument with anyone?"

"How curious you sound." He led her to her chair at the dining table. "But the answer is no, I did not argue with anyone and yes, I did meet someone new."

"Oh, do tell me everything!"

"Prayers first." Constance's enthusiasm was halted by her father's declaration.

Grace was said over the meal with a special offer of thanksgiving for their health and safety. With that put aside, dinner was served and a fine, succulent pork roast drew the attention of the Blackwell family.

"So, who did you meet?" Constance questioned, while Pierce cut into a piece of meat.

"I met Father's tailor, Abraham Lewy, and his daughter, Darlene. She's very pretty with black hair and dark eyes like yours. Oh, and they have a man who works for them, but I can't remember his name. He's only a little older than you and quite dashing."

Constance blushed. "Is Darlene my age?"

"No," Pierce replied with a glint in his eye that was not missed by his aunt. "No, she's definitely older. Probably eighteen or so."

"She's twenty," his father declared. "And quite a beauty."

"She's a Jewess," Eugenia said as though it should put an end to the entire discussion.

"That's true enough," Pierce replied, "but Father is correct. She's quite beautiful."

"What's a Jewess?" asked Constance.

"It's a woman of the Jewish faith." Dennison replied.

Eugenia sniffed indignantly. "It means she's not one of us and therefore need not be further discussed at this table."

"Will she go to the Valentine's Ball?" Constance refused to let the matter drop.

Pierce shook his head. "She's never even had a valentine sent to her. Much less danced at a party for such a celebration."

"I should very much like to go to such a dance." Constance's voice was wistful.

"You've not yet come of age," Eugenia declared. "There are the proprieties to consider and if no one else in this family holds regard for such traditions, then I must be the overseer for all." She sounded as though it might be a tremendous burden, but Pierce knew full well how much Eugenia enjoyed her dramatic role.

"You should ask Miss Lewy to the dance," Constance told her brother. "If she's especially pretty and likeable, you could probably teach her all of the right steps."

Pierce nodded and gave her a conspiratorial wink. "Or, I could just have you teach her. You dance divinely."

Dennison laughed. "Perhaps our Constance could open her own dance school right here."

"Perish the thought!" Eugenia exclaimed. "I have enough trouble trying to manage the child without you putting improper ideas in her head."

Dennison smiled at his children and waved Eugenia off. "It was nothing more than good fun, sister. Do still your anxious mind or you'll have a fit of the vapors."

Dinner passed in relative silence after that. Eugenia's nose was clearly out of joint and Pierce had little desire to pick up the conversation again if it meant listening to some cold disdain towards Darlene and her kind.

Finally, Eugenia and Constance dismissed themselves to the music room while Pierce and Dennison remained at the table to linger over coffee.

"You seem to have a great deal on your mind."

Pierce looked at his father and nodded. "I keep thinking about the Lewys."

"One Lewy in particular, eh?"

"Perhaps Darlene did capture my attention more than Abraham, but you seemed to have him engrossed with the topic of Christianity."

Dennison pushed back a bit and sighed. "Abraham and I have been having regular talks about our religious differences."

"How did that get started?"

Dennison looked thoughtful. "His wife died in childbirth fifteen years ago."

"Just like mother?"

"Yes, it was a strange similarity. They were still in Germany and Darlene was only five.

Abraham lost both his wife and their new son."

"When did they come to America?"

"Only about five years ago. Tensions seem to follow the Jewish people and for a number of reasons Abraham considered the move a wise one. I believe his choice was God-directed. He worked hard to save enough money to make the move and to set up his shop here in New York. I happened upon his work through a good friend of mine and I've taken my business to him ever since."

"How is it I've never heard you talk about them?"

Dennison smiled. "You've been a very busy man, for one thing. I can't tell you how good it is to have you back from Europe."

Pierce finished his coffee and stared thoughtfully at the cup for a moment. "I've never been at home in New York. I can't explain it. I wasn't at home in London or Paris either. I guess I know that somewhere out there, there's a place where I will be happy, but stuck in the middle of Aunt Eugenia's social calendar isn't the place for me."

Dennison chuckled. "Nor for me, although my dear sister would believe it so. After your mother died, God rest her soul, Eugenia hounded me to death to remarry. Of course, there was Constance to consider. Such a tiny infant and hardly able to find nourishment in that weak canned milk cook gave her. Hiring a wet nurse was the only thing that saved that girl's life."

"It is a strange connection between us and the Lewys. Both mothers perished and they lost their baby as well. It must have been very hard on Darlene as well. A five-year-old would have a difficult time understanding the loss. I was eleven and struggled to understand it myself."

"Yes, but you had faith in the resurrection. You knew that your mother loved Christ as her Savior. I think the death of his wife caused Abraham to question his faith rather than find strength in it. When I first met him we discussed things of insignificant value. Darlene was much like Constance, gangly and awkward. A little girl running straight into womanhood. Oh, and very shy. She would scarcely peek her head out to see what her father was doing."

Pierce smiled, trying to imagine Darlene in the form of Constance. "I'll bet she was just as pretty as she is now."

Dennison looked at his son for a moment. "Don't buy yourself a heartache."

This sobered Pierce instantly. "What are

you saying? Surely you don't follow Aunt Eugenia's snobbery because the Lewys are not of our social standing?"

"No, not at all. Social standing means very little if you have no one to love or be loved by. Money has never been something to offer comfort for long." Dennison leaned forward. "No, I'm speaking of the theological difference. You are a Christian, Pierce. You accepted Christ as your Savior at an early age and you've accepted the Bible as God's Holy Word. Darlene doesn't believe like you do, nor will she turn away from the faith of her fathers easily. Marrying a woman who is not of your faith is clearly a mistake. The Bible says to not be unequally yoked with nonbelievers."

"But I wasn't talking marriage," Pierce protested and looked again to his coffee cup.

"Weren't you?" Dennison looked hard at his son and finally Pierce had to meet his father's gaze. "Be reasonable, Pierce. You found yourself attracted to this young woman. Where would you take it from this point? Friendship? I find it hard to believe it would stop there, but there it must stop."

"You've worked to change Abraham's mind. Why can I not work to change Darlene's?"

"I have no problem with you desiring to

35

share your faith with others. But, I think you should seek your heart for the motivation. If this is a personal and selfish thing, you may well cause more harm than good. However, if you truly feel called of God to speak to Darlene, then by all means do so, but leave your emotions out of it."

Pierce tried to shrug off his father's concerns. "You worry too much about me. I know what's right and wrong. I won't throw off my faith or be turned away from God." He got to his feet. "I believe I'll retire for the evening. I have a good book upstairs and I'd like to spend a bit of time in it before I go to bed."

Dennison nodded. "Sleep well, and Pierce, it is good to have you home again."

Pierce smiled. "It's good to be home."

Upstairs, comfortably planted in his favorite chair, Pierce picked up his book and opened to the marked page. He was just about to begin the fifth chapter when a knock sounded on his door. By the heavy-handed sound of it, Pierce was certain he'd find Eugenia on the opposite side.

"Come in," he called, sitting up to straighten his robe.

"It's a bit early for bed, isn't it?" Eugenia asked rather haughtily.

36

"I thought I'd like to read for a while."

"I see. Nevertheless, I've come to express my deep concern about our dinner conversation."

"Concern?" Pierce closed the book and shook his head. "What possible concern could our dinner conversation have given you?"

Eugenia drew back her shoulders and set her expression of disdain as though it were in granite. "I simply cannot have the scandal of you being indiscreet with that Jewess."

"I beg your pardon?" Pierce felt his ire rise and struggled to keep his temper under control.

"I could clearly read your mind and the interest you held for the Lewy girl. I must forbid it however. I cannot imagine anything more sordid than you taking up with that . . . that woman."

"Her name is Darlene and she is very pleasant to be around. And whether or not I hold any interest in her is none of your concern." Pierce got to his feet and crossed the room. "Aunt Eugenia, I love you and care a great deal about your comfort, but I am a grown man and I will no longer tolerate your interference in my life. I left this house three years ago because of such discomfort and I will not be driven from it again."

"Well! I've never heard such disrespect in all of my life. I've done nothing but see to your welfare. When my dear husband departed this earthly life, I knew it was my duty to help poor Dennison raise you children properly. If I instill culture and social awareness in your life, then you will find yourself the better for it and not the worse."

Pierce felt the heat of her stare and refused to back down. "Since you came to me with this matter, I am going to speak freely to you. I am certain Father appreciated the companionship and assistance you offered him with Constance. As you will recall, however, I was already a grown man of twenty-three when you came into this house. I need neither your care nor grooming to make my mark upon society, because I have no such plans for myself or society. These are things of importance to you, but certainly they do not concern me."

"They concern the well-being of this family. Would you see your father's reputation ruined because you chose to marry a Jewess?"

"Why must everyone assume I mean to marry the girl? I've only just met her and I thought she was a lovely creature with a fiery spirit."

"So I'm not the only one to broach this subject, eh? Perhaps I'm not the lunatic you make me out to be." Eugenia's face held a smug regard for her nephew.

"I've never thought you to be a lunatic, Aunt Eugenia. Meddlesome and snobbish, yes, but never a lunatic."

"Well!" It seemed the only thing she could say.

Pierce continued, "I will go to your charity balls and I will allow you to parade me before your society friends. I will use the proper silver and talk the proper talk. I will dance with impeccable skill and dress strictly in fashion, but I will not be dictated to in regards to the woman I will choose as my wife. Is that clear?"

"You have to marry a woman of your standing. To marry beneath your station will do this family a discredit. Then, too, imagine the complications of marrying a pauper. You must marry a woman of means and increase the empire your father has already begun."

Pierce could take no more. He walked to the door and opened it as a signal to his aunt that the conversation was at an end. "I will marry for love, respect, admiration, and attraction, be that woman of Jewish heritage or not. I seem to recall the Word of God saying we are all the same in the eyes of the Lord, and that whosoever shall call upon the name of the Lord will be saved. I realize the importance of marrying a woman who loves God as I do, and if that woman should turn out to be a Jewess who embraces Christianity and recognizes Christ as the true Messiah, I shan't give her social standing or bank account a single thought."

Eugenia stepped into the hall, clearly disturbed by Pierce's strong stand. "You'd do well to remember the things of importance in this world."

"I might say the same for you, Aunt. My father admonishes me to marry a woman of Christian faith, and that is clearly set in scripture. By what means do you base your beliefs?" He closed the door without allowing her to reply and drew a deep breath. "I've only just met the girl," he muttered to himself, "yet everyone has me married to her already."

CHAPTER 3

And it shall be, if thou do at all forget the
Lord thy God, and walk after other gods,
and serve them, and worship them, I
testify against you this day that ye shall
surely perish.

DEUTERONOMY 8:19

Nearly a week after her encounter with
Pierce Blackwell, Darlene felt herself getting back into the routine of her life. She
could almost ignore the image of the handsome man when he appeared in her daydreams, but it was at night when he haunted
her the most. And in those dreams, Darlene
found that she couldn't ignore the feelings
he elicited inside her. Never in her life had
she given men much thought. Her father
urged her to seek her heart on the matter
and to find a decent man and settle down.
He spoke of wanting grandchildren and
such, but Darlene knew that down deep

inside he was really worried about her, should something happen to him.

"Tateh," she called, gathering on her coat and warm woolen bonnet. "I'm leaving to go to Esther's."

Abraham peered up from his cutting board. "You should not go out on such a cold day."

"I'll be fine. It's just down the street. You worry too much." She smiled and held up a bundle. "We're making baby clothes for Rachel Bronstein." Her father nodded and gave her a little wave. "I'll be back in time to dish up supper. Don't work too hard."

She hurried out of the building, firmly closing the door which stated LEWY & CO. behind her. It was a brisk February morning and the skies were a clear, pale blue overhead. The color reminded Darlene of watered silk. Not that she ever had occasion to own anything made from such material, but once she'd seen a gown made of such cloth in a store window.

The sky was a sharp contrast to the muddy mess of the streets below. Gingerly, Darlene picked her way down the street, trying her best to avoid the larger mud holes. The hem of her petticoats and skirt quickly soaked up the muck and mud, but she tried not to fret. No one at Esther's would care because their skirts would be just as messy as hers.

The noises of the street were like music to her ears. Bells ringing in the distance signaled the coming of the charcoal vendor. She'd not be needing him to stop today, and so she only gave him a brief nod when he passed by.

"Fresh milk! Freeeesh milk!" another man called from his wagon. Cans of milk rattled in the wagonbed behind him and Darlene grimaced. She had never gotten used to what she deemed "city milk." It wasn't anywhere near as rich as what she'd been used to in Germany. Rumor had it that dairymen in the city were highly abusive with their animals, and that not only were the conditions unsanitary and unsavory, but the cows were fed on a hideous variety of waste products. Vegetable peelings, whiskey distillery mash, and ground fish bones were among the things she'd heard were used to feed New York's dairy cows. Even thinking of such a thing made her shudder.

A young boy struggled by with bundles of wood over each shoulder. "Wood, here! Wood!" Behind him another boy labored to entice a mule to bring up the wood-laden cart.

All around her, the smells of the city and

of the working class made Darlene feel a warmth and security that she couldn't explain. She thought of the people who lived in their fine brick houses on Broadway and wondered if they could possibly be as happy as she was. Did fine laces and silks make a home as full of love as she had with her father? *Certainly not,* she mused and jumped back just in time to avoid being run over by a herd of pigs as they were driven down the street.

Let the rich have their silks and laces. Her life with Tateh was sweet and they had all that they needed — the Holy One, blessed be He! But in the back of her mind Darlene remembered her father's conversation with Dennison Blackwell and then her own with Pierce. It was as though another world had suddenly collided with hers. Pierce knew what it was to live in fine luxury. He could work figures in his head with complete ease, and he was more than a little bit handsome.

Esther's tiny house came into view. It was there, tucked between a leather goods shop and a cabinetmaker, and although it was small, it served the old widow well. Trying to scrape the greater portion of mud from her boots, Darlene gave a little knock at the door.

A tiny old woman opened the door. She

was dressed in black from head to toe, with nothing but a well-worn white apron to break the severity. Her gray hair was tightly wound into a bun at the back of her neck, leaving her wrinkled face to stand out in stark abandonment. "Ah Darlene, you have come. Good. Good. I told Rachel and Dvorah you would be here."

"The streets are a mess. If you take my things, I'll leave my boots here at the door."

"Nonsense!" Esther declared. "The floor will sweep. Come inside and sit by the fire. You are nearly frozen." The old woman led her into the sitting room. "See Rachel, our *Hava* has come." Hava was Darlene's Hebrew name.

Rachel, looking as though she were in her eleventh month of pregnancy, struggled up from her chair and waddled over to Darlene. Bending as far over as she could to avoid her enormous stomach, Rachel kissed Darlene on each cheek and smiled.

"I was afraid you would be too busy. Hayyim told my husband the shop is near to bursting with customers."

"Yes, the rich *goyim* have come to extend their social season wardrobes. They won't have us at their parties, but they wear our suits!" Darlene said with much sarcasm.

"Who would want to go to a Gentile

45

party, anyway," Esther said, taking Darlene's coat. "You couldn't eat the food."

"Feh! *Kashruth* is such a bother anyway! We'd just as well be rid of it, if you ask me," a dark-headed woman said, entering behind Esther.

"Ah, but what does God say about it, Dvorah?"

Dvorah was much more worldly than the rest of the women Darlene knew. Her father was a wealthy merchant and could trace back a family history in New York nearly one hundred years. Nevertheless, they were Jewish and no matter how liberally they acted among the Gentiles, they would never be accepted as one of them.

"I leave God's words to my father's mouth," Dvorah replied, swishing her lavender gown with great emphasis. "I'm much busier with other things." She smiled sweetly over her shoulder before picking up her sewing.

"We all know what Dvorah is busy with," Esther said in a disapproving tone. "And I tell you, it is an honest shame to watch a young woman of your upbringing chase after the men the way you do. You need to refrain yourself from acting so forward, Dvorah. Your mother, *oy vey!* What she must go through."

Dvorah shrugged, indifferent to Esther's interfering ways. Darlene saw this as a good opportunity to change the subject. "So, Rachel, how are you feeling?"

By this time Rachel had waddled back to her chair and was even now trying to get comfortable. "I'm fine. Just fine. The baby should come any day and since you've been so good to help me sew, he will have a fine assortment of clothes to wear."

"What 'he'?" Esther questioned. "So sure you are that the child is a male?"

Rachel blushed and Darlene thought she looked perfectly charming. "Shemuel says it will be a boy."

Esther grunted. "Your husband doesn't know everything."

"May God make it so," Darlene proclaimed.

The women worked companionably for several hours and when the hall clock chimed noon, Esther offered them something to eat and drink. They were gathered around the table enjoying a fine stew when Esther brought up the one subject Darlene had hoped to avoid.

"So how is it with your father?"

"He's well, thank you." She slathered fresh butter on bread still warm from Esther's oven and took a bite.

Esther narrowed her eyes and leaned forward. "I've heard it said that he's talking matters of God with the goyim."

How Esther managed to know every private detail of everyone's life was beyond Darlene, but she always managed to be right on top of everything. She swallowed hard. "My father has many customers and, of course, they speak on many matters."

Esther looked at Darlene with an expression of pity. "Hayyim said that there are talks of why the Christians believe we are wrong in not accepting their Messiah."

"Hayyim should honor my father's goodness to him and remain silent on matters of gossip." Darlene knew her defense was weak, but what could she say? To admit that her father's conversations concerned her would only fuel Esther's inquisitive nature.

"So has *Avrom* betrayed the faith of his fathers?" Esther questioned, calling Abraham by his Yiddish name.

"Never!" Darlene declared, overturning her teacup. It was like all of her worst fears were realized in that statement. Without warning, tears welled in her eyes.

Rachel reached out a hand to pat Darlene lovingly. "There, there," she comforted, "Of course Avrom would not betray our faith."

At this Darlene choked back a sob. "He

talks with Mr. Blackwell." It was all she could manage to say, and for some reason it seemed to her that it should be enough.

"It will not bode well, I tell you," Esther commented, refilling Darlenc's cup.

Rachel ignored Esther. "Why are you so upset? Has your father said something that causes you to worry?"

Darlene shook her head. "No, but . . . well," she paused, taking time to dry her eyes. "I can't explain it. I just have this feeling that something is changing. I try to tell myself that I'm just imagining it, but I feel so frightened."

"And well you should. If Avrom turns from his faith he will perish," Esther declared.

"Oh, hush with that," Dvorah replied. "Darlene does not need to hear such talk."

"There will be plenty to hear about once word gets around," Esther said rather smugly.

"Yes, and no doubt you will help to see it on its way!" Dvorah's exasperation was apparent. "Leave her be. Come, Darlene, I'll walk you home and the air will cool your face." She got up from the table without waiting for Darlene's reply.

Esther shook her head in disapproval. "You should speak with the cantor, Hava."

Their congregation was too small to support a rabbi and Reuven Singer, a good and godly man, took on the role of cantor for their group. He led the prayers on Shabbes and was always available to advise his people regarding God's law.

"Mr. Singer could speak with Avrom, if you're worried," Rachel offered.

Darlene nodded and drew a deep breath to steady her nerves. She accepted her coat from Dvorah who even now was doing up the buttons on a lovely fur-trimmed cape. After enduring another suggestion or two from Esther and a sincere thank you from Rachel for the baby clothes, Darlene followed Dvorah outside.

"That old woman!" Dvorah declared. "Busybody Esther should be her name!"

This made Darlene smile. "She always seems to know exactly what everyone is up to. I don't dare make a wrong move with her only two blocks away."

Dvorah laughed. "She told me my dress was too exciting. Six inches of mud on the hem and she thinks I'm dressing too fine."

"It is lovely." Darlene had thought so from the first moment she'd laid eyes on it, but with Esther, who would dare to say such a thing?

"Thank you. Oh, look, a hack. I'd much

rather be driven home than walk." She waved her handbag once and the driver brought the carriage to a stop. "Don't forget what I said." Dvorah waved from the hack and then was gone.

"I won't," Darlene muttered to no one. But already, thoughts of the luncheon conversation were racing through her mind. So much so, in fact, that as Darlene set out to cross the muddy, bottomless street, she didn't see the freight wagon bearing down on her.

Just as she looked up to catch sight of the horses' steaming nostrils, Darlene felt strong arms roughly encircle her and pull her to safety. Gazing up in stunned surprise, she nearly fainted at the serious, almost angry expression on Pierce Blackwell's face.

"Were you trying to get yourself killed?" he asked. Then without waiting for her reply he pulled her against him and asked, "Are you all right? You didn't get hurt, did you?"

"No. I mean yes." She shook her head and sighed. "I'm fine. You can let me go now." He only tightened his hold and Darlene actually found herself glad that he did. Her legs felt like limp dishrags and she wasn't at all certain that she could have walked on her own accord.

"Let's get you inside and make sure you're

all right," he half-carried, half-dragged her the remaining distance to the Lewy & Co. door. Opening it, Pierce thrust her inside and immediately called for her father.

"Mr. Lewy!"

"Don't!" Darlene exclaimed, trying to wrench free from Pierce. "You'll scare him out of ten years of life."

Pierce ignored her complaint. Abraham hurried into the room with a look of concern on his face. His gaze passed first to the man who had called his name and then to the pale face of his daughter.

"What is it? What is wrong?"

"Nothing, Tateh. I'm fine." Darlene hoped that by hurrying such an explanation, her father would breathe easier.

"She was nearly killed by a freighter," Pierce replied. "I believe she was daydreaming and didn't even see him coming. There was no way the poor man could have stopped."

"I'm fine, Tateh. I'm just fine."

Abraham seemed to relax a bit. "You are certain?"

"Absolutely. I wouldn't lie to you." Darlene smiled sweetly, more than a little aware that Pierce watched her intently.

With the moment of crisis in the past, Abraham turned his gaze to Pierce. "You saved my *Havele.* You have my thanks and never ending gratitude."

Pierce looked at him with a blank expression of confusion. "Havele?"

"*Hava* is Hebrew. It means Eve. Havele is just a way of saying it a little more intimately. Perhaps you would say, Evie?"

"But I thought, I mean, I remember my father saying her name is Darlene."

"Don't talk about me as though I'm not here!" Darlene suddenly exclaimed. Gone was the fear from her encounter with the freighter. "My mother liked the name Darlene and that is what I'm called. Now please let me go."

At this, Pierce released her with a beaming smile that unnerved her. He bowed slightly, as if to dismiss the matter, but Abraham would have nothing of it.

"I have no fitting way to reward you," he began, "but I shall make for you six new suits and charge you not one penny."

"Tateh, no!" Darlene declared without thinking of how ungrateful she must sound. She knew full well the cost of six suits and while they were living comfortably at this point, there was no telling what tomorrow could bring. They shouldn't become indebted to this man.

But they were indebted. Pierce Blackwell

53

had saved her life.

It was only then that the gravity of the situation began to sink in. With a new look of wonder and a sensation of confused feelings, Darlene lifted her face to meet Pierce's. "I'm sorry, I just mean that suits hardly seem a proper thanks."

"I completely agree," Pierce replied. "And that is why I must say no. I did not rescue your daughter for a new wardrobe. I have funds aplenty for such things. I happened to be here because I have a fitting appointment. God ordains such intercessory matters, don't you think?"

"I do, indeed," Abraham said and nodded with a smile. "I do, indeed."

His acceptance of Pierce's words only gave Darlene reason to worry anew. It was exactly these matters which had caused her to walk in front of the freighter. Certainly such thoughts could only cause more trouble. What if her father thought Pierce's God was more important and more capable of dealing with matters? What if her father gave himself over to the teachings of the Christians! Esther's words came back to haunt her. *He will perish,* Darlene thought. God would turn His face away from her beloved Tateh and he would surely die.

CHAPTER 4

By faith Abraham, when he was called to
go out into a place which he should after
receive for an inheritance, obeyed; and
he went out, not knowing whither he
went.

HEBREWS 11:8

Pierce closed the door to Abraham's shop
and hailed his driver. He could still feel the
rush of blood in his ears and the pounding
of his heart when he'd seen Darlene about
to die. She'd nearly walked right into the
path of that freighter and all with a sad,
tragic look on her face. It was almost as if
she were facing an executioner. Surely she
hadn't intended to kill herself!

Pierce ordered his driver to take him to
his commission merchants office, then
relaxed back into the plush leather upholstery of the carriage. No, Darlene wouldn't
kill herself. There'd be no reason for that.

But perhaps there was. Pierce didn't really know her at all. He toyed with several ideas. Perhaps she'd just been rejected by a suitor? No, she'd told him there were no suitors in her life. Perhaps she'd lost the will to live? Pierce was certain she couldn't bear to be parted from her father. Then what had caused such a look of complete dejection?

His Wall Street destination was only a matter of a few blocks away, and before he could give Darlene another thought, his driver was halting alongside the curb. Pierce alighted with some reservations about the meeting to come. His man, Jordan Harper, was quite good at what he did, but Pierce had never gotten used to letting another man run his affairs. Of course, when he'd been abroad it was easy to let someone else take charge. He knew that his father would ultimately oversee anything Harper did, and therefore it honestly didn't appear to compromise matters in Pierce's mind. The only thing he'd ever disagreed on with his father had been the large quantities of western land tracts Pierce had insisted on buying. The land seemed a good risk in Pierce's mind, and it mattered little that hardly anyone had ever heard of the dilapidated Fort Dearborn or the hoped for town of Chicago.

Climbing the stairs, Pierce pulled off his top hat and entered the brokerage offices where Harper worked. A scrawny, middle-aged man of questionable purpose met Pierce almost immediately.

"May I help you, sir?"

Pierce took off his gloves, tossed them into the top hat and handed both to the man. "Pierce Blackwell. I'm here to see Jordan Harper."

"Of course, sir. Won't you come this way?" the man questioned, almost as if waiting for an answer. At Pierce's nod, he whirled on his heels and set off in the direction of the sought-after office.

Black lettering stenciled the glassed portion of the door, declaring HARPER, KOMSTED, AND REGAN. The older man opened the door almost hesitantly and announced, "Mr. Blackwell to see Mr. Harper."

The room was rather large, but the collection of books, papers, and other things related to business, seemed to crowd the area back down to size. Three desks were appointed to different corners of the room, while the fourth corner was home to four rather uncomfortable-looking chairs and a heating stove.

Jordan Harper, a man probably only a few years Pierce's senior, jumped up from his chair and motioned to Pierce. "Come in. I've been expecting you." The scrawny man took this as his cue to exit and quietly slipped from the room, taking Pierce's hat and gloves with him.

"Take off your coat. Old Komsted keeps it hot enough to roast chestnuts in here." The man was shorter than Pierce's six foot frame, but only by inches. He ran a hand through his reddish-brown hair and grinned. "I've made quite a mess this morning, but never worry, your accounts are in much better shape than my desk."

Pierce smiled. He actually liked this man whom he'd only met twice before. "My banker assures me I have reason to trust you, so the mess is of no difference to me."

Harper laughed. "Good enough. Ah, here it is." He pulled out a thick brown ledger book and opened it where an attached cord marked it.

Pierce settled himself in and listened as Jordan Harper laid out the status of his western properties. "You're making good profits in the blouse factory. They're up to eighty workers now and I found foreign buyers who are ready to pay handsomely for the merchandise. Oh, and that property you hold near Galena, Illinois is absolutely filthy with lead and has netted you a great deal of money. Here are the figures for you to look over. Here," he pointed while Pierce took serious consideration of the situation, "is exactly what the buyer paid and this is what your accounts realized after the overhead costs were met."

"Most impressive," Pierce said, sitting back in his seat. "I see you've earned your keep."

Jordan smiled. "I've benefited greatly by our arrangement, Mr. Blackwell, but you don't know the half of it yet. It was impossible to catch up to you while you were abroad. It seemed every time I sent a packet to you, you'd already moved on. Several of my statements were forwarded, but eventually they'd be rerouted back to New York and, well, they're collecting dust in the files downstairs."

"I kept pretty busy," Pierce commented, "but my father trusted your work, and so I felt there was nothing for me to concern myself with. Of course, I was a little younger and more foolhardy three years ago."

Jordan laughed and added, "And a whole lot poorer."

Pierce raised a brow. "Exactly what are you implying, Mr. Harper?" There was a hint of amusement in his tone.

"I'm not implying one single thing. I want

59

you to look here." Jordan Harper quickly flipped through several pages. "As you will see, I took those tracts of land which you purchased at the Chicago site and in keeping with your suggestion that should prices look good, I should sell as much as two-thirds of the property, I did just that."

Pierce again leaned forward to consider the ledger. At the realization of what met his eyes, Pierce jerked his head up and faced Jordan with a tone of disbelief. "Is this some kind of joke?"

"Not at all. In fact, it's quite serious. I take it from your surprise that you haven't bothered to check on all of your accounts when you were visiting the banks?"

"No, I suppose I didn't concern myself with it," Pierce admitted. "But you're absolutely sure about this?"

"The money is in the bank, and I get at least twenty offers a week to buy the balance of your land in Chicago."

Pierce looked at the figures again. "But if I understand this correctly and I'm certain I do, the original $100,000 investment I made has now netted me over one million dollars?"

"And that's after my commission," Jordan said with a smile.

Pierce shook his head. Who could have

imagined such an inflation of land prices? "I knew it would be a valuable investment, but I figured it would be ten or twenty years before I realized it."

"Chicago is bursting at the seams. It's growing up faster than any city I've ever seen the likes of. People are taking packets across the Great Lakes and making their way to Chicago every day. The population has already grown to over three thousand. Why just yesterday I saw an advertisement offering passage from Buffalo to Chicago for twenty-five dollars. Everybody's getting rich from this little town."

"And you saved out the tracts I asked you to?"

"Absolutely! You can sell them tomorrow if you like or build your own place."

"Sounds to me," Pierce said thoughtfully, "that hotels and boarding houses would be greatly in need."

"All those people have to live somewhere, Mr. Blackwell."

Pierce smiled. "Indeed they do."

Hours later, Pierce was still thinking about Chicago. He'd picked up all the information he could find on the small town and while contemplating what his next move should be, wondered if his next move might ought not to be himself.

He left the papers on his bed and went to stand by the window, where heavy green velvet curtains kept out the world. Pulling them back, Pierce thought seriously about leaving all that he knew in New York. It had been easy enough to go abroad. European cities were well-founded and filled with elegance, grace, and fine things. But Chicago was in the middle of nowhere. It hadn't been but three years since the Indian wars had kept the area in an uproar. There was no main road to travel over in order to get to the town, and even packets to Chicago were priced out of the range of the average citizen. Perhaps Pierce could invest in a mode of transportation that would bring that price down. New railroads were springing up everywhere and canals were proposed for the purpose of connecting Lake Michigan to the Mississippi River. It was easy to see that this was a land of opportunity. But could he leave all the comforts of home and travel west?

A light snow was falling again, and with it came images of the young woman he'd held so close earlier in the day. He liked the way Darlene fit against him. He liked the wide-eyed innocence and the look of wonder that washed over her face when he refused to release her. He liked the smell of her hair, the tone of her voice, even the flash of anger in her dark eyes. He let the curtain fall into place and sighed. If he went west, there would be no Darlene to go with him. At least here he could see her fairly often on the pretense of embellishing his wardrobe. But, a man could own only so many suits of clothing.

He sat down again on the bed and looked at the papers before him. Then without knowing why, he thought of Valentine's Day and the dance. Darlene had declared herself unfamiliar with both, and this had truly surprised Pierce. A thought came to mind and he toyed with it for several minutes before deciding to go ahead with it. He grinned to think of Darlene receiving her first valentine. What would she think of him? Perhaps he could leave it unsigned, but of course she'd know it was from him.

Deciding it didn't matter, Pierce jumped up and threw on his frock coat. Valentine's Day was a week from Saturday, so there was plenty of time, but Pierce wanted to have just the right card made.

CHAPTER 5

Wherefore the children of Israel shall
keep the sabbath . . . It is a sign between
me and the children of Israel forever: for
in six days the Lord made heaven and
earth, and on the seventh day he rested,
and was refreshed.

EXODUS 31:16,17

Darlene worked furiously over the cuffs of
Pierce Blackwell's long-tailed frock coat. It
would soon be dark and the Sabbath would
be upon them. There was never to be any
work on Shabbes, for God Himself had
declared it a day of rest and demanded that
His people honor and keep that day for
Him.

Esther sat companionably, for once not
making her usual busybody statements, but
instead helping to put buttons on the satin
waistcoat which Pierce would wear the following night. Such deadlines made it neces-

sary for Darlene and Abraham to elicit additional help, and the fact that Valentine's Day came on a Saturday made it absolutely necessary to have everything done as early on Friday as possible.

Shabbes began on Friday evening when it was dark enough for the first stars to be seen in the sky. By that time, all work would have to be completed and put aside. No work was to be done, not even the lighting of fires on such cold, bitter mornings as February in New York could deliver. For this purpose, Abraham paid a Shabbes goy, a Gentile boy, to come and light fires and lamps. Darlene knew that many families could not afford to pay someone to come in, and for them she felt sorry. They were strictly dependent upon the goodness of neighbors and sometimes they went through Shabbes without a warm fire to ward off the cold.

Finishing the cuff, Darlene held up the coat and smiled. She knew Pierce would be handsome in the black, redingote-styled, frock coat. The tapering of the jacket from broad shoulders to narrow waist only made her smile broaden. Pierce would need no corset to keep his figure under control. Of this she was certain.

"Such a look," Esther remarked, staring at Darlene from her work.

Darlene laughed. "I was only trying to imagine what it might be like to dance at a party where men dress so regally."

"Oy vey! You should put aside such thoughts. Next, you'll be considering marriage to some rich goy, if you could find one who'd have you."

Darlene felt her cheeks flush and instantly dropped the coat back to her lap and threaded her needle. She prayed that Esther wouldn't notice her embarrassment, because just such thoughts had already gone through her mind.

"So, you do think of such things!" Esther showed clear disgust by Darlene's breach of etiquette. "*Bist blint* — are you blind? Such things will only lead you to heartache."

Darlene waved her off. "I'm not blind and I'm not headed to heartache or anything else. I simply wondered what it might be like to own fine things and not be looked down upon by the people in the city. Is that so bad?"

Esther studied her closely for a moment. "There is talk, Havele. Talk that should make your father take notice. The cantor knows that Avrom's faith is weakening."

"Never! It's not true!" Darlene shouted the words, not meaning to make such an obvious protest.

"If he turns from God, he will be a traitor to our people. No one will speak to him again. No one of Hebrew faith will do business with him. If that happens, Havele, you will come and live with me." She said it as though Darlene would have no choice in the matter.

"I will not leave Tateh. Such talk!" She got up from her work and excused herself to tend to Sabbath preparations upstairs. Hurrying up the rickety backstairs, Darlene couldn't help but be upset by Esther's words. It was true enough that her father would be considered meshummad — a traitor, if he accepted the Christian religion of Dennison and Pierce Blackwell. But surely that could not happen. They were God's chosen people, the children of Israel. Surely her father could not disregard this fact.

She finished putting together the *schalet,* a slow-cooking stew that would simmer all night long and be ready to eat for the Sabbath. This would enable her to keep from breaking the day of rest by preparing meals. Turning from this, Darlene set about completing preparations for their evening Sabbath meal. This was always a very elegant dinner with her mother's finest Bavarian china and a delicate lace tablecloth to cover the simple kitchen table.

Setting the table, she hummed to herself and tried to dispel her fears. Surely things weren't as bad as Esther implied. The small roast in the oven gave off a succulent, inviting smell when Darlene peered inside. It would be done in plenty of time for their meal and it was a favorite of her father's. Perhaps this would put him in a good frame of mind and give him cause to remember his faith. Perhaps a perfect Shabbes meal would focus his heart back on the teachings of his fathers.

Filling a pot with water and potatoes, Darlene left it to cook on the stove and hurried back to finish the Blackwell suit. Hayyim was to deliver the suits before Sabbath began, and with this thought, Darlene silently wished she could go along to see where Pierce lived. No doubt it was a beautiful brick house with several stories and lovely lace curtains at each and every window. With a sigh, she pushed such incriminating thoughts from her mind and joined Esther.

"It is finished," Esther announced. "I must get home now and make certain things are ready."

"Thank you so much for helping me. Did Tateh pay you already?"

"Yes, I am well rewarded," Esther said,

pulling on her heavy coat. Darlene went to help her, but she would have nothing to do with it. "I may be an old woman, but I can still put on my coat."

Good, Darlene thought. *She has already forgotten our conversation and now she will return home and leave me to my dreams.* But it was not to be. Without warning, Esther turned at the door and admonished Darlene.

"You should spend Shabbes in prayer and seek God's heart instead of that of the rich goyim."

And you should mind your own business, Darlene thought silently, while outwardly nodding. She did nothing but present herself as the most repentant of chastised children. With head lowered and hands folded, Darlene's appearance put Esther at ease enough to take her leave.

"*Gut Shabbos,* Hava."

"Good Sabbath to you, Esther."

With Esther gone, Darlene breathed a sigh of relief and called to Hayyim. "The Blackwell suits are finished. You can take them now." She let her fingers linger on Pierce's coat for just a moment before Hayyim took it.

"Darlene, you look very pretty today," Hayyim said, lingering as if he had all the time in the world.

Darlene felt sorry for him. She knew he was terribly taken with her, but her heart couldn't lie and encourage the infatuation. "Thank you, Hayyim. You'd better hurry if you're to get home in time for Sabbath."

Hayyim nodded sadly. Darlene watched him take up the rest of the clothes in a rather dejected manner. Better she make herself clear with him now, than to lead him on and give him reason to hope for a future with her.

Just as she was about to go upstairs and finish with the meal, a knock sounded at the back door. Wondering if Esther had forgotten something, Darlene glanced quickly about the room, then went to open the door.

Five children ranging in age from four to twelve stood barefooted and ragged in the muddy snow. These were her "regulars," as Darlene called them. Destitute children who came routinely on Friday afternoon to beg for food and clothes.

"Ah, I thought perhaps you had forgotten me," she said with a smile. "Come in, come in. Warm yourselves by the fire." She motioned them forward and they hurried to the stove, hands outstretched and faces smiling.

Darlene stuck her head out the door and noted that two older youths, probably in their middle teens, waited not far down the alleyway. She smiled and motioned for them to join in, but they shook their heads and went back to their conversation. They only watched over the little ones. Darlene knew they were probably older siblings who realized the younger children could persuade better charity from sympathetic adults, without being expected to work in return.

She closed the door to the cold and turned to meet the sallow faces and hopeful eyes of the little ones. "I have a surprise for you. I hope you like sweets."

The children nodded with smiling, dirt-laden faces.

"Good. You wait here and I'll be right back." Darlene hurried into the next room where she had saved them a collection of things all week long.

Nebekhs — the poor things! They had nothing, and no one but each other. Their parents were most likely involved in corrupt things that took them away from wherever they called home. If they had parents. Some were orphans who roamed the streets only protected by the various street rowdies who had taken residence in the area. The hoodlums taught them to steal and to beg and in return, they provided some semblance of a family.

Gathering up armloads of remnant cloth and a small brown bag of sweets, Darlene went back to the children. "I think you'll like this," she said, putting the cloth down and holding out the bag. "There's plenty inside for everyone, even your friends outside."

One little girl, barely wrapped in a tattered coat, reached her hand in first and pulled out a peppermint stick. "Ohhh!" she said, her eyes big as saucers. This was all the encouragement that the others needed. They hurriedly thrust hands inside the sack and came up with sticks of their own.

"Now, here are some nice pieces of cloth which can be made into clothes. And I have a small sack of bread and several jars of jam." Darlene went to retrieve these articles and returned to find five very satisfied children devouring their peppermint.

"Can you carry it all or should I call for your friends?"

"Ain't no friends. Them's my brothers Willy and Sam," one little boy replied.

"Well," Darlene said, opening the door, "would you like for them to come and help?"

"No ma'am," the oldest boy of the group

announced. He had the remains of a black eye still showing against his pale white face. "We can carry it." And this they did. The children each took responsibility for some article with the youngest delegated to carrying the candy sack.

"I'll see you next week," Darlene said and waved to the elusive Willy and Sam. They didn't wave back, but Darlene knew they saw her generosity. How sad they were trudging off in the filthy snow. Little feet making barefoot tracks. Silent reminders of the children's plight. Darlene wanted to cry whenever she saw them. No matter what she did for them it was never enough. Scraps of material and sweets wouldn't provide a roof over their heads and warmth when the night winds blew fierce. *How could God allow such things?* she wondered. How could she?

Without willing it to be there, the image of Pierce Blackwell filled her mind. She wondered if the Blackwells in all their finery and luxury ever considered the poor. The Valentine's ball Pierce and his father would attend was purported to be for charity. Would children like these know the benefits of such a gala event or would the rich simply line their pockets, pay their revelry expenses and advertise for yet another charity ball?

The children had passed from view now and only their footprints in the snow remained to show that they'd ever been there at all. Noting the fading light, Darlene rushed to close the door and get back to her work. There was still so much to do in order to be idle on the Sabbath.

An hour later, Darlene breathed a sigh of relief and brought two braided hallah loaves to the table. Stowing images of the ragged children and Pierce Blackwell away from her mind, Darlene set her thoughts to those of her Shabbes duties. She could hear her father puttering in his bedroom and had a keen sense that in spite of her worries, all was well. Taking down long, white candles in ornate silver holders, Darlene placed them on the table and went to the stove. In a small container beside the stove, long slivered pieces of kindling were the perfect means for lighting the Shabbes candles. Darlene came to the table with one of these and, lighting the candles, blew out the stick. Then with a circular wave of her hands as if pulling in the scent from the candles, she covered her eyes and recited the ritual prayer.

"*Baruch ata Adonai, eloheinu melech haolam, ahser kiddeshanu bemitzvotav, vetsivianu le'hadlik ner shel Shabbos* — Blessed art Thou, Oh Lord, who sanctifies us by His commandments, and commands us to light the Sabbath lights."

CHAPTER 6

Wherefore by their fruits
ye shall know them.

MATTHEW 7:20

Pierce lightly fingered the edge of a starfish shell and waited for his name to be called. He hated with all of his being the very fact that he was seated in the City Hotel ball-room, waiting to be auctioned off to the highest bidder. What would happen if Aunt Eugenia failed to top the bidding and buy him out of harm's way? Then again, what if Aunt Eugenia's way was one and the same?

The City Hotel's ballroom had been transformed into a lush underwater world. Heavy blue nets hung overhead to give the illusion of being underwater with a greedy fisherman hovering dangerously overhead. Many considered it pure genius to compare catching an eligible bachelor to amassing a good catch of fish, but Pierce wasn't among their numbers. He was literally checking his pocket watch every fifteen minutes and remained completely bored by the entire event.

"And bachelor number twelve is Pierce Blackwell. Mr. Blackwell, please come forward."

Pierce sighed, adjusted his new coat, and went up to the raised platform where he would be auctioned to the highest bidder. Putting on his most dazzling smile, Pierce pretended to be caught up in the evening's amusements.

"Pierce is with us after a three-year absence in Europe, and the ladies here tonight are no doubt in the best of luck to be a part of this gathering. As you can see, Mr. Blackwell would make an admirable suitor for any eligible young woman." Giggles sounded from the ladies in the audience.

"The bidding will open at one hundred dollars," the speaker began.

A portly matron in the front waved her fan and started the game. Pierce remained fixed with the facade of congeniality plastered on his face. He nodded to each woman with a brilliant smile that he was certain wouldn't betray his anguish.

"The bid is at eight hundred dollars." The crowd ooohed and ahhhed. The heavy-set woman holding the eight hundred dollar bid blushed profusely and fanned herself continuously.

"One thousand dollars," Eugenia Blackwell Morgan announced and a hush fell across the room. She stepped forward in a heavy gown of burgundy brocade. Multiple strands of pearls encircled her throat and in her hand she held an elaborate ivory fan. She cut a handsome figure and appeared to know it full well. Pierce personally knew many men who would love to pay her court — if she was a less intimidating woman.

"The bid has been raised to one thousand dollars. Do I hear one thousand, one hundred?" Silence remained and there was not one movement among the bidding women. Pierce wondered if by prior arrangement, Eugenia had forbid any of them to outbid her.

"Then the bid is concluded at one thousand dollars." Applause filled the air and Pierce bowed low as he knew he was expected to do.

Stepping down from the platform, he went to his aunt and bowed low once again. "Madam," he said in a most formal tone.

"Oh, bother with you," Eugenia said, and swatted him with her fan. "Come along."

Pierce offered his arm and Eugenia took

it without a word. Although it was proper for a gentleman to lead a lady, Eugenia clearly made their way through the crowd to the table she had reserved to be her own. Sitting there waiting was an incredibly beautiful young woman. Her thick dark hair reminded Pierce of Darlene, but that was where the similarities ended. The haughty smile, sharply arched brows, and icy blue eyes of the woman clearly drove the image of Darlene from his mind.

"Pierce, this is Amanda Ralston. She is the only daughter of Benjamin Ralston."

Pierce bowed before the woman and received her curt little nod. "Your servant," he said and looked to his aunt for some clue as to how the game was to be played.

"No doubt you are familiar with her father's name and their family," Eugenia said with pale tight lips. "I will leave you two to discuss matters of importance and to dance the night away."

Inwardly, Pierce groaned. Outwardly, he extended his arm. "Would you care for some refreshment? The bidding will no doubt continue for some time."

With a coy, seductive smile, Amanda put her gloved hand on Pierce's arm. "Perhaps later. Why don't you join me and tell me about your time in Europe?"

He took the chair opposite her. "What would you like to know?" He was evasive by nature and with this woman he felt even more of a need to maintain his privacy.

"You were away a very long time. Did you perhaps lose your heart to some young Parisian woman?"

Pierce's expression didn't change. "No, I simply had no reason to return to America."

"No reason? There's a fortune to be made in this country and men like you are the ones to do the making."

Well, thought Pierce, *she certainly has no trouble putting her thoughts into words.* "America did fine in my absence."

She laughed a light, stilted laugh. "Mr. Blackwell, you do amaze me. This is a time of great adventure in America. A great deal of money is changing hands. Don't you want to be a part of that?"

"Money changes from my hand all the time," he replied smugly.

"Well, the more important thing is that it returns tenfold," she fairly purred.

Pierce thought of his land deals in Chicago and wondered if she'd swoon should he be as vulgar as to mention figures. She was clearly a woman looking out for her best interest and as far as Pierce was concerned, her interests were far removed from his.

"I find this conversation rather dull for a party," Pierce finally spoke. "Surely a young woman of your caliber would rather discuss dances and debuts rather than banking ledgers."

Amanda lifted her chin slightly in order to stare down her slender, well-shaped nose. "My father believes the banking system is doomed to fail. What say you to that, Mr. Blackwell?"

Pierce looked at her thoughtfully. She was incredibly beautiful. Maybe too much so. Her emerald green gown was a bit risque for her age, at least by Pierce's standards. Should Constance ever show up in such a gown, he'd be persuaded to throw a wrap about her shoulders. Amanda seemed fully comfortable, if not motivated by, the daring low decolletage of the gown. Her creamy white shoulders glowed in the candlelight, while the ecru lacing of her gown urged his gaze to travel lower. Pierce refused to give in to the temptation and pulled his thoughts away from Amanda. Music was beginning at the far end of the ballroom. No doubt the auction was completed and now the dance could start again.

"Would you care to dance?" Pierce asked politely.

"I suppose it would be expected," Amanda replied.

With the grace of a cat, Pierce was at her side. He helped her from the chair and led her across the room to where other couples were already enjoying the strains of a waltz. Pierce was not entirely certain he wished to waltz with Amanda. It was such a daring dance of holding one's partner close and facing each other for a time of constant consideration. But, he'd been the one to open his mouth and bring her this far. He supposed there was little to do but carry through.

He whirled her into the circling dancers and tried not to think about the way dancing seemed to further expose her figure to his eyes. Didn't she realize how blatantly obvious her assets were being admired by every man in the room?

"Perhaps," he said a bit uncomfortably, "this gown was not intended for such dancing."

Amanda looked at him with complete bewilderment. "Why, whatever do you mean, Mr. Blackwell?"

Pierce coughed, more from nervous energy than the need to clear his throat. "It's just that the cut of your gown seems, well, a bit brief."

Amanda's laughter rang out in a melodious tinkling sound. "Why, Mr. Blackwell, that is the idea."

Pierce felt his face grow flushed. There was no dealing politely with this woman. "Miss Ralston, I am not in the habit of keeping company with women whose sole purpose in designing a gown is that they should overexpose themselves to the world."

"My father says that beautiful things should be admired," she replied curtly. "Do you not think I'm beautiful?"

Pierce wanted to say no, but that would be a lie. "Yes, your countenance is lovely. Your spirit would raise some questions however."

"My, and what is that supposed to mean? Spirit? Why you sound as though you were some sort of stuffy reverend from the downtown cathedrals."

Pierce turned her a bit too quickly, but he held her fast and she easily recovered the step. "I am a man of God, but not in the sense you suppose. I am of the Christian faith and I believe in women keeping themselves discreetly covered in public."

"Ah, but what about in private?" She tripped and fell against him. Only then did Pierce realize it was deliberate. "Oh my, have I compromised you, Mr. Blackwell?"

she asked with a hint of a giggle.

Pierce could stand no more. He set her back at arm's length and admonished her. "If you cannot contain your enthusiasm for the dance, madam, perhaps I should lead you from the floor."

"Remember, you're mine for the evening. Charity and such, you know." She was amused with his discomfort and it registered clearly on her face and in her voice.

Without warning, Pierce pulled her rudely from the circle of dancers. "It seems I've winded myself," he said with a look that challenged her to suggest otherwise. "I'll take you back to our table."

She said nothing as he escorted her back and only after she had been seated did Pierce excuse himself to bring back refreshments. "I won't be a moment," he promised and left her very clearly alone.

Rage coursed through him. She was no better than the women of the night, only she wore expensive satin and jewels. He would throttle Constance if she ever dared to toy with men in such a fashion. Taking up two glasses of punch, Pierce tried to steady his nerves before returning to the table. Without thought he downed both cups before realizing what he'd done. Smiling sheepishly, he put one cup down, offered his for a refill, and picked up another for Amanda.

He walked slowly back to the table. Maybe too slowly for by the time he'd returned there had gathered a number of seemingly unattached young men. He wondered silently if he could just slip away unnoticed, but Amanda hailed him in her bold and open fashion.

"Oh Pierce, darling," she announced, "I thought I'd simply perish before you returned. You gentlemen will excuse me now, won't you?" She batted her eyes coyly at the group and smiled as though promising each of them something more than she could deliver.

The men graciously but regretfully took their leave, and Pierce was finally able to place the cup of punch on the table at her fingertips. "It was good of them to keep watch over you in case you expired before I returned," he said sarcastically and took his seat.

"Why, Pierce Blackwell, you're jealous." She laughed and took a long sip of her punch.

Pierce couldn't decide the path of least resistance and so said nothing. This only added fuel to Amanda's imagination. "Mrs. Morgan told me that your father is quite anxious to settle you down with a wife. I must say, I was honored to be singled out for such consideration. You know my father has made himself a tidy sum of money, nothing compared to your father of course." She stopped for a moment, took another sip of punch, and continued, "But together, we would clearly stand as one of New York's wealthiest couples."

"I'm not going to live in New York," Pierce finally announced.

"Oh well, Paris then? Or perhaps Boston?"

Pierce shook his head. "Chicago." He couldn't help but get satisfaction from the expression of disappointment on her face.

"Chicago? My, but where in the world is that?"

"It's a little town in Illinois. It sits on Lake Michigan."

"And why would you ever plan to live there?" She was obviously filled with horror at such a thought.

Pierce smiled. "Because this is a time of great adventure in America." He used her own words against her, but she didn't seem fazed by his strategy.

"Yes, of course, but moving to such a place would be complete foolishness for one of your social standing. Such moves as those are justified by the poorer classes who seek to set up a new life for themselves."

"But I seek such a life for myself. I've grown quite weary of the life I've known here in New York."

Amanda was aghast. "But I could never agree to marry you unless we lived in New York City."

"I never asked you to," Pierce said smugly. "Perhaps my aunt presumed too much. Perhaps she led you to believe a falsehood about me, but I assure you I am no more interested in marrying you than you are in marrying me. Now, I suggest that I deliver you back to your father's protection and end this farce."

Amanda's face betrayed her anger. "No one treats me like this. I am a Ralston!"

"That you are, madam, and if left up to me, that you would remain."

The gasp she made was not very ladylike and certainly louder than polite society would have accepted, had the room been quiet enough in which to hear it. Pierce merely got to his feet, offered his arm once again, and waited for her to make up her mind.

"I haven't all night, Miss Ralston. Come, we'll tell your father that something has prevented my staying out the evening. No harm should be done, as it was Blackwell money which secured me as your companion this evening." With that, Pierce nearly dragged her to her feet.

It was a stunned and openly hostile Amanda which Pierce delivered to the care of her mother. Mrs. Ralston was ever so sorry to learn that Pierce was suddenly called away. Pierce begged their forgiveness, then hurried from the gathering before Aunt Eugenia could spot him and force him to stay.

Outside the hotel, Pierce quickly found his driver and urged him to spare no time in exiting the scene. Cold and uncomfortable in the emptiness of his carriage, Pierce had thoughts for only one thing. One woman. Darlene.

For the first time that evening, he smiled. He thought of how he'd arranged for his valentine to be delivered that afternoon and wondered what Darlene thought of the impulsive and rather brazen gesture. Suddenly he felt warmer. Just the thought of her made him push aside the discomforts of the night. There would be much to answer for tomorrow. His aunt would be unforgiving for his rude escape. But he was much more concerned with how Darlene would react to his card.

His father's warning words came back to

haunt him and Pierce was suddenly filled with an uneasiness born of knowing the truth. Darlene was not of his faith and she would reject everything about his Christian beliefs, just as he would reject her disbelief in Christ. Unless God somehow persuaded Darlene to open her heart to the truth of who Jesus really was, further consideration of her could only lead to heartache. But Pierce knew that in many ways it was too late. He was rapidly losing his heart to Darlene, and the thought of rejecting his feelings for her was more than he wanted to deal with.

"She's a good woman, Lord," he prayed aloud in the privacy of the carriage. "She's responsible and considerate, and she loves her father and respects his wishes. She's beautiful, although I don't think she knows it, and I admire her greatly. Surely there's some place for her in my life. Surely there is some way to share with her the Gospel of Christ." But even as Pierce prayed, he knew his words were born out of self-desire.

CHAPTER 7

And he shall be for a sanctuary; but for a
stone of stumbling and for a rock of
offence to both the houses of Israel, for a
gin and for a snare to the inhabitants of
Jerusalem.

ISAIAH 8:14

Darlene looked apprehensively at the envelope in her hands. It had arrived during the
Sabbath and because she knew it was nothing in regards to keeping the day holy, she
had put it aside until Sabbath had concluded. Now, however, there was no putting
off her curiosity. With breakfast concluded
and her father already occupied with something in his room, Darlene sat down to the
kitchen table and opened the envelope.

The card slid out quite easily and caused
Darlene to gasp. It was cream colored with
gold-foil trim and a lace-edged red heart in
the center. The words, *"My Valentine,"*

topped the card, while at the bottom tiny Cupids held a scroll with a more personal limerick.

My heart I do give and display,
For this, our first Valentine's Day.
Let me say from the start, I will never
 depart,
My heart from yours never will stray.

Darlene stared at the card for several moments before turning it over. There was no other word, no signature, nothing at all to indicate who had sent it. But Darlene was already certain who had sent it. There was only one possible person. Pierce Blackwell!

After the initial shock wore off, Darlene began to smile. She fingered the lacy heart and wondered if Pierce had ordered this especially made for her. Perhaps it was a standard card he sent to all women, for surely there must be many fine ladies of his acquaintance. A twinge of grief struck her. Perhaps he had sent this as a way of laughing at her. Maybe it was his only means of making sport of her ignorance. She frowned and looked at the card with a more serious eye.

Hearing her father come from his bedroom, Darlene quickly put the card back into its envelope and tucked it in her apron pocket. Glancing up, Darlene was startled to find that Abraham was not dressed in his shop clothes, but in his best suit with hat in hand.

"Tateh?" she questioned. "You are going out?"

Abraham seemed a bit hesitant to discuss the matter. "I am."

Darlene shook her head. "But I don't understand. Is there something we need? Some errand I can help you with?"

"No." He placed his hat on the table and smiled. "I should talk to you about the matter, but it was not my wish to cause you grief."

"What grief?" Now she was getting worried.

Abraham took a seat beside his daughter and reached out to take her hand in his. "I'm going to the Christian church today with Dennison Blackwell and his family."

"What!" Darlene jumped up from her seat, snatching her hand away.

Abraham lowered his head and it was then that Darlene noticed his head was bare. The yarmulke which he had religiously worn all of his life, was absent. This was more serious than she'd imagined.

"Tateh, I don't understand." Her voice

betrayed her concern.

"I know."

His simple statement was not enough. Darlene came back to the table and sat down. She was stunned beyond words, yet words were the only way to explain her father's decision. He looked so sad, so old, and for the first time Darlene considered that he might die soon. Now he wanted to change religions? After a lifetime of serving God in the faith of his ancestors?

"Why don't you explain and I'll try to be quiet," she suggested.

Abraham looked up at her. His aged face held an expression of sheer anguish. "I've wanted to explain for some time. I know there are rumors among our friends. I know you have had to deal with many questions."

It was true enough. Yesterday, after going to the synagogue with her father, Darlene had found herself surrounded by friends and neighbors, all wanting to know what was going on with her father. Still, she'd not expected such an open showing of defiance. There was no way she could hide the fact that Abraham Lewy was going to the goy's church.

When she said nothing, Abraham continued. "There are many questions in my mind about the Christian faith. The Israelites are the chosen people of God, but Dennison showed me scripture in the Bible which makes it hard to deny that Jesus was truly Messiah."

"The Christian Bible is not the Torah," she protested.

"True, but the scriptures Dennison shared are from Isaiah and those scriptures are a part of our Bible as well."

"This is so confusing," Darlene said, feeling as though the wind was being sucked from her lungs. "Are you saying to me that you believe their Jesus is the Messiah we seek?"

"I'm saying that I see the possibilities for such a thing."

Very calmly, Darlene took a deep breath. "How? How can this be? You told me as a child that Jesus was merely a man. You told me the disciples who followed Him took His body from the tomb and hid it away in order to support their lies of His resurrection." Her voice raised and the stress of the situation was evident. "You told me the goyim served three Gods not one, and now you tell me that Isaiah's words have caused you to see the possibilities of the Christian faith being right and the Jewish faith being wrong?" She felt as though she might start to cry at any moment.

"Neshomeleh, do not fret so. You must understand that I do not consider this matter lightly. I am seeking to know the truth."

"But if Jesus is the Messiah, who needs Him? Still our people suffer, for hundreds of years they suffer. Even now, we are misfits, and less than human in the eyes of some. If Jesus is Messiah, where is His Kingdom? Where is our deliverance?" Darlene knew the words sounded bitter, but she didn't care.

Abraham patted her tightly gripped hands. "I only seek the truth. My love for you is such that I would not seek to put your soul in eternal jeopardy. If there is even the slightest possibility that I am wrong, then I wish to learn the right and teach it to my children before my days are finished.

"You see the mezuzah?" Abraham looked up to the small ornate box which graced the side of the kitchen door. "Within that box are precious words from Deuteronomy. We kiss our hands and touch the mezuzah as a representation of our love and obedience to God's commands."

Darlene looked to the box with its silver scrolling and tiny window. They'd brought this particular mezuzah with them from Germany, and she knew full well it had come from her mother's family. Others were nailed to the wall beside other doors, but this one was very special. The ritual of the mezuzah was as automatic and commonplace as breathing. She touched it reflexively whenever she entered the room and because it was so routine, she seldom reflected on the parchment words held within.

"On that paper God speaks saying, 'And these words, which I command thee this day, shall be in thine heart. And thou shalt teach them diligently unto thy children, and shalt talk of them when thou sittest in thine house, and when thou walkest by the way, and when thou liest down, and when thou risest up.' God has commanded me to train you, Darlene. I cannot fail you by ignoring the truth. Should my choices have been wrong, should I be too blind to see, it would be a tragedy. Would you not rather know the truth?"

"But how can you be certain that the truth isn't what you already believe it to be?" she questioned softly.

Abraham gave a heavy sigh. "Because my heart is troubled. There is an emptiness inside that won't be filled. I used to think it was because of your mother's death. I reasoned that she was such an important part of my life, that the void would quite naturally remain until I died. But with time,

I realized it was more than this. I felt a yearning that I could not explain away. When Dennison Blackwell began to speak to me of his faith, a little fire ignited inside, and I thought, 'Ah, maybe this is my answer.' "

"But Tateh, how can you be sure? You can't give up your faith and embrace the Christian religion without absolute certainty. How will you find that?"

"Because I don't have to give up my faith in order to embrace Christianity. That is the one thing I continue to come back to. Of course, the Jews believe differently about Messiah, but they still believe in Messiah. To acknowledge that Jesus of Christian salvation is also Messiah seems not so difficult a thing."

Darlene was floored by this and longed to ask her father a million questions, but just then a knock sounded loudly on the door downstairs.

"That will be Dennison," Abraham said, getting to his feet. He took up his hat and placed his arm on Darlene's shoulder. "Do not grieve or be afraid. God will direct." He paused for a moment. "You could come with me?"

"No!" she exclaimed, then put her hand to her mouth to keep from saying the multitude of things that had suddenly rushed to her mind. Tears flowed from her eyes and a sob broke from her throat when Abraham bent to kiss the top of her head.

He left her, touching the mezuzah faithfully, but this time it impacted Darlene in a way she couldn't explain. Suddenly her world seemed completely turned upside down. This Jesus of Christian faith seemed to be at the center of all of her problems. How could she ever be reconciled to her father's new search for truth, when all of her life the truth seemed to be clear? Now, her father would have her question whether their beliefs were accurately perceived.

Her father's absence made the silence of the house and shop unbearable. Darlene had no idea when he might return and all she could do was busy herself with the handwork he'd given her. Hayyim was hard at work in the cutting room when she came to take up her workbasket. He looked up and smiled, but quickly lost his expression of joy and rushed to her side.

"You've been crying. *Vos iz mit dir?*"

She tried to shake her head, but couldn't. "Nothing's the matter. I'm all right."

"No, you're not. You look like something truly awful has happened. Here," he led her to a chair, "sit down and tell me what's wrong."

All Darlene could remember was that Hayyim had shared information from the shop with Esther. Of course, Esther was an old woman, butting in wherever she could in order to learn whatever there was to learn. Still, Hayyim should have been more discriminating.

"I'm fine," she insisted. "There's much to be done and Tateh won't be back for several hours. He has a meeting with Mr. Blackwell."

"On a Sunday? I thought that rich goy went to synagogue, I mean church, on Sunday."

Darlene shrugged. "It is no concern of mine . . . or yours." She narrowed her eyes at Hayyim. "You mustn't talk about my father to other people. There are those who say you gossip like an old woman and I won't have it, do you understand? My father is a good man and I won't have people look down upon him because of loose, idle palaver."

Hayyim looked genuinely sorry for his indiscretion. "Esther has a way of getting it out of you," he said by way of explanation. "I didn't even realize I was talking until I was well into it. I meant no harm."

Darlene pitied him and for a moment she thought he might cry. "I know well Esther's way. Just guard your mouth in the future."

"You know I would never hurt you, Darlene. You know that I would like to speak to your father about us."

"There is no 'us,' Hayyim. I do not wish to marry you and I will not leave Tateh."

"I would never ask you to leave him. I would work here as your husband and make a good life for you and your father. I would care for him in his old age and he would never have to work again."

Darlene smiled because she knew Hayyim was most serious in his devotion. She shook her head. "I could not take you for a husband, Hayyim."

"Because I am poor?" He sounded the question so pathetically.

Darlene touched her hand to his arm. "No, because I do not love you, nor would I ever come to love you."

She left him at that, knowing that he would not want her to see him cry or show weakness. He was still a child in some ways, and although being orphaned by his parents and losing his brothers all to cholera had grown him up, Hayyim was not the strong, intelligent man she would hope to call husband.

A fleeting image of Pierce Blackwell came to mind and Darlene reached into her pocket for the valentine he'd sent. She pulled it from the envelope and for a moment, remembering that Pierce's father was the cause for her heavy heart, thought to throw it in the fire. But she couldn't destroy it. For reasons quite beyond her ability to understand, Darlene put her work aside and went quietly to her bedroom. Going to her clothes chest, she gently lay aside her nightgowns and put the envelope safely away. Replacing the gowns, she felt a strange tugging at her heart. Pierce might be a Gentile, but he was considerate and intelligent and very handsome. It was difficult not to be persuaded by such strong visual enticements.

Going back downstairs, Darlene picked up her sewing and began her work. There was much to consider. Her father's words still haunted her and the questions in her mind would not be put aside. Perhaps she would go later and speak with Mr. Singer. Without a rabbi to consult, perhaps Mr. Singer could advise her. But to do so would betray her father's actions and bring about harsh reprisals. Still, to say nothing and have no knowledge of what she should do could only cause more grief. Perhaps if she knew more, she could persuade her father to give up this foolish notion of accepting Christianity as being truth. Otherwise, this issue of Jesus as Messiah was going to be quite a barrier to overcome.

Chapter 8

I know that ye are Abraham's seed; but
ye seek to kill me, because my word hath
no place in you.

John 8:37

Darlene walked bitterly into spring with a
heaviness of heart that would not be dis-
pelled. She listened to her father's words
and knew him to be quite excited about the
things he was learning. There were phrases
he spoke, words which meant something
different than they'd ever meant before.
Salvation. Redemption. The Holy Spirit. All
of these frightened Darlene to the very core
of her being.

Now, with less than a week before Passover, Darlene didn't know whether to make
preparations for a seder meal, or to just plan
to spend Passover with Esther. By now,
everyone knew that her father was a man
torn between two religious views. He went

faithfully to the synagogue on Friday evening and Saturday, but on Sunday he went to the Christian church with Dennison Blackwell. He was rapidly viewed as being both crazy and a traitor, and neither representation did him justice as far as Darlene was concerned.

The ringing of the shop doorbells caused Darlene to jump. Nervous these days from a constant barrage of Esther's questions, Darlene had decided that every visitor could possibly represent some form of gossip or challenge related to her father. This time, her assessment couldn't have been more accurate. With a look of pure disdain, Reuven Singer filled the doorway. He wore a broad-rimmed black hat, with a heavy black overcoat that fell to the floor. His long gray beard trailed down from thick, stern lips and one glance into his pale blue eyes caused Darlene to shiver.

"Good morning, Mr. Singer. Tateh is out, but I expect him back soon."

"I know full well that your father is out. I know, too, where he has gone. He's at the church of his Christian friends, no?"

"It's true," Darlene admitted. She felt sick to her stomach and wished she could sit down. "You're welcome to wait for him upstairs. Come, I'll make tea."

"No. Perhaps it is better we talk."

Darlene glanced around her. Hayyim was on the third floor moving bolts of cloth. She knew he'd be busy for some time and would present no interruption for the cantor. "We can sit in here or go in the back."

"The back, then."

She nodded and led the way. Her hands were shaking so violently that she wondered if the cantor was aware of her fear. She offered him the more comfortable of two stuffed chairs and when he had taken his seat, she joined him. Barely sitting on the edge of her chair, Darlene leaned forward, smoothed her skirt of pale blue wool, and waited for Mr. Singer to speak.

"Miss Lewy, it is believed by many that your father has fallen away from the teachings of his fathers. I cannot say how much this grieves and angers me, nor can I stress enough the dangers you face."

Darlene swallowed hard. What should she say? To admit to everything she knew might well see her father ostracized by his own people. Deciding it was better to remain silent and appear the obedient child, Darlene did nothing but look at her folded hands.

"Avrom has feet in two worlds. It cannot remain so. He is a Jew or he is a traitor to his people."

Darlene could not bear to hear him malign her father. Squaring her shoulders, Darlene looked him in the eye. "Mr. Singer, may I ask you a question?"

The old cantor seemed taken aback by her sudden boldness. He nodded, his gray beard bobbing up and down with the motion.

"I've heard it said," she hesitated. She wasn't a scholarly woman and all of the things she was about to say had come straight from her father's mouth. She could only hope to accurately translate the things she'd been told. "I've heard it said," she began again, "that the words of Isaiah make clear the coming of Messiah. The Christians believe Isaiah speaks of Jesus, but we believe it speaks of Israel. Is this true?"

The cantor eyed her quite sternly for a moment. "It is true."

"The Christians also believe that Jesus is not only Messiah, but that He offers salvation to anyone who comes to Him."

"And what salvation would this be?" the cantor questioned. "Would it be salvation from the persecution our people have faced from their kind? Would it restore Israel and Jerusalem back to our people? Salvation from what, I ask?" The deep, resonant voice clearly bore irritation.

"Well . . ." Darlene was now sorry to have brought up the subject. So much of what her father had shared regarding the Christians seemed reasonable, but confusing. "I thought it to mean salvation from death."

"You are of God's chosen people, Miss Lewy. By reason of that you are already saved."

"But the Christians believe . . ."

"Feh! I care not for what the goyim believe. You are responsible for three things. *Tefillah* — prayer. *Teshuvah* — repentance. And *tsedakah* — righteousness. If you do what is right in God's eyes, make your prayers, and turn away from your sins, God will look favorably upon you. The only salvation we seek is for Israel. Why do you suppose we say, 'Next year in Jerusalem'? We mourn the destruction and loss of our beloved homeland. We long with fervency to return. Messiah will rebuild Jerusalem and the Holy Temple and restore His people to their land. The Turks now control it. Would you have me believe that the Christian Jesus came to earth but was unable to establish such restoration?"

"I don't know," she answered honestly. "I suppose that is why I ask."

The cantor seemed to soften a bit. "It might be better if you were to leave this place. Esther has already told me there is room for you in her home. She would happily take you in and keep you."

"Leave my father? How could this be in keeping with the scriptures to honor him?" Darlene was devastated by the suggestion.

"He is a traitor to his people if he believes that Jesus is Messiah. He will be forsaken and there will be no fellowship with him. He will become as one dead to us and you will be as one orphaned."

Darlene couldn't help but shudder. She thought of the tiny, homeless children who frequented her doorstep. Would she be reduced to begging scraps of food and clothing from the friends and neighbors who would deem her father unfit — *apostate* — dead? She shuddered again. "I could not leave Tateh. He isn't well and he might die. He needs me to care for him."

The old man's harsh demeanor returned. "He will surely perish if he turns from God. As will you. Will you become meshummad — traitor to your faith and people? Will you trample under foot the traditions of your ancestors and break the heart of your dear, departed mother? If you follow your father into such betrayal, you will leave us no option but to declare you dead as well."

Darlene felt shaken and unsure of herself.

"I . . . I'm not . . ."

The cantor got to his feet. "Christians have sought to destroy us. They treat us as less than human and disregard us, malign us, and even kill our people, all in the name of Christianity. Can you find acceptability in such a faith?" He didn't wait for an answer, but strode proudly from the room.

Darlene sat silently for several moments. She could feel her heart racing and perspiration forming on her brow. Why did such things have to be so consuming? The ringing of the bells caught her attention, and Darlene thought perhaps Mr. Singer had returned. Jumping to her feet, she was surprised to find her father standing in the door. A quick glance at the clock on the wall showed her that more time had passed than she'd been aware of.

"Tateh, you're back!"

Abraham smiled broadly. "That I am and I have news to tell you. Come upstairs and we'll sit together."

Darlene followed her father, wondering what in the world he had to tell her. His countenance was peaceful and his smile seemed to say that all was well, but in her heart Darlene feared that this talk would forever change their lives.

"Let me check on your dinner," she said,

barely hearing her own words. She opened the oven to reveal a thick-breasted chicken roasting golden brown. Poking a fork into the center of it, she was satisfied to watch the succulent juices slide down the sides and into the pan.

"Come, dinner will wait," Abraham stated firmly.

Darlene closed the oven and took her place at the table. It was always here that they shared important matters. It was at a similar table in Germany that her father had told her of her mother and brother's death. It was at that same table he had announced their departure for America. What could he possibly wish to share with her now?

"What is it, Tateh?"

Abraham smiled. "I have invited the Blackwells to share Passover with us."

Passover? Her heart gave a sudden lurch. If Tateh was considering Passover, perhaps things weren't as bad as she supposed. But to invite the Blackwells to their seder was a shock.

"You've asked them here? For our seder?"

"Yes. The message this morning at their church was all about Easter and the last supper of Jesus Christ. The last supper was a celebration of Passover. Pierce said that he wondered what that Passover feast might have been like, and I told him he should come see for himself."

"And they accepted?"

"Dennison and Pierce did. Mrs. Morgan, Dennison's widowed sister, declined interest. I don't think she much cares for our kind." His words were given in a rather sorrowful manner. "Of course, she also takes a strong stand where Dennison's youngest child is concerned and refused for both herself and Constance Blackwell."

"I see." Darlene felt a lump form in her throat. "Well, I suppose I have preparations to see to."

"You are unhappy with this?" Abraham looked at her so tenderly that Darlene couldn't distance herself from him.

"No, not really." She considered telling him about the cantor, but decided against it. "I'm just surprised that they would want to come."

Abraham chuckled. "I think Pierce would make any excuse to come. He seems most anxious to see you again. He always asks about you and wonders how it is that you are ever away when he comes for fittings."

Darlene blushed, feeling her cheeks grow very hot. She thought no one had noticed her purposeful absences. "I suppose it is because I have much to do."

Abraham laughed even more at her feeble attempt to disguise the truth. "Daughter, you are not so very good at telling falsehoods. I've seen the way your face lights up when I speak of him. Perhaps you have a place in your heart for him?"

"No!" Darlene declared a bit too enthusiastically. "He's not of our faith and besides, I would never leave you."

"You will one day. It is important for a woman to marry and I will see you safely settled into a marriage of love and security before I die. So, if you think you can prolong my life on earth by simply refusing to marry, think again."

Darlene saw the glint of amusement in his eyes. She loved this man more than any other human being. Falling to her knees, she threw her arms around his waist and with her head on his lap began to cry. "I love you, Tateh, please do not jest about your death. I'm afraid when I think of you dying and leaving me behind. I think of how much it hurt to lose my mother and I can't bear the thought of your passing."

Abraham stroked her hair and tried to reassure her. "That is why the truth is important to me, Darlene. I want to be absolutely sure of my eternity. Does that sound like a foolish old man who is afraid to die?"

"Of course not!" she declared, raising her gaze to meet her father's eyes.

"Well, it's the truth. I am a foolish old man and I'm afraid to die. Dennison Blackwell isn't afraid to end his life on earth because he has great confidence in what will happen to him after his earthly life is completed."

"And you don't have such faith in your beliefs?" She dried her eyes with the back of her sleeve and waited for his answer.

He gently touched her cheek with his aged fingers. "If I could say yes, I would and put your mind forever at ease. But I cannot say yes."

"I'm afraid, Tateh."

"I know." He smiled sympathetically. "I suppose it would do little good to tell you not to be afraid."

"Very little good," she said with a hint of a smile on her lips. She got to her feet and Abraham stood too, wrapping her in his arms.

"You will make for the Blackwells a fine seder?" he questioned softly.

"Of course, Tateh. It will be the very best."

"Good. Now, I must go to work and earn for us the money for such a feast."

Darlene let him go without another word. She made her way to her bedroom and closed the door quietly behind her. Standing there in the stark, simple room, Darlene couldn't help but wonder where the future would take them. Surely if her father converted to Christianity, they'd find it impossible to remain in the neighborhood. Mr. Singer had already made it clear that they would be cut off from the community and called dead.

Drawing a deep breath, Darlene went to her bed and sat down. *No matter what happens,* she thought, *no matter where I am led, I will not forsake my father. I will not be blinded by the prejudice and stupidity of my own people.* She saw her reflection in the dresser mirror and tried hard to smile. Her eyes were still red-rimmed from crying and her face rather ashen from the shocks of the day, but deep inside, Darlene knew that her spirit thrived and that her heart was complete and whole. She would not be defeated by these things. She had trusted her father all of her life. To deny his ability to look out for her very best interests now would be to subject all of his ways to speculative guesses.

Dropping her gaze, Darlene caught sight of the chest where Pierce's valentine lay hidden away. She'd never spoken to him of the matter. In fact, her father was quite right to mention her disappearances when Pierce was scheduled to arrive in the shop. She felt nervous and jittery inside whenever she thought about Pierce Blackwell. There was no future with him, but he stirred her imagination in a way that could be quite maddening. With very little thought, she went to the chest and retrieved the pristine card.

She traced the letters, *"My Valentine"* and wondered if Pierce had ever given it a single thought after having it delivered to her. He must think her terribly rude to have never thanked him for his thoughtfulness. And she truly believed that the act had been inspired by thoughtfulness and not because Pierce wanted to mock her inexperience with the day.

And now they were coming for Passover.

Pierce and his father would arrive to share her favorite celebration. Would they mock her faith, or would they understand and cherish it as she did? She thought of the recited words of the Passover dinner. The questions which were always asked and the responses which were always given. "What makes this night different," she whispered and replaced the valentine in the chest. And indeed, she couldn't help but know that this night would be most different from all the others she had known.

CHAPTER 9

And it shall come to pass, when your
children shall say unto you, What mean
ye by this service? That ye shall say, It is
the sacrifice of the LORD's passover, who
passed over the houses of the children of
Israel in Egypt, when he smote the
Egyptians, and delivered our houses. And
the people bowed the head and
worshipped.
EXODUS 12:26, 27

Darlene had worked diligently to rid the
house and shop of any crumb of leaven. She
swept the place from the top floor down and
burned every bit until she was satisfied that
the house was clean. This was in keeping
with the teachings of her Jewish faith, and it
made her proud to be such an important
part of Passover. She remembered asking
her bubbe why they had to eat unleavened
bread and why the house had to be kept so

clean of crumbs. Bubbe had told her the story of Israel's deliverance out of Egypt and it came to be a story she remembered well, for it was retold with every Passover celebration.

"When our people were in Egypt," Bubbe had said, *"they were slaves to the Pharaoh. They suffered great miseries and God took pity upon them and sent out Moses to appeal to Pharaoh to let God's people go. But of course, Pharaoh was a stubborn man and he endured many plagues and sufferings upon his own people before finally agreeing to let the Israelites go free. The last of these great plagues was the most horrible of all. God told Moses He would take the life of every firstborn in the land of Egypt. Our people smeared blood over the doors and windows and the destroyer passed over, seeing this as a symbol of obedience unto God. Then, they had to rise up with haste to make the great journey to freedom. There was no time for the bread to rise and so they ate unleavened bread. Thus Passover became the Feast of Unleavened Bread."*

Darlene still shuddered to think of such a monumental judgment upon the land. She remembered the verses Bubbe had quoted. *"For I will pass through the land of Egypt this night, and will smite all the firstborn in the land* of Egypt, both man and beast; and against all the gods of Egypt I will execute judgment: I am the Lord."

Darlene felt a deep sense of awe in that statement. It was such a moving reminder. "I am the Lord." Baruch Ha-Shem, she thought. Blessed is the Name.

With her mind focused on the preparations for Passover, Darlene forgot about the Blackwells. Instead, she wondered if her father would participate with the same enthusiasm he had once held for the ceremony. Surely he still felt the same about the deliverance of God's people from bondage. Freedom was a most cherished thing in the Lewy household and Darlene knew full well that her father didn't take such matters lightly. But perhaps the Christians in their faith were not so concerned with such things. What if the Blackwells had convinced her father that such freedom and remembrances were unimportant?

This was her first conscious thoughts of Pierce and his father. She grew nervous trying to imagine them at the seder table. Would they wear yarmulkes? Would they recite the prayers? Would they scoff and laugh at the faith of her people?

Somehow, Darlene couldn't imagine Pierce or his father being so cruel, but she reminded herself that she really didn't know either one all that well. Putting aside her worries, Darlene began to think about Pierce. She'd caught a glimpse of him leaving the shop one day and couldn't help but notice the way her heart beat faster at the very sight of him. Why did he have to affect her in such a way? Why could she not forget his smiling face and warm brown eyes? Sometimes it hurt so much to imagine what life with Pierce might be like. She knew what it felt like to be held securely in his arms. Would he hold her in that same possessive way if they were married? Would his smile be as sweet and his manners as gentle if she were his wife?

"No!" she exclaimed, putting her hands to her head as if to squeeze out such thoughts. It was sheer madness to imagine such things. Pierce was a Christian and she was a Jew. There was no possibility of the two coming together as one.

The Blackwell carriage drew up to the shop of Abraham Lewy. Pierce felt the anticipation of seeing Darlene mount within him and he found himself anxious to push the evening forward. If his father sensed this, he said nothing. In fact, little talk had been exchanged between them because two hours earlier, Pierce had announced his desire to move to Chicago. Dennison hadn't taken the news very well. A number of protests to such an idea were easily put forth, but Pierce had answers for all of his father's concerns. Hadn't they been his own concerns when first the thought of such a trip had come to mind? *How will you live? How will you travel there? How will you survive in the wilds of Illinois?* They were legitimate questions and Pierce couldn't pretend that he had all of the answers.

Seeing his father's brooding face, Pierce offered him a word of consolation. "Don't fret about this which hasn't come to pass. I promise I won't make any rash decisions, and I will discuss everything with you first."

"Discuss, but not necessarily heed my advice," Dennison muttered.

Pierce realized that nothing he said would offer comfort and gave up. He sprang from the carriage and without waiting for his father, went to knock on the shop door. Closed for Passover, the window shade on the door had been pulled and even the shop windows were shaded for privacy. As his father came to stand beside him, Pierce couldn't help but feel the racing of his heart and wondered if his father would make some comment about the inappropriateness of Pierce's interest in Darlene. But before any word could be exchanged, Abraham Lewy opened the door and smiled.

"Ah, you have come. Shalom."

"Shalom, my friend," Dennison replied. "And, my thanks for this invitation to your home and celebration."

It was a most somber occasion, and yet Pierce could hardly contain himself. He knew that just up those wooden stairs, Darlene would be scurrying around to make everything perfect for the occasion. He wanted to see her more than anything, and all other thoughts were wasted on him.

"Come, my Darlene has already made ready our table," Abraham said. "Oh, and here." He pulled out two yarmulkes and handed them to Dennison and Pierce. "You will not mind wearing a headcovering for prayer, will you?"

"Of course not," Dennison announced and promptly placed the yarmulke on his head.

Pierce held the small black piece for a moment and smiled. "My pleasure," he announced, putting it into place. All he could think of was that this might in some way bring about Darlene's approval. He certainly didn't believe it necessary for prayer, but he knew it was something she would expect.

They made their way up the stairs, slowly following Abraham's aged form. Pierce felt the yarmulke slip off his head just in time to replace it. Dennison was having no better luck. As they entered the dining area, Pierce saw Abraham touch his hand to his lips and then touch a small metal box at the inside of the door. He pondered this for a moment, wondering what the box represented, but then Darlene appeared, and he thought of nothing else for a very long time.

She was lovely, just as he'd remembered her. She wore a beautiful gown of amber satin and lace, and her hair had been left down to cascade in curls below her shoulders. Her response was friendly and open, but Pierce saw a light in her eyes when she met his gaze and it caused a surge of energy to flow through him.

"Good evening, my dear," Dennison said first. "Thank you for the invitation to share such an important celebration with you." The yarmulke slid off his head and onto the floor. Dennison laughed and bent over to pick it up, just as Pierce's did the same.

Everyone laughed, but it was Abraham who spoke, "For you, Darlene could fetch some hat pins?"

They all laughed again and Pierce and Dennison replaced the yarmulkes.

Then it was Pierce who spoke. He tried to steady his nerves and keep his voice even. "Darlene, it's wonderful to see you again. I see you've managed to avoid the freighters."

She blushed as he knew she would at the reminder of their last meeting. "Good evening, Mr. Blackwell," she said rather shyly.

"Nonsense, my name is Pierce. You must use it and give me the honor of addressing you by your given name."

Darlene looked hesitantly at her father and Dennison Blackwell before nodding. "Very well, Pierce."

She hurried away after that and Pierce wished that he could follow her. "Do you need help with anything?" he called after her.

"No. Everything is ready."

She was only a few feet away, but space seemed to represent an unbreakable wall to Pierce. Her rejection of his help left him with nothing to do but listen to the conversation of his father and Abraham, and to make an occasional comment when asked for one.

"Come," Abraham said, "we'll begin our seder."

Pierce took in every detail of the setting. A beautiful lacy cloth lay over the table and two lighted candles, in intricate silver holders, were placed atop this. There was also a strange tray of some sort with six circular indentions. Each indention held some food article, but none held the same appeal as the delicious aroma of whatever Darlene had in the oven. Pulling out a chair, Pierce saw that there was a cushion on it. Gazing around he noted a cushion at the back of every chair. Perhaps the Lewys feared that their guests would expect luxury.

Darlene took her seat opposite Pierce, looking up for a moment to meet his gaze. He smiled, hoping that it would both charm and relax her. She seemed tense in his presence and he wondered if perhaps she would have rather he not share her Passover seder.

Abraham began the opening prayer and from there the ceremony seemed to pass in a blur of fascination for Pierce. It was all so different from anything he'd ever known, yet there was also an air of familiarity. Had he not been taught from the Bible about Moses and the slavery of Israel? Yet for Darlene and Abraham, there seemed an appreciation for this remembrance that Pierce had no understanding of. He had known an easy life. He had known a life of privilege. Thinking this, Abraham's next words caught

Pierce's attention and seared a place in his heart.

". . . We speak this evening of other tyrants and other tyrannies as well. We speak of the tyranny of poverty and the tyranny of privation, of the tyranny of wealth and the tyranny of war, of the tyranny of power and the tyranny of despair, of the tyranny of disease and the tyranny of time, of the tyranny of ignorance and the tyranny of color. To all these tyrannies do we address ourselves this evening. Passover brands them all as abominations in the sight of God."

Abominations in the sight of God? Pierce could only wonder at the meaning for surely God had no problem with wealth and prosperity. Unless, of course, it led to greed and cruelty. He thought of Amanda Ralston. The tyranny of ignorance and color gave him thoughts of Eugenia and her fierce dislike of the Jews in their city. All the things named as tyrannies were the very essences of those things which separated one people from another.

The ceremony continued and Pierce was surprised when Darlene got up and retrieved a pitcher of water, a bowl, and a towel. Abraham noted his confusion and smiled.

125

"It is recorded in the Talmud, the hands should be washed before dipping food."

Pierce watched as Darlene placed the bowl at her father's side. He held his hands over the bowl and she poured a small amount of water from the pitcher. Abraham rubbed his hands together and accepted a towel from Darlene on which to dry them. This process was repeated for Dennison, and finally for Pierce. He sensed her anxiety and nervousness. Without looking up, he held his hands as he'd seen the others do and when she handed him the towel, their fingers touched for just a moment. He heard her draw in her breath quickly and kept his face lowered. Such a sobering ceremony deserved his respect, but he really felt like smiling because he was growing ever more certain that Darlene felt something powerful for him.

After washing her own hands, Darlene retook her place and the seder continued. There was a passing of raw parsley which was used to dip in salt water and Abraham directed them all in the recitation of the blessing, first in Hebrew and then in English.

"Praised be Thou, O Lord our God, King of the universe, who created the fruit of the earth."

There were more prayers and the breaking of the unleavened bread, or matzah as Abraham called it, and Pierce was completely mesmerized by the process of this ceremony. There were symbolic reasons for everything and he suddenly found that he wanted to understand it all at once.

Without warning, Darlene spoke in a soft, but clear voice that reminded Pierce of a little girl. "Why is this night different from all other nights?"

He wondered if this was part of the ceremony or just a reflective thought because of his presence at her seder. He didn't have long to wait before realizing that this was yet another portion of recitations. Abraham spoke out in his deep authoritative voice.

"In what way do you find this night different?"

"In four ways," Darlene answered, "do I find it different."

"What is the first difference?"

Pierce paid close attention as Darlene replied. "It differs in that on all other nights we eat bread or matzah, while on this night we eat only matzah."

"And what is the second difference?"

"It differs in that on all other nights we eat vegetables and herbs of all kinds, while on this night we must eat bitter herbs."

Abraham nodded. "And what is the third difference between this night and all other nights?"

"It differs in that on all other nights we do not dip vegetables even once, while on this night we dip them twice."

"And what is the fourth difference?"

"It differs in that on all other nights we eat in an upright or a reclining position, while on this night we recline at the table."

Pierce began to realize the purpose for the cushion at his back. There was so much that he was unaware of and he felt like an outsider intruding on something very precious.

"The four differences," Abraham concluded, "that you have called to our attention are important and significant. They are reminders that freedom and liberty are cherished values not to be taken for granted."

The words touched Pierce as Abraham continued to explain. "To appreciate what it means to be free we must be reminded of how it feels to be enslaved."

Pierce felt a chill run up his spine. He took his freedom for granted. He took his wealth and the privileges he enjoyed for granted. He didn't know what it was to be enslaved, with the possible exception of the way

Darlene had enslaved his heart.

Abraham continued with a recitation of the enslavement of the Israelites under the Egyptian taskmasters. He stressed the importance of retelling the story of deliverance lest any man forget God's blessings and the importance of freedom. There were other stories and a remembrance of the ten plagues God had brought upon Egypt when Pharaoh would not let the children of Israel go.

Then came another phase of the seder and Abraham raised a bone which lay upon the seder tray. This was symbolic of the Paschal Lamb which was eaten on Passover eve when the Temple stood in Jerusalem. "What does this bone remind us, and what does it teach us?" Abraham questioned and then continued. "It reminds us of the tenth plague in Egypt, when all the firstborn of the Egyptians were struck down. It reminds us of the salvation of the Israelites whose homes were spared. For *Pesach* means more than Paschal Lamb; it has another meaning. It means, 'He skipped over.' The Lord skipped over the houses of those whose doorposts bore the blood of the lamb." Abraham lowered the bone and said very seriously. "The willingness to sacrifice is the prelude to freedom."

Pierce felt a trembling in his body and clearly knew the hand of God was upon him. Perhaps he was in more bondage than he knew. He wondered if he had a heart for sacrifice and whether he could give up all that he loved, for the sake of freedom in God.

Abraham then raised the matzah. "This matzah that we eat reminds us of the haste with which the Israelites fled from Egypt. The dough that they were baking on the hot rocks of the Egyptian fields was removed before it could leaven, and so it remained flat."

He lowered this and picked up the *maror,* bitter herbs represented here by horseradish. "The bitter herbs symbolize the bitter lot of the Israelites who were enslaved in Egypt. Pesach, matzah, and maror are the symbolic expressions that represent freedom in all ages. Today we might say they symbolize sacrifice, preparedness, and hope. These are necessary elements in the fight for freedom."

Pierce's thoughts were turned inward as the seder concluded. He barely heard the words while going through the motions of the ceremony. His heart and conscience were pricked with the meanings and representation of the things he did. When he'd agreed to come to the seder, Pierce had thought nothing of how it might affect him. He'd only thought of Darlene and how she might affect him. But now, in the humble quiet of their home, Pierce's mind ran in a multitude of directions. To have freedom from the greed and prejudice of New York society, he would have to sacrifice his comfort. To go forward in a positive and clearly mapped out manner would require preparation. And, to serve God more directly and in a completely life-changing way would require hope. Hope in that which he could not see, but was certain existed.

The seder meal was completed and the symbols cleared away by Abraham, while Darlene brought out a most extensive feast. Pierce watched her intently, wondering quietly to himself whether she'd ever consider leaving New York as his wife.

As they sat around the table enjoying a huge beef roast, Pierce was surprised when Abraham spoke. "Your celebration of Easter seems to share something with our Passover."

"It shares a great deal," Dennison replied. "We remember that Jesus ate the Passover seder with His disciples before going to His death on the cross. This time of year reminds us, too, of freedom. We Christians

131

have freedom from eternal death because of Christ's sacrifice on the cross. He prepared a way for us to be reconciled with God, and because of this we have hope that He will come again for us."

Darlene's expression seemed to change from indifference to revelation. She said nothing, but Pierce saw the change and wondered if God had somehow stirred her heart to understanding.

"And," Pierce added quickly, hoping that his words would reach her, "the blood which Christ shed for us is like that of the lambs' blood sprinkled over the doorposts of the Israelites, although more precious because it was the sacrifice of God's Son rather than that of a simple beast. But both represent the shedding of blood in exchange for death passing us by. Christ died that we might not have to."

Darlene looked at him for a moment, and in those few precious seconds, Pierce believed that God had finally made Himself known to her. Perhaps there would be no instantaneous revelation. Perhaps it would be years before she would understand what had happened. However long it took, Pierce knew that seeds had been planted and he was confident that God could harvest Darlene's heart for His own.

CHAPTER 10

But God commendeth his love toward us,
in that, while we were yet sinners, Christ
died for us.

ROMANS 5:8

After sharing Passover with the Blackwells,
Darlene knew that she'd never be the same.
It was impossible to stop thinking about the
words Dennison and Pierce had shared.
Also, it was impossible to not remember the
joy in Father's face and the certainty in
which he shared his heart on the matters of
Christianity and Judaism. And, alas, it was
also impossible to forget Pierce Blackwell.
His gentle smiles pervaded her thoughts.
His searching eyes and questioning expressions made her realize that he wanted to
know more about her. But why? Why was
Pierce paying her so much attention? In the
months that had passed since that seder
dinner, he had come by for visits, brought

candy and trinkets (always for both herself and her father), and he seemed completely determined to better know her mind on certain issues.

What did she think of westward expansion? What did she know about the new railroads? What had she read about the western territories and states? Did she like to travel? Would she ever consider leaving New York City?

Oy vey! But the man was annoying!

That night had not only given her reason to consider her heart and soul, it had also changed forever her relationship with her father. Abraham now openly attended church with the Blackwells and more frequently was absent from the synagogue. This made Darlene depressed and discouraged, but even more so, she found herself consumed by a deep, unfillable void. Why did Tateh have to embrace Christianity and turn away from the Hebrew faith? He hadn't announced the rejection of Judaism, so Darlene tried to keep hoping that her father was merely studying the goy's faith with a scholarly interest. But deep down inside, she knew it wasn't true.

In his bedroom, Darlene could hear her father at prayer. He would wear his *tallis,* the fringed prayer shawl of black and white.

He would also have his *tefilin,* leather boxes, strapped to his forehead and left arm. Inside these boxes were the scriptures of Exodus thirteen, verses one through ten, dealing with the remembrance of God bringing the Hebrew children out of bondage and commanding them to keep God's laws. On his head would be his yarmulke and from his mouth would come the familiar prayers she'd heard all of her life. These were the markings of his Jewish faith. Why then would he lay them aside in a few moments, eat breakfast with her, and go to the goy's church with the Blackwells?

Tears came to her eyes and she wiped at them angrily with the back of her sleeve. It wasn't right that her father should leave her so confused and alone. Why must she struggle through this thing? Why should there be such despair in her heart?

She brought bread and porridge to the table and set it down beside a huge bowl of fruit. She loved the summer months when fruits and vegetables could be had fresh. Fetching a pitcher of cream, Darlene tried to rally her heart to gladness. They had plenty and were well and safe. Her father's health had even revived a bit with the warmth of summer. Surely God was good and His protection was upon them, in spite of her father's search to better understand Christianity.

"Good morning, Neshomeleh," Abraham said, coming into the kitchen. He reached a hand to his lips and touched the mezuzah as he always had.

Darlene smiled and came to greet her father with a hug. "Good morning, Tateh. Did you sleep well?"

"Yes, very well." His smile warmed her heart, just as his kiss upon her forehead put her at ease. "And you?"

"It is well with me also."

They ate in companionable silence, but when Abraham had finished, he eyed Darlene quite seriously and said, "I have a favor to ask of you."

Darlene put down the dish she was clearing and asked, "What is it?"

"Sit."

She did as she was asked, but in her mind whirled a thousand possibilities. What was it that he would ask of her that required she sit down? "What do you want of me, Tateh?"

"Come with me today. Come to the Blackwells' church and be at my side. It is important to me and I only ask because it would mean a great deal."

"But why now? Why is it suddenly so important to you?" Darlene felt fear constrict her chest. It was difficult to breathe.

Abraham smiled lovingly and put his hand upon her arm. "Because today, I will accept Jesus into my heart."

"What!" She jumped up from the table. "You can't be serious!"

"Darlene, I have never been more serious. These long months I have searched for answers to questions that have eluded me all of my life. The knowledge given to me through the *Tanakh* and the New Testament has answered those questions."

"New Testament?"

Abraham smiled tolerantly. "It's the story of Jesus and His followers. It tells how believers in Christ should act and live. It filled my longing and took away my emptiness."

Darlene thought of her own longing and the emptiness that haunted her. She swallowed hard and sat back down in a rather defeated manner. "Then you are no longer of the faith. What of your friends and the shop? You will become as dead to them."

"Most likely," Abraham agreed. "But then, they haven't exactly been very friendly these last months anyway. I make a good living from people who are not Jewish, so the shop should not suffer overmuch."

"But Hayyim will leave us. How will you

manage to work without help?"

"I'll advertise for a Christian. There must be plenty of Christian young men who would take up the job of tailoring."

Finally Darlene had to ask the one remaining question. "What of me? What of us? The cantor says I should leave you and live with Esther. He says you are a traitor and that should you reject your faith, I must leave or face the possibility of becoming a traitor as well."

Abraham shook his head. "There is nothing between us that must cause us to part. Come with me today and I believe you will come to understand my choice. In time, you may well come to make that choice for yourself and when you do, I want to be at your side."

Darlene stared at the table rather than meet her father's joyous expression. How could she be so sad when he was obviously so happy? How could she, who had listened to the words and advice of her father for all of her life, now reject his words because they seemed rash and contradictory to everything he had taught her?

"Please come with me today."

His pleading was more than she could bear. In that moment Darlene knew that should she be forever branded a traitor, she would still go with her father wherever he asked her to go. "I'll come with you," she whispered in a voice that barely contained her grief.

Abraham leaned over and kissed her on the head. "Thank you, my little soul. You are all that is left to me on this earth."

Darlene was still thinking about his words when the Blackwells' carriage arrived and Dennison Blackwell stepped down to greet them. Darlene had put on her best gown, a pale blue muslin with huge gigot sleeves and lace trimming around the neck. It was a simple dress, yet it was her finest. In her mind she had imagined Pierce taking her by the arm to lead her into his church, and it was then that she wanted to look her very best.

"Good morning, Abraham, Darlene," Dennison said in greeting. "Have you ever known a more perfect day?"

"It is very lovely," Abraham said, then took hold of Darlene's arm. "My daughter will come with us today. Is there room in your carriage?" He looked up at the open landau where Eugenia and Constance Blackwell sat on one side, while Pierce occupied the other.

Dennison was at first quite surprised, but

quickly enough a broad smile crossed his face. "There is plenty of room and you are very welcome to come with us, my dear."

Darlene felt her heart give a lurch when Pierce stood up and held out a hand to assist her up. "We're very glad to have you join us," he announced, while Eugenia gave her a harsh look of disdain. "You may sit here with Constance and my aunt Eugenia."

Darlene put her gloved hand in his and allowed him to help her into the carriage. Eugenia looked away, while Constance smiled most congenially and made room for Darlene to sit in the middle. Abraham took his place between Pierce and Dennison and without further fanfare, they were on their way.

Immediately, Darlene was painfully aware of the contrast to her best gown and the Blackwell women's Sunday best. Constance wore a beautiful gown of pink watered silk. The trimmings alone were worth more than Darlene's entire dress. Tiny seed pearls decorated the neckline and heavy flounces of lace trimmed the sleeves and skirt. Her hair had been delicately arranged in a pile of curls and atop this was a smart looking little hat complete with feathers and ribbons. A dainty pink parasol was over one shoulder to shade her from the sun and around her throat lay a strand of pearls, all perfectly white and equally sized.

Eugenia, of course, was attired even more regally in mauve colored satin. Darlene tried not to feel out of place, but it was obvious to anyone who looked at her that she felt completely beneath the standing of her companions.

Dennison introduced her to his sister and daughter, but only Constance had anything to say. "It's so nice to have you with us."

"Indeed it is," Pierce said with great enthusiasm.

The church service was unlike anything Darlene had ever known. The women and men sat together for one thing, and somehow Pierce had managed to have her seated between himself and Constance. She was very aware of his presence. The smell of his cologne wafted through her head like a delicate reminder of her dreams. She couldn't suppress the fantasies that came to her mind and while they joined in to sing and share a hymnal, Darlene wondered what it might be like to marry Pierce and do this every Sunday.

What am I thinking? She admonished herself for such thoughts, while in the next moment her heart betrayed her again. To be the wife of Pierce Blackwell would mean every manner of comfort and luxury. It would mean having gowns of silk and satin. It would mean never having to worry about whether enough suits were made to pay the rent and grocer. She stole a side glance at Pierce. He caught her eye and winked, continuing the hymn in his deep baritone voice. Marriage to such a man would also mean love. Of this she had no doubt. Pierce Blackwell would make a most attentive husband.

The minister began his sermon by praying a blessing upon the congregation. Darlene watched for a moment, then bowed her head and listened to his words.

"Heavenly Father, we ask Your blessing upon this congregation. We seek Your will. We seek to know You better. We ask that You would open our hearts to the truth, that we might serve You more completely. Amen."

Well, Darlene thought, *that wasn't so bad.* She relaxed a bit. Maybe this wasn't going to be such an ordeal, after all.

The minister, a short, older man, seemed not that different from the cantor. He wore a simple black suit and while he had no beard, his muttonchop sideburns were full and gave the appearance of at least a partial beard.

142

"It is good to come into the house of the Lord," he began. His words were of love and of a deep joy he found in God. Darlene couldn't help but be drawn to his happiness.

"God's love is evident to us in many ways," the minister continued. "God watches us with the guarded jealousy of a Father to His child. You fathers in the congregation would not allow a thief to sneak into your homes and steal your children from under your watchful eye, and neither does God allow Satan to sneak in and steal their hearts and souls.

"Just as you provide for your children, so God provides for us, His children. If your child was lost, you would seek him. If he was cold, you would warm him. If your son or daughter was hungry, you would give your last crumb of bread to feed them. So it is with God. He longs to give us good things and to care for us in His abundance." Darlene was mesmerized.

"God wills that none should be lost. He gave us His Son Jesus Christ as a gift of love. Seeing that we were hopelessly lost, separated by a huge cavern of sin and despair, God sent His Son Jesus, to reconcile us to the Father. Is there anyone here who would not try to rescue your child from a burning house? Would any of you stand idly by and watch your children drown? Of course not. And neither would God stand by and watch us sink into the hopeless mire of sin and death, without offering us rescue.

"But what if you reached out a rope to your drowning child and they refused to take it? What if you tore open a passage in the burning house, but your child refused to come forward? So it is with God, who extends to us salvation through Jesus Christ, only to have us refuse to accept His gift." Darlene felt as though the minister was speaking to her alone. She'd never heard such words before. No wonder her father found himself confused. No wonder he questioned his faith.

"Will you be such a child?" the minister asked. "When God has offered you a perfectly good way back to Him, will you reject it? Will you throw off the lifeline God has given you in His Son? Will you die without knowing Christ as your Savior?"

Darlene could hardly bear the now serious expression on the minister's face. He seemed to look right at her and, inside her gloves, Darlene could feel perspiration form on her hands. She wanted to get up from her seat and flee from the building, but she couldn't move. Should the building have caught fire and burned down around her, Darlene knew that it would have been impossible to leave.

The minister spoke a short time more, then directed those who would receive Christ to step forward and publicly declare their repentance. Her mouth dropped when Abraham stood. She had known he would do this, but somehow watching it all happen, she didn't know what to think. A kind of despair and trepidation washed over her. It was as if in that moment she knew a wall had been put in place to forever separate her from her beloved Tateh. A wall that she could only remove if she accepted Christ for herself.

As if sensing her fears, Pierce put his hand over hers and gave it a squeeze. This gesture touched Darlene in a way she couldn't explain. It was as if he knew her heart, and that somehow made it better. *Does he understand my loss?* she wondered.

Hearing a confession of faith from the man who had nurtured her so protectively, Darlene felt all at once as though he'd become a stranger to her. And yet, was it this that disturbed her most? Or was it the words of the minister? Words that made more sense than she would have liked to admit?

■ ■ ■ ■

The ride back home was spent in animated conversation between Dennison and Abraham, and Pierce and Constance. Eugenia remained stubbornly silent, while Darlene felt her mind travel in a million directions. All of which brought her continuously back to the dazzling smile and penetrating brown eyes of Pierce Blackwell.

"I'm glad you took time from the shop to accompany us today," Pierce told her.

"Do you work in your father's shop?" Constance asked in complete surprise.

Darlene nodded. "Yes. I do sewing for him."

"How marvelous. Tell me all about it," Constance insisted.

Eugenia harrumphed in obvious disgust and with that simple gesture, Darlene saw all her girlish dreams of marriage to Pierce fade. Of course, there had never been any real possibility of a lowly Jewess marrying a rich Christian socialite, but she had felt at least comforted by the possibility.

"My father is a tailor, as you know. We make suits and shirts, just about anything a man could possibly need for dressing."

"And they do it very well," Pierce added.

146

"I have never owned such fine clothes."

"And you work with your father? Did you help with my brother's suit?" Constance asked, completely fascinated by this.

Darlene eyed the rich green frock coat and nodded. Pierce's gaze met hers and his lips curled automatically into a smile. "I didn't know that," he said, running his hand down the sleeve of his coat. "It only makes it all the more special."

Darlene felt her face grow hot. It made it special to her as well. She could remember running her hand down the fabric and wondering what Pierce would look like when it was completed. She had sewed the buttons onto the front with a strange sort of reverence, imagining as she worked how Pierce's fingers might touch them later.

"How wonderful to do something so unique!" Constance declared.

"It is hardly unique to do a servant's labor," Eugenia finally said. With these words came a silence in the carriage and a sinking in Darlene's heart.

Dennison frowned and Eugenia, seeming to sense that her opinion would meet with his disapproval, fell silent again. The damage was done however. Darlene grew sullen and quiet, while Pierce looked away as if disgusted by the reminder of her station in life. There would never be a bridge between their worlds and the sooner Darlene accepted that, the happier she would be. But even forcing thoughts of Pierce from her mind did nothing to dispel the stirring memory of the minister's words that morning. Nor would it displace the image of her father going forward into acceptance of Jesus as Messiah. There was no going back now. There would be no chance of changing her father's mind about Christianity. But what worried Darlene more was that she wasn't sure she still wanted to change his mind.

CHAPTER 11

But the wisdom that is from above is first
pure, then peaceable, gentle, and easy to
be intreated, full of mercy and good fruits,
without partiality, and without hypocrisy.

JAMES 3:17

Pierce listened with bored indifference to
Amanda Ralston's description of the new
art museum her father had arranged to be
built. The truth of the matter was, he was
bored with the entire party. Amanda's party.
Amanda and all her shallow, haughty
friends.

The only reason he'd even come was that
Eugenia had insisted on the matter until
there was simply no peace in the house and
even his father had asked him to do it as a
favor to him. So it was because of this,
Pierce found himself the center of Amanda's
possessive attention.

"Darling, you haven't had any champagne," Amanda said with a coy batting of her eyes.

"I don't drink champagne and you know that full well." He tried not to frown at her. No sense having anyone believe them to be fighting.

Amanda pouted. "But then how shall we toast our evening?"

Pierce looked at her and shrugged. "I have nothing to toast, my dear. Why don't you go find someone who does?"

Amanda refused to be dealt with so harshly. "I had this gown made especially with you in mind. Don't you think it's lovely?" She held up her glass and whirled in a circle. The heavy gold brocade rippled in movement.

"It looks very warm," he said noncommittally. "I'm certain it will ward off the autumn chill."

Amanda was clearly losing patience with him. "Pierce, this gown cost over sixty dollars. The least you could do is lie about it, even if you don't like it."

"I see no reason to lie about it, and the gown is quite perfect for you. Sixty dollars seems a bit much. I know a great tailor, if your seamstress insists on robbing you."

"Oh, bother with you," she said, stomping her foot. "You are simply no fun at all."

"I didn't come here to have fun. I came because you and my aunt decided it should be so. There would have been no rest in my house if I'd refused."

"But Pierce," she said in a low seductive whisper, "didn't you want to see me? Don't you enjoy keeping company with me?"

Pierce looked at her in hard indifference. "I'd rather be mucking out stables."

"That's hideous!" She raised her arm as if to slap him, then thought better of it and stormed off. Pierce saw her exchange her half-empty glass for a full one before moving out of the room.

The rest of the evening passed in bits of conversation with one group and then another. Pierce, finally relieved of Amanda's annoying presence, found a moment in which to discuss westward expansion with several other men.

"It seems to me that we must settle this nation of ours or lose it," a broad-shouldered man with red hair was saying. "There's plenty who would take it from us. I say we move off the Indians and pay people to settle out west. Give them the land for free, although not too much land. Just enough to spark an interest."

"How would you move them all there?" asked an elderly gentleman. "There's not a decent road in this country. Even the civilized towns suffer for want of better roadways."

"True enough," said Pierce. "Perhaps the government could develop it. There's surely enough money in the US coffers to plow a few roads."

The redheaded man nodded. "Even so, it would take months, years, to make decent roads. We need people in the West now!"

His enthusiasm gave fuel to the spark already within Pierce's heart. "I've allowed myself some investments in Chicago. I've given strong thought to the possibilities of life there." This caused his companions to stare open-mouthed at him.

"You don't mean to include yourself in such a thing?" the older man questioned.

"Why certainly, I do." Pierce couldn't figure out why they should so adamantly declare the need for people in the West, yet find it unreasonable that he would consider such a thing.

"No, no. That would never do. You would have to deal with all manner of corruption and lowlife."

Pierce eyed the old man with a raised brow. "And I don't have to here? New York City is worse than ten western cities put together. Greed runs so rampant in this town that a man would sell his own soul if it promised a high enough return."

The redheaded man laughed at this. "Well, buying your soul out of hock seems a great deal easier than uprooting yourself and leaving the comforts of home behind. Monetary investments are one thing. Flesh and blood is quite another."

Pierce smiled. "I couldn't agree with you more. It is exactly for those reasons that I consider the possibilities of such a move."

It was then that Amanda chose to re-appear. "What move are you talking about, darling?" She placed her hand possessively on Pierce's arm.

"It seems your friend would like to move out amongst the savages." The older man chuckled while the redheaded man continued. "I can just picture you at his side, Amanda dear. Dirt floors dusting the hems of your expensive gowns, six children grabbing at your skirts."

Amanda's laughter filled the air. "Oh, certainly Mr. Blackwell is making sport of the subject. He has too much here in the city to ever go too far. Isn't that true, darling?"

Pierce shook his head. "No, actually I'm quite seriously considering the move. Perhaps when spring comes and the weather allows for long-distance travel, I will resettle myself in Chicago."

"You can't be serious, Pierce." Her facade of genteel refinement vanished.

"I've only been telling you of my interest for months now."

Amanda waited until the other gentlemen had considerately moved away. She pulled Pierce along with her to a balcony off the main room and turned, prepared for a fight.

"Pierce, this is ridiculous. Your aunt assures me that it is your father's wish you marry and produce heirs. Now, while I have no desire to find myself in such a confining predicament, I would see fit to participate at least once in such a matter."

Pierce laughed. "Are you talking about giving life to a child, or suffering through a party for fewer than sixteen people?"

"This is a matter of grave importance; I won't stand your insults."

"Indeed it is a matter of grave importance." Pierce almost felt sorry for the young woman. She was clearly in a rage of her own creation. Her face was flushed and her eyes blazed with a fire all their own. She would have been pretty had she not been so conniving and self-centered. "Please hear me, Amanda. I have no desire to marry you. Not now. Not ever. I am not in love with you, which is the most important thing I believe a marriage should have. Without a mutual love and respect for each other, marriage would be nothing more than a sham of convenience. That kind of thing is not for me."

Amanda seemed to calm a bit. "Marriage is more than emotional entanglements, Pierce, and you know it as well as you know your bank account. To marry my fortune to yours would ensure our future. It would set forever our place in society. Imagine the possibilities, Pierce."

"I have, and they do not appeal to me."

"You aren't that stupid," she said, the caustic tone returning. "You are too smart to throw away your future. You've worked hard to set it into place."

"You are exactly right," Pierce replied.

She smiled with a seductiveness that ordinarily would have been charming. "I knew you'd see it my way."

"Oh, but I don't. I merely said you were right about my being too smart to throw away my future. I'm not about to sit around in houses that look fit only to be mausoleums, stuck in the middle of a city that's driven by greed and avarice and married to a woman who concerns herself only with parties and the value of her possessions."

He turned to leave, but Amanda reached out to hold him.

"If you leave, I'll see you ruined!"

"Do what you will, Amanda, but do it without me."

He strode from the room without so much as a backward glance. He heard the sounds of the party behind him, the tinkling of glass, the faint strains of the stringed quartet, the laughter of shallow-minded associations. It was all a facade. There was absolutely nothing real or of value here for him.

He hailed a hack and gave the driver his address. Chicago loomed in his mind like an unattainable prize. Somehow, he would make his way west. Somehow, he would leave New York behind.

Darlene. The name came unbidden to his mind. Could he leave her as well? Could he walk away from a woman he was now certain he loved? He couldn't suggest marriage, not with their religious differences. He couldn't take her away from her father, and even if he suggested Abraham accompany them west, Pierce didn't know if the old man was well enough to do so.

Chicago would mean leaving Darlene. Chicago would mean throwing off every matter of security ever known to him and going into the unknown alone. Could he do it? Could he leave the comforts of life as he knew it, and forge into the wilds of Illinois?

The hack pulled up to the redbrick house and stopped. After paying the driver, Pierce made his way inside and found the house quiet. Grateful for this blessing, he made his way to the library. Tossing his frock and waistcoat aside, Pierce undid his cravat and eased into a plush leather chair. On the small table beside him, a copy of the newspaper caught his eye.

Picking it up, he scanned the pages for anything of interest. IRISH RIOTS ON THE WABASH AND ERIE CANAL, titled one article. Another announced the cause of some shipping disaster. He looked for something related to Chicago or travel west and found only one tiny article related to the suggested building of a railroad from New York State to the rapidly growing towns of Cincinnati and Chicago. It was such a small article and told with such a negative slant that Pierce was certain no one would have paid it much mind.

He folded the paper, tossed it aside, and stretched out his long legs. *Dear God,* he began to pray, *what is it that I should do? I have no peace here. No happiness within my soul. I am as out of place as a fish taken from water. Society bids me be greedy when I would be generous, and tells me to have nothing to do with those who are beneath my status, when I would take all mankind to my heart.* He sighed. *Oh God, please show me the way. Give me peace about the direction I should take. Give me a clear path to follow. Amen.*

"Whatever are you doing in here?" Eugenia questioned from the door. "I heard a carriage and couldn't imagine what you were doing home so early."

"I left because the party was not to my liking," he answered simply.

Eugenia frowned. "But what of Amanda? Surely she compensated you where the party was lacking."

"She was the one lacking the most," Pierce replied.

Eugenia looked behind her before entering the room and closing the door. "Pierce, you and I need to talk."

"We've talked aplenty as far as I'm concerned. Just leave it be." Exhaustion registered in his voice.

"I don't wish to cause you further grief, but you must understand," Eugenia began, "it is very important to your father that you settle down and marry. Amanda Ralston is everything you could ever hope to find in a wife. She'll be congenial. She'll run your home efficiently and she'll never interfere in your business. She's been groomed for just such a job since she was old enough to walk. Amanda knows her place and she'll benefit you in many ways."

"But I don't love her. I could never love her."

Eugenia grimaced. "Who could you love? That little Jew?"

Pierce narrowed his eyes. "Don't think to bring Darlene into this matter."

"Why shouldn't I? She clearly is a part of this matter. You fancy yourself in love with her, and I say forget it. She is not of your kind."

"And which kind would that be? The greedy kind? The selfish kind? Oh, wait, I know, maybe it's the kind who look down on others because they are different." Pierce got to his feet. "I'm glad she's not of those kind. But what you tend to forget because you're so mired in it yourself, is that I'm not of that kind either!"

"You are better than she is!" Eugenia said, blocking his escape by throwing herself between him and the door.

"No," he said, shaking his head. "I'm not. I'm not better than Darlene. I'm different in some ways, I'll give you that much. But I

159

am not better. The Bible says that we should love one another, even as God loves us. Do you suppose God loves Darlene less because she's of Hebrew lineage? Jesus, Himself, is of such lineage! What if God loved me less because I'm not?"

"You cannot marry a Jew. Even by your own standards and beliefs you cannot do such a thing. You'd forever link yourself to a woman who would never believe as you do. Think of the irreparable harm you could do yourself."

Pierce picked up his coats and with little trouble, maneuvered Eugenia out of his way. "I'm finished discussing this. If you ever bring up the subject again, I will leave this house for good."

"I'm only trying to be wise about this, Pierce."

He realized that she truly believed this. Turning, he said, "Man's wisdom and God's are often two very different things. I've tried it man's way. Now I seek God's."

CHAPTER 12

The preparations of the heart in man,
and the answer of the tongue,
is from the LORD.

PROVERBS 16:1

"So who are the flowers from?" Abraham asked his daughter.

Darlene stood holding a newly arrived bouquet of roses and the blush on her cheeks felt as warm a red as the flowers. "They're from Pierce Blackwell. He's coming this afternoon to . . . well . . . see me."

Abraham smiled and nodded. "That's good. I think he likes you."

"For whatever good that could ever do him," Darlene muttered and took the flowers upstairs to put on the kitchen table. Then, without thinking consciously of what she was doing, she hurried into her bedroom and changed her clothes.

Wearing a simple gown of green cotton

161

and ivory ruching, Darlene tried to steady her nerves as she sewed a silk lining into a frock coat. Pierce had sent her flowers before, but never roses and never such a large bouquet. She felt a surge of anxiety and drew a deep breath. *I mustn't let him see me so jittery,* she thought. *I don't want him to think I'm drawing unmerited conclusions in this matter.* But she was. She was already imagining all of the most wonderful things that Pierce could come and tell her. Furthermore, she imagined how she might respond to just such things.

Even though Darlene knew and anticipated Pierce's arrival, it was still a surprise when he bounded through the door. He was dressed in a stylish brown suit which her father had made. His waistcoat of amber and orange might have appeared too loud on another man, but it seemed just right on Pierce.

"Hello," he said with a dashing smile and deep bow. "You look very pretty today."

Darlene put aside her sewing. "Thank you." She didn't know what else to say, so she folded her hands and said nothing more.

"You received my note, I presume."

"Oh yes." She nodded, then remembered the roses. "The flowers are simply beautiful. I've put them upstairs. I was afraid down here someone might knock them over." She was also afraid that if Esther saw them she'd immediately begin questioning Darlene for all the facts.

"I thought you might enjoy them. I was passing a shop and saw them in the window. With winter coming on, I thought they might perk up the place a bit."

"They brighten the kitchen considerably."

The silence seemed heavy between them and Pierce searched for another topic. "And your father, is he well?"

"Yes. Well, he has a cold, but I'm hoping it won't be anything serious."

"Good."

"What of your family?" Darlene asked, raising her eyes to look upward.

"They are well. Constance had a birthday last week. She's sixteen now and feels very grown up."

"I remember sixteen quite well," Darlene replied. "I didn't feel very grown up at all. Of course we'd not been long in this country. I was struggling to improve my English and to make a good home for Tateh."

"I wish I could have known you then," Pierce said in a soft, almost inaudible tone.

Just then Abraham returned from an errand. His arms were full of brown paper-wrapped packages, and Pierce and Darlene hurried forward to take the burden from him.

"Tateh, you shouldn't have carried all of this yourself. I could have gone back and brought it home."

"Nonsense." He waved away her concern. "I'm an old man, but I'm still good for some things, no? Ah, Pierce, good day to you. I heard you were coming this afternoon."

"Yes," Pierce replied, putting the packages where Darlene motioned. "I would like very much to take Darlene for a walk. Would that be acceptable to you?"

Abraham smiled and struggled out of his coat. "It would be very acceptable. She works too hard now that Hayyim is gone."

"And you haven't found another assistant to help with the work, I take it?"

"No, but God will provide. He always has." Abraham's words would normally have comforted Darlene, but since all of the changes in her father's life, she was never certain whether she should take hope in such things.

"Of course He will. If I learn of anyone who might be adequate help, I'll advise them to come to you." Pierce then turned to Darlene. "Would you mind walking with me? It's a bit chilly, but otherwise very nice."

"I'll get my shawl," she replied. Now

curiosity was taking over her fears. She had never known Pierce not to discuss every single matter of interest in front of her father. What was it that he wanted to say to her in private? And, if it wasn't a matter of discussing something with her, then why was he suggesting the walk? For a fleeting moment she hesitated. What if Esther saw her? Oy! What mutterings and innuendos she'd have to answer to then!

She pulled a cream-colored shawl around her shoulders. She'd only finished knitting it two days earlier, and this was her first real opportunity to show it off. Pulling a bonnet over her dark brown hair, Darlene hurried to join Pierce. If Esther saw her, she'd just deal with it later.

"I'm ready," she announced. "Tateh, are you sure you can spare me?"

"Be gone with you already," Abraham said with a chuckle. "You can do Pierce more good than me."

And then they were outside and walking amicably down the street. When Pierce offered his arm, she hesitantly took it. Outside in the public eye it would mean dealing with more than just Esther. What would any of her friends say if they saw her walking with the goy? She squared her shoulders. It didn't matter. They'd all turned their backs on her father and she wasn't going to concern herself with what they thought. Oh, they were nice enough to her face and Esther still invited her over from time to time, but she knew they were all talking about her behind her back. And, she figured the only real reason Esther still called on her was for the simple purpose of gathering information.

"You don't seem to be listening to me."

Darlene looked up with an apologetic smile. "I do tend to get caught up in my thoughts."

"Yes, I know. That's why I suggested walking with you. I'll keep an eye for the freight wagons while you daydream. But, it comes with a price."

"Oh?"

"Yes," he nodded and added, "you must tell me what those dreams are about."

She shook her head. "They weren't really daydreams. I was actually thinking of the old neighborhood and how much it has changed."

"Has the neighborhood changed, or have you changed?"

"Some of both," she admitted. They walked past a fishmonger's cart and the heady scent of fish and other seafood assailed her nose. "Some things never change," she said, wrinkling her nose.

Pierce laughed and pulled her a little closer. "But change can be good, don't you think?"

"Is that why you've come to talk to me today?" *There,* she thought. *I've just come right out with it and I don't have to wonder anymore what he's up to.*

Pierce wasn't phased by her boldness. "Yes," he answered simply.

"So what change is it that you wish to discuss?"

"I'm leaving New York."

The words hit her like boulders. "Leaving? Where are you going?" She tried hard to sound distant and unconcerned.

"Chicago. It's a fairly new town in Illinois. It's quite far to the west and there's great opportunity to be found there."

"I see." She focused on the ground.

"Darlene, I wondered if you and your father might consider moving there also. I mean, I know what your father has experienced here in the neighborhood. He's told my father about some of the ugly letters . . ."

"What letters?" Darlene interrupted. "I've heard nothing of letters."

Pierce looked genuinely embarrassed. "I'm sorry. I presumed that you knew."

"Tell me everything," she demanded, and halted in the middle of the street as they crossed. "I have to know what has been said."

"Surely you know already," he pulled at her arm, but she held her place. "Come now, Darlene. I will share what I know, but not in the middle of the roadway."

She allowed him to take her along and waited silently, although impatiently, for him to tell her the truth.

"Apparently there have been some threats," Pierce said as delicately as he could. "I believe the letters are harmless enough, but they probably bear consideration. I know the shop has been vandalized twice."

"But that was probably only street urchins," she said, even now wondering about the truth of the matter.

"Your father thinks perhaps it is more than that." Pierce pulled her into an alleyway and stopped. "You must know that he doesn't wish to worry you, but Darlene, I do fear for both of you. I know the ugliness of those who cannot accept what is different from what they know. Your Jewish friends can be just as prejudiced as my Christian friends."

She nodded, knowing that it was true. She could remember well the haughty stares of neighbors when her father stopped going to the synagogue. It was as if the Lewy family simply ceased to exist. Oh, they tried to be kind to her whenever she was alone, but ridicule followed even her. Especially when people asked her why she didn't leave Avrom and go to live with Esther.

"Chicago could be a new start for you both. I have property there and would be happy to set up a new shop for you. It could be as big as you like and I'm certain we could entice someone to sign on as an assistant to your father."

Darlene felt a single moment of excitement, then shook her head. "Tateh would never leave."

"Well, well. What have we here?"

"Looks like rich folk to me."

Pierce thrust Darlene behind him as he turned to face a group of filthy street rowdies. "What do you want?"

"Money, same as you uppity dandies," one of the taller boys said, coming a step closer.

"And jewels," another boy said. "Give us your lady's jewels."

There were five of them, with another two watching the street at the end of the alley. One of the boys produced a club and began whacking it in his hands. "Let's have it," he said in a low menacing tone.

169

Pierce moved a step back, pinning Darlene in place against the brick wall behind her. "I think we can work this out with no need of violence. Let the lady go and you may have my wallet."

"We'll have your wallet and the lady if we want," the boy replied.

Darlene peered around Pierce's shoulder. They couldn't be much more than teenagers, certainly not men. She was about to say something, but just then one of the five pointed at her.

"Wait a minute, Willy. That's the lady that helps us from the tailor shop. We can't rob her."

Pierce relaxed enough for Darlene to slip out from behind him. "I know your little brother. You must be Sam."

The boy nodded, looking rather sheepish. "Come on, guys. These are good folk."

The gang backed off and ran down the alley, signaling to their conspirators as they passed by. Pierce started to go after them, but Darlene reached out and took hold of him.

"Please let them go. They're only trying to survive. They wouldn't have hurt us."

"It didn't look that way to me," Pierce said angrily. "Scum and lowlife! That's all they're good for. The filth and despair of this neighborhood are all they know. Probably all they care to know. The lower classes always breed this kind of criminal element. Something should be done to clean up this neighborhood and rid it of the vermin."

"But Pierce," she said in a calm, soothing tone, "I am this neighborhood. My friends and family all live here. If you condemn them all because of the actions of a few, then you must surely condemn me as well."

This sobered him and he pulled her quickly back onto the main street before something else could happen. "I didn't mean it that way and you know it. I have only the highest admiration for you."

"But there are many in your circle of friends who believe we are nothing but Jewish scum. The Christ-killers. That's what they call us."

"But they can't blame you or your people for what a few . . ." he fell silent.

Darlene smiled, knowing that his words were about to match hers. "People can be cruel without even knowing it. We came to this country for many reasons. One of the most inspiring was the growing hatred of Jews in my native home of Germany. That hatred started innocently enough with whispered insults and indifference. Gradually the name calling and assaults on our homes resulted in our being unable to live in certain areas and work at certain jobs. Can you imagine allowing such hatred to dictate the laws of the land?"

"How can you not hate them in return?" Pierce asked.

"I don't know. I suppose it is like Tateh says, 'To hate another requires that you keep the ugliness of their deed written on your heart so that you might hold it up to remember them by.' "

"Your father is very wise. Perhaps that is why his heart was so open to the Word of God regarding Jesus."

Darlene nodded. "It may well be." She felt the familiar stirrings and knew that, more than anything else, she would like for Pierce to better explain Jesus to her. "I wonder if you would tell me a bit about your Jesus."

If Pierce was surprised by her words, he didn't say so. "Jesus came as a baby to this world. You know of the Christmas celebration?" Darlene nodded. "We celebrate His birth and give gifts to each other in honor of the day. In truth, Jesus came to a lowly Jewish couple, a carpenter and his wife. Joseph and Mary. He was a gift from God to the world. He came among men, because God wanted to draw all men to Him. He wanted to give man a path to forgiveness and eternal life. Jesus said in John fourteen, 'I am the way, the truth, and the life: no man cometh unto the Father, but by me.' So you see, we believe that by accepting Jesus as Messiah and repenting of our sins, we accept the way to God and eternal life."

They were back to the shop by now, but Darlene wished they could walk on forever. She found her heart clinging to every single word Pierce said. Could it be true? Could Jesus really be the Messiah her people looked for? Had they simply missed the signs or had they willingly ignored them?

"And you believe all of this, without any doubt at all?" she asked softly, looking up to find Pierce's tender expression.

"Without any doubts or fears," he whispered, taking her small hands in his own.

"But what makes you so certain?" She felt a tingle of excitement shoot up her arms and goosebumps form on her skin.

"He makes me certain," Pierce replied. "He makes me certain deep within my soul."

CHAPTER 13

And she shall bring forth a son, and thou
shalt call his name JESUS: for he shall
save his people from their sins.

MATTHEW 1:21

They stood by the shop door for what
seemed a long time before Darlene finally
turned the handle and went inside. Pierce
followed her, but paused just inside the
door.

"Think about what I said," he told her.

Darlene couldn't help but think of all the
things he'd said. Things about leaving New
York, wanting her and her father to go to
Chicago, and that Jesus loved her. "I will,"
she promised. And then without warning,
he gave her one more thing to think about.

Taking her face in his hands, he placed a
very light kiss upon her lips. "I love you,"
he whispered. Darlene opened her eyes in a
flash of confusion and wonder. She stared

up at him, not really believing she'd heard the words accurately.

As if reading her mind, he repeated them. "I love you. I think I always have."

Before she could say a single word, he turned and left the shop, gently closing the door between them. To Darlene it was a moment she would always remember. Pierce Blackwell loved her and had kissed her as a token of his affections. Touching her hand to her lips, she could scarcely breathe. *He loves me?* It wasn't mere infatuation on her part? She thought of the hundreds of daydreams she'd had about him. Dreams of marriage and love, romance, and a future as Pierce Blackwell's wife.

"Darlene, is that you?" her father called from upstairs.

"Yes, Tateh." She could barely say the words. Her voice seemed incapable of working properly and her legs felt like leaden weights.

"Are you all right? Is Pierce still with you?"

"No. I mean, yes I'm all right, but Pierce has gone home." At least, she presumed he'd gone home.

She forced her legs to work and pulled the bonnet from her head as she made her way upstairs. She thought about Pierce and his words about Jesus. *Tateh believes in Je-*

sus, she thought. *Pierce believes in Jesus. Why should I not believe in Him just because all of my life I've been taught one way?*

At the top of the stairs she paused. The only person in the entire world who could help her now was her father. "Tateh," she called, coming into the kitchen where he sat eating a bowl of soup, "I need to talk to you."

Abraham put down his spoon and motioned her to take a chair. "Is something wrong? You look as though you bear the weight of the world."

Darlene put aside her bonnet and shawl and sat down. "Tateh, there are things I want to know about."

"What things?"

She took a deep breath. "Pierce told me that Jesus came to make people a way back to God. He said Jesus said that He was the way and that no one could get to God except by going through Jesus."

"That is true."

"But our people do not believe in Jesus as Messiah. They don't believe that they need someone to make a way for them to God." She paused, reflecting on a lifetime of training. "They believe each man is responsible for his own sin, so therefore how could Jesus take on the responsibility for all mankind

176

and settle the matter for even those people yet to come?"

Abraham smiled. "Because God loves us, He showed mercy. He gave Jesus as a means to demonstrate His love. Not only for the people of His own time, but for the future generations. He was born purposefully to save His people, and Darlene, we are His people, even before the Gentiles."

"But our people rejected Him as Messiah. They saw Him die and presumed that He couldn't possibly be what they expected."

"Not only that, but Jesus made a great many people, especially those who were high Jewish authorities, very uncomfortable. His way would bring change and people often resent change."

Darlene thought instantly of Pierce and his words about change being good. "But if Jesus was the Messiah we looked for, why have our people suffered so? Are we being punished for rejecting Him? Is God reckoning with us for something we didn't understand?"

"Who can know God's mind?" Abraham said with a shrug. "I suppose I look at the world and our place within the bounds of mankind and I say, 'There are many problems here.' Not only the Jews suffer. Think about history. Even the Christian Church has had its bloody times. The world has seen plagues and sufferings throughout. Even here in America the plight of the slave is evidence of injustice. They were taken from their homes and forced away from families and loved ones in order to work for people they didn't know. Many people are hurting and suffering. I don't think God has forgotten us. Remember the sufferings of Job?"

"Yes, but how can God continue to let such things go on? Can't He see what is happening?"

Abraham shrugged. "I think He keeps better watch than you imagine. It's a matter of trusting, Darlene. We have to have faith just as the children of Israel had faith that God would lead them through the desert."

"Yes, but God allowed them to wander for forty years," she added.

"But was that because of God's indifference or their sin?"

Darlene nodded. "I guess I see what you're saying. We often suffer our lots in life because of our own disobedience. By our own hand we create the miseries of the world, is that right?"

"I believe so," Abraham replied.

"Then the Jewish rejection of Jesus could well have something to do with our people's miseries. Not because God is angry that we rejected the Messiah, but because we continue in blindness to seek another way."

"Perhaps."

Darlene looked at her father and in her heart she felt the birth of something very precious. It was a trust in God that she'd never before known. "Tateh, is Jesus the Messiah?"

Abraham smiled. "He is."

"And you are certain? There is no room for doubt in your heart?"

"None."

"That's what Pierce said."

"And what did you think of that?"

Darlene sat back and breathed a deep breath. What did she think of it? Wasn't that part of the reason she was seeking out her father's advice? "He seemed very confident. I suppose I envy that confidence. When I am with my friends, I feel there is an emptiness which no one can explain. When I was little, I thought like you, that it had to do with Mother's death. When I got older, my women friends told me that I was simply yearning for a husband and family. But Tateh, I don't believe that's what I'm looking for.

"There are many women in our community who are married with many children of their own, and yet, I know there is a void within them as well. I've talked to Rachel and Dvorah and even Esther and all of them have known this emptiness. Esther says she fills it with work and other things."

"Mostly gossip and sticking her nose where it doesn't belong, no?" Abraham said with a smile.

"It's true Esther is an old busybody, but perhaps she is one because she is empty and lonely inside. Who knows?" Darlene replied with a shrug.

"God knows and He sees all."

"I do believe that." She thought of Pierce's certainty and of her father's unwavering faith. "And you believe that the Messiah has already come and that He is Jesus. You believe that the Christians are right and that we Jews are wrong."

"I believe that Jesus came to save all people. I believe the faith of my fathers is valid and important, but falls short of a complete understanding of God's love and mercy. You must understand, Darlene, I do not throw away my Jewish heritage to take up one of Christianity. I am a Jew, but I also believe in Jesus."

Darlene shook her head. "I don't see how this can be so. I've been taught since I can first remember that you cannot be both Jewish and Christian. I've been taught that

Jesus is not the Messiah we seek, for if Jesus was Messiah why did He not set up his Messianic Kingdom and restore Jerusalem? I so want to believe what you say is true, but a lifetime of beliefs stand between me and Jesus."

Abraham took hold of her hand and patted it lightly. "God will make a way through the desert. Just as He made a way for the Israelites so long ago. You mustn't be afraid to let God show you the way however. Pray and trust Him, and let Him show you the truth."

"But how will I know that it is the truth, Tateh?" She searched his face, knowing that her expression must surely register the pleading of her soul.

"You will know," he said smiling. "You will know because God will give you peace of heart and mind."

In the warmth of his bed, Pierce awoke in the middle of the night with only one thought: He had to pray for Darlene! He felt the call so urgently that it wouldn't let him be. "Dear God, what has happened? What is it that I should pray about?" He struggled with the covers of his bed and went to the fireplace to rekindle the flames.

The fire caught and grew, bringing with it

181

a warm orange glow to the room. Sitting cross-legged in front of the hearth, Pierce reached up to the nightstand and took down his Bible. He read for several minutes, but again the urgency to pray was upon him. He buried his face in his hands, struggling against the image of Darlene's innocent expression after his kiss.

"Father," he began in earnest. "I love Darlene, but I know Your Word tells me not to be unequally yoked with unbelievers. I can't help loving her though. She is a special part of my life and I've already told You that I will walk away and go to Chicago without her, if that's what You want me to do."

Utter misery took hold of him and it felt as though a part of his heart was being ripped in two. When had she become so important to him? When had he lost his heart so completely to her? There had to be a way to bridge the distance. There had to be an answer he was not seeing. *I love her, and I want her to be my wife!* But even as he acknowledged this truth, God's Spirit overshadowed it with the Word. What fellowship could light have with darkness?

"But God, she's not evil. She's faithful to serve You in her own way."

The words seemed to echo in his mind. "Her own way." Not God's way.

This did nothing to lay aside the need to pray and so Pierce tried to refocus his thoughts and pray just for the woman he loved. "Darlene needs to know You, Father. She needs to know that You love her and she needs to accept Jesus into her heart. Please dispel her fears and let her mind be open to the truth. Give her peace, dear God. Let her come unto You and know the joy and contentment of being reconciled."

Assurance flooded Pierce's soul. This was good and right and exactly what he needed to do. Until the wee hours of the morning, Pierce continued to pray for Darlene and her father. It was as if a spiritual battle was raging somewhere and Darlene's soul was the prize. Pierce was not about to let go of her, and he knew that God would not let go of her either. Feeling a stillness within, Pierce collapsed into bed just as the horizon brought the first signs of morning light.

"I love her, God," he whispered, "but I give her to You."

CHAPTER 14

For we know in part, and we prophesy in part. But when that which is perfect is come, then that which is in part shall be done away.

1 CORINTHIANS 13:9, 10

December came in with bitter cold and strong winter winds. Darlene found it impossible to keep the house warm, and in spite of her efforts, Abraham grew weaker. When he finally succumbed to his illness and remained in bed, Darlene knew that her worst fears were coming true. Somewhere, deep down inside, she knew that her father was dying.

She tried to busy herself so as not to think about such morbid things. She took what few orders she could get for suits and cut them herself, relying on the briefest of measurements lest she cross over the line of propriety by measuring the men herself. She was up before the light of day and still working long into the hours of the night. Cutting patterns out of heavy wool, stitching through thick layers until her fingers bled, and constantly worrying about her father. And through it all, her heart reflected on the words of her father and of Pierce. She thought of God's love and the hope that was found in the belief that Messiah would one day come and properly restore all things. If only Messiah would come now.

Every week when Sabbath came, she would light the candles and ask the blessing, but her heart sought something more. Her soul yearned to understand in fullness the mystery that eluded her. Sometimes when her father slept, she would creep in to sit by his side, and as she sat there she would pray for understanding. Once, she even picked up his Yiddish New Testament, a gift from Dennison Blackwell. Thumbing through the pages she found a most intriguing passage in a section marked, "The First Letter of Paul the Apostle to the Corinthians." Chapter thirteen was all about love. The writer said, in his own way, that even if he were really good and had the best of intentions and kept the faith, but didn't have love, it was all for nothing.

Verse twelve caught her attention and

stayed with her throughout the days which followed. *"For now we see through a glass, darkly; but then face to face: now I know in part; but then shall I know even as also I am known."* That's how she felt. Like she was seeing God and the world through a dark, smudgy glass. There were parts that seemed glorious and too wondrous to speak of. Like Messiah and God's ability to forgive. There were also parts which seemed clouded and vaguely open to understanding. Like eternity and Messiah's coming and whether her people had been wrong to reject Jesus.

Sitting as close to the kitchen stove as possible, Darlene worked at her sewing and allowed her thoughts to drift to Pierce. She hadn't seen him in weeks and she couldn't help but wonder if he'd already left for Chicago. He'd said that he loved her, but apparently there was nothing more he could say or do, for he'd never written or come back to say more. Perhaps it was just as well. They lived in two very different worlds.

Darlene tried to imagine him at home. No doubt the comfort of his wealth kept him from too seriously considering his love for a Jewess. Still, he had asked her to come west with him. He'd promised to help her and Tateh. A shop in Chicago! She tried to envision it. Pierce had said it could be as large as she liked. How wonderful it would be to plan out such a thing. She would make all the rooms on the ground floor so that her father wouldn't have to trudge up and down the stairs. She'd put their rooms at the very back and make it so that the shop could be completely closed away from the living quarters. And they'd have huge fireplaces and stoves to keep the building warm.

A loud knock sounded on the downstairs door, causing Darlene to nearly drop her scissors. She put aside her sewing and hurried down the stairs. *What if it's Pierce?* she wondered and smoothed back her hair with one hand while adjusting her shawl with the other.

She peered through the window shade and was surprised to find Esther standing on the other side. "Esther, it's freezing outside; you shouldn't have come out!" she chided.

"It was colder in the old country. I can bear a little cold," she said, hurrying through the door nevertheless. She held out a covered pot. "It's soup for your father. I've heard it said he is ill."

Darlene took the pot. "Yes, he is. He's bedridden and I'm afraid it will be a long, slow recovery. The doctor says he's sick with consumption."

"Feh!" Esther spat out in disgust. "He is

sick because he has angered God!"

"How can you say such things?" Darlene asked angrily. "Did my father not provide for you when you had nothing?"

"It is true enough, but he had not forsaken the faith of his ancestors then. Now he has and God is punishing him for his waywardness. Mark my words, Darlene, you will fall into corruption and be lost as well. Don't think I haven't heard that you keep company with the goyim. You will be forever lost if you turn from God."

"I'm certain that is true," Darlene replied. "But neither I nor my father have done that." She paused and some of the anger left her. "Esther, have you never wondered about Messiah?"

"What's to wonder? Messiah will come one day and that will be that. Of course, we should live so long!" The wind picked up and played at the edges of their skirts.

Darlene shivered and she knew that Esther must be cold. "Do you want to come upstairs and talk?"

"No," Esther replied. "Rachel and Dvorah are helping me to make a quilt for Mrs. Meyer."

"And you didn't ask me to help?" Darlene tried not to show how hurt she was. She would no doubt have begged off anyway.

"It is better you decide your loyalties first. There's been a great deal of talk about you and Avrom. You should set yourselves right with God and seek His forgiveness. Then we will talk again."

"But my heart is right with God," Darlene protested. "I've done nothing wrong."

"You are the daughter of your father. Avrom's house is in danger because his heart is corrupt with *goyishe* reasonings. You must convince him to repent and then perhaps God will heal him of his afflictions. Don't forget about the sins of the fathers being revisited upon the children."

"And just what are you saying by that?"

Esther's forehead, already wrinkled with age, furrowed as she raised her snowy white brows. "Only that you are close to corruption by staying here."

Darlene felt her temper dangerously close to exploding. Exhaustion was making her bold and unfearing. "Tateh has God's wisdom and a peace of soul that I have yet to find in our congregation. We say that Messiah will come and make all things right, and I'm telling you that Messiah may well have already come to try."

Esther put her hands to her ears. "I'll not listen to any more. You're a *meschuggene* just like your father! Better you should leave him now!"

"No, I won't desert him like everyone else. It was good of you to bring him soup. I will bring you back the pot later tonight."

Esther seemed to have nothing more to say and quickly left the shop. Darlene took the soup upstairs, poured it into her own pot, then put it on the stove to keep warm. She went to check on her father and found him awake and seemingly better.

"Tateh, Esther has brought you some soup. Would you like some now?"

"No, just come and sit with me," he said in a weak voice. "I would tell you some things before it's too late."

"Shh, Tateh! Don't say such things."

Abraham tried to sit up, but he was too weak. Falling back against his pillow, he reached out a hand to Darlene. "Please hear me," he said, breaking into a fit of coughing.

She took his hand and sat down on the edge of his bed. He looked so very old and fragile now. Once her Tateh had been a pillar of strength and she looked to him for the courage she lacked. Now, she wished with all of her heart that something could be done to help him. But the doctor said there was nothing to be done. Nothing could help rid him of the consumption which seemed to ravage his lungs.

Darlene waited in silence, not moving so much as a muscle lest she cause him to cough even harder. He struggled for breath and finally the spell subsided. "I'm going to a better place," he said softly. "You must promise me that you will not be afraid."

Darlene knew better than to argue with him. "I promise," she said, wondering if she could really keep her word.

"And another promise," he whispered.

"What is it, Tateh?"

"Promise me that you will think about Jesus. I don't want to die knowing that you might forever be lost."

Tears came to her eyes as she hugged his hand to her face. "I can't bear for you to talk about death. I can't bear to think of life without you."

"Jesus is the true Messiah. I want very much for you to know that. Don't be afraid of the world and the things which would hide the truth from you." He began coughing anew and this time when the attack subsided, there was blood at the corners of his lips.

"I want to know that Jesus is truly the Messiah," she said. Tears fell upon his hand as she kissed it. "I don't want you to leave me."

"We'll never be parted again if you accept Jesus as your Atonement," he said in a voice filled with as much longing as Darlene felt in her heart.

"What must I do?"

Abraham's eyes seemed to spark with life for a brief moment. "You must only ask Him into your heart. Ask His forgiveness for your sins, and He will give it to you!"

Darlene thought of this for a moment. A peace filled her and she knew in an instant that it was the right thing to do. There was no image of Pierce or her dying father, or the ugliness of her friends and neighbors; there was only this growing sensation that this was the answer she had sought all along. Jesus would fill the void in her heart and take away her loneliness.

"Then let it be so," she whispered. "I want Jesus to be my Savior."

"Baruch Ha-Shem," Abraham gasped and closed his eyes. "Blessed be the Name."

Darlene saw the expression of satisfaction that crossed her father's face. It was as if a mighty struggle had ceased to exist. Was this all that had kept him alive? Was this so important that he couldn't rest until he knew Darlene believed in Jesus?

Outside the wind howled fiercely and Darlene remembered that she needed to return Esther's pot. "Tateh, I must go to Esther's and take back her soup pot. I won't be gone but a minute."

"Wait until tomorrow," he said in a barely audible whisper.

"I think it might well snow before then and I'd rather not have to go out in it. I'll only be a few minutes and besides, no one will bother me. Ever since that day when Pierce and I were accosted by the rowdies, I've had the assurance of Willy and Sam that we'd be safe. They even keep an eye on the building in case anyone wants to vandalize it. I think they're the reason our so-called friends haven't broken any more windows in the shop."

Abraham drew a ragged breath and opened his eyes. "Then God go with you."

She leaned down and kissed his cold, dry forehead. "And with you."

Pausing at the door, Darlene kissed her hand and touched the mezuzah. The action was performed as a reminder of how she should always love God's Word and keep it in her heart. In that moment, it became more than an empty habit. In that moment, Darlene was filled with a sense of longing to know all of God's words for His people. She glanced back at her father and felt a warmth of love for him and the Messiah she had finally come to recognize.

"Jesus," she whispered the name and smiled.

CHAPTER 15

And the world passeth away, and the lust thereof: but he that doeth the will of God abideth for ever.

1 JOHN 2:17

Pierce sat with his shirt sleeves rolled up and his collar unbuttoned — a sure sign that he was hard at private work. Within the confines of his room, he couldn't help but wonder if he'd miss New York when the time came to leave. When in Europe, home had been all that he could think of. But then thoughts of Eugenia's demanding ways, his father's constant absences, and Constance being torn between the two adults she loved most in the world would dissolve any real homesickness. Perhaps it would be the same when he moved west to Chicago.

He looked at the latest letter he'd received from Chicago. He'd hired a well-respected contractor and was already the proud owner of a hotel. Well, at least the frame and foundation were in place. The five-story building was, as the letter put it, enclosed enough to allow indoor work during the harsh winter months. There would, of course, be a great deal of interior work to be done. Pierce remembered the blueprints with pride. The hotel would stand five stories high and have one hundred twenty rooms available for weary travelers. Located close to where packets of travelers were deposited off of Lake Michigan, Pierce knew his hotel would be the perfect money-maker. And, with more than enough room to expand, Pierce had little doubt he could enlarge his establishment to house more than two and maybe even three hundred people.

Leaning back in his chair, Pierce tried to imagine the finished product. Brick with brass fixtures would make a regal first impression. Especially to that tired soul who longed for nothing more than a decent bed and perhaps a bath. There were also plans for a hotel restaurant, and Pierce had felt a tremendous sense of satisfaction when he'd managed to secure one of the finest New York chefs for his hotel. It had cost him triple what it would have cost to hire a less experienced man, but Chef Louis de Maurier was considered a master of cuisine and Pierce knew his presence would only improve the hotel's reputation.

Of course, the fine imported oak and mahogany furniture he planned to ship would be a tremendous help as well. Each hotel room would be supplied with the very best. Oak beds with finely crafted mattresses. The best linens and fixtures money could buy would also draw the better paying customer. He thought of how there would be many people who couldn't afford such luxury and immediately thoughts of a lower-priced, less formal hotel began to formulate in his mind. He could build a quality hotel and supply it with articles which were sturdy and durable, but not quite as fine. Each room could have several beds and this way poorer folks could share expenses with several other people. He could charge by the bed, instead of by the room. *Chicago was going to be a real challenge,* he thought, and scratched out several of his ideas onto paper.

Then, as always happened during his daydreams, Pierce's mind conjured images of Darlene. He'd purposefully left her alone after suggesting she and her father come west. More importantly, he'd left her to consider that he loved her. He hadn't intended to tell her that, but there was a desperation in him that hoped such words just might turn the tide. If she knew how he felt, perhaps she would encourage her father to consider the trip to Chicago. And already, Pierce was prepared for just such a decision. He'd managed to locate a doctor whose desire it was to relocate to Chicago. For passage and meals, the man had agreed to travel with Pierce and act as private physician to Abraham Lewy. This way, Pierce was certain that Darlene could find no objections to the idea of going west.

He frowned as he thought of the stories he'd been told by his father. Stories of how Darlene's friends had turned away from the Lewy family. Stories of how Darlene was forced to sew what few orders she could obtain by herself. He tried not to think of her shoulders bent and weary from the tasks she bore. He tried, too, not to think of her face marred with worry over the health of her father, which Dennison had already told him had been considerably compromised by the cold winter weather.

I love her, Lord, he prayed. *I love her and want her to be my wife, but I won't go against You on this. If You would only turn her heart toward You and open her eyes to the need for salvation, I would happily take her as my wife and love her with all of my heart.*

"Pierce? Are you in there, son?" Dennison Blackwell questioned.

"Yes, come in." Pierce yawned and straightened up.

Dennison opened the door. "I wondered if you would join me for coffee in the library. There are some things I think we should discuss."

"Things? Such as?"

"Such as Chicago and your insistence to cast away the world you know for the wilds of the West and what you do not know."

Dennison seemed so genuinely upset that Pierce instantly got to his feet. "I would be happy to put your mind at rest."

He followed his father down the hall and into the library which stood at the top of the main staircase. Dennison closed the door and motioned Pierce to take a seat, while he himself began to pace.

"I know you're a grown man and have every right to the future of your choosing, but I cannot say that this idea of yours doesn't bother me. Chicago is hundreds of miles away and travel is precarious at best." He held up his hand lest Pierce offer any objections. "Yes, I know the Erie Canal is making travel to the Great Lakes much easier. I've even managed to obtain informa-

199

tion on a variety of wagon trains and stage-lines that go west."

"You've left out the possibility of taking a sailing vessel to New Orleans and then going up the Mississippi and across Illinois," Pierce said with a grin. "Oh Father, you really shouldn't be so worried. I know this is where God is directing me to go. There's so much to be done and men of my standing, with the capital to back them, can not only make a huge fortune, but benefit the masses who also are dreaming of a new start. Chicago has nearly four thousand residents and it is projected that by 1840 there will be twice that many people."

"That's all well and good, but . . ."

"Father, why don't you come west with me? We could build an empire! I still own a great deal of land in Chicago and we could develop it together."

Dennison smiled sadly at this. "I thought we were doing that here in New York."

"But I can't bear the snobbery of this town much longer. The prejudices are enough to drive me mad."

"And you think Chicago will be without its own form of prejudice?"

Pierce knew his father had a point. "I'm sure they do have prejudice, but they aren't formed around the tight little society that

New York has made for itself. I've never known another town, with the exception of Boston, that holds its lofty council above all others and looks down its nose at those considered beneath it."

"Then you haven't looked very close," Dennison said with a smile. For some reason this seemed to put him at ease and he took a chair across from Pierce and poured a cup of steaming black coffee. "I've traveled to some of the same places you have. London. Paris. Munich. They all have their 'tight little societies' as you put it. You know as well as I do how laws have been passed in Germany to discriminate against the Jews. Some towns are even forbidden for them to live in, and others are denying them the right to own property and businesses. I'm telling you, Pierce, there is no place in this world that is without its own form of prejudice."

Pierce poured his own coffee and sighed. "I know you're right. It just seems a shame to watch people so divide themselves. Their greeds and lusts take over and they give little consideration for those who suffer."

"It was no different in Jesus' time. You must understand, Pierce, there will always be those who suffer injustices. All you can do is your very best to see that you aren't a part of it and that you render aid where you can."

"But don't you understand? That's what I'm trying to do now. In leaving New York, I leave behind their ways and their snobbery. I say to them, in essence, enough is enough and I will no longer be party to your corruption. And I am already prepared to render aid. I found a Jewish doctor who is a new Christian. He desires to go west and I have offered to pay his passage to Chicago in turn for his acting as private physician to Abraham Lewy."

"Abraham? He has agreed to go with you to Chicago?"

"No, but I'm certain that once I speak to him of the benefits he will want to go."

"And if he doesn't?"

Pierce shrugged and pushed back thick brown hair which had fallen onto his forehead. "I don't know. I guess I kind of figured if I made him an attractive offer, he'd naturally want to come along."

"And Darlene? Was she a part of the attractive offer?"

Pierce grinned. "Well, of course Darlene is included. I mentioned to her the idea and told her I'd help her father establish a new shop and home."

"And what did she say?" Dennison eyed

his son quite seriously.

This question took some of the wind out of Pierce's sails. "She didn't think he'd want to go."

"I thought as much. You see, Abraham and I have often discussed the matter of moving west. Many of the Jews who came here over the last ten years have done so only with westward expansion in mind. They aren't comfortable in the large eastern cities where people are cruel with hate and prejudice. They are more inclined to migrate west and form their own towns and societies. Abraham considered such a thing, but he was sure that his age was against him. Thinking he was too old, he settled here and found friends he could trust."

"But I want very much for them to know peace and to be accepted into the community. Now that Abraham is a Christian, surely people will take him in and treat him respectfully."

"They will always be Jewish by blood. They look like Jews, they sound like Jews, they have Jewish names. People are going to know. Whether they worship in a synagogue or a church, people are going to think of them as Jews. And, you're forgetting one very important thing. Darlene is still of the Jewish faith."

"But it is my prayer that she'll come to know Christ."

"But until she does, Pierce, she is still very much separated from you in her beliefs. You have fallen in love with this woman, I know that. But I'm telling you that marriage to one such as her can only spell disaster for you both."

Pierce only frowned and sipped at the hot liquid in his cup. He felt the familiar resentment of wanting something that he knew he couldn't have.

"If you were to marry her without her having accepted Christ, who would perform the ceremony? A rabbi? A minister? Then, too, would you attend a church or a synagogue and when would you actually honor the Sabbath? On Saturday or Sunday? What happens, even if you both amicably decide to worship God your own way, when children come along? Will you raise them as Christians or as Jews? Can't you see, Pierce, there is no peace in a divided house. You cannot walk both paths and remain true to either one. You are a Christian. Your foundation for living is in the salvation you know in Christ. You base your beliefs on the Christian Bible and you know that the teachings there are absolute truth. To marry Darlene would be to cast off all that you know as right."

"But Darlene is only one small issue. Even men in the Bible married women of other cultures and nations."

"That's true. But Ahab married Jezebel when she was still an idolatress and it was a disaster. Samson fell in love with Delilah and it led him into tragedy."

"But what of Ruth the Moabitess?"

"Yes, she accepted the Jewish faith and culture and so became acceptable for Boaz to marry. Do you see Darlene giving up her faith and culture for you?"

Pierce put down the cup and shook his head. "I wouldn't want her to do it for me. I want her to know Jesus for herself. I want her to be saved because God has opened her eyes to the truth."

Dennison nodded. "I'm glad to hear you say that, because if she changes faiths for you, and not because God has so moved her heart, it will never take root and grow in her heart."

"I know," Pierce replied, and indeed he did know it full well. Wasn't it the same thing that had given his heart hours of frustration and grief? Wasn't it the very burden he had laid at his Savior's feet, begging for hope and a satisfactory solution?

"Are you completely certain that God is

leading you to Chicago?"

Dennison's question hit a spot deep in Pierce's heart. "Yes. I feel certain."

"How do you know for sure that it is right?"

Pierce sighed. "Because I have such peace about going. Even," he paused, "when I count what I must leave behind, I know that it is the right thing to do."

"And if those things left behind include Darlene Lewy?"

"I told God I'd leave her, too." Pierce looked up, his eyes filling strangely with tears. "Don't think it's easy for me to say these things. Don't think it's easy for me to leave you and Constance either. But I know that I have to do it. I know this is right. I've prayed and considered the matter and always the answer is, 'Yes, go to Chicago.' I can't forsake what I know is God's will for my life."

"Nor would I ask you to," Dennison said, leaning forward to place his hand over his son's. "It won't be easy to let you go again, but if you are this convinced that God is leading you, then I must have peace in it and trust Him to know the way that is best. It won't be easy for me either. It will be lonely here without you, and there will be a void that only you can fill. But, alas, children do grow up and find their own way. I'm gratified to know that you seek God's counsel. It makes me confident that I have done right by you."

"Of that you may be certain," Pierce replied, putting his hand in his father's. He squeezed it gently.

Outside, the wind died down a bit and as it did the sound of distant bells could be heard clanging out in the night. Fire was a common thing in New York and the fire departments were the best in the world. Each station had its own signals and this was clearly a signal for their own neighborhood.

Pierce jumped up and ran to the window, wondering if he could see where the fire might be. An eerie sensation ran through him and the hairs on the back of his neck stood up. Inky blackness shrouded the town and even the bit of moon overhead did nothing to light the darkness. His heart began to race faster with each clang of the bell.

"I can't see anything!" he declared.

"Perhaps Mack knows," Dennison suggested.

Three of the Blackwells' coachmen, including Mack, were volunteers with the neighborhood fire department, so Pierce lit out of the room on a dead run, hoping to hear some bit of news. For reasons beyond his understanding, he couldn't shake off the sensation that something was terribly wrong. It was more than the simple signal of the fire. Fires were commonplace things. Poorly built clapboard buildings and careless vagrants were well-known reasons for fires, not to mention those finer houses which went up when lamps were knocked over or fireplaces were left unattended. It was more than this and he had to know what it was that drove him to concern.

"Where's the fire?" he shouted, passing through the kitchen into the breezeway.

"Don't know," the cook answered in her brusque manner. "Nobody tells me anything."

Pierce felt the stinging cold bite at him through the thin material of his shirt. He went to the stable, refusing to turn back for a coat. "Where's the fire?" he asked again, this time to one of his remaining groomsmen.

"Lower end. Business district. They're calling out extra help because the Old Slip is up in flames and their department's hoses and pumps are frozen solid."

"The Old Slip? Are you certain?" Pierce's heart pounded in anticipation of the answer.

Darlene and Abraham were less than two blocks up from the harbor and well within the Old Slip district.

"Aye, I'm certain. We had a rider come through afore the bells even sounded. Charlie and Mack grabbed up their gear and took off just as the signal came through. It's going to be a bad one."

"What about Ralph?" Pierce questioned, referring to the third Blackwell volunteer.

"He's in bed with a blow to the head. That new bay we bought got a bit out of control."

"Saddle my horse," Pierce said, ignoring the news about the injured man. "No, wait, a carriage! Get the landau ready and I'll drive it myself!" The groomsman stared at him in stunned silence. "Get to it, man! I'm going for my coat and I want it ready when I return. Oh, and throw in a stack of blankets."

Darlene! It was all he could think of. *Darlene and Abraham are in danger!*

He raced up the stairs, taking them two at a time. His father's concerned expression did nothing to slow him down. "It's the Old Slip," he called over his shoulder. "It's bad."

Nothing more needed to be said. Pierce knew that his father would understand his need to go. Dangers notwithstanding, Pierce had to find a way to get Darlene and Abraham to safety. His father would expect no less.

In his room he grabbed his frock coat and heavy woolen outer coat. Forgetting his top hat, he barely remembered to take his gloves and muffler.

"Bring them back here," his father said as he passed him in the hall.

"I will," Pierce replied and hurried off into the night. He had to find them. He had to save them. *Dear God, please don't let me be too late!*

CHAPTER 16

When thou passest through the waters, I
will be with thee; and through the rivers,
they shall not overflow thee: when thou
walkest through the fire, thou shalt not be
burned; neither shall the flame kindle
upon thee.

ISAIAH 43:2

After placing a kiss upon her sleeping
father's forehead, Darlene secured her bonnet and did up the buttons of her coat. She
felt a new peace and excitement that she
couldn't put into words. She had accepted
Jesus into her heart and the wonder of it
consumed her. She felt giddy, almost like
laughing out loud. What was it Pierce had
told her? Something about having great joy
in knowing a personal relationship with
God. Was that why she felt so wonderful?

Grabbing up Esther's newly washed pot,
Darlene hummed to herself, nearly skipping

down the stairs. She felt so good! Her father had been very pleased with her choice and while she knew that pleasing him was important, it wasn't the reason she'd accepted Jesus as Messiah. No, God had done a work in her heart and she had come to Him in the full belief that there was more to life than laws and traditions.

She pulled the door to the shop closed and sniffed the air. There was a faint scent of woodsmoke on the breeze, but on a night as cold as this, it wasn't unusual for the air to hang heavy with the smoke of coal and wood. She snuggled her face into the fur collar of her coat and hurried down the street to Esther's. She was already determined to share her new faith with Esther, even knowing that the old woman would call her a traitor and crazy. For reasons beyond what Darlene could understand, however, she knew that she had to try to make Esther see what Christianity was all about. It wasn't leaving the Jewish faith behind. It was fulfilling it in the Messiah they had always known would come.

In the distance she could hear the clang of the fire bells. *How sad,* she thought, *that someone would suffer through the cold of the night while fire consumed their home or shop.* She instantly asked God to put out the blaze and keep the unknown folks from harm. New York seemed always to suffer with fires and Darlene couldn't help but wonder if Pierce's Chicago would be any different.

Pierce! The very thought of Pierce Blackwell caused her to tremble. Always before she'd been hesitant to dream of the words he'd told her. *"I love you,"* he'd said and Darlene had pushed them aside knowing that a Jew could never marry a Christian. *But now we share faith in Christ,* she thought, and a smile broke across her painfully cold face. Just as quickly as it had come, however, it faded. *I'm still poor and unworthy of his social standing. Nothing can change that.*

She knocked on the door of Esther's tiny house and waited for some reply. After several minutes of stomping her boots to keep her feet from freezing, Darlene was happy to see the old woman peek from behind her curtained window.

"Hava!" Esther exclaimed, opening the door, "You should not have come out. The pot could wait until tomorrow."

"I know," Darlene said, coming into the house. She waited for Esther to close the door and take the pot before continuing. "I wanted to talk to you for a moment. I wanted to apologize for my attitude earlier."

Esther had just returned from her kitchen

213

and the look upon her face was one of surprise. "You have changed your mind? You will live with me now?"

Darlene shook her head. "No, I didn't change my mind about that. Look," she hesitated, knowing that her words would not be well received. "I know you've worried about Tateh ever since he accepted the Christian Jesus as Messiah, but Esther, there are things you do not know. Things which I myself do not know, but am trying hard to understand. Tateh told me that Jesus didn't come to cancel out the laws of Moses, but to fulfill them. He said if we do the things Jesus commanded, we will still be keeping the laws."

"Feh!" Esther said indignantly. "Jesus commanded! What right does He have to command anything?"

"Because He's Messiah. He's God's Son and God sent Him into the world to save us from our sins!"

"Oy vey!" Esther said and pulled at her hair. "You haven't allowed such talk to fill your head, have you?"

Darlene smiled. "No, it's filled my heart. Oh Esther, you must listen to me." She reached out and held the old woman's hand. "I know how hard this is for you. It was hard for me as well. I listened to the

214

things Tateh said, I worried about his standing in the community and whether or not his friends would desert him, but God's peace is upon him. You don't understand and I'm not very good at explaining it. Tateh is very sick, but he's not afraid. God has given him great peace through Jesus. And He's given me the same peace."

Esther's face registered understanding. "Get out of my house. You and your father are dead to me from this moment on." She jerked her hand away and opened the door.

Darlene moved to the door, but turned back. "Please, Esther. We've been good friends all these years."

Her pleading fell on deaf ears. It was just as it might have been months ago had someone tried to talk to her about Jesus. No, that wasn't true. Because the words Pierce and her father had shared caused Darlene to think and ponder them over and over. She had been angry about them and rejected them as truth, but she always listened and later reflected. All she could do was hope that Esther would do likewise.

"I'll go, but I'll also pray for you."

The clang of fire bells suddenly grew louder and from somewhere in the darkness came shouts and screaming. Darlene looked up and even Esther came outside to see what might be the problem. Gazing up one way, Darlene saw nothing but the occasional glow of lamplight shining through the windows and a street lamp here and there. Turning, however, to look down the street from where she'd only come moments before, Darlene cried out, putting her hand to her mouth at the sight of bright orange and yellow flames. The wharves were on fire!

"Tateh!" Darlene rushed down the street, mindless of Esther's cries that she not go. Her father would be in danger and far too weak to move even if he was aware of the fire. She ran as fast as her legs would carry her, but the cold had made her stiff and with each step her feet felt like a million pins and needles were pricking them.

She was appalled to see the flames grow brighter. The fire was less than a half block from her shop. The heat was already warming her and thick black smoke was choking out her breath. A crowd had started to gather on the street and Darlene was startled when a policeman grabbed her.

"There, there. You can't be going in!" he declared.

"I have to. My father is in there." She pointed to the building, now only a block away.

"You can't go in. Leave the rescues to the

fire department. Besides, I'm sure your papa will have seen the fire by now and made his way out."

"No, you don't understand. He's very sick." She wrenched away from him, but saw he wasn't about to let her pass. Just then a group of rowdies could be seen down the block breaking out the glass window of a shop and stealing what they could take.

The policeman called out for them to halt, and the distraction was enough to allow Darlene time to slip down the alley and make her way to the back door of the shop. Thick smoke poured down the alleyway as though it were being sucked through the narrow channels by some unseen force. Darlene buried her face in the fur of her collar and felt her way along the buildings. Stumbling over trash and other abandoned articles, Darlene finally reached the shop and turned the handle. The door didn't budge. It was locked!

"Of course it's locked," she muttered. She pushed up against it, but it refused to give. She ran at it, thrusting her shoulder against the door, but while it bowed ever so slightly, it wouldn't give in and only managed to cause Darlene a great deal of pain. She would have to gain entrance by going through the front, but how?

The smoke was most caustic now and she began to cough. Her eyes were burning fiercely and she knew there was no time to waste. She would go back to the front and if anyone tried to stop her, she would fight them any way she could.

Retracing her steps, Darlene found that the crowd had grown larger and that the policeman was now moving them even further up the street. He had been joined by three other members of his profession and no one seemed to notice Darlene as she slipped through the shadows and into the shop.

Panting, she slammed the door shut behind her. Inside, the smoke was not as bad, and with the light of the flames growing ever brighter, Darlene didn't even need a lamp to make her way up the stairs.

Still coughing, she choked out her father's name and hurried up the steps. She thought to grab some of their most precious articles and instantly reached up to take the mezuzah from the kitchen door. She tucked this into her coat pocket and for some reason thought of Pierce's valentine. She ran to her room, but just then a tremendous boom rattled the very floorboards beneath her feet. It sounded like a building collapsing, and instantly Darlene forgot about gathering up anything else and went to get her father. She had already formed a plan in her mind. She would help him from the bed and once they were downstairs and outside she would call those ever-efficient policemen and get them to help her carry her father to safety.

"Tateh!" she exclaimed, hurrying into the room. "Tateh, there's a fire. It's got the entire Old Slip in flames. Come, we must hurry!" She pulled back the covers and went to get her father's coat.

Abraham remained silent and still. Darlene shook him hard. "Tateh, wake up."

And then, without waiting for any sign that he had heard her, Darlene suddenly knew that he was gone. "No!" she screamed into the smoky night air. "No!" She threw herself across his body and cradled him against her. "Don't die. Please don't die."

But it was too late. Abraham Lewy was dead.

The sound of bells and firemen mingled with breaking glass and the shouts of desperate people. There was no time for mourning, and though Darlene felt as though a part of her heart died with her father, self-preservation took over and she suddenly knew that she must hurry or perish in the fire.

Unable to consider leaving her father to be consumed by the flames, Darlene pulled his cover to the floor, then rolled his body off the bed and onto the cover. It wasn't an easy process, for even though her father had lost a great deal of weight, Darlene wasn't very big.

"Oh God," she prayed aloud, choking against the thickening smoke. "God, help me please. I believe You have watched over me this far. I believe You have taken Tateh to Your care, but I don't want to leave him here. Please help me!"

She struggled against the weight of her father and placed him in such a way that she could pull him along on the cover. How she would ever make it down the stairs without losing control of the body, she had no idea. But she was determined to try.

Pausing at the landing to draw her breath, Darlene screamed when hands reached out to close around her arm.

"It's me, Darlene."

"Pierce?"

"Yes, come on. I've got to get you to safety. Where's your father?"

"He's dead," she said, so matter-of-factly that it sounded unreal in her ears.

"Dead?"

"Yes, he's here on the floor. I have him on

his cover and I was taking him out of the building." Her mind seemed unable to accept that Pierce had come. "Are you really here?" she asked suddenly.

Pierce laughed, but it was a very short, nervous laugh. "Yes, I'm really here. Now come on." He reached down and hoisted Abraham to his shoulder. "The building next door is already in flames. We'll have to hurry or we'll never get out in time." He coughed and gasped for air and this seemed to open Darlene's senses to the gravity of their situation.

"Hurry," she called over her shoulder, making her way down the stairs. She had just reached the bottom when the east wall of the shop burst into flames. It lit up the smoky room and instantly ate up the dry wood of the shelves.

"We'll have to go out the back way!" she yelled above the roar of the fire. Pierce nodded, and pushed her forward.

"Hurry up," he said. "Hurry or we'll die!"

Darlene pushed through the putrid smoke as if trying to cut a way through to the back room. There was no way to see in the smoke now, and suddenly she grew frightened wondering if Pierce was still behind her. There was no breath to be wasted on words, however, and all she could do was pray that

God would allow them both to find their way.

Flailing her arms before her, Darlene finally hit the wall of the back room and then the door. She fumbled with the latch and slid back the lock. Pulling the door open only brought in more smoke and by now her head was growing light from the lack of oxygen. She felt dizzy and wondered if she could possibly make it another step. Slumping against the doorframe, she was startled when Pierce pushed her through. He seemed to have the strength of ten men as he pulled her along the alleyway.

Hazy images filtered through Darlene's confusion. She knew they were in danger, but now, gasping for each breath, she couldn't imagine that anything mattered as much as fresh air. She wondered where they were going. Her mind played tricks on her and she became convinced that if she could just rest for a few moments, all would be well.

They had reached the front of the building and now the entire shop was in flames. Darlene still felt Pierce's iron-clad grip on her wrist, but her legs were growing leaden. She turned to see the walls of her home collapse and knew that the end of her world had come.

"My valentine!" she cried, suddenly trying to jerk away from Pierce.

"What?"

The air was only marginally better here, but Darlene felt her senses revitalized. "My valentine, the one you gave me!"

"I'll buy you a hundred others. You can't go back now; the place is completely destroyed." He pulled her along and made his way down the block to where he had hidden his buggy. *Thank You, God,* he offered in silent prayer. His one consuming worry had been that someone would find the landau and steal it for their own transportation.

Putting Abraham in the back, Pierce grabbed up several blankets and pulled Darlene to the driver's seat with him. He tucked blankets around them and then urged the nervous horses forward.

They made their way down the alley and side streets until they'd reached Wall Street. From here they could see the bright flames and eerie glow in the night sky, but the air was clean and only marginally scented with smoke.

"I don't even know if Esther made it out," Darlene suddenly murmured.

"But you're safe." Pierce put his arm around her shoulder and pulled her close.

"I was so afraid I'd lose you."

Darlene looked up at him. The landau lantern swung lightly in the breeze making a play of sending out shadowy light to fall back and forth across their faces. "My father is dead." She said it as though Pierce could possibly have forgotten.

"I know," he answered. "I'm so very sorry, Darlene." He pulled her closer and wrapped his arms around her very tightly.

Crowds of people were lining the streets and as some went running to help with the fire, others were struggling to carry possessions to safety.

"The fire's comin' this way!" a man yelled out and encouraged people to flee.

"Nothing will be left," Darlene said softly. She lay her face against the coarse wool of Pierce's coat. "I have nothing now."

"You have me," he whispered. "You've always had me."

CHAPTER 17

Wherefore he saith, Awake thou that
sleepest, and arise from the dead, and
Christ shall give thee light.

EPHESIANS 5:14

Darlene's first waking moment was filled
with panic. She had no idea where she was
and the thought filled her with a consuming
urgency. Sitting up abruptly, she looked
around the room and found nothing that
she could recognize. Early dawn light filtered through the gossamer-like curtains
and gave the room only a hint of the day to
come.

Flowered wallpaper lined the walls and a
very soft mauve carpet touched her feet
when Darlene got off the bed. She hurried
to the window and was greeted with the
stark reality of a cold winter's day. The
neighborhood, an avenue lined with leafless
trees and shrubs, was elegant even in this

setting. Black wrought-iron fencing hemmed in the yard, and beyond this Darlene could make out the brick street.

Then the memories of the night before flooded back into her mind. The fire. Her father's death. Pierce. She sank to her knees on the carpeted floor and wept. Everything was gone. All lost in the fire. Her father had died, succumbing to consumption and now she was truly alone. She wrapped her arms around her and felt the soft folds of the nightgown. *It isn't even my gown,* she thought. The only thing left to her in the world were the clothes she'd worn out of the fire. *And Pierce.*

The last came as a tiny ember of thought. Pierce had said that she would always have him. But even that seemed lost and unlikely. How could he ever take her to be his wife? Especially now that she had nothing to offer him in the way of a dowry. The shop had burned to the ground, no doubt, and with it went every possible material article she could ever have offered a husband.

She cried even harder at this loss. Burying her face in her hands, she pulled her knees to her chest and thought of what she was going to do. It was all too much. She would have to bury her father, but even the idea of this caused her more misery than she could deal with. Who would perform the service? Her father was a Christian and would require a Christian burial, but she had no idea what that entailed. Who would prepare the body? The *hevra qaddish,* Jewish men from her community, would have normally prepared her father for burial and Kaddish would have been recited. Would anyone recite Kaddish over Abraham now? Would he have wanted them to? She was so confused.

Drying her eyes against the lacy edge of her sleeve, Darlene tried to remember if her father had ever made mention of such things.

Just then a light knock sounded upon the bedroom door. Getting to her feet, Darlene scrambled into the bed and pulled the covers high. "Come in," she called out and was surprised when Dennison Blackwell appeared.

"Are you up for a visitor?" he questioned.

She nodded, not really feeling like company, but knowing that this man had been her father's best friend in the world seemed to be reason enough to endure his visit.

He was dressed in a simple shirt and trousers. On his feet were slippers and a warm robe was tied loosely over his clothes to ward off the morning chill. "Forgive me for such an early visit, but I heard you crying and I felt compelled to come to offer you whatever comfort I could."

Darlene felt tears anew come to her eyes. "I tried very hard to be quiet," she said, snuffing back the tears.

"My dear, there is no need for that. Should you desire to cry down the very walls around you, you would be perfectly in your rights." He brought the vanity chair to her bedside and sat down wearily. "I am so very sorry about your father. He was my dearest friend and I will always feel the loss of his passing."

"He held you in very high regard," she replied, feeling the need to comfort him.

"And you?" Dennison said. "Are you going to be all right? Did you suffer any injuries during the fire?"

"I'm well," she said, feeling it was almost a lie. "I'm devastated by Tateh's death, but the fire did not harm me." *Other than to take everything I hold dear,* she thought silently.

"I thank God for that. When Pierce left here last night, all I could do was drop to my knees and pray. I feared for his safety, for yours and your father's, and I grieved for those I knew would be destroyed by the fire."

"I was so shocked when Pierce showed up

that I could scarcely comprehend that he was really there. The smoke made my mind confused and incapable of clear thought and there was no way I could have carried Tateh to safety." She paused here, wiping away an escaping tear. "I couldn't let him be burned up in the flames. I knew he was already dead and I knew that he would be in Heaven with God." Dennison eyed her strangely for a moment, but she hurried on before he could speak. "I even knew that I would see him again, because he told me we would all be joined together in Heaven. But the pain of losing him and then the idea of leaving him to the fire, was just too much. I hope you don't think me terribly addlebrained."

"Not at all," Dennison murmured. His mind was clearly absorbed and this concerned Darlene.

"I don't know how to ask you this," she struggled for words. "I mean . . . well you see . . ."

"What is it, child?" he said, suddenly appearing not at all preoccupied. He reached out to pat her reassuringly. "You have only to name your request."

"It's my father's burial. You see, I have no idea what should take place, and I have no money. Everything was lost in the fire."

Dennison smiled. "You have nothing to

worry about. I will see to everything and I insist on paying for the funeral myself. This will be one thing I can do in Abraham's memory and honor. I will see to it all." He paused, his face sobering. "But tell me, my dear, will you be grieved by the Christian service? Should I also plan for some type of service in your Jewish faith?"

Darlene shook her head. "I'm no longer of that faith. At least not like I was. Tateh said that Jesus is the fulfillment of our Jewish faith, but I'm still very new at this."

"Are you saying that you've accepted Jesus as your Savior?"

"Yes. Last night, before Tateh died. We talked and I felt such a peace. I know my friends would say that losing Tateh and everything I had on earth is my just punishment for forsaking the faith of my fathers, but I don't believe that. I don't know why, but I still have a peace inside that the fire didn't consume. Does that make sense?"

Dennison's face seemed filled with light. "It makes wonderful sense. I'm so very pleased to hear about your acceptance of Christ. Oh Darlene, how happy your father must have been. He could die in blessed assurance of seeing you again in Heaven. It must have given him a great deal of peace."

"Yes, I believe it gave him the peace to

die. At first, I was angry and very sad, but I lay here thinking last night that Tateh wouldn't want me to grieve. He would want me to trust God and not be angry that God took him from me."

"That's very wise coming from one so young."

Darlene swallowed hard and tried to smile. "I can't repay you for what you've done. At least, not yet. I don't know where I'll go or what I'll do. My Jewish friends will have nothing to do with me now that they know I believe in Jesus as Messiah."

"You've told them already?"

"I told Esther last night and that's as good as telling them all." This did make her smile and Dennison couldn't help but grin in a way that reminded her of Pierce. "They'll believe me to be a traitor and so I'll be an outcast."

"It won't be easy to face such a thing."

"Oh, I don't think I'll go back," Darlene said in a thoughtful way. "I don't know what I'll do just yet, but the old neighborhood is behind me now. I'm sure there's very little left after the fire anyway."

"Well, that much is true. They're still trying to put out the flames. I'm afraid it burned all the way up to Wall Street and consumed most everything in its path."

231

Darlene nodded. "Somehow, I thought it would be that way." She squared her shoulders. "But God will provide, right?"

"Of course!" Dennison said and patted her hand again. "He already has. You are welcome to stay here for as long as you like. We've plenty of room and I know Pierce will be very happy to have your company here."

Darlene felt her cheeks grow warm. "I'm very thankful he came to us last night."

"As am I. Does he know about your new faith?"

Darlene shook her head. "No. There was no time to speak of such things and all I could really think about was Tateh being dead."

"He's going to be delighted," Dennison said with a huge smile. "I think it will be an answer to his many prayers concerning you."

"Concerning me?"

"You sound surprised. Surely you know he has deep feelings for you."

Her face grew even hotter. How could she explain that Pierce's feelings couldn't possibly be as strong as her own? Then, too, how could she speak to this man, his father, of the love she felt for his son? The Blackwells were rich and quite esteemed in society; surely Dennison Blackwell would not want to hear of her love.

"I see I've embarrassed you. Not to worry, I won't say another word. But, you should tell Pierce of your acceptance of Jesus at the first possible moment. It will probably answer a great many questions for you." With these mystic words he rose to his feet. "I will leave you to rest. You are not to get up from that bed for at least two days. Doctor's orders."

"What doctor?" Darlene questioned in confusion.

Dennison shrugged. "Doctor Blackwell," he said with a laugh. "A poor excuse for a physician if ever there was one, but nevertheless, I insist. I may not be a doctor, but I know that you've endured far too much for your own good. Two days of bed rest and pampering and you'll feel like a new person."

"Mr. Blackwell?"

"Yes?"

"Thank you for being so kind. You and Pierce have both been so generous. I know that my father came to an understanding of Jesus through you."

"You are most welcome, my dear."

"Would you extend my thanks to Pierce? Tell him that his prayers were answered."

Dennison looked confused. "You want me

233

to tell him that you have found Jesus for yourself? Don't you want to wait and tell him yourself?"

"I think he will take great peace of mind from it and since he's partially responsible, I think he should know as soon as possible. Do you mind?" she asked, suddenly concerned that she'd expected too much.

"Not at all," he said in a fatherly way that implied great pride. "It shall be my honor."

He left her with that, and Darlene relaxed back against the pillows. Her heart felt much lighter for the sharing of her concerns. Mr. Blackwell said that she could remain in his home for as long as she liked. This gave her great comfort, and that he would tell Pierce that Darlene was now a Christian. She yawned and snuggled down into the warmth of the bed. She tried to imagine Pierce's reaction, but before she could consider anything else, her eyelids grew very heavy and finally closed in sleep.

Several hours later, Darlene awoke to the sound of someone puttering around her room. Groggily opening her eyes and forcing herself to sit up, she found a young woman in a starched white apron and high-collared black work dress standing at the foot of her bed.

"Good morning, ma'am. I'm Bridgett. I've brought your breakfast. Mr. Blackwell said to remind you that you're not to set foot out of the bed, except for the hot bath I'm to draw for you after you eat."

A hot bath? Darlene thought. But Tateh had only died the night before! Did these goyim have no sense of propriety? How could she indulge in such comforts during the mourning period? Then it suddenly hit her. Perhaps bathing in such circumstances was a Christian tradition. Oy vey! but there was so much to learn.

Darlene smiled weakly. Bridgett's immaculately ordered red hair caused her to smooth back her own tangled curls. "I'm a frightful mess," she declared.

Bridgett made no comment, but instead brought Darlene breakfast on a lovely white wicker bed tray. Poached eggs, toast and jam, and three strips of bacon were neatly arranged on a delicately patterned china plate. Beside this was an ornate set of silverware, a linen napkin, and a steaming cup of tea.

"Thank you," she said, but the girl only bobbed a curtsey and took herself off through a side door.

Darlene looked at the breakfast and almost laughed out loud at the bacon. Oy vey! but what would Esther say? She wondered how it was with Christians and how she would ever learn the right and wrong thing to do. Were there things which Christians didn't eat? Studying the plate a moment longer, Darlene decided against the bacon.

The toast and jam were safe enough and it was this that she immediately began to eat on. Gone was the headache of the night before and the only reminder was the heavy smell of smoke on her body and in her hair.

When the maid returned, Darlene had finished her tea and toast and set the tray aside.

"The bath is in here, ma'am."

Darlene stared after Bridgett and finally followed her. She found herself in a charmingly arranged room. A huge tub of steaming water awaited her and beside it was a tray with a variety of bath salts and scented soaps. On the other side stood a lovely vanity with so many lotions and powders that Darlene couldn't imagine ever using them all.

"I'll take your gown, ma'am," Bridgett said, obviously waiting for Darlene to disrobe.

Feeling rather self-conscious, both because of the stranger and the finery around her, Darlene hesitated. Thinking of the *mikveh,* the ritual bath used by Jewish women for cleansing before marriage, and after child-birth or menstruation, Darlene no longer felt shy. The mikveh required that her body be inspected before immersion and there-fore it was far more personal. Bridgett merely wanted to take the gown away and leave her to privacy of her bath.

"Do your people bathe during times of mourning?" Darlene asked hesitantly.

Bridgett's expression contorted. "My peo-ple?"

Darlene twisted her hands anxiously and rephrased her question. "Do Christians take baths . . . well, that is to say . . . is it all right to take a bath after a loved one has died?"

Bridgett looked at her strangely for a mo-ment. "They take a bath whenever it suits them. Cleanliness is next to godliness or so my mother says."

Darlene nodded, feeling torn between old traditions and new. Well, she'd put aside the bacon, so perhaps accepting the bath wasn't too bad. After all, Bridgett said it was perfectly acceptable. Slipping out of the gown, she handed it to the maid and stepped into the tub.

Darlene sank into the hot water with a grateful smile on her face. She let the water come over her shoulders and finally dipped her head below and enjoyed the sensation of warmth. She was at peace and her heart, though heavy for the passing of her father, was not worried. She allowed her mind to think of Abraham and of the happiness he'd had in knowing that she'd found Jesus. It was the most important decision she could ever make, he'd told her once. And now she knew for herself that it was.

After her bath, Bridgett reappeared with a fresh gown of soft pink lawn and a robe to match. After helping Darlene dress, Bridgett took her to a chair beside the fireplace and proceeded to dry her long wet hair. Darlene had never known such care and thoroughly enjoyed the pampering. It wasn't long before Bridgett had the long, tangled mess dry and brushed to a shining, orderly fashion. They agreed to leave it down before Bridgett led Darlene back to bed where fresh linens and covers replaced the smoke scented ones from the night before.

She'd barely gotten back into bed when the door was flung open and Eugenia Blackwell swept into the room.

"That's enough, Bridgett. You may go," she said in her haughty, superior way.

Bridgett bobbed again and hurried from the room, taking Darlene's towels with her.

Eugenia frowned at her for a moment, leaving Darlene to feel rather intimidated. She thought perhaps she should say something, but couldn't imagine what it might be.

"Well, I see you have composed yourself," Eugenia said, staring down at Darlene.

"Yes, you've all been very kind to help me." *There,* thought Darlene. *I've said something complimentary and surely she'll realize I only mean to be a congenial guest.*

"Yes, of course. But then, what else could we do? It wasn't as if we had a choice."

Darlene frowned. "Mr. Blackwell assured me it was no trouble."

"But he would say that, my dear. That's how it is done in proper society."

Darlene cringed inside at the coldness in her voice. It was clearly evident that Eugenia did not share her brother's hospitality towards Darlene.

"May I be frank with you?" Eugenia suddenly asked.

This surprised Darlene who thought Eugenia had done quite a complete job of that up till now, without seeking anything closely resembling permission. "Of course," she finally managed to say.

Eugenia took up the chair vacated earlier by her brother. Sitting across from Darlene, she maintained her rigid, austere posture and frowned. "You must understand that what I am about to say should remain strictly confidential." Darlene nodded and Eugenia continued. "I am, of course, quite sorry to learn of your father's death. However, your presence in this house creates a bit of a problem for us. I find my nephew easily confused by you and because of this he has begun to question the things that should matter most in his life."

"I don't know what you're talking about," Darlene said in complete confusion.

"But I'm sure you do," she replied rather snidely. "Pierce fancies himself in love with you. Whether or not he's mentioned this to you is of little concern to me. Eventually he will come to his senses and you will be forgotten. Pierce will marry Amanda Ralston, a woman chosen for him by his father and myself. Amanda is of a proper New York family and can offer Pierce much by their marriage." Darlene felt as though Eugenia had actually struck her a blow. "You, my dear, simply cannot be so heartless as to want Pierce to give up the things which make him happiest."

"Certainly not."

Eugenia smiled rather stiffly. "I'm glad to hear you say it. Therefore, you will understand when I say, also, that you cannot remain in this house. Pierce will continue to be confused by you and I'm afraid that if you remain, his father will have no other choice but to cut him off entirely. This would be a grave tragedy."

"But, I thought, well . . ." Darlene fell silent. She wasn't about to try to explain her thoughts to Eugenia Blackwell Morgan. The woman obviously could not care less that her words had pierced Darlene through to the soul.

"The kindest thing you can do is to leave as soon as possible. Don't make a scene and don't even say goodbye. I will give you assistance in reaching whatever destination you like."

"But I have no one now and Mr. Blackwell is arranging my father's funeral. I certainly can't just walk away from that."

"I suppose you are right," Eugenia said, as if only considering this for the first time. "After the funeral, then. I will come to you and supply you with the proper funds. You can take yourself to a hotel until you find somewhere to board permanently." She got to her feet, acting as though the matter was entirely resolved. "You can only mean disaster to Pierce, and if you care at all about his well-being, you will go as soon as possible and give him nothing more to dwell on."

Darlene wanted to scream at her to mind her own business, but frankly the shock of Eugenia's forward nature was more than enough to silence her. She was still staring at the chair Eugenia had just vacated when a loud knock on her bedroom door signaled yet another visitor.

"Come in."

Pierce burst through the door with a huge smile on his face. "Father just told me your news. Darlene, I'm overwhelmed." He paused for a moment as though stricken by her appearance. "You are so beautiful!" he declared.

Darlene tried to smile, but Eugenia's words came back to haunt her. Perhaps she was bad for Pierce and perhaps her love for him would spell disaster if left unchecked.

Pierce crossed the room and took hold of her hands. Raising each one to his lips he kissed first one and then the other. "I'm very happy that you've accepted Jesus as your Savior. I can't begin to tell you how I've prayed for this very thing."

"I know," she whispered. "I remember you said you would pray for me to know the truth. Before Tateh died, he helped me see that truth for myself."

Pierce pulled up the chair so that it touched the side of the bed. "I can't tell you how sorry I am that he's gone. I wanted so much for you and your father to come west with me. I even secured a physician to travel with us. He's a man of your own people who also believes in Jesus."

The idea that Pierce would do this for her father deeply touched Darlene. "How very kind."

"I suppose I had my motives," he grinned. "I wanted to leave no stone unturned, so to speak. I wanted there to be no arguments, nothing which would stand in the way of your coming along. Now that he's dead, I realize you will feel his loss very profoundly, but I know too that you need to make decisions about your own future. A future I hope will include me."

Darlene lowered her face and looked at her hands. Eugenia's cold eyes and haughty stare seemed to be all that she could think of.

"I know this is a bit overwhelming, and I won't say another word on the matter until after the funeral. I just want you to have heart and be assured that you needn't worry for tomorrow." He leaned over and surprised her by kissing her gently on the cheek. "I still love you."

243

He left without expecting any reply and Darlene could feel her cheek burning where his lips had touched it. *He loves me, but I'm no good for him.* She fell back against the pillows and at once wished more than ever that her father could be there to advise her. *Pray,* an inner voice seemed to whisper. *Pray to your Heavenly Father and He will advise you.* This thought gave her peace. Perhaps God would show her what to do.

CHAPTER 18

And the LORD God said, It is not good
that the man should be alone; I will make
him an help meet for him.

GENESIS 2:18

Darlene reflected on her father's funeral in
the silence of her bedroom. The Christian
funeral had been quiet and simple and very
comforting. The minister had spoken of a
day when all things would be passed away
and the resurrection of those in Christ Jesus
would take place. She tried to imagine what
a reunion it would be and how very happy
her father would be to see her again, and
how he wouldn't be sad or sick.

She looked down at her sober gray gown.
Eugenia had insisted that black would be
more appropriate, but this was a dress borrowed from Constance and Darlene didn't
want anyone to go to the expense of dying
it black and making it unusable to the young

girl again.

"Borrowed clothes and somebody else's room," she muttered to the walls, "that's all I have left." Well, that wasn't entirely true. Dennison had told her of a small insurance policy that her father had taken on the shop. It seemed that the policy was protection against fires and would allow, in cases of complete destruction, a small amount of money for rebuilding. He had promised to see to the situation in a few days and to take care of all the necessary paperwork. Darlene was relieved, even if it only amounted to several hundred dollars. It would give her enough money to take care of herself for a while and it would allow her more freedom to decide her future.

She went to the window and stared out on the false spring day. For all appearances it would seem spring was just around the corner, but she knew better. They all did. Sometimes fair weather came in the middle of winter, just like this. It would lull you into a false sense of security and then render you helpless in a blizzard or ice storm. Maybe that's what she was allowing to happen to her in regards to the insurance money. Was she being lulled into a false sense of security by placing her values in monetary needs? Tateh had said, "God will provide." And of course, He always did. So why should she fret so now, and seek all manner of solutions, all of which had nothing to do with God?

"Oh God," she whispered the prayer, "I'm afraid and I don't know very much about how to follow Jesus. I need help and I don't know where else to turn, but to You. You've always been there and Tateh said You were the same God of my childhood, that You are now of my adulthood. Tateh said You would never fail and never desert me and that I could come to You with all of my hopes and fears and You would take care of my needs." She saw the empty branches of the trees rustle slightly in the breeze. "I need You, God. I need to know what I must do and where I should go. I love Pierce so much, but I know that his aunt is right. I can never be the wife he needs. Please help me."

She felt so torn apart. Tateh was gone and Pierce soon would be. She had no idea where to go or what to do, and she wanted so much to please God and be brave.

"I'll never be good enough," she said with a sigh, and then the words of the minister came to mind. At Abraham's funeral, he had said that no one was saved because they were good enough. He said they were saved by grace and that one need only have faith in that grace in order to find their way to God.

"I can have faith," she whispered and the words gave her heart strength. "I can have faith. I might have no answers and very little money, but faith is the one thing I can surely dig up from within." She smiled and knew that if Tateh were here, he'd be quite pleased with her.

The door to her room opened abruptly and Darlene knew without turning around that it would be Eugenia. She was the only one bold enough to simply enter the room without knocking.

"I see you haven't yet changed back into your own clothes," Eugenia announced. "Well, I suppose there is still time."

Darlene looked at her, but said nothing.

"I've brought you enough money to keep yourself in decent style until you can find a job or other friends to take you in." Eugenia tossed a small cloth bag onto the bed.

"I don't want your money, Mrs. Morgan."

"Nonsense. You will take it and I will have the carriage ready to take you wherever you might instruct him to go. I think it would be best if you were to make your departure before the evening meal. Any delay you make will only create further problems."

"But Mr. Blackwell is handling my affairs

and . . ."

"You are no good for this family and even worse for Pierce."

"I would disagree with you, Madam," Pierce said, entering the open door without warning. "I believe quite the contrary. Miss Lewy is excellent for me and I intend to see that she never gets away from me. Now, stop interfering and leave us to talk."

Eugenia was stunned by his comeuppance. "How dare you speak to me like that?"

Pierce put a protective arm around Darlene's shoulders. "You've stuck your nose into my business one too many times, Aunt. Father and I have already discussed Darlene's future and I have great plans for her."

"But this is nonsense," Eugenia stated firmly. "You must marry a woman of means and one with a social bearing that matches your own. You cannot dally with this little Jewess and expect your future to know anything but heartache. I have already spoken with Amanda and she assures me that she'll take you back, no questions asked."

"As I said earlier," Pierce replied, his voice rather cold and unemotional, "you are interfering where no one wants you and I won't tolerate your attitude towards Darlene any longer. Either see your way fit to treat her with respect, or leave." He dropped his hold on Darlene and stepped forward as if to create a barrier between Darlene and his aunt.

"Well!" Eugenia declared and left without another word.

Pierce turned. "It seems I am ever saving you from runaway freighters or burning buildings or destructive old women," he said with a smile. "I'm sorry for Eugenia's attitude. I promise you that she doesn't speak for me or for my family."

Darlene sobered a bit. "She's right though. I don't fit into your world."

Pierce laughed. "So what? I don't fit into my world. I despise the rhetoric and snobbery. I've long planned to leave it, as you well know. There's only been one thing stopping me."

"What?"

"You," he said softly.

Darlene looked up into his face and felt her protests melt away. His dark eyes seemed to drink her in and his face beckoned her touch. Denying herself no longer, Darlene reached a hand to his cheek and found his hand quickly covering hers to hold it in place.

"I love you," he said.

Darlene knew her moment of truth had

come. She lowered her gaze. "I love you," she whispered in a barely audible tone.

"What was that?" He lifted her chin with his free hand. His eyes sparkled with amusement. "I couldn't quite hear you."

"I love you," she stated quite frankly. "Although I've tried not to."

"But why?" He sounded almost hurt.

Darlene shook her head. "Right now, I can't think of one reason."

"I'm serious. If there's something I should know . . ."

She put her finger to his lips and felt a current of excitement course through her. "I thought you should marry someone of your own standing. I can never serve proper teas in proper parlors and I will never be accepted by your society friends. To them a Jew is a Jew is a Jew, whether he believes in Jesus or not."

Pierce pulled her tightly into his arms. "I'm not marrying my society friends, nor do I care one whit what they think. God knows our hearts, Darlene. He has brought us together and brought you to an understanding of His Son Jesus. Do you suppose He would desert us now?"

Darlene melted against him, feeling such a strange sensation of emotion. She truly did love him, but she loved him enough that she couldn't bear the thought of saddling him with an improper wife. "But what of Chicago?"

"What of it? I plan to go there and build us a new life. I will build you the finest house ever seen that far west and people will come from miles around and say, 'Look what that man did out of love for his wife!' "

"Oh Pierce, be serious."

"I am. I want to spend the rest of my life showing you just how serious I am," he said in a low husky tone that put goosebumps on Darlene's arms. "I want you for my wife. I've wanted it since last year when I came for my Valentine's suit. Remember?"

"I couldn't forget. I lost my valentine in the fire," she said sadly. "It was quite precious to me because I knew, even though you'd not signed it, that it was from you."

"Marry me," Pierce whispered against her ear. He kissed her lightly upon her hair, then her cheek, and finally her lips. Hovering there, he whispered again. "Marry me and be my Valentine forever."

"But . . ."

He silenced her with his lips in a passionate kiss and when he pulled away, Darlene smiled. "I suppose I should give in on your ability to kiss alone, but I won't." Pierce frowned and she continued. "You must consider that people in Chicago might well not like you being married to a Jewess. You have to think about this because it might well ruin your reputation and end your prosperity. *Di libe iz zis — nor zi iz gut mit broyt.*"

"And what's that supposed to mean?"

"Love is sweet — but it's better with bread. In other words, love won't put bread on the table and it won't fill your belly when you're hungry. If people in Chicago should act harshly towards you because of me, it won't matter how much we love each other."

"Nonsense," Pierce said, holding her close. "You will be Mrs. Pierce Blackwell and your beauty and graciousness will win them all over. Now, stop putting me off and say yes."

Darlene grinned and nodded with a sigh. "Yes." It seemed so right and in her heart she knew that God had answered the prayer she'd pleaded only moments before.

EPILOGUE

I will bless the LORD at all times: his praise shall continually be in my mouth.

PSALM 34:1

Darlene flushed at the passionate kiss Pierce placed upon her lips. The minister cleared his throat and both Dennison and Constance Blackwell could be heard to chuckle. When he pulled away, Darlene shook her head and smiled.

"I present the happy couple, Mr. and Mrs. Pierce Blackwell," the minister announced.

"Oh Pierce!" Constance said, coming to hug her big brother. "I'm so happy for you! How wonderful to get married on Valentine's Day!"

"He only did that so he could avoid going to the bachelor ball again," Dennison teased, then added, "My dear, you are a radiant bride. Welcome to our family." He kissed her lightly on the cheek and hugged her gently.

"Thank you," Darlene whispered. "Thank you for everything."

Eugenia Blackwell Morgan's absence from the wedding did nothing to spoil the fun. The house staff laid out a wonderful wedding breakfast and everyone gorged themselves until they could hold no more. Pierce had worried that Darlene would regret such a small wedding, but she assured him over and over that it was only important that he be there, whether the rest of the world showed up or not.

When evening came and the couple made their way to the privacy of their first bedroom as man and wife, Darlene felt an uneasy nervous flutter in her stomach and trembled when Pierce lifted her to carry her across the threshold.

"I love you," he said, gently putting her down again. "I will always love only you."

Darlene's nerves instantly settled. She stared up into the face of her husband and smiled. "And I love you and so long as I live, you'll be my only Valentine."

"That reminds me," Pierce said. He went to the large bureau and pulled open a drawer. Fishing out an envelope he brought it to her and grinned. "Happy Valentine's Day."

"But I didn't get you anything," she protested.

He nuzzled her neck with a kiss. "I'm sure we'll work that out."

She blushed, feeling her face grow hot. Concentrating on opening the card, she found it to be an identical replica of the one she'd lost in the fire. But this time it was signed as well.

" 'To Darlene, my darling wife, with all my love, Pierce,' " she read and tears came instantly to her eyes. She looked up at him and saw the tenderness in his expression and knew that God had done a wonderful thing in her life. Stepping into his arms once again, she thought of the future and the hope that lay before them. It was good to know that they would face it together. It was good to know they'd have God to guide their way.

"Thank you for my valentine," she said, pulling away. "I'll cherish it always." She turned to place it on the bureau, but Pierce reached out and pulled her back with a deep, mischievous laugh.

"I'm not letting you get away," he said, then grinning in a roguish manner, he pulled loose the ribbon from her hair and whispered, "Now, about my valentine . . ."

■ ■ ■ ■

LITTLE SHOES
AND MISTLETOE

BY SALLY LAITY

■ ■ ■ ■

CHAPTER 1

New York, 1898

Newly-fallen snow transformed Manhattan into a magical fairyland, hushed and glorious and glistening in the November sunshine like millions of diamonds scattered by an unseen hand. Every object in view sported a coating of frothy whiteness. Even the bottommost branches of the twin hemlocks out front drooped beneath the heavy blanket. Admiring the charming Currier & Ives scene from the parlor window of Harper House, Eliza Criswell almost forgot her melancholy.

"Quite peaceful, considering the way the wind howled around us half the night," her aunt Phoebe Harper said as she swept into the room, the hem of her russet morning gown swishing softly over the emerald-and-gold carpet.

Dragging her gaze from winter's unexpected but breathtaking spectacle, Eliza released the lace undercurtain and turned to her widowed aunt with a thin smile, the best she could muster. "Oh. You've brought breakfast. You should have let me carry that tray for you, Auntie."

"Nonsense." The birdlike woman shrugged beneath the crocheted shawl draping her shoulders. "This old body of mine might have a few aches and pains now and again, but I'm not completely infirm yet." Resting the edge of the silver tray on one of two lace-covered tables gracing the bright front room, she removed the coffee carafe and other accoutrements that gleamed in the warm glow from the crackling fire.

Eliza helped set out embossed napkins, utensils, and china plates bearing warm, cranberry-raisin scones, then flicked a glance around her aunt's combination tea parlor and gift shop. An assortment of cabinets and shelves fairly overflowed with tasteful, handcrafted items of particular interest to women. "What if customers come while we're eating?"

Aunt Phoebe remained nonplused. "It takes awhile for folks to clear their walks after a sudden snow. One of my greatest blessings is having young Peter Bradley living next door. That boy has taken it upon himself to look after me since my beloved

Captain Harper went down at sea. I think the world of him; I surely do. If I'd had a son of my own . . ." A slight sigh punctuated the unfinished thought.

Eliza recalled the shoveling sounds that had drifted to her second-floor bedroom while she dressed. "How thoughtful. I've often wondered how you managed after Uncle Amos passed on. Even though New York and Pennsylvania share a common border, Manhattan might as well be in Europe, the way Father's business affairs prevented our family from traveling. I'd have loved being able to visit you more often."

"Yes, well, the good Lord never forgets His own." She gestured for Eliza to be seated, then took the needlepoint-cushioned chair opposite her. "And the people at church take His instructions to heart, too. They see that the widows of the flock are cared for."

"Sounds like a splendid congregation. I shall look forward to attending services with you."

The older woman nodded and reached out to take Eliza's hand for grace.

The feeling of the frail, gnarled fingers caught at Eliza's heart. Upon her arrival yesterday, she'd been shocked to see how much her aunt had aged in the last ten years. Though Aunt Phoebe remained spry for the ripe old age of sixty-four, even the most casual observer could detect her occasional halting step, the slower movements which quickly sapped her energy. Eliza well understood the reason she had received the recent invitation to come live with her aunt.

It couldn't have arrived at a more opportune time either, Eliza conceded bitterly, slamming mental doors shut against an assault of painful memories. When the realization dawned that her aunt had finished praying, she smoothed the napkin over the lap of her sapphire gown and met the faded blue eyes across the table. "How long have you been running a gift shop, Aunt Phoebe?"

The older woman sipped her coffee and set down the fragile cup. "Oh, about two years now. It seemed an excellent way of supplying niceties for special occasions. Not that I need the extra income, you understand. The Captain left me quite comfortable, even with the expenses it takes to keep up Harper House. But I like to be able to give regularly to the needy. Orphans in the city, to be more precise."

Such selflessness touched Eliza. "But where do you get all the beautiful stock? Everywhere I look I see something exquisite

— porcelain dolls, intricately scrolled stationery, crocheted furniture scarves, handmade
lace. Wherever do you find such a lovely
selection?"

"I make it."

Eliza stopped chewing and touched her
napkin to the corners of her lips. "All of
this?"

"That's right, dear. When a body spends
so much time alone, there are scores of
empty hours to fill. From the time I was a
young wife, coping with solitude when the
captain was off at sea, I would pull my rocking chair close to the hearth and work on
whatever new project happened to catch my
fancy at the time. Some of my handiwork I
gave to friends on birthdays and what have
you, but over the years I accumulated far
too much for personal use. Then the thought
came to me to open a little shop." She
paused. "Of course, my stock always dwin-
dles rapidly as Christmas nears. I'm hoping
now that you've come, you might learn a
few skills, help me keep up with the de-
mand."

"I'd be delighted." The possibility of
becoming accomplished at those arts ap-
pealed to Eliza's own creative nature. Her
gaze drifted once more to the decorative
objects.

Aunt Phoebe nodded and took another sip of coffee. "Did you sleep well with that storm carrying on outside?"

"Oh yes. I must have been more tired than I realized after the train trip. And the feather bed in your front bedroom is simply delightful."

"Well, I'm just glad to have you here. I've been rattling around this big place by myself much too long." She finished the last bite of her scone, her shrewd eyes peering kindly at Eliza through rimless eyeglasses. "I know it was not the happiest of occasions that made you willing to leave Harrisburg, my dear."

Eliza felt a stinging in the back of her eyes and averted her attention to the cup she held.

"But if it brought you to me," her aunt went on, "it must have been part of God's mysterious workings. Perhaps when you're up to talking about things, you'll feel free to confide in your old auntie. These bony shoulders may not look like much, but they'll do for a good cry now and again."

Giving a perfunctory nod, Eliza managed to swallow the remainder of her scone.

The front door opened just then, emitting a blast of icy air, and the silver bell suspended above the entrance tinkled the arrival of a customer.

Glancing toward the visitor as her aunt rose, Eliza did a double take, almost choking on a sip of hot coffee. For a second the man had looked exactly like — she swallowed more calmly — *Weston*. A wave of nausea raged through her at the feasibility that Weston Elliot might have had the gall to follow her. She sloughed off the foolish pounding of her heart and stood to begin clearing the table.

"Good morning, my dear Mrs. Harper," came the newcomer's cheery voice.

"And good day to you, Micah. Right on time, as always."

"Just trying to match your faithfulness," he said smoothly. "And it's on my way, actually, to my first call."

"I'll just get this week's money from the drawer. How have things been going?"

"Surprisingly well, until I find myself suddenly frustrated and rebuffed at every turn. But we can't afford to give up, not when there's so much dire need."

From time to time during the exchange, Eliza sensed his gaze move to her. And linger. Still shaken by the mistaken notion of his identity, she almost lost hold of the cut-glass sugar bowl she was about to set on the tray. Taking a firmer grip on the handle, she put it in place, then reached for the matching cream pitcher.

"Oh Micah," Eliza heard her aunt say. "You haven't met my new housemate. She just arrived yesterday from Harrisburg and will be living with me now."

"Is that right?" he asked politely.

"Eliza, come here, dear," the older woman said. "There's someone I'd like to introduce to you."

Chagrined that she hadn't quite made her escape to the kitchen, Eliza cringed. Nevertheless, setting her burden back down, she acted the dutiful young niece and approached the two with an aloof smile.

"Micah," Aunt Phoebe said, gesturing with one arm, "I'd like to present my favorite niece, Miss Eliza Grace Criswell. Eliza, this is Micah Richmond from my church. He works with Child Placement Services, a true servant of the Lord."

"Miss Criswell." He took Eliza's hand and bowed over it gallantly. "It's a pleasure to meet a relative of this wonderful lady. She's been extremely unselfish in support of my work, and I'm not alone in the great admiration I feel for her."

Finally raising her lashes, Eliza met the young man's eyes. The identical light brown she'd dreaded stared back at her, and they were even framed in a squarish face. Quite startling, even unnerving, the similarity between this man and that wretched Weston. Realizing she was gawking at him in a most unladylike fashion, Eliza reclaimed her fingers and moistened her lips. "Pleased to meet you."

"And I you. I hope you enjoy New York City. A touch larger than Pennsylvania's fine capital, but it has its friendly side, as I'm sure you'll discover."

"Y–yes, I'm sure," she stammered while a few more pertinent details registered. *Hair that same shade of sandy brown, corresponding height and bearing . . .*

"Eliza." Aunt Phoebe's voice broke into her reverie. "Is there more coffee left in the carafe? I'm sure Micah would like to warm up before going back outside into the cold."

"Oh no, no." He raised his hand. "Thank you for the offer, ladies, but I'm afraid I'll be late for my appointment if I tarry a minute more. Next time, perhaps?" Pocketing the contribution the older woman had given him, he tipped his head respectfully. "Mrs. Harper. As always, I'm grateful for your boundless generosity." He then smiled at Eliza. "A pleasure meeting you, Miss Criswell. No doubt we'll see one another at Sunday services, to say nothing of my future visits here."

"No doubt," she parroted with a slight nod. "Mr. Richmond."

Plunking his felt bowler atop his thick light brown hair, he turned toward the door and took his leave, setting the little bell to tinkling again. His descending footfalls echoed from the wooden porch steps, fading into the distance.

"A fine, fine young man, that one," Aunt Phoebe remarked. "He has a deep burden for the immigrant children in the tenements and works night and day trying to find homes for little ones who've been orphaned by the rampant diseases."

"You don't say. Aren't there orphan asylums in the city?" Hoping that conversation would help her to gather herself, Eliza returned to the table for the breakfast tray.

"Several. And every one of them bulging at the seams with forlorn and destitute youngsters. It's a fair shame, that's what it is, but we do what we can to help." She heaved a thoughtful sigh, then gave Eliza a thin smile. "Well, if you don't mind washing up those dishes, I'll dust the shop and see which of my handicrafts seem in the shortest supply. We'll start that lesson first."

"Fine, Auntie. I won't be long."

Once in the solitude of the roomy kitchen, Eliza carried the breakfast things to the sideboard, grateful for an opportunity to calm nerves frazzled by the visitor's uncanny resemblance to her former fiancé. At her first glimpse of the man, a wave of nausea had surged through her. Thankfully that had subsided as quickly as it had come.

She sank to the seat of the nearest spindle-backed chair, her gaze idly reacquainting herself with the massive coal stove, the polished wood floor, and the ruffled chintz curtains gracing the double window. Everything appeared tidy and charming as she'd remembered, and oddly comforting in her distress.

Coming when it had, Eliza had latched desperately onto the invitation to relocate to New York. How she loved this glorious pale yellow cottage with its rounded turrets and abundance of gingerbread trim. It was one of a limited number of dwellings constructed of something other than brick or the varieties of stone so liberally used throughout the city. Inside and out, her aunt's loving touches lent rich beauty and homey grace wherever one's eye might fall. And here, far from Harrisburg, Eliza intended to put the past to rest and make a new start for herself.

Here she vowed to forget Weston Elliot and all his smooth words, the smiling lips that could bring all her dreams to life even as his cold heart could bring them dashing back to Earth again. She'd been a fool, so trusting, so naive. But she wouldn't make that mistake in the future, not with a man — and *definitely* not with someone she considered a friend. Better to live and die friendless and a spinster than suffer such humiliation a second time.

Bitter anger at Melanie Brown had successfully repelled that young woman's intrusion into Eliza's thoughts since she'd fled Harrisburg. But how would she ever banish her former betrothed from her mind when she'd be crossing paths with someone whose very appearance would be a constant reminder of the man who had stolen her untried heart and thoughtlessly smashed it into a million pieces?

CHAPTER 2

Guiding his buggy away from Harper House, Micah gave his scarf an extra wrap about his neck. The storm had ended hours ago, and the last remnants of the clouds had long since moved out over the vast expanse of the Atlantic Ocean. The temperature, however, remained nippy even in the bright sunlight — especially with the breeze blowing across the ice-fringed Hudson River off to one side. Manhattan's close proximity to the sea both moderated and lessened the length of winter's cold snaps, so doubtless this one would dissipate soon enough.

Thinking of the funds provided by Mrs. Harper, he smiled to himself. The goodly sum would purchase a number of coats and mittens for the ragged orphans, plus some staple foods. The widow's giving spirit humbled Micah. For someone living alone for nigh unto a dozen years, she never once complained about her circumstances. She merely kept abreast of the needs of those less fortunate and did whatever she could to help out.

But his keen eye perceived that her health had been on the decline for some time now. How providential for God to send her a companion. Perhaps with extra hands and a caring person to look after her, the dear soul would gain new strength and find restored health. The world needed more folks as kindhearted as she.

Micah's recollections then drifted to her niece, whose delicate beauty seemed as appealing and fresh as Mrs. Harper's was creased with age. The young woman wore her sable hair parted in the middle with the back fashionably confined in a hair net, but tiny curls framing her face added a tangible softness. And despite the age difference between the two, Micah thought he'd ascertained a family resemblance in both features and carriage.

But there appeared no subtlety about Miss Eliza Criswell's reserve, he admitted. Her veiled eyes scarcely met his gaze long enough for him to identify their particular shade of blue. And in one unguarded moment he'd caught a glimpse of something that could only be termed anguish.

Well, no doubt she'd make some new

friends once she began attending church services, and then perhaps her burdens would lighten. He would suggest to his fiancée, Anabelle, that she befriend Miss Criswell.

With that plan in mind, he snapped the reins sharply against the horse's back to pick up the pace.

Eliza looked forward all week to the arrival of Sunday. Her spirit was in dire need of bolstering. Other times in her life when she'd faced disappointments and heartaches, she'd withdrawn from the Lord, becoming lax in her personal prayer and Bible reading. But that only led to more misery, more emptiness, and hopelessness.

This time — perhaps from the utter shock of having been betrayed by two people she loved dearly — she turned to God for comfort and sanity, finding His grace sufficient, as the Bible promised. And here, far away from the pitying eyes of people who had known her all her life, she'd have the freedom to enter fully into the worship service.

To the casual observer, Faith Community Church definitely lacked the grandeur of the city's older and larger cathedrals. The steepled, redbrick building sported a new coat of pristine white paint around the windows, and the dormant shrubbery and trees flanking it were taller than Eliza remembered. Inside, however, its dark plank floor and walnut pews appeared much the same as they'd been years ago.

Relaxing beside Aunt Phoebe in the older woman's customary fourth row, she allowed her gaze to wander over the hushed sanctuary. There seemed to be very few people her own age, except for a slim, golden-haired organist playing a reverent prelude on the pump organ. Eliza focused on the young woman, noting the smoothness of her touch on the keys, the contrast between her fair complexion and the rich burgundy of her gown. With her every graceful move, muted colors from arched, stained glass windows fell in a kaleidoscope of pastels over the wine velvet, accenting her lissome figure.

Eliza suddenly thought of Micah Richmond, remembering she hadn't seen him among the worshipers when she and her aunt made their way to their seats. Not that she was looking for him, especially, but his would have been the only other familiar face in this congregation of strangers.

Returning a few polite smiles from people around her, she shifted her attention forward.

Just then, the Reverend Thomas Norman rose from one of three large chairs on the platform and moved to the pulpit. He adjusted the sleeves of his charcoal suit as he surveyed his flock through gold-rimmed spectacles.

"I bid you all good morning on this lovely Lord's Day," he said, his smile warm and welcoming. "I'm certain Wilf Perkins has chosen some stirring hymns to lead off our service, but first, let us open with prayer." He bowed his graying head and spoke in a solemn voice. "Almighty God, who sustains, guides, and protects us, we gather in Thy presence in humble thankfulness for Thy unfailing goodness and mercy to us all. Grant that we may worship Thee in spirit and in truth this day as we endeavor to glorify Thy Son, in whose name we pray. Amen."

Something about the pastor's manner greatly encouraged Eliza, and as the closing bars of the last hymn before the sermon faded and the man once again stepped to the lectern, she eagerly anticipated his words.

"Our text this morning is found in the fourth chapter of Philippians," he announced, "a passage with which I'm certain many of you dear folk are acquainted."

Eliza turned to it during the ensuing shuffle of crisp pages throughout the room.

"In this letter . . ." Pastor Norman's voice took on a booming quality, reverberating through the sanctuary. "The apostle Paul testified, 'I have learned in whatsoever state I am, therewith to be content.' And in writing to Timothy, upon another occasion, he proclaimed that 'godliness with contentment is great gain.' But how could someone who had suffered the magnitude of adversity which Paul endured ever find contentment in such troubled circumstances? That's what we are about to find out, dearly beloved, as we examine in depth the apostle's own words."

Eliza, musing over her own recent adversity, somehow gave the minister her whole attention while he continued relating the great saint's trials and suffering. She easily found the alternate passages used during the discourse. Many were already underlined in her Bible.

"But even a man as great as this," Pastor Norman continued, holding forth his large, frayed copy of the scriptures, "was flesh and blood. He laughed, cried, got angry, became perplexed — and he was deeply conscious of his weaknesses. At times he openly acknowledged not only fear, but despair of life itself.

"Yet through it all, one thing held true. From his very conversion and subsequent trials, Paul was being drawn closer to the Lord, to His love and His power. He was being made like Him. Small wonder he could write, 'For to me to live is Christ, and to die is gain.' "

The words sounded oddly discomfiting to Eliza as she compared them to her own situation. Perhaps she hadn't shut herself off from God in this heartbreak, but she had yet to reach the point where she could forgive Weston for taking her love and throwing it back in her face. And Melanie's betrayal had seemed doubly cruel. Those wounds were still so fresh, the pain so intense. Eliza knew it would be a very long while before she could say in truth that she was becoming more like Christ — if ever. She needed to give the matter serious contemplation.

The minister paused and swept a glance around his congregation. "I'll close with this thought. The more satisfied we are with Jesus, the more we draw our strength from Him, the more firmly we'll stand up through all the bitter gales of adversity. Every believer can learn to find contentment in Him. It is, my friends, a matter of the heart.

Let us pray. . . ."

Engrossed in her own thoughts, Eliza scarcely noticed as Mr. Perkins again took charge for the closing hymn and benediction.

Afterward, Aunt Phoebe took her hand and made the rounds, joyfully introducing her to the ladies of the church, a few deacons, and last of all, the pastor. But when her aunt became involved in a lengthy discussion with some friends from the Ladies' Benevolent Society, Eliza felt suddenly out of place. She meandered to the front of the sanctuary where the young woman in burgundy stood collecting her music.

"Excuse me," Eliza said tentatively.

The golden-haired girl turned, her gray-green eyes alight. "Yes?"

"I wanted to express to you how much I appreciated the music you played during the service."

"Why, thank you." A faint blush revealed a shy nature.

"I hate to admit it," Eliza continued, "but I was absolutely dreadful at my piano lessons, so I recognize a gift when I hear one."

The young woman smiled. "I'm Anabelle Dumont, and you're . . . ?"

"Eliza Criswell, Phoebe Harper's niece,

from Harrisburg."

"Oh, of course." An airy quality to her voice indicated a growing ease. "Micah told me about you. I believe you've already met him? Micah Richmond?" She scanned the departing crowd and frowned. "He was hoping to make the service this morning, but something else must have arisen."

"Yes, we've met," Eliza replied. "He came by my aunt's shop a few days ago."

"Well, I'm very pleased to meet you, Miss Criswell."

"Eliza. Please."

"Eliza then. And you must call me Anabelle. I assume we'll have many opportunities to get to know each other, now that you're living here in New York."

"I would imagine. Well, thank you — for the music, and for letting me bother you and all."

Anabelle blushed again. "It was no bother. Welcome to Faith Community. I hope you'll soon feel at home among us."

Eliza nodded and turned, rejoining her aunt, who was bidding the reverend good day. With a parting smile, she took the older woman's arm and assisted her down the steps to their waiting hired carriage.

"I see you met our fair Anabelle," Aunt Phoebe remarked as they plodded homeward. "She . . . keeps company, shall we say, with young Micah Richmond."

"Oh?" For some odd reason, Eliza's interest piqued, then flattened again in relief. Yet another reason she needn't waste thoughts on that particular man.

"Yes," her aunt went on. "Seems their families have enjoyed a close, lifelong relationship, so Ana and Micah have grown up together. Their parents naturally assume they'll wed one day."

"How nice." Eliza paused, choosing her next words with care. "I felt drawn to Anabelle, somehow. Her music, her . . . spirit. Something I can't name. Not that I'm seeking new friends, just now. But I couldn't help but notice there were very few young people in your church."

Her aunt's silver brows arched high. "Not seeking friends? Why, I've never heard of such a thing — especially since one couldn't find a sweeter companion than Anabelle Dumont. Most of her peers have married and moved elsewhere, so I would imagine she would appreciate a new friend herself."

The mild rebuff made Eliza smile with chagrin.

"And you certainly don't need to be cloistered for days on end with no one but an old woman for company. I'll ask Ana over to tea," Aunt Phoebe determined. "I don't get out to many of the church functions or socials anymore, and I never go out at night in the winter. These old bones can't seem to take the cold the way they used to. But I'm sure she will manage a visit. I'll pass on the invitation through Micah when he stops by next."

Eliza gave a noncommittal nod and averted her attention to the passing scenery. This day, too, was clear and sunny, even though quite cold. Couples strolled arm in arm along the snowy path that ran alongside the Hudson River, happy and smiling as they exchanged adoring looks.

The reminder of her own loss brought a sharp jab of pain. Was her former fiancé even now parading his new *wife* along some wintry park setting for all the world to see? Anger rose up within her, stealing the pleasure of the day and, along with it, the joy she had derived from the music and the church service.

After reaching home and enjoying a light repast, Aunt Phoebe took advantage of the shop closure to lie down.

Eliza picked up the project she'd been working on and went upstairs to her room.

Cheery and bright, and looking out upon a broad expanse of the river several dozen yards away, the boudoir's entirely feminine decor displayed yet more of her aunt's artistry. It was papered beautifully with pale blue-and-white stripes on the lower portion and miniature roses above, and a hand-painted rose vine trailed above and below the white wainscoting. Eliza had spent a good part of her first day at her aunt's just admiring the perfectly rendered blooms.

Lowering herself onto the blue velvet chaise positioned to take advantage of the window's light, she set to work again on the tatted border around the edge of a handkerchief. It would be some time before she would feel adroit at this delicate skill, but eventually she hoped to produce the quality of work someone might buy. Determined to master the art as quickly as possible, she worked carefully.

Mulling over the day's events and conversations brought to mind her new acquaintances. So Anabelle Dumont and Micah Richmond were keeping company, as Aunt Phoebe put it. It was easy enough to deduce what he saw in the organist, but what about the reverse? For the life of her, Eliza could think only of Weston when recollections of the child placement worker crossed her mind. And those thoughts were far from pleasant.

She frowned. She certainly wasn't being fair to the gentleman from Aunt Phoebe's church. After all, he'd been nothing but proper when they'd met. Perhaps she'd only imagined a resemblance between her former betrothed and this young man. Yes, that was it. She'd always been plagued by an overactive imagination, and in her present frame of mind, she might mistake anyone for the fiancé who had consumed all of her waking thoughts for the past few years.

Well, she certainly didn't need any reminders of Weston Elliot. She planned to erase him from her mind for good. She did not want to think about him — ever. For the rest of her life.

CHAPTER 3

Ships and warehouses lined busy South Street along New York's East River, where piers stretched for a distance of three miles, in what was termed "Packet Row." The bustle of activity knew no season. Summer and winter, ocean vessels and packets of every size and purpose lay at anchor as passengers lined the quays and milled about, chattering to the small groups of individuals who had come to offer welcomes or bid farewells.

The area teemed with the clamor of street traffic, seabirds, and ships' whistles. Seamen of countless nationalities hollered to one another while hefting bulky ropes and moving cargo alternately aboard or ashore, according to their bills of lading. And not to be outdone, hawkers yelled above the melee, trying to entice customers to buy their wares.

Used to the confusion of the wharves,

Micah paid it scarcely any mind as he hastened along, intent on his errand. A dockworker had informed him of a little homeless girl who'd been appearing out of nowhere whenever a new ship arrived. Belonging to no one, and with no other means to support herself, she would stand on the quay and sing, depending on some kind soul for a few pennies or dimes with which to buy her next meal.

This was not the first "singing girl" he'd heard of. The practice was heartbreakingly common among immigrant children orphaned by cholera or influenza. Such youngsters often sought meager shelter for the night in trash barrels or sometimes huddled against a closed door — anything to get out of the biting wind. Micah intended to find this little one a place to stay, even if only temporarily. Knowing the timid urchins feared the authorities, he kept a casual pace, his eyes darting about, searching likely hiding places.

At last he caught a movement on the edge of his vision. He turned his head slowly, feigning interest in some goods a passing peddler had for sale. Sure enough, he spied a street child. Painfully thin and ragged, bare-legged and hatless even in the bitter cold, she was scavenging in a refuse container. *Dear Father, she can't be more than seven or eight. And she needs help. Please give me wisdom in how to handle this situation.*

Experience taught him to go slowly in these instances. He took up a position behind an object that would prevent her from noticing him, then forced himself to stand by and do nothing except keep watch.

At that moment, the faraway blast from an incoming ship announced its approach.

Her head snapped in that direction, a tiny smile appearing in her dirty face as she meandered toward the available dock.

He smiled inwardly and followed. With her absorbed in performing for disembarking passengers, he just might manage to blend into the crowd . . . and have her sing for him. *Thank You, Father.*

It seemed to take an interminable amount of time for the vessel to chug its way into the harbor, drop anchor, and be secured. But at last Micah saw the gangplank lower into place. Passengers started down the wooden walkway.

As they neared the bottom, the little ragamuffin stepped out into plain view. Trembly at first, her thin, high voice broke forth in a hymn, gathering strength with each phrase.

Most folks completely ignored her.

Their callousness caught at Micah's heart. *Look at her!* he wanted to shout. *But for the grace of God, she could be your own little one!* But the new arrivals had more important things on their minds. Precious few tossed even a single coin in her direction.

Determined now, Micah merged into a group of descending folk and eased his way across to the other side of the gangplank, heading straight for the child.

"A song for ye, mister?" she asked shyly as he came nearer.

"Why sure, young lady." He grinned, stopping to give her his whole attention. "Happen to know 'Abide with Me'?"

She nodded, her stringy hair bobbing with the motion. Opening her rosebud mouth, she sang the words perfectly, her grimy face shining with hope.

All the while he listened, Micah had to steel that portion of his heart that ached for each child such as this he encountered, willing the sorrow not to bring forth tears of anger, frustration, and grief.

"What do you suppose that song means?" he asked when she finished.

The thin shoulders beneath the threadbare coat shrugged.

"Do you know about God?"

Another shrug. "He lives up in heaven."

"Did you know He cares about you and wants to be your Friend?"

At this, her wary brown eyes took on a dubious look. "Are ye gonna give me money?"

Reaching into his coat pocket, Micah withdrew a pair of silver coins and dropped them into her tiny hand. When she appeared about to bolt, he dug for another. "Say, I was just about to go have something to eat. I don't suppose you're hungry?"

She stared for a moment before giving a grudging nod.

"Well, I know a place where there are lots of children, and they're just about to sit down to some hot soup and fresh bread. And after a while, they'll be sleeping in warm, soft beds. Doesn't that sound nice?"

Her gaze dropped to the money in her palm, and she averted her eyes to the ground.

"And it doesn't cost one copper penny," Micah added quickly. Watching the play of emotions in her face, he took a risk. "You know, honey, God happens to be a Friend of mine, and He told me you needed help. Would you let me help you? There's another snowstorm coming." His sober expression gave emphasis.

288

Until he said that, she remained passive. But then her eyes swam with tears.

It took every ounce of strength he possessed not to sweep her up into his arms. Instead, he offered a hand.

Turning her watery gaze to his, she hesitated briefly before placing her fingers into his palm.

Micah covered her tiny hand with his other one and smiled down at her. "My name is Micah. What's yours?"

"Rachel," she whispered, the gleam of hope in her eyes slowly overtaking the despair.

"My, but you're quiet this evening." Bringing a tray of tea and sliced nut bread into the parlor of her parents' home on fashionable Lexington Avenue, Anabelle set it on the coffee table before taking a seat beside Micah on the indigo brocade sofa. Matching gas lamps had been turned down low, and the soft, dim light gave the room an intimate air.

He smiled gently. "I had a rather long day."

"So I noticed," she said pointedly as the grandfather clock in the hall of the comfortable brownstone house chimed eight times. She poured each of them some of the rich amber liquid, handing one cup to him before helping herself to the other.

Micah reached for the cream pitcher and added a dollop as she stirred her usual two sugar cubes into hers. With the golden firelight as a backdrop, Anabelle's hair shone like a halo, and when she settled back against the sofa, her perfect profile appeared outlined in molten light. As always he admired her flawless, fragile beauty.

"What detained you?" she finally asked.

"I came across a street child this afternoon, one who needed food and a place to stay. It took awhile to arrange things."

"You were successful, then." Her words were more statement than question.

He nodded.

Anabelle sipped delicately from her cup, returning it to the saucer with an almost inaudible clink. "You know, Micah, I can't understand why you feel compelled to make all the city's orphans your personal responsibility."

He braced himself for the comments he knew would follow.

"There will always be needy children. Even the Bible says that. But here in New York the problem is almost overwhelming. You should be able to put in a day's work and then leave at a regular time, as does everyone else."

Her sentiments were not new. It seemed she'd said the same thing a thousand times before, in as many ways. Lacking energy to suppress his ragged sigh, he didn't fight it. "You know I feel called by the Lord to do what I do. It's not just a job; it's my ministry."

She gave a doubtful shrug. "I only know that the church provides considerable aid to the unfortunates through prayer and contributions and our benevolent activities. That should be enough."

"Well, it isn't enough, Ana. And it never will be . . . at least, not for me." Draining his tea, he set the cup onto the tray and started to rise.

Anabelle stopped him with a hand on his forearm. "Oh, please don't rush off, sweetheart. I haven't even had a chance to tell you I met Mrs. Harper's niece yesterday at service."

He sat back down. "Oh?"

"Yes. She seems ever so nice. Even lonely . . . perhaps because she's only recently arrived in the city."

"It's fortunate that her aunt will now have someone around to look after her. But by the same token, I'm sure Miss Criswell could use a friend, if you happen to be so

291

inclined."

"I do, actually. We can always use extra hands on quilting days at church, and I'm thrilled at the prospect of having someone my age there. Those old biddies are forever talking to me as if I'm a schoolgirl."

He had to smile. "Well, at twenty-two, you're not all that far removed from being at Miss Witherspoon's Academy, you know."

Anabelle smiled dryly.

Micah brushed the curve of her fine cheekbone with his fingertips and gazed into her eyes — more gray than green in the subdued light. "Well my dear, I am kind of tired. If you don't mind, I think I'll call it a night. Maybe tomorrow I'll be better company."

"Whatever you say." She took no offense from his early departure. "I'll make some taffy for when you come. Would you like that?"

"Sure. Sounds delicious." Rising, he pulled her lightly into his arms and gave her an equally soft kiss, attributing his own lack of passion to bone-weariness from his long day. "Take care, Ana. I'll see you tomorrow."

Sliding her arm about his waist, Anabelle rested her head against his shoulder and strolled with him to the door.

Outside once more in the cold night wind, Micah willed aside his nagging disappointment that the woman he planned to marry cared so little about what was most important to him. Perhaps that would change after they wed.

But what if it did not?

Clothed in her warmest nightgown, Eliza stood at the mirror and removed her hair net and hairpins, allowing her long tresses to fall free of their usual confinement. She took the silver-handled brush her grandmother had given her years ago and began the habitual one hundred strokes.

Though this grand old mansion felt toasty during a sunny day, at night the wind's cold breath filtered through tiny cracks and crevices around the windows and along the floorboards. She hoped the warming pan had chased the chill from the bedsheets.

Finally reaching a hundred, Eliza set down the brush and padded to the fourposter. She removed the long-handled pan and climbed into the bed, arranging the fluffy quilts over herself before reaching for her Bible on the night table.

Pastor Norman's sermon still rang in her mind. And try as she might, she couldn't justify the ill feelings she still bore in her heart toward Weston — whom she blamed for everything, even Melanie's betrayal. After all, the girl had always been gullible to a fault. But determined to ease her own inner turmoil, Eliza read over the verses covered in the message, then clutched the Holy Book to her breast and bowed her head.

Dear Heavenly Father, I thank You for this lovely day and for Your presence even in our trials. I know that eventually I must let go of my anger and humiliation . . . and perhaps in time, I'll be able to do just that. But for now, I ask only that You stay close to me. Help me to remember that Your Son forgave even His murderers. Please don't let me forget His example. And if You can change my heart to be more like His, I am willing.

Even as that small admission came, Eliza realized she meant it and took that as an encouraging sign. She placed her Bible on the small table again and lay down with a sigh.

She loved being here with Aunt Phoebe. She hadn't particularly intended to seek out a new friend, yet it appeared the Lord was replacing Melanie with Anabelle Dumont. And Eliza was learning skills she had always coveted but somehow never found time to master.

Nevertheless, the future stretched before her, a bleak and empty road to nowhere. One she would travel alone, thanks to Weston Elliot. The wedding which she'd been planning for such a long time — and one which should have taken place by now — would never be.

She hoped her mother had returned all of the lovely gifts to which she was no longer entitled. And as for the pillowcases and other linens she'd so lovingly embroidered ever since girlhood for her married life, Eliza almost wished she had brought them along with her for the perverse pleasure of setting them ablaze!

No. On second thought, she'd sell them to help the needy . . . sell off her own chest of hopes, stop feeling sorry for herself, and find another purpose for her life just as her aunt had done.

But how, when she couldn't even find all the pieces of her shattered heart?

Hot tears she had long held back flooded her eyes, rolling down into her hair and onto her pillow. Eliza wept until she could weep no more.

CHAPTER 4

"Utterly fascinating." Eliza peered over her aunt's shoulder at the exquisite lace collar being created by the aged fingers. Without missing a beat, Aunt Phoebe picked up a hand-carved bobbin from the myriad of wooden spools encircling her lace board. Then she wound the silk thread around and between the clusters of tiny pins positioned to form the intricate pattern she had designed. To Eliza, the finished portion appeared to be made of nothing but gossamer and air, and she felt reasonably certain she would never possess such skill.

"It's not really as difficult as it looks," her aunt said, "though it does require considerable practice."

"Indeed."

"My grandmother taught me when I was just a young girl. But with these old eyes, I dare not attempt it except on a bright morning like this. And that's one reason why I made this sunroom my work area."

"Still," Eliza marveled, "I wouldn't know where or how to start."

The white bun atop her aunt's head jiggled as she nodded, and she paused in her work to meet Eliza's gaze. "Making lace always reminds me of life," she began thoughtfully. "We're the pins on the board, and God is the great Weaver. He picks up a thread from some faraway corner and winds it around us. We might not feel a particular strand is so very comfortable as He first pulls it taut. But there's no point in struggling against it. From His viewpoint, He's fashioning a design that brings glory to every aspect of His handiwork. And one day, when we look back on our lives, we'll see things of beauty even in the places we thought were dark and hard."

The lovely sentiments touched Eliza, and she mused over them momentarily before focusing again on her own task. "Well, I'll be satisfied if I can master tatting." With a critical grimace, she sank back into her chair in the workroom and held her own project at arm's length to assess her stitches.

"I wouldn't fret overmuch," Aunt Phoebe said kindly. "From what I've seen of your labors so far, I'd say those handkerchiefs will not remain in the shop very long before someone buys them."

As if on cue, the bell above the parlor door reverberated through the hall, signaling the arrival of a customer.

The older woman stood. "I'll tend to this one."

"And I'll see about dinner. It's nearly noon." Laying her task aside, Eliza rose and headed for the kitchen. But she couldn't dismiss the mental picture her aunt had painted. Could being rejected and cast aside like some unwanted, disdainful object ever be part of her own life's beautiful pattern? She had her doubts. No matter how she attempted to distance herself from her circumstances, they would forever appear cruel and ugly.

In the kitchen, Eliza opened the icebox, removed a pair of eggs and set them to coddling, then sliced two thick chunks of bread to toast and butter. Small dishes of canned peaches with sweetened cream, ladyfingers, and a pot of tea topped off the light midday meal. Putting all the items on a large tray, she carried them to the parlor.

Her aunt, she discovered upon her approach, had not as yet finished with the customer. Not wanting to intrude, Eliza hesitated before entering the room.

"As always, we can only do our best,"

came Micah Richmond's familiar voice. "Things are going from bad to worse as winter settles in. Conditions at the tenements are deplorable beyond words, as you know."

"Yes, and it's such a pity," her aunt replied. "Let us pray that the good ladies at Faith Community will be able to step up their provisions in the weeks to come. I've been saving material scraps left over from some of my own projects. I'll add them to the quilt supplies at the church."

"I'm sure that'll be much appreciated. You are a good friend."

Eliza surmised from the tone of the conversation that the young man was about to depart. She waited for the sound of the door. When it didn't come directly, she sighed and propped the heavy serving tray against a hip.

With her movement, a teaspoon fell over the edge and clattered noisily to the floor.

"Is that you, Eliza dear?" Aunt Phoebe called out.

Eliza knew it would be pointless — and rude — not to respond. "Yes." Forcing a smile, she gripped her burden more firmly and stepped into the room, heading for the nearest table.

"Ah, Miss Criswell." The young man gave

a slight bow of his head as she moved into view. "Good day."

"And a good day to you, Mr. Richmond." Eliza had all but convinced herself she had only imagined the resemblance between the man and her former fiancé, but to her dismay, the merest glance proved the opposite to be true. She caught her breath at the amazing similarities and purposely refrained from meeting his gaze as she turned away and put all her efforts into setting a proper table.

"Oh, that reminds me, Micah," her aunt said, "Eliza and I would love for Anabelle to come to tea. Tomorrow afternoon, if it's convenient. Would you be kind enough to deliver this note to her?"

"Delighted to be of service, Mrs. Harper. It's not often I get to do something in return for your kindnesses. I shall take my leave so you ladies can enjoy your meal." Plunking his hat on, he tipped his head politely and exited with a carefree wave of the hand.

Last week's snow had melted days ago, and the sound of his footfalls drifted from the front walk as he strode out to his carriage.

"Such a nice, nice young man," Aunt Phoebe said, coming to take a seat at the table. "Oh, this looks lovely, dear."

A fairly steady stream of patrons, mindful of the approaching Christmas season, came to the shop the next morning. Aunt Phoebe had assigned kitchen duty to Eliza, and Eliza suspected that her aunt hoped the chore of providing an array of freshly baked treats for afternoon tea would help occupy her until their guest arrived. But she wondered if her aunt felt more nervous than she did. From bits of conversation, Eliza guessed that Aunt Phoebe didn't want her niece being cut off with other young people simply because she was living with an older woman. With the exception of Micah's brief visits, the afternoon tea with Anabelle would be the first time they had entertained someone Eliza's age since she'd moved from Harrisburg.

Finally four o'clock arrived, and with it, the carriage bringing Anabelle. Aunt Phoebe ushered the fair-haired beauty inside and turned the CLOSED sign outward.

"Lovely to see you both again," Anabelle said airily as she hung her fur-lined wrap on the hall tree beside the door and tucked her long gloves into its roomy hood. Her cheeks glowed pink from the brisk temperature, a

301

fitting contrast to the rich emerald gown she wore. Its sleeves fairly dripped with rich ecru lace every bit as delicate as her soft skin.

"We're so pleased you could come," Eliza answered, thankful that she'd taken the time to change into a dressier frock after the day's baking was finished.

"Why don't we all be seated?" Aunt Phoebe motioned to the lace-draped table, and the three of them took chairs.

Eliza felt her face flush with pride when Anabelle glanced appreciatively at the assortment of fancy cookies, fudge, and teacakes she had labored over most of the day. She had done her best to prepare something that Anabelle would enjoy, and she sighed with thankfulness that everything had turned out perfectly.

Aunt Phoebe offered a brief prayer over the food, and then filled the floral-patterned teacups.

"Everything is just exquisite," Anabelle said, her tone completely sincere. "I've often envied your talents, Mrs. Harper." Scooping two sweet cubes from the silver sugar scuttle, she stirred them into her tea before taking a sip.

Aunt Phoebe smiled. "If you're referring to the array of gifts about the room, I am happy to announce that my niece is acquiring some splendid proficiency along those lines already. If you're speaking of our refreshments, however, I must confess they are all Eliza's doing."

"You don't say." Anabelle turned a gracious smile on Eliza. "Well, music might come easily to me, Eliza, but I'm afraid my accomplishments in the kitchen lag far behind yours."

"Thank you," she replied demurely.

"Speaking of music," Aunt Phoebe chimed in, "we'd love it if you would favor us with a piece when we've finished eating. Something from the classics, perhaps."

"As you wish." Sampling one of the dainty cookies on her plate, Anabelle switched her attention to Eliza once more. "Are you enjoying your stay in New York?"

"Very much. I've been quite busy and have met many friendly folk at the church and here at our shop. Of course, Auntie always makes me feel at home whenever I come to visit."

The honey-blond nodded in agreement. "All of us at Faith Community have basked in her hospitality on occasion. I'm pleased to hear you're fitting in so well. In fact, it would be a boon to the sewing circle if you would consider joining us on Thursday afternoons. At present, we're working on quilts for the unfortunates. Micah delivers them where they're most needed."

"Why, I'd be delighted to help out, if Aunt Phoebe can spare me for a few hours each week." She flashed a questioning glance at her aunt, who nodded.

"Wonderful!" Anabelle exclaimed. "I'll have my driver come by for you on Thursdays at one o'clock." She laughed lightly. "At last, someone near my own age! You cannot imagine what it's like to be among ladies who treat me as if I'm still in pigtails."

With a pointed look at the two of them, Aunt Phoebe finished the last of her tea and got up. "I hope you'll both excuse me if I leave you two *youngsters* to visit while I do a bit of dusting and rearranging of goods on the store shelves."

"Not at all," they both answered.

Anabelle bit into a piece of fudge as the older woman left the room. When she spoke again, her tone was soft, almost conspiratorial. "I know quite a number of eligible bachelors who might enjoy your company also, Eliza. I'd be happy to introduce you around. Perhaps Micah and I could escort you and —"

Eliza blanched. "Thank you, but no. I'm not at all interested in that sort of thing."

"Oh." Her color heightening, Anabelle readjusted her napkin. "What a pity. Well, all the same, I shall be glad for your company at the sewing circle."

Sensing her guest's discomfort, Eliza decided to change the subject. "So, what other interests do you have that occupy your time beside music and needlework?"

The slender blond relaxed noticeably. "I'm an avid reader, absolutely devouring whatever new fiction comes into the bookseller's. And of course," she added on a note of chagrin, "my mother insists I prepare supper at least twice every week. She's bound and determined to marry me off to Micah at the earliest opportunity."

The constant references to the young woman's beau were oddly comforting to Eliza, instilling in her a deeper conviction that she need not be ill at ease in his presence. After all, he wasn't Weston; he had no designs on her. And she truly did want to become friends with Anabelle. Seeing that the girl seemed to have finished eating, Eliza folded her own napkin. "Shall I show you to the piano now?"

"Oh yes. I'm sure that my fingers have finally thawed sufficiently."

Half an hour and a dozen etudes later, Eliza felt completely at ease with Anabelle

Dumont. "I shall never cease coveting your talent," she finally admitted. Resting against her aunt's ebony satin upright, she watched the girl's nimble fingers caressing the ivory keys. "When I think of how I detested all those dreary scales and tiresome arpeggios, it's no wonder I drove many a music tutor mad."

Anabelle's laugh sounded as fittingly musical as her ability. "And I, on the other hand, could not get enough of playing. My mother often threatened to put a leash around my neck so she could drag me away from the piano for meals."

At this, Eliza sputtered into a giggle, and Anabelle nearly doubled over with mirth.

"Now that's what's been missing from this old house," Aunt Phoebe murmured, coming into the room. "The sound of music and youth and laughter."

"I've just been trying to absorb a measure of Anabelle's gift," Eliza said, gathering her composure again. "It reminds me how foolish it is to waste one's opportunities in life."

"So what is it you desire?" her new friend asked. "A second chance?"

"Are you offering to teach me?" Eliza, only half jesting, sobered. "Because, if you're serious, I think I truly would like to study the piano again. I'm older now. The

306

thought of scales and practice aren't nearly so unbearable as they seemed in my girlhood."

"Agreed." Anabelle crossed her arms and gave a decisive nod. "We'll do it on Fridays, then. That is, assuming my coming here won't upset your schedule, Mrs. Harper." She swept a glance up to the older woman, who at this point appeared to be in shock.

With a shake of her snowy head, she recovered nicely. "No, no. Whatever you two decide is fine with me. I'll still have Eliza to help me the rest of the time."

But when Eliza searched her aunt's lined face, she saw something she hadn't been aware of before . . . a deep love for her. Concern for her welfare. She couldn't resist the urge to hug the kind woman.

As she did, the future which had seemed to hold nothing but bleakness and despair such a short time ago shone with brighter facets. She may not have become the new bride she had expected to be — and possibly never would — but the Lord held her life in His hands. And for the most fleeting of seconds, Eliza could almost glimpse a measure of beauty taking shape in the pattern He'd chosen.

CHAPTER 5

The smartly fitted black-and-red barouche rolled smoothly behind matched chestnut geldings. Despite Eliza's best intentions to put her unhappiness behind her, the grayness of the afternoon sky cast a pallor over her spirit as she rode with her new friend to the quilting circle meeting.

"You'll just love the dear ladies who come every week to sew," Anabelle gushed. "Especially the Madison sisters, Francine and Frederica. Sadly enough, they nursed their sickly parents for so many years, life has passed them by. But a kinder, more selfless pair of spinsters you'll never find, to say nothing of their blithesome natures. They inspire the rest of us to accept whatever befalls."

Eliza stifled a grim smile, wondering if one day someone would make a similar comment about her. *Poor Eliza Criswell. For an old maid, she remains amazingly cheerful. I hear she came near to marrying at one time, but her beau ran off with her best friend. Tsk, tsk.*

"It's to be commended, don't you think?"

Realizing Anabelle was awaiting her response, Eliza felt a flush crest her face. "Forgive me; I was thinking about something else and missed what you said."

"No matter," Anabelle said, her fair complexion a stark contrast against the coat's deep blue hood. "I get rather carried away at times with my chattering. It's one of my worst faults. I didn't mean to bore you."

"Oh, you weren't boring me. Not at all. Please, do continue with what you were saying."

As if to make sure the plea was sincere, Anabelle scrutinized her for a few seconds, then picked up the thread of conversation. "I was merely stating that Faith Community Church provides many kinds of aid to the immigrants, and thanks to the efforts of the Madison sisters, many other city churches have now undertaken similar programs."

"Yes, that is splendid. From what I've heard, the need is great."

"Quite true. I confess, however, that I fail to share Micah's obsession for the unfortunates. How he can set foot in those horrid, smelly places, I'll never know. But after all, some of us labor best from behind the lines."

"I heartily agree."

At this, a broad smile lit Anabelle's blithe countenance. "I knew it. From the moment we met, I've had a most profound conviction that we're kindred spirits."

"So did I!" Eliza returned the smile. "I'm glad we've become friends."

The carriage slowed upon nearing the neat, steepled church, then drew to a stop.

Anabelle pushed aside the fur lap robe covering their legs as the lanky, black-coated driver hopped down from his seat.

"I'll call back for you at half-past three, miss," he said pleasantly, lifting his prominent chin when he helped Anabelle and Eliza alight from the conveyance.

"Thank you, Graham; that will be fine. Come, Eliza." Gathering her skirt in one hand on her way up the church steps, Anabelle waited at the top landing for Eliza, and together they entered the building. "We use the basement for our work, since it's near the furnace and therefore the quickest to heat."

Once inside, they hung up their outer wraps and immediately took the stairwell off to the right. Quiet voices from below floated up to meet them, growing louder on their descent.

When they emerged into the open, Eliza saw that long worktables had been pushed end-to-end, dominating the center of the large room, their flat surfaces sporting piles of assorted materials and works in progress. A dozen or more seamstresses lined both sides.

"Good day, ladies," Anabelle sing-songed.

The workers turned their heads, light glinting off an array of eyeglasses perched on the various noses.

Eliza manufactured a brave smile.

"I've brought a newcomer to join us," Anabelle went on. "I'm sure many of you met Eliza Criswell this past Sunday at service. She lives at Harper House now and will be helping with our projects."

"Splendid," a frail waif of an elderly woman said, her voice crackling. "The more the merrier."

"Yes, we're thrilled to have additional hands," a second, plumper matron added.

Recognizing a number of faces as Anabelle rattled off everyone's names, Eliza released a small breath of relief. She wasn't going to feel so much like a stranger here after all.

"And you must get to know this charming duo." Anabelle moved to drape her arms about the shoulders of two bony but handsome ladies of advanced years. "These are the Madison sisters, Miss Francine and Miss Frederica, our mainstays here at Faith Community."

"So good to make your acquaintance," the more outspoken of the two said, while her sister gave a beaming nod. "You girls make yourself right at home." She waved a spindly, blue-veined hand in the direction of an available spot where they could sit together.

Anabelle perused the multicolored quilt draping the work space between the sisters. "Oh, I see you've nearly finished that one. Eliza and I will begin piecing a new top." She helped herself to the scissors, needles, and thread they would need, then rooted through the available scraps, which she placed in close proximity for working.

The afternoon went swiftly for Eliza, listening to the chatter and gentle teasing passing back and forth among the workers, but she couldn't help wondering how Aunt Phoebe was making out on her own.

Idly surveying the work going on around her, she noticed a lovely finished coverlet similar to one her mother had pieced years ago for a hope chest better forgotten. Before the memory could inflict pain, she centered on the need to write home and let her parents know that being here in New York agreed with her.

As the session wound down to a close and two ladies folded a newly finished quilt, the heavy clomp of masculine footsteps sounded from the stairs. Micah Richmond entered, his face red from the outside chill. "Greetings, ladies. Thought I'd come by for the latest offerings." He rubbed his gloved hands together as if to generate some warmth.

"We've done three more this afternoon," one of the Madisons informed him. "Now that we've got a new helper —" She smiled at Eliza graciously. "We should be a little more productive each month."

"Wonderful." He grinned at the older woman before turning his deep-set hazel eyes upon Eliza. "I assure you, we can use as many of these as your nimble fingers can provide."

Eliza watched Anabelle move to his side, the young woman's gaze and her smile dreamy as they rested on his manly features. When Micah drew her within the crook of his arm, the sight sent a sad remembrance through Eliza. She lowered her lashes and busied herself helping the others set the work area to rights once more.

Micah would have had to be blind not to notice the bright spots of color both Anabelle and Eliza provided amid this gathering of somberly attired matrons and widows. Not only had the pair dressed in rich jewel hues, but they were the only two whose hair was neither white nor some shade of gray. Even their faces bore a youthful radiance, with Miss Criswell's taking on a deeper rose whenever he looked her way. Curious, how she never quite met his eyes, but perhaps she was shy.

"Well, now," he said casually, tightening his arm about Anabelle's slender form, "I know some folks who will truly appreciate your tireless labors. I thank you from the bottom of my heart. We'll waste no time in delivering them where they're most needed."

"Will I see you this evening?" Anabelle asked as he released her and moved away to pick up the neat stack of quilts waiting at the end of one table.

"Most likely."

"Marvelous. We'll expect you for supper then."

"Fine. I'll be there." Leaning to plant a quick peck on her cheek, he gave her chin a loving tweak with his free hand, then waved good-bye to the others. "Thanks again, ladies. God bless you all."

Mounting the stairs two at a time, he hurried to his waiting buggy. He'd head directly to Child Placement to collect his assistant, Mrs. Wallace, and the two of them would take the coverlets to some needy tenement families. And after that, he'd go to Ana's.

Thoughts of his intended rambled through his busy mind, and he smiled. She seemed much happier since Eliza Criswell's arrival in town. The pair seemed to get along royally, which was gratifying, considering he'd suggested Anabelle befriend Mrs. Harper's niece mainly for the newcomer's benefit. But whatever the outcome of this blossoming friendship, he appreciated seeing those green eyes of Anabelle's sparkling again.

He only wished he had generated some of that dazzle himself.

When Eliza got home, she found her aunt in her favorite rocking chair, working on a needlepoint case for spectacles.

The older woman looked up. "Did you enjoy your outing, my dear?"

"Oh yes. It's rather amazing to see how much a group of women can accomplish in a single afternoon. And it's a joy to be with Anabelle." She drew a hesitant breath. "Her beau stopped by when we were finishing up."

"Is that so?" Aunt Phoebe nudged her

special sewing glasses a notch higher but continued to peer over them at her.

"Yes, to pick up the finished quilts." Even as she elaborated on Micah Richmond's visit, Eliza wondered why she'd bothered to mention it. Nevertheless, she could not restrain her tongue. "It seems he delivers them almost the moment the last thread has been tied."

"That does not surprise me. I've yet to meet a more industrious lad. His parents would have been proud of his generous spirit. Of course, to be truthful, he is much like they were themselves. It was a great loss to our church when his dear mother passed away suddenly, to be followed soon after by his father. Of course, Micah's family and Anabelle's were very close friends, and the Dumonts treat him like their own son. He will be, soon enough, I expect."

Eliza nodded thoughtfully, reflecting on the striking couple Anabelle and Micah made.

The older woman studied her for a moment. "It does my heart good to see you perking up, dear. I don't mind telling you, I was quite concerned over you when you first arrived from Harrisburg."

"I suppose I'm destined to live after all," Eliza admitted candidly, then paused with a sad smile. "But still, there are certain things I can't allow myself to dwell on just yet."

Her aunt nodded. "I never met that young man of yours, so I realize I'm making a rash judgment when I speak ill of him. But I've known you all your life, Eliza, and it boggles this old mind that anyone could treat you shamefully."

With suppressed tears so very near the surface these days, Eliza fought hard to keep them at bay.

"But never you mind about him, my dear. It has always been my experience that the Lord never takes something away from us without replacing it with something better. And I'm sure He has someone wonderful and more deserving of you in store. Wait and see." She picked up her needlepoint and resumed working.

Watching her, Eliza pondered those last statements. She sincerely doubted she wanted to be that vulnerable again — ever. Just now that was about the last thing on her list of desires. But considering her aunt's optimistic statement, Eliza felt the need to clarify it. "Auntie, when the Lord took Uncle Amos all those years ago, did He send you someone . . . better?"

The old hands stilled once more, and the watery blue eyes turned to her. "Yes and no. Of course, I could never imagine loving another man the way I did my Captain. It was like losing a part of myself when his ship went down. Took me ages to stop looking out the window, expecting to see him coming up the walk with those long sweeping strides of his, hearing that jaunty whistle that so cheered my days."

A wistful expression gentled the creases in the aged countenance. "But gradually I became aware of the soothing presence of the Comforter whom God tells us about in His Word. The Holy Spirit became very real to me, in a way I'd never experienced before. And He is a great blessing and has been through the years. That is what has sustained me since Cap's been gone."

Eliza felt the gathering tears trembling on her lashes. Her heart ached for Aunt Phoebe's loss and for her own. Perhaps the day would come when she could think of Weston and Melanie without wanting to scream or cry. But at the moment she felt compelled to go and hug her aunt, perhaps absorb some of that peaceful spirit that somehow radiated from her very being.

Tonight, she would ask God to make His presence more real in her own empty life. Anything to fill the aching void that gaped within her heart.

CHAPTER 6

Thanksgiving, a quiet affair for two, provided a time of challenge, with Eliza and her aunt Phoebe trying to outdo one another in relating their blessings. Though it started out in all seriousness over dried apple pie after a small but delectable feast, it soon became apparent that neither wanted to relinquish the opportunity to have the last word.

"Well, I am thankful to still be living here at Harper House," the older woman said, "where so many of life's precious memories still bring me joy."

Eliza tipped her head respectfully. "And I am glad you're still here, making precious memories with me."

"How sweet. And now that you mention it, I am thankful to have company at last. To hear someone else's footsteps and laughter besides my own."

"Then, both of us are grateful to Weston

for furnishing me with a reason to come!" Even though Eliza had spoken without thinking, the fact that she truly meant it made her sputter into a giggle. Her aunt joined in, and they laughed until tears ran down their faces.

For a brief moment, Eliza feared she would not be able to stop crying, and the astute older woman's expression gentled.

"It hurt very deeply, I would expect."

Eliza blotted the corners of her eyes on her napkin and nodded. "Perhaps it might have been easier to bear if —" She could hardly utter the words. "Why did he have to choose my very dearest friend?" Tears again blurred her vision, and she rushed to say the rest before her throat closed up. "I could have turned to Melanie for solace, but instead, I've had to learn to live without her, too."

"I know, child." Aunt Phoebe inhaled slowly, deeply. Her loving fingers stroked Eliza's arm, letting her cry as long as she needed to. "Sometimes I wonder how we manage to endure some of the losses we are asked to suffer. And all I can say is that our heavenly Father's heart breaks right along with ours, and then He gives the strength we need."

When Eliza's inner turmoil subsided, she

gathered herself together. She searched the kind, frail face across the table, and her heart swelled with love. "You know, Auntie, not too long ago, I wondered if I would ever be happy again. But somehow, since coming to be with you, I've actually started 'forgetting the past,' as the apostle Paul put it. Not that I have come up with any grandiose plans for my future, mind you. I don't care to look that far ahead. But at least I can trust God for today without fearing what tomorrow may bring. Does that sound strange?"

"Not at all, my dear, not at all." Closing her crooked fingers over Eliza's, she smiled. "I would say it's an answer to prayer." Her blue eyes sparkled again. "For which I am deeply grateful."

"Oh no!" Eliza laughed in feigned shock. "Now you've made it my turn again. . . ."

November ended and December took its place, bringing shorter, changeable days which featured brilliant sunshine or banks of endless gray clouds. Holly boughs and evergreen wreaths tied with crimson ribbons lent a festive air to lampposts and front doors all over the city.

In view of the coming holidays, Aunt Phoebe set out an abundance of red candles and velvet-bowed decorations. And the bell above the gift shop door rang with more frequency, necessitating long evenings of labor to replace merchandise which had been sold.

Eliza took pride in the quality of work she now turned out, both at home and in the quilting circle at church. But most of all, she treasured her times of solitude in her room when she sought the company of the loving Comforter whose soothing presence her aunt so appreciated. Morning and evening Bible reading and prayer became less a duty and more a joyous communion with a dearest Friend. And in the light of the indescribable peace that now filled Eliza, past disappointments faded into insignificance as she began to pray that her life would have meaning and purpose.

On Thursday, Anabelle stayed home in bed with a cold but sent her driver as usual to transport Eliza to church. While she was glad to go, Eliza found the activity rather lonely without the willowy young woman's company and good-natured chatter. Nevertheless, the afternoon did pass swiftly, with four more coverlets completed.

It was Eliza's turn to tidy up at the close of the sewing session, so after the other ladies put away the supplies and took their leave, Eliza swept the loose threads from the floor. The silence of the almost-empty building magnified the peculiar creaks and groans caused by the wind, sounds that had been scarcely noticeable earlier amid the banter and conversation. Now they echoed hollowly from wall to wall. Eager to be finished with the chore, she hurriedly dumped the dustpan into a waste bin in the storage closet.

A door opened upstairs. Eliza assumed Anabelle's driver had come for her.

But the heavy footsteps that clambered down to the basement brought Micah Richmond instead, his shoulders sporting a dusting of snowflakes. "Where is everyone?" he asked jovially.

Eliza smiled, his sudden appearances no longer catching her off guard. "You just missed them. They went home not five minutes ago."

"And left you with the drudgery, I see," he teased.

"We take turns, actually."

"Ah." He scanned the room. "Ana's not here?"

"Sorry, no. She's under the weather this afternoon."

"Oh yes. She complained of a chill last evening, as I recall. I'll run by later and look in on her."

Eliza nodded and gathered her belongings together.

"I assume these are today's completed quilts?" He tipped his head toward the end of the table.

"Yes. Four this time."

"Wonderful." Micah picked them up and took a few steps toward the doorway, then turned. "Uh, Miss Criswell? I don't suppose —"

"What is it?"

"Must you go home directly?"

Her eyes widened. "Well, naturally Aunt Phoebe expects me soon after the close of the quilting circle. I did tell her and Anabelle's driver that I would be detained a few minutes after the session. But Graham might be waiting for me." Noticing Micah's troubled expression, she paused. "Why do you ask?"

"It's nothing. Never mind." Filling his lungs, he started away, but halted again. "On second thought, I might as well come out with it. I'm in dire need of a favor."

"I beg your pardon?"

A sheepish grin appeared on his lips. "I was hoping to deliver these right away, but my assistant was called out of town to her daughter's home on an emergency. I was wondering if you could possibly accompany me."

Eliza merely stared, unsure how to respond.

"Many women at the tenements have been widowed or deserted by their husbands," he explained, "and they're more at ease if I bring a female companion along. I promise not to keep you a moment longer than absolutely necessary."

"I — I don't know what to say."

He released a disappointed breath. "I understand. It was just a thought. Sorry to impose on you."

His deflated expression tugged at her heart and made her change her mind. She'd probably regret doing so later, but after all, he wasn't asking that much of her. "Wait!"

He halted on the steps and looked back.

"If you're sure it would help, I suppose it couldn't hurt for me to go along this once."

Micah's strong, manly features took on a boyish quality with his grin. "Splendid. I'll not keep you long, I assure you."

But even as Eliza followed him up the stairwell, she wondered if her decision had been a rash one. Hadn't Anabelle told her he often went to disreputable areas of town?

Outside, the Dumonts' coach indeed stood waiting. Micah went to thank the driver for his trouble and sent him on his way. Then he assisted Eliza into his much plainer buggy, climbed aboard himself, and took the reins. "I truly appreciate your willingness to help me out, Miss Criswell."

He clucked the horse forward, guiding it out among the assortment of other conveyances on the busy street. "Would you think me terribly forward if I were to call you Eliza? Since you're such a good friend of Ana's, and she speaks of you so often, I thought perhaps you'd consider me a friend as well."

The brief recollection of the last man who called her by her first name brought a pang, but Eliza ignored it. "As you wish." Her breath crystallizing in the cold air, she tucked her hands into the fur muff which complemented her winter coat. Soft feathery snowflakes swirled around them.

"Then you must call me Micah. It will save time, not to mention be less cumbersome."

She gave a perfunctory nod and averted her attention to the passing residences on either side of the unfamiliar Manhattan thoroughfare as the horse's hooves clopped in regular cadence over the pavement. Stately and well-tended, the grand homes had lovely grounds whose summer glory could only be imagined. But even beneath winter's cold spell their subdued beauty was a sight to behold as the profusion of old trees reached lacy crowns toward the heavens.

Micah didn't seem very talkative, and Eliza sensed he had a lot on his mind. Without the need for polite conversation, she concentrated on the sights that were completely new to her as the buggy turned onto Broadway. There her gaze drank in the limitless variety of stores and tall buildings whose tops scraped the sky. Signs of the approaching holiday season abounded in colorful window displays of the latest in fashion and children's toys.

When they passed city hall and neared the East River, however, the scenery took a turn for the worse. The streets became narrower and more crooked. Dwellings looked gloomy and wretched and crowded together. And despite the salt-laden breeze coming from the vast Atlantic, whose briny waters mingled with that of many of the large rivers along the eastern coastline, a foul stench from the refuse-filled gutters pervaded the air.

Eliza surveyed the conglomeration of grim, multistory dwellings in Manhattan's lower East Side. In various stages of disrepair, all of them fairly teemed with inhabitants. She was appalled at the cheerless appearance of the tenements, to say nothing of the hordes of hopeless-looking people and ragged children seemingly everywhere. Dismal, frozen clothing and diapers flapped from clotheslines strung high above the narrow road from windows opposite each other, and Eliza couldn't begin to discern the number of foreign languages being bandied about.

"I can't believe people live like this." Having actually uttered that thought aloud, she cringed with embarrassment.

"You haven't seen anything yet." Drawing the horse to a halt midway down one of the cobbled lanes, Micah got out and helped her down, then reached for the quilts. "Just stay close to me."

He needn't have said it. Nothing would have made Eliza venture anywhere by herself.

As bad as the exteriors of the tenements looked, the interiors proved even worse. In her wildest imaginings she wouldn't have dreamed such filth existed, or that people could actually spend their days in such horrid conditions. Clutching her skirt to keep the hem out of the grime, she doggedly followed Micah into the common hall of one of the buildings, their footsteps echoing off the cracked plaster walls and bare floors. A rickety staircase, out of reach of the faint light struggling to penetrate the single window at the other end of long corridor, ascended into utter darkness.

"Mr. Micah! Mr. Micah!" The gleeful, boyish voice carried the entire length of the dreary hall. The patter of little feet followed immediately as a curly-headed boy sprang up from where he'd been sitting in an open doorway and flew to throw his arms around Micah's legs. His shirt gaped where a button was missing, and his trousers were too short, but his exuberant greeting lacked nothing at all.

"Hi there, Vinnie." Micah knelt to return the hug, the bulky quilts clutched in the crook of one arm. "What's up, buddy?"

By now, other little ones peeked out into the hall from the same room as well as other rooms lining the hallway. They all came running.

Eliza stood back in amazement, watching her companion tousle hair, hug shoulders, and pat heads in turn. The sight warmed her heart, and she returned each timid glance with a smile she hoped appeared friendly.

"Guess'a what, Mr. Micah?" a scraggly-haired girl of about five said in a conspiratorial tone. She toyed with the torn pocket of her faded dress. "Rosa and Gabriella's mama, she gone'a to da angels. Dey both'a stay'a wit us."

His cheery expression turned somber. "I thought she was getting better." Then he gave a nod of resignation. "Well, I'm on my way to see your mother right now. Come on, Gina. Think you can show my friend, Miss Eliza, the way?"

The little one gave Eliza a dubious glance, but with a sigh, took her hand. "Dis'a way."

Trying not to reveal her dismay at the grubby little fingers and dirt-smudged face, Eliza allowed herself to be led along.

Two doors farther down, Micah rapped on the jamb. "Mrs. Garibaldi?"

The youngsters clustered around him, their huge brown eyes adoring as they stroked the fine material of his winter coat.

"Eh? Who'sa dere?" came a voice from inside. Seconds later, wiping her hands on the soiled apron covering her threadbare cotton dress, a large-boned, frazzled woman of indeterminate age appeared. "Oh. Mr. Richmond. Come in'a, come in." She eyed the bounty he carried, then glared pointedly at the children. "Hey bambinos. Whatsa matta you bother da nice'a man, eh? Go.

330

Play." Waving them away, she leaned out the door to watch them go down the hall.

Micah peeled off the top quilt. "This is for you. You said last time that you could use another one."

"*Graci*. Vittorio and'a me, we appreciate dis."

While Micah talked to the lady of the house, Eliza couldn't help looking around the bleak, narrow room in the feeble glow from a kerosene lamp. She could smell the stew simmering in a pot on the stove at the far end. Worn, sparse furnishings in no particular arrangement filled most of the wall space. Her heart went out to the young, curly-haired baby sitting on a blanket remnant on the otherwise bare floor, sucking on a worn baby shoe. Surprisingly, though cramped and cheerless, the place seemed somewhat tidy, even quite clean.

"Gina told me Mrs. Riccio passed on. Is that true?" Micah asked.

"*Si*. Yesterday, noon. Dey already take'a da remains. Vittorio say to me, 'Sophia,' he say, 'Giuseppe and Anna Marie our friends'a since Naples, eh? We should keep'a Rosa and Gabriella for our friends.' So, bambinos, dey stay wit us, like'a before. Where else dey go?"

Micah gave a noncommittal shrug. "Won't

331

they be a bother with your own children to look after, your sewing, and all?"

"What else friends'a do, eh? Dey live here when'a we all come to America. Dey play wit our Maria an' Gina, you know?"

"Well, if they get to be a burden, tell me. I might be able to find a place for them."

She nodded, albeit reluctantly.

"Where are the girls now?" Micah asked.

"Asleep. Dey cry an' cry. Dey finally sleep."

"Mind if we look in on them?"

Just then the baby toppled over and let out a wail.

"Go look. Dey all right." She pointed toward the next room, then stooped to pick up her own little one.

Following behind Micah, Eliza almost bumped into him when he stopped abruptly. She peered around his shoulder into the dim interior of what was hardly more than a closet, where sleeping pallets were crammed so closely together that not a spare inch of floor remained. Ragged, threadbare blankets were strewn every which way among the lot. A lump rose in her throat.

On one mattress, two slumbering girls, about six and three years of age, clung to one another in sleep, their thin bodies still racked by occasional sobs.

Micah turned to Eliza, his expression taut with concern. And without another word, he took another quilt from the three remaining and spread it over the motherless sisters.

"I've never witnessed such despair," Eliza murmured a short time later on the homeward journey, her thoughts still on the impoverished recipients of the quilts. The rest of the coverlets had been distributed to other needy families.

"You might be surprised to hear that many of these folks are well-educated and had highly respectable jobs in their homelands," Micah answered evenly, his light brown eyes warm in the fading light. "But they left everything they had just to come to America. Home, family, friends, their livelihoods, all in hope of providing their children with a better life in a new country. Granted, a few are in such poor health the voyage itself claims them before they ever reach our shores. And with the lack of nourishing food, the rest are susceptible to any sickness that comes along."

"But the children! They haven't proper clothes. Some of them look as if they haven't seen a bathtub in months, if ever. And I even saw a rat scurrying along the hallway of that building. How can people continue to live in such squalor?"

"They've nowhere else to go. Most don't even speak the language when they first arrive. They're dependent upon go-betweens, often ministers or social agents, who set them up in language classes and find jobs for them — usually work no one else will do. The immigrants labor hard and long, and in time some of them actually do save enough money to start businesses of their own. But sad to say, those are often the minority."

"And those little girls whose parents passed away. What will become of them?"

"That's a common occurrence here in the tenements. That pair is lucky, since family friends will assume the responsibility of caring for them. So many in similar situations are left to fend for themselves. Child Placement shelters quite a number of orphans until we can find new families willing to adopt them. And, of course, there are other asylums in the city with similar facilities."

"But it's . . . it's just overwhelming."

"My sentiments exactly. And more shiploads arrive every day."

By the time the buggy pulled up outside Harper House, Eliza felt completely spent, emotionally as well as physically. It was all she could do to make her way up the front walk.

Micah took hold of her elbow and assisted her. "Well, thanks again. I appreciate your willingness to help me today. I could have gone alone, but as I mentioned before —"

"I understand. Truly. The experience was rather enlightening, to say the least. I shall never complain again."

His lips spread into a smile.

Eliza glimpsed then, for a brief moment, Micah Richmond's soul, the depth of his caring and the concern that motivated him to work beyond the normal hours of his employment. And she fully understood his calling. She wanted to say something to commend him for his efforts, something profound, but nothing worthy enough came to her weary mind.

The door opened then, and Aunt Phoebe leaned out into the snowy air, some of the flakes landing on the crocheted shawl worn about her shoulders. Worry creased her face. "There you are, at last, Eliza! I was wondering what had detained you."

"The fault is all mine, dear lady," Micah explained. "I imposed on your niece's good nature to help me out this afternoon. Which she did most graciously, I must say."

"I'm just glad you delivered her safely

home. Would you like a cup of hot tea before you go?"

"No, but thank you kindly. I'm expected at Anabelle's." He switched his gaze to Eliza as she was about to enter. "Again, I can't thank you enough for filling in for Mrs. Wallace. I'll endeavor not to take advantage of you again."

She merely smiled. "Good evening. Give Ana my love when you see her, and tell her that her presence was sorely missed at the sewing circle."

"I'll do that. Good evening to you both." Touching the brim of his bowler, he gave a polite tip of his sandy head and returned through the falling snow to his buggy.

Eliza stepped into Harper House, its golden lamplight casting intricate shadows among the finery, and closed the door. Hanging up her warm wrap, she turned, her gaze drinking in the array of splendor before her. And she closed her eyes in reproach. *All of this, for two people.*

There had to be more she and Aunt Phoebe could do to help.

CHAPTER 7

After a short visit with Anabelle and her parents, Micah returned to his rented room on Columbus Avenue . . . the sum total of his living quarters the past few years. Reluctant to spend the time or money it would require to keep up his late parents' sprawling house, he had leased it out to a young couple with a growing family and moved his personal things into a one-room apartment in a row of brick townhomes. Simple and cheerless, it at least freed him from having to get caught up in repairs and other mundane chores involved with owning property.

Now, alone with the ticking of the mantel clock and the slowly dying embers of the fire he'd lit earlier, Micah rose from his knees and extinguished the bedside lamp before climbing between the cool sheets on his bed. The light snow which had begun earlier that afternoon now fell in earnest outside, muffling the normal night sounds in almost eerie stillness. And because he wasn't especially tired, it seemed a good time for reflection. Retrospection.

He couldn't help but think back on his day, on the heart-rending thankfulness expressed by the recipients of the latest quilts. Having just prayed for those folks and so many others with whom he'd dealt over the past several months, he imagined them warm and toasty beneath the thick coverlets provided by the nimble-fingered ladies of Faith Community Church.

He also thought of newly orphaned Rosa and Gabriella Riccio, who'd found refuge with family friends, the Garibaldis. But with the kind couple already stretched to the limit with an abundance of offspring of their own, Micah could only hope and pray that the sad little girls would adjust to life without their parents and not be too much of a drain on the Garibaldis.

And he could not entirely dismiss from his consciousness the memory of Eliza Criswell's presence this afternoon. He knew the young woman's gentle upbringing had sheltered her from the sort of reality found in Manhattan's lower East Side and most likely she'd been shocked over the whole grievous situation. But thinking back,

Eventually
d fervor
heart,
nding
share
else
was
o

d also been obvious. .ened or repulsed .ad she'd seemed .Most especially, her .the little Riccio sisters. .e ride homeward, he'd .shimmer of tears in those .yes of hers, though she'd pre- .smattering of snowflakes had stung .ce on a gust of wind. Micah sensed .t the immigrants now had another concerned ally on their side, and a very beautiful one, at that.

With chagrin, he willed his thoughts to Anabelle, suffering through a cold, her pert nose pink and puffy, her eyes watery, sipping endless cups of tea laced with glycerine and honey to soothe her sore throat. Micah had grown up knowing her. She'd been a part of his life for as far back as he could remember. They shared a multitude of each other's secret dreams and fears and felt completely at ease with each other.

If only she understood his calling.

He had invited — all but begged — her to come with him upon occasion when he'd needed to drive to the tenements. But her constant refusals stopped just short of being adamant. Not only did Ana not wish to go there, she was just as determined about him

something else had also been obvious. She hadn't appeared sickened or repulsed by what she'd seen. Instead she'd seemed touched. Humbled. Most especially, her heart had gone out to the little Riccio sisters.

Once during the ride homeward, he'd even caught the shimmer of tears in those wide blue eyes of hers, though she'd pretended a smattering of snowflakes had stung her face on a gust of wind. Micah sensed that the immigrants now had another concerned ally on their side, and a very beautiful one, at that.

With chagrin, he willed his thoughts to Anabelle, suffering through a cold, her pert nose pink and puffy, her eyes watery, sipping endless cups of tea laced with glycerine and honey to soothe her sore throat. Micah had grown up knowing her. She'd been a part of his life for as far back as he could remember. They shared a multitude of each other's secret dreams and fears and felt completely at ease with each other.

If only she understood his calling.

He had invited — all but begged — her to come with him upon occasion when he'd needed to drive to the tenements. But her constant refusals stopped just short of being adamant. Not only did Ana not wish to go there, she was just as determined about him finding some new line of work. Eventually he'd given up asking.

Every night he prayed with renewed fervor that she would have a change of heart, become burdened for the sad, never-ending stream of America's newcomers and share in his ministrations to them. How else would their marriage last? Until he was convinced that his life's work would not cause strife between them, he was in no hurry to take that step.

Realizing that his eyelids had grown heavy, Micah slowly filled his lungs and rolled over, nuzzling into the warmth of his own blankets as remembrances of this day's most pleasant companion crept into his thoughts. Again.

"My goodness, but you're quiet this morning." Aunt Phoebe's voice came from across the breakfast table.

Eliza became aware that she had yet to take a sip of coffee from the cup she'd been holding for who knew how long. "Sorry, Auntie. I suppose my thoughts were occupied elsewhere." Sampling the now-lukewarm liquid, she set it down and took up a square of toast, spreading on a thin coating of marmalade.

"Elsewhere. I see." The older woman's

discerning blue gaze didn't miss much. "Considering you've been like this ever since you returned late yesterday afternoon, it must have something to do with that 'errand of mercy' Micah took you on."

Eliza tried to smile but failed miserably as her eyes filled with tears. "You have no idea how those poor people live, Aunt Phoebe. If you could just see the shabby hovels they are forced to call their homes, smell the filth, listen to the hopeless crying of children. It's far more than I can bear. Especially —" About to blurt out a bold remark about their own overabundance of blessings, she bit her lips and averted her gaze to her toast once again.

"Oh, but I have seen some of what you experienced, child," her aunt said softly. "Up until it became difficult for me to get around the way I could in my younger years, I was far more active in acts of benevolence. Personally, I might add."

The news surprised Eliza and also filled her with remorse. "I'm sorry. I had no idea. But don't you find yourself wishing you could do more? I mean, here we are, living in this grand old home, just the two of us, when not so very far away there are needy folks who exist with practically nothing. And more of them, it seems, arriving every week."

"Yes, it is a shocking reality. Which is why, even I, an old woman, endeavor to keep contributing all the funds this shop brings in. Little as it is, it's the best the Lord has enabled me to provide at this time in my life." Her aged face gentled with a wistful smile. "Truth is, I'd love to wrap up in a warm shawl and pull the rocker up close to the hearth for the simple joy of basking in ease. But as soon as I did that, we'd run out of stationery or hankies or scarves or some other item that brings in money I wouldn't have otherwise. Do you know what I'm saying?"

Eliza nodded. She had misjudged this kind relative and could only hope she hadn't hurt her as well. Coupled with the distress she'd felt ever since yesterday, it made it even harder to contain her unshed tears. "Please, forgive me for speaking out of turn. This is just so completely new to me that I'm having trouble dealing with all the emotions I'm feeling inside."

"I know, dear. How it must grieve the very heart of God to witness the often needless suffering of those unfortunates. I believe that must be why He lays the burden on the occasional younger, stalwart heart, like

Micah Richmond. Through that sensitive man and others of similar character He is able to accomplish much more than we can ever realize to alleviate some of the woes of the poor."

Eliza chewed the last bite of toast in thought. Yes, Micah had a personal hand in what she now viewed as an incredible ministry. Never had she met such an unselfish, giving young man. Anabelle was truly fortunate to know she would one day wed such a champion of the downtrodden.

Champion. For all his advantaged upbringing, he had no qualms about picking up and hugging a dirty, ragged child. On the contrary, little ones ran to him with their arms outstretched, their eyes shining with adoration. It made quite a picture . . . one Eliza did not expect would ever completely fade from her most priceless memories.

Then, conscious that harboring such notions about her best friend's fiancé was bordering on betrayal, Eliza purposely pushed all thought of Micah Richmond from her consciousness.

As she had a thousand times since yesterday.

"Splendid!" Anabelle turned away slightly to dispose of her sniffles in her handkerchief before replacing it in the pocket of her indigo skirt. "You've been practicing."

"Yes, an hour a day actually." Eliza rested her fingertips lightly on the ivory keys. "I've been committing to memory those pieces you loaned me on Sunday."

"And it shows. Well my friend, all I can say is that if you continue to keep at it, I'll not be of much use as your teacher. After all, this skill is acquired through diligence and single-mindedness."

"I know. Practice, practice, practice," Eliza said wryly. "Seems I've heard that before. But somehow, I don't seem to mind it now as I did when I was young and flighty. I've even enjoyed the scales, tiresome as I once thought them to be." She began at the beginning again, playing smoothly through the piece. The lilting melody resonated back from the papered walls of the sitting room.

Out of the corner of her eye, she saw Anabelle tuck her chin. "Were you very flighty? I find that hard to imagine. You've appeared so serious since you came here to live."

Thinking back on her arrival, not to mention the reasons for her hasty departure from Harrisburg, Eliza could only agree. "Well, I hope I haven't put you off with my dreary moods."

"Not at all. I haven't found you to be

moody in the least. That word is better used to describe Micah these days."

Eliza's fingers fumbled on a chord, and she stopped and turned to Anabelle. "He hasn't struck me that way at all."

Recognition dawned on Anabelle's fragile features, and her brows arched higher. "Oh yes. He told me he implored you to accompany him on his errand of mercy yesterday afternoon." She shuddered, and her jade eyes took on a pained look. "How you could subject yourself to go among those ragamuffins is a mystery. I could never do that. Never."

Observing her friend's dark expression, Eliza could not bite back the urge to speak out in Micah's defense. "I, too, looked upon the occasion with dread, almost regretting that I'd allowed him to persuade me. But once we reached the tenements and I actually saw the horrors those poor families suffer every day of their lives, I could not help but be moved to tears. They so need someone who cares, which Micah does most admirably. You'd have been extremely proud of him, Anabelle, the way he reaches out to them and makes them feel important."

"Indeed. Well, the fact is, he's not the only kindhearted soul who looks after their needs. He's just the one who seems to draw his very life's breath from doing so." Ana gave a huff of consternation. "I do sorely wish he'd pass that *burden* on to someone else." Shuffling determinedly through some music sheets in her tote, she drew one out. "Here, try this. It's becoming quite the rage."

" 'Sweet Songbird of Love.' " Eliza perused the title as she tried to dismiss Anabelle's criticism of her fiancé. "Do you know the lyrics? I'll play it through once, and then you can sing as I go over it again."

Ana shook her head, her golden pompadour moving slightly with the motion. "Just play it, Eliza. I'm afraid I haven't much of a voice just yet."

"Oh. Of course. You're looking so well, I forgot you're still recovering from a cold."

Aunt Phoebe breezed into the room just then, bearing a silver tray with tea and cakes. "I thought you might enjoy some refreshments."

"Why, thank you, Auntie." Eliza rose and accepted the tray, placing it on a small, drop-leaf table by the window. "Won't you have some with us?"

The older woman shifted her slight weight to her other foot. "Oh, I wouldn't want to intrude. It's pleasure enough to listen to the music drifting from here to the parlor. No sense in getting in the way of two young ladies who want to talk."

"We wouldn't mind at all," Anabelle assured her with a smile. "In fact, I'm sure we can prevail upon Eliza to play the new song I brought today."

When at last the house had been locked for the night, the fires banked and curtains drawn, Eliza snuggled deeper into her fluffy bedding. The chilly air in her room hardly seemed noticeable as the blankets absorbed her warmth and multiplied it. *Part of the heat radiating from me surely must come from my face,* she thought in vexation. She had no right to be entertaining thoughts of Anabelle's beau. Nevertheless, visions of Micah Richmond had come unbidden to her mind amazingly often today.

He had reminded her so much of her own fiancé, Weston Elliot, when her aunt first introduced them. But Eliza couldn't picture Weston showing such concern for immigrants — or for anyone else other than himself, for that matter. His strong, patrician features at times seemed carved in stone, whereas Micah's possessed the ability to reflect an abundant range of emotions, depending on the moment. Weston would definitely frown upon that sort of spontaneity. Everything had to be kept to a strict schedule and work in precise order to suit him.

What had she ever seen in that egotist in the first place?

The question had come from nowhere, and Eliza gave herself a mental shake. Such ridiculous musings would be better spent if turned into prayers. So in the comfort of her warm bed, Eliza poured out her heart to God, trusting Him to make sense of the muddled ramblings of her overburdened mind as she lifted up two recently orphaned little girls in prayer.

CHAPTER 8

Despite a concentrated effort to occupy her every moment, Eliza found her thoughts returning time and again to the plight of Manhattan's underprivileged inhabitants — particularly to Rosa and Gabriella. Their heartbreaking loss caused a wrenching memory from Eliza's own past to surface. She'd been just a little child herself when her long-awaited baby sister fell prey to a fever and passed away in her infancy. A raft of girlish plans and dreams had been laid to rest with tiny Emily. But in her grief, Eliza had had loving mother arms to comfort her and dry her tears. She prayed that these two little ones would find solace with the kind friends who had taken them in.

Returning her attention to the violets she'd been embroidering on the front of a tea cozy, Eliza cast a critical eye at several uneven stitches and released a ragged sigh.

"Something troubling you, dear?" her aunt asked.

Already clipping the threads to make them easier to remove, she grimaced. "I'm afraid my mind insists upon wandering. I'll just have to redo this section."

The slight woman set her tatting on the lamp table beside her and got up. "Why don't we take a break? We've been laboring for more than an hour already, and I was just thinking fondly of some hot tea."

Eliza lay the scissors and tea cozy down and rose also. "I'd say that's a splendid idea. In fact, I'll even go and prepare it. I'll just be a moment."

"Thank you, dear. It does feel good to stretch these old legs a little after sitting for so long in one spot." She took a few cautious steps to the nearby window and moved a curtain panel slightly to peer outside.

Heading for the kitchen, it dawned on Eliza that her aunt's movements had lacked their normal perkiness. Perhaps an extra log on the fire would help dispel some of the dampness brought by the stormy sky. She'd see to that on her return.

The kettle on the back burner of the massive stove always retained a good supply of heat, so Eliza knew the water wouldn't take long to boil. She moved it to a hotter front burner, then went to the cupboard to take down the tea things. Soon enough, she returned to the workroom bearing the refreshment tray.

Just then, the doorbell tinkled.

"I'll see to the customer, love," the older woman said. "You sit and enjoy your tea. Don't bother waiting for me."

Eliza nodded and watched after her aunt, noting the halting footsteps. The room did indeed seem chilly, so she crossed to the hearth and stoked up the fire, adding two small logs. On her way back, her gaze took in the dwindling supply of thread in the spool basket on the table between their chairs. With Aunt Phoebe occupied, it would take scarcely any time at all to run upstairs for more supplies before pouring the tea.

When Eliza opened the door of the spare room on the second floor, cold air wafted toward her from its unheated confines. She quickly found the needed thread and slipped several spools into her apron pocket. Turning, she glanced around as she strode slowly toward the door. Such a shame, a nice bedroom like this sitting virtually empty. It was larger than the one common sleeping chamber in the Garibaldi apartment. Yes, a true shame.

■ ■ ■ ■

"And so, dear friends," Pastor Norman said, focusing his attention on the congregation of worshipers, "it behooves us to remember what this passage in Matthew chapter twenty-five is telling us. 'I was an hungred, and ye gave me meat: I was thirsty, and ye gave me drink . . .'

"As I studied these verses in preparation for today's sermon, I saw something quite interesting. Something I would like to point out to you as well. Notice, the Bible says it was the *righteous* who didn't understand what Jesus was saying — the very people who are most apt to be conscious of doing service to God. The Lord had to explain the deeper meaning of His words to the people of His own flock. This is His answer: 'Verily I say unto you, Inasmuch as ye have done it unto one of the least of these my brethren, ye have done it unto me.' "

Peering up from the open Bible on his lap as the preacher droned on, Micah thought of scores of destitute folk he'd met since becoming associated with Child Placement. He had to admit that much was being done for them by a host of righteous people. Nevertheless, those efforts barely scratched the surface of what actually needed to be done. He couldn't help wondering, if every person who truly wanted to serve God did as much as humanly possible to relieve the circumstances of the immigrants, would there still be such deep need?

Even as he contemplated that question, Micah felt an even more disturbing one rise to the fore: Could he fault someone else, when he himself might not be doing as much as he possibly could? Perhaps his own efforts left much to be desired.

" 'Unto one of the least of these my brethren,' " the minister was saying, his voice cutting across Micah's musings, " 'ye have done it unto me. Come, ye blessed of my Father, inherit the kingdom prepared for you from the foundation of the world.' "

The man's discerning eyes surveyed his audience. "Next time you are faced with an opportunity to do good to someone less fortunate, beloved, think back on this passage of scripture. Remember that the service you render unto others is, in reality, service to Almighty God. Can you do less than make it your very best?" He paused. "Let us bow in prayer."

The pastor's message rang a chord in Eliza's heart as Anabelle's fingers rendered a quiet postlude to the departing church members. All she could think about was that spacious, almost empty room at Harper House, whose purpose was for nothing more than cast-off furniture, cartons of unused items, and a selection of sewing supplies. Wouldn't it be of better service if occupied? Dare she even mention the notion to Aunt Phoebe?

One look at the older woman's pale countenance at the close of the service, and Eliza immediately dismissed all thought of the spare room as she moved nearer and placed an arm about the bony shoulders. "Are you not well this morning, Auntie?"

She fluttered a veiny hand. "Oh, it's probably just a chill. Once I get home and take a nice rest, I'm sure I'll feel more like myself. You'll see."

But Eliza had her doubts. Gently taking her aunt by the arm, she maneuvered the dear woman past the clusters of widowed friends who normally waylaid her to chat and led her aunt toward the entrance.

"Good day, Eliza," Micah said, coming alongside. "And to you, Mrs. Harper. Always nice to see some bright faces on such a gloomy day."

"Yes, hasn't it been dreary of late?" Aunt Phoebe remarked, her voice lacking its usual vibrancy.

Eliza watched concern register in the young man's expression as he centered his attention on her aunt, then flicked a questioning glance to her.

"I'm afraid Aunt Phoebe is feeling a bit under the weather. I'm taking her out to the buggy."

Without hesitation, he sprang to the opposite side and offered his arm. "Then I shall be honored to assist." He steered them around the departing worshipers bidding good-bye to the pastor and pushed the door open with his free hand.

"Fuss and bother," Aunt Phoebe muttered, but a sparkle in her eye belied her frown. "A simple chill is nothing to concern oneself about."

"Perhaps not," he said. "Nevertheless, we shall see that you get home as quickly as possible."

When they reached the bottom step and the driver of the buggy pulled forward to the end of the walk, Micah effortlessly picked Aunt Phoebe up and deposited her onto the leather seat, then assisted Eliza and spread the lap robe over them both. "I'll check in on you later," he said, touching the older woman's sleeve, then nodded to Eliza and the driver.

A flick of the reins set the gelding in motion.

The sincerity she'd glimpsed in Micah's hazel eyes touched Eliza deeply, and she drew much comfort in knowing he truly cared about her aged aunt. No doubt his prayers would join her own wordless pleas for the older woman's welfare.

And perhaps God, in His mercy, would grant renewed health one more time. Trying to rest upon this assurance, Eliza swallowed and relaxed against the upholstery.

Once they reached Harper House, Eliza paid the stocky driver and hopped down from the buggy.

He followed a second later. "Always glad to lend a hand to fair ladies," he said in explanation, and gently helped Aunt Phoebe to alight and guided her to the door.

"Thank you, kind sir," the older woman whispered, utterly spent.

"Yes. Thank you so much." With a grateful smile, Eliza ushered her aunt inside and to her bedroom, thankful that the older woman occupied a first-floor chamber. She dispensed with both their outer wraps as Aunt Phoebe sank onto her featherbed.

"There, that's better," Eliza crooned. "Let me cover you up, then I'll go make some nice broth and tea for you."

"Later, perhaps," came her aunt's labored whisper. "I'll sleep now." And almost as soon as her silvery hair touched the pillow, her eyelids fluttered closed.

Not quite ready to take her leave, Eliza remained where she was for several moments, listening until the uneven breaths became more regular. Then she tiptoed out, leaving the door slightly ajar.

The big house seemed unnaturally quiet at this hour, even though Aunt Phoebe's Sunday naps had been a custom since before Eliza's arrival. She felt at a loss and paced the sitting room aimlessly as she tried to relinquish control of the situation to the Lord. *Please, please, Father . . . make her well again. She has so much to do here. . . .*

True to his word, Micah Richmond stopped by a few hours later.

At the sight of him, Eliza's heart skipped a beat, but she convinced herself she'd have been just as glad to see any friendly face after being alone with her disquiet all that time.

He hung his coat on a wrought-iron hook just inside the door, followed by his scarf and bowler. "How's our patient faring?" he asked and blew into his chapped hands.

She shrugged, hugging herself. "She seems to be sleeping peacefully whenever I peek in on her. See what you think."

He nodded. "I stopped by her doctor's house on the way here. He wasn't home, but I took the liberty of leaving word for him to call first thing in the morning."

"Thank you. I —" At his kindness, the floodgates behind Eliza's eyes threatened to collapse. She'd successfully banked her anxieties in her aunt's presence, and then later when she'd been by herself. But now those defenses started to crumble, and the thought absolutely mortified her. She just couldn't fall apart now, not in front of Micah, of all people.

He seemed to sense her distress and took a step closer.

A jolt of alarm shot through Eliza. She almost expected him to put his arms around her.

But he merely gave her shoulder an empathetic squeeze. "Everything will be all right, my friend. As I prayed for your aunt on my drive here, a feeling of great peace came over me. I believe the Lord will bring her through."

Eliza blinked away telltale mistiness and managed a smile.

He stared for a few seconds, then, appearing satisfied, he strode quietly up the hallway to the older woman's room.

The scent of his hair balm lingered in his wake, as did the warmth and strength of his touch.

Eliza scolded herself. *It was only a friendly gesture, for pity's sake.*

But, oh, the comfort her soul had drawn from it.

Quickly reining in her wayward imaginings before they turned utterly ridiculous, she attributed her momentary weakness to a touch of homesickness for her demonstrative parents. She must have missed a hundred hugs since she'd left . . . some of which should have been Weston's embraces.

Weston. No doubt all of his displays of affection were lavished on Melanie now. . . .

Surprisingly, that thought didn't carry the usual sting. *That saying about time and its healing powers must be true.*

An almost imperceptible squeak from the other end of the hall brought Eliza back to the present. But before she could compose herself, her breath caught as Micah came into view. *Oh Anabelle, I sorely wish you had come, too.* "H–how is she?"

"Resting quietly, as you said. Her color appears to be improving also."

Eliza touched a hand to her throat in relief. "Truly?"

Micah nodded. "She awakened for a few

moments, so I offered a short prayer, and that seemed to comfort her. She drifted off to sleep again."

"Well, thank you. For coming, I mean. I know my aunt thinks the world of you."

"And I of her." His expression turned unreadable. "You share some of your aunt's finer qualities, you know."

The heat of a blush crested Eliza's cheeks. Speechless, she had no idea whether to accept the statement or challenge it. She said nothing.

If he noticed her reaction, Micah gave no indication as he crossed to the wall peg, took down his coat, and pulled it on. "Well, the doctor should come by in the morning. I'll keep the two of you in my thoughts and prayers this evening."

"Thank you," Eliza murmured, knowing he should leave, wishing he would stay, and aware that she had no right to wishes concerning Micah Richmond.

And with a buoyant wave, he was gone.

Chapter 9

Eliza peeked in at Aunt Phoebe, then went upstairs to her own room. Her cheeks still burned with shame at the brazenly wanton thoughts regarding Micah. Falling to her knees beside the bed, she clasped her hands and bowed her head.

Dear heavenly Father, I'm truly mixed up and have no one to turn to except You. I beg Your forgiveness for my foolishness. When Weston tossed me aside, I almost hated him — as much for breaking my heart as for depriving me of Melanie, my dearest friend in the world. But with the passing of days and weeks, I realized I had no choice other than to accept my sad fate. With Your help, and Aunt Phoebe's kindness and love, I've done just that. I no longer harbor ill feelings toward Weston. I don't love him or hate him, and I'd rather spend the rest of my life alone than to be that vulnerable ever again.

But what I cannot understand is why I feel so drawn to Micah Richmond. I do not want someone to replace Weston — and it's not as if he were inclined to do so anyway. He's not free, Father. He belongs to Anabelle, and she is the best friend I have in this world just now. Please help me not to be untrustworthy or unfaithful to this new friendship.

I'm just being a silly goose, and I know it. So, please, help me to think clearly again and act rationally. Don't let me lose myself to daydreams and fantasies. I want You to fill all the needs of my heart. Help me to be the person You want me to be, and may my life glorify You always.

A new peace came over Eliza, enveloping her in its warmth. She stood to her feet and removed her Bible from the bedside table, then sank into the comfort of the chaise. Opening to the book of Psalms, she feasted upon the bounty before her.

"My, but you seem preoccupied this evening," Anabelle remarked, setting the tray of scones and tea on the lamp table. She smoothed her butternut gabardine skirt with her fingers.

Micah gave her a one-sided smile and took her hand, drawing her down to the settee next to him. "Forgive me, sweetheart. I was just thinking of Mrs. Harper. She had a spell this morning at church."

"Oh yes." Snuggling closer, she rested her golden head against his shoulder. "I thought I noticed Eliza leading her away after the service, rather than allowing her to visit with the other ladies as she normally does." She turned her face upward, meeting his gaze. "Is it something serious? Has there been word?"

He traced a finger lightly along her delicate jawline, catching the sincerity in her eyes, and his heart contracted. "I really couldn't say, just yet. I stopped by the house on my way over here to see how she's doing. She seemed to be resting and looked a little better than she did at church. I prayed with her and left. No doubt the doctor will run by there tomorrow."

"Then I shall pray for her tonight when I go to bed. How was Eliza coping?" she asked casually.

"Same as always. Had her aunt all tucked in bed with a tea tray waiting for when she awakened. Naturally she's worried, but she seems determined to leave the matter in God's hands."

Ana gave a consenting nod. A quiet moment elapsed before she spoke again. "Eliza is very . . . lonely."

"Think so?"

Another nod. "She left all her friends behind, you know, in Harrisburg. I think she's getting a bit homesick."

"Could be."

"I wish she'd agree to attend some Christmas concerts with us. In the company of, say, Phillip Madison. Or even Charles Sprocket. A foursome would be such fun."

"Why don't you suggest it?" Even as he asked, Micah tried to picture gentle Eliza in the company of slick-handed Phillip or nasal-voiced Charles. He grimaced.

Ana toyed with the lace edging on her ivory silk sleeve. "Oh, but I have. She says she's not in the least interested."

"Well, then, we should accept her decision."

Leaning forward, Anabelle poured tea into the china cups, handing one to Micah. She added her customary two sugar lumps to hers and stirred it, the spoon making soft clicking sounds with her movements. Then she took a sip and set her cup down again. "I think Eliza was jilted."

Micah swallowed too quickly and held his breath as the scalding liquid singed his throat. He took a bite of a raisin scone, trying to envision the kind of rat who could inflict pain on someone like Eliza.

"She hasn't told me so," Ana admitted. "At least, not in so many words. But she's alluded to something sad. I'm sure she'll come out with the whole story one of these days."

"Let's wait, then. No sense making up stories that might or might not be true."

"And in the meanwhile, why don't you check with Phillip or Charles and see if either of them would consider escorting our new friend about town? I'm sure if I keep after her, Eliza will agree to join us."

"Whatever you say."

"Splendid." A sweet smile spread across Anabelle's lips.

"Oh, I think complete bed rest for a week or so should suffice," Doctor Jenson said, tucking his instruments into the old black bag he'd brought with him before slipping into his equally worn black suit coat.

"A week!" Aunt Phoebe groaned.

"Only a week?" Eliza could not mask her elation that her aunt's spell hadn't been more serious. Or that it hadn't been her imagination that the older woman looked more like herself this morning, even if a touch pale. Thinning hair draped the shoulders of her nightdress in two slender braids.

"That's what I said, ladies. A week." The white-haired old man winked at Eliza, then glared pointedly through his monocle at his patient. "And you'd best follow my orders, Phoebe, or I'll put you in the hospital myself. You manage to get yourself in a fix every year at this time, seems like, working yourself to death for that shop out front."

"Well, if I didn't, there'd be a lot of people without gifts for Christmas," she said in her own defense. After the good night's sleep, her voice had regained some of its force.

"Be that as it may, I expect you to stay in bed. This niece of yours appears perfectly capable of seeing to business." He glanced at his silver pocket watch, then tucked it into the fob pocket of his vest. "I'll check back day after tomorrow to see how you're doing. Good day, Phoebe. Miss."

"Thank you, Doctor." Eliza came around from the other side of her aunt's bed. "I'll show you out." As she led the way, she had to ask the question, had to satisfy herself. "She's really going to be all right? She's just overtired?"

"That's right. Wears herself out every holiday season, regular as clockwork. The old gal must think she's still a spring chicken."

Eliza smiled. "Well, I'll see that she obeys your orders. You can count on me."

He flicked a teasing grin over his shoulder. "Kinda thought that, just looking at you. Good day, miss." Plunking his hat atop his head, he nodded and took his leave.

Eliza all but skipped back to her aunt's room.

The next morning Eliza had the shop dusted and open for business bright and early and discovered she enjoyed dealing with the customers, many of whom asked after her aunt and expressed their regards. Mostly women, they appreciated the quality of the goods. Eliza took singular pleasure when a patron would stop to admire something she'd done herself.

"Does this tea towel come in other designs?" a heavy-set lady asked as she browsed among the wares that afternoon, perusing, touching this and that with plump, bejeweled fingers.

"Yes. In fact, we've a selection of floral patterns in stock. Let me show you." Crossing to her, Eliza bent to open a drawer beneath the display of towels and brought out several others for the woman to examine.

After some consideration, she pursed her lips and inclined her head. "I'll take these two. My daughter's to be married in the spring. She loves getting pretty things for her hope chest."

"Then you've made a fine choice. A young wife would be proud to have these in her kitchen. Will there be anything else, madam?"

"Yes, that lily of the valley tablecloth." Her index finger indicated the folded linen cover displayed to one side. "It's simply exquisite." She dug into her handbag.

Having finished embroidering the design in the cloth's four corners scarcely a week ago, Eliza tried not to blush as she wrapped the items and made change.

"Thank you, miss. Good day."

The bell above the door tinkled on her departure.

Eliza swivelled to refold a few items that needed to be tidied before turning the CLOSED sign outward.

"So, how's our patient today?" Micah's resonant voice rang through the quiet room.

Eliza jumped, inadvertently knocking a stack of crocheted doilies to the floor. Before she could stoop to gather them, he beat her to it and handed them over with a smile. "Forgive me. I didn't mean to startle you."

"No harm done. I — I just didn't hear anyone come in," she said inanely, hating the flush rising upward from her collar.

"I happened to arrive just as that last lady was leaving."

"I see." Eliza's hands began an irritating tremble. Hoping it was not obvious, she reached to tuck a loose strand of hair into her hair net, then purposely laced her fingers together behind her back.

"Thought I'd stop by for the weekly donation," Micah went on. "But first I'd like to see Mrs. Harper, if I may."

"Of course." Gradually regaining her equilibrium, Eliza smiled. "The doctor's making her stay in bed all week, so she's a mite testy, but I'm sure she'll be happy to see you."

"Splendid." He spun on his heel and stepped into the hall.

His temporary absence gave Eliza a chance to call herself a few names for being so flustered. *A fine way to act,* she thought scathingly, *considering that fervent prayer just last evening.* She simply had to conquer her silly tendency to go all aflutter whenever Micah Richmond appeared. To start with, she drew several calming breaths, which did help. She repeated the procedure off and on while he remained with her aunt. *He is merely a friend,* she lectured inwardly. *A friend who is spoken for.* "And you are a goose," she added for good measure.

"Did you say something?" Exactly when Micah had exited Aunt Phoebe's room would remain a mystery, but those long strides of his quickly brought him into the parlor.

Eliza turned her eyes skyward. "Counting," she blurted. "I was merely counting stock." *Bother. Now I'm resorting to lying? This just has to stop.*

"Oh. Well, it appears the Lord has seen fit to answer our prayers and restore your dear aunt to health once again."

The small reminder of the Lord's constant presence reinforced Eliza's guilt. "Yes. I'm so thankful. She was able to take some broth and toast earlier. And I can tell from her temper she'll soon be back to feeling like herself."

He chuckled, a warm, low rumble that made Eliza smile.

"I'll get the funds she left for you." Aware of his gaze following her movements, but unable to do anything about it, Eliza somehow managed to get to the drawer and find the packet quickly. She held it out to him.

A broad grin appeared as he closed his fingers around the envelope. "I do thank you immensely. Both of you. As I mentioned before, everything helps."

"I've been wondering, have there been any new developments for the little girls since our visit? Rosa and Gabriella, I mean?"

Micah tipped his head slightly in thought. "I was there just yesterday, actually. The family's doing their level best to cope with the extra mouths to feed, now that there's less income to live on. It's not easy, by any stretch of the imagination."

"Do you . . . do you think they'll be all right?"

"I sincerely hope and pray so, but only time will tell." He regarded her evenly. "You really do care about them, don't you?"

She had to be honest. "How could I not? Such heartbreak to deal with at such a young age."

"But that's only two out of thousands. We can only do what we can do and trust that it helps." He paused, pocketing the funds from Aunt Phoebe. "Guess I'll be off. Thanks again, Eliza. You'll be in my prayers."

And you will be in mine, her heart answered.

As the bell jangled above the door, a

second, smaller one sounded from Aunt Phoebe's room. Eliza turned the CLOSED sign outward and went to answer the summons.

CHAPTER 10

By closing time the following afternoon, Eliza's feet ached from having been on them all day. It seemed the nearer it got to Christmas, the more customers came to buy gifts. No wonder Aunt Phoebe had been so worn out, she conceded, what with tending the shop most daylight hours and then working on projects until late at night.

Eliza bristled to think she had allowed the older woman to carry most of that burden, while she herself traipsed off to quilting circle every week, practiced the piano most mornings, and whiled away untold hours that could be better spent in making Aunt Phoebe's life easier. After all, hadn't that been the reason she'd come to New York in the first place?

Grimacing at her thoughtlessness, Eliza went to turn the CLOSED sign around. Her frown turned into a smile at the sight of a visitor coming up the walk, and she threw open the door to admit her friend. "Anabelle! How nice of you to come by!"

Ana handed her a basket of baked treats. "I thought you might be in need of some company."

"Oh I am, I am. With the exception of Aunt Phoebe, I see only strangers most of the time. And thank you for the goodies. I'll make us some tea."

"While you do that, I'll look in on the dear lady, if you don't mind. I've brought her a book of poetry. I'll be just a few moments."

"How sweet of you. She will love it, I'm sure."

With a hopeful smile, Anabelle hooked her wrap over one of the wall pegs, tucking her gloves into the hood before removing a small wrapped book from the pocket. Straightening her jade gown, she went down the hall.

Eliza headed for the kitchen and got out the teapot, tidying up a few things she'd been too busy to tend to while the shop was open. By the time the water was boiling and she had measured tea into the silver tea ball and filled the pot to the brim, her visitor joined her.

Anabelle pulled out a spindle-back chair and sat down. "As Micah reported, your aunt seems to be improving. I didn't stay long, though, lest I tire her. He's been quite anxious about the two of you."

"Your Micah tends to worry about a lot of folks," Eliza replied. "I just wish we hadn't added to his concerns." She set out matching cups and saucers, then brought the teapot to the table and placed it between them. "I could have jumped for joy when the doctor said Aunt Phoebe's just worn out — although I must confess, I feel somewhat responsible."

"Why is that?"

"I could have done so much more to help, but instead, I chose to occupy myself with my own activities. That had to be a factor in her having taken ill." Watching Ana's expression cloud over, she pressed on. "So, I've decided to stop going to the sewing circle — at least until after the holidays."

"Oh, I'm sorry to hear that. I do understand though." She paused. "Just don't become a recluse yourself. That's one of the reasons I came by, actually."

Eliza frowned in curiosity.

"Micah and I would like you to attend a holiday concert with us. Us and a friend. A foursome, you know."

"A *gentleman* friend?"

Anabelle nodded, raising a hand to dismiss all of Eliza's objections. "It's just for an evening. I can't bear for you to be sequestered at home for the rest of the Christmas season when so many churches put on festive programs. And afterward we can go to some quiet spot for pie and coffee."

"I don't know. . . ."

"Come on, Eliza. I promised Micah I would be able to persuade you to accompany us."

Envisioning herself in some quiet little spot across the table from Micah Richmond did strange things to Eliza's insides. But, her conscience reasoned, perhaps that was just what she needed. Being in his company when he was with Anabelle. Watching the two of them making doe eyes at one another. Witnessing their mutual love. It might just render a mortal blow to her absurd fantasies about the Weston Elliot look-alike.

Against her better judgment, she acquiesced. "All right. As soon as Aunt Phoebe can be left alone for an evening, I'll go out with you — *and* your gentleman friend."

A new glow filled Anabelle's eyes. "Splendid!"

"But only once," Eliza amended.

"As you wish. I can't wait to tell Micah!"

But even as Eliza poured the tea, she hoped fervently that she wasn't making a huge mistake.

■ ■ ■ ■

Eliza brushed out her aunt's silvery hair, fashioning it into its customary knob at the crown. She fluffed a few loose tendrils around her face, then stepped back to assess her work. "I do declare, you're looking positively chipper this morning, Auntie."

Crossing her arms over her bosom, the older woman emitted a huff. "All I know is it feels downright ridiculous to have to spend one more day in this bed with Christmas a scant three weeks away. I need to be up and doing more than just crocheting."

"Now, now," Eliza scolded good-naturedly. "You know what Dr. Jenson said. You don't want him to hustle you off to the hospital, to be poked, prodded, and peered at, when a few more days' rest will only help you to get stronger."

"Yes, yes, I've heard that lecture more times than I care to admit. I'll stay here, more's the pity, but I don't have to like it." She made a face at the books on the bedside table. "Are there any more classics in Cap's library? I've read these a dozen times already."

"I'll take a look. I'm sure there must be something. Have you finished the poetry book Anabelle brought?"

"Twice." Her countenance softened with a smile. "It was sweet of her to come by and wish me well, though, her and Micah. They'll make a good match — assuming he ever gets down to marrying the girl, that is. Can't imagine why he's dragging his feet."

Eliza didn't respond, instead stepping to the window and opening the draperies to allow the bright sunshine in. "Looks like another glorious day. No doubt dozens of customers will come by the shop."

"How's the stock holding up?"

"Fine, Auntie. Just fine. Stop worrying." Bending to bestow a kiss to her companion's silken cheek, she hugged her as well. "I'll bring your breakfast tray directly."

Her gnarled fingers squeezed Eliza's hand. "Do forgive my orneriness, dear. I truly appreciate your kind attention to an old lady. It's just —"

"I know," Eliza murmured gently. "It won't be much longer. The doctor's sure to notice how much you've improved since he was last here."

"Largely thanks to you," she admitted with a grudging smile. "Now, about my breakfast . . ."

Micah looped the horse's reins through the

hitching post in front of the tenement building and helped his assistant to alight from the buggy. He handed her one of the sacks of groceries they'd brought and took the remaining two himself, and they started toward the cluttered stoop directly ahead.

"Mercy," Mrs. Wallace exclaimed, her short legs stepping over a greasy-looking puddle in her path. "One naturally expects winter to improve a dreary spot, what with new snow falling from time to time."

"It'll take more than a few inches of snow to alleviate some of this gloom," Micah said dryly. "A raging blizzard, maybe."

The pleasant-faced woman chuckled, and the cheeks beneath her feather-trimmed hat plumped with her smile. Then she sobered. "Ah, but then some of these poor souls would have it all the harder, wouldn't they?"

Micah could only agree.

"Here," she offered. "I'll get the door. You have your arms full."

He grinned his thanks, and the two of them paused just inside while their vision adjusted to the dimness of the long hallway.

As always, children swarmed around them both, eyes wide and expectant. They did not, however, display a lack of manners by so much as hinting about the penny candy that typically appeared whenever Micah arrived with sacks. He rarely kept them waiting. Setting down one of his bags, he reached into his coat pocket and withdrew some peppermint sticks. "Here, Tony, Vinnie, Gina. One for everybody."

Beside him, Mrs. Wallace had her own cluster of youngsters vying for attention. "Little Rosa, Maria, Gabriella." She handed a treat to each one in turn, and almost en masse, the gaggle of little ones skipped away with their treasures. She turned to Micah. "Now, where do we start?"

He gave her a lopsided grin. "First two apartments, then the Garibaldi household." Gesturing with his head for her to follow, he strode toward the nearest flat.

Once a portion of the groceries had been delivered to the intended parties, he and Mrs. Wallace approached Gina and Vinnie's place. Micah rapped on the doorjamb.

The olive-skinned housewife appeared almost instantly. Looking more tired than usual, dark circles shadowed her eyes as she dried her hands on the soiled apron covering her faded dress and stepped aside. "Mr. Richmond. Mrs. Wallace. Come in'a, come in." She pretended not to notice the burden Micah held.

"Thought we'd come by and see how you're doing," he said evenly. "We hoped you might put some of this to good use." With that, he pressed the bulging sack into her arms.

Her dark eyes misted over, and she swallowed. "Oh, you shouldn't have done'a dis. But Vittorio an' me, we say graci."

"How is everyone?" Mrs. Wallace asked.

The woman released a weary sigh. "Some days'a good, some days'a not so good. We make do."

"And the girls, Rosa and Gabriella," Micah prompted. "Are you managing all right with them?"

She cast a surreptitious look over her shoulder, as if not wanting to be overheard, then met his gaze. "I tell'a you, it'sa hard. We love dem, you know. But we got our own to feed and clothe. It'sa not easy to do for our own." A self-conscious shrug finished the unspoken thought eloquently.

Micah gave a reluctant nod.

"We try. We make do."

"I understand. That's all we could hope, right? I'll check back again in a few more days."

"You do dat. And graci for da food . . . and da caring. *Arrivederci.*"

"God bless," Micah said. He glanced at Mrs. Wallace, and they turned for the door.

Their footsteps echoed hollowly from one

end of the deserted corridor to the other, all the way to the exit. Neither of them spoke until they reached the buggy.

"Well, I guess we know what that means," his companion said under her breath on a sigh of resignation.

Micah nodded. "Might as well start looking for a family who'd like to adopt two little Italian girls." But how, with so many prejudiced against their foreign culture, their Catholic faith? The best he could do for now was try to find a temporary shelter. And pray that God would touch someone's heart.

Handing Mrs. Wallace up to the seat, Micah gathered the traces and climbed in beside her. The afternoon was starting to cloud over again, and there was a definite nip to the air. He'd best drive her directly to the office before seeing to the errands that still awaited him.

For some reason — most likely because she asked about the children only yesterday, he told himself — his thoughts drifted to Eliza. This new development would likely disturb her almost as much as it did him. *If* he mentioned it, that is. She already had worries enough caring for Mrs. Harper. It might be prudent not to say anything.

If only Ana showed some of that concern,

he mused in his despondency. Or even just listened sympathetically while he unburdened himself after a particularly trying day. After all, wasn't that part and parcel of being a wife?

When they married, she'd have to be more accepting of his ministry. If he could only convince her to go with him on one of his benevolent calls, she'd see he was involved in something of real value. Anyone with a heart as tender as Anabelle's could hardly escape being affected if she witnessed the deep need herself.

Releasing a shuddering breath, he turned the matter over to God in silent prayer.

CHAPTER 11

When Aunt Phoebe at last dropped off to sleep, Eliza extinguished the downstairs lights and trudged upstairs to her bedroom. Every bone in her body ached, and her stomach growled from hunger, but she was too weary to care. A letter had come from home in response to her most recent missive, and she had yet to read it. Taking the envelope from the pocket of her skirt, she placed it on her bedside table and lit the lamp. Then she broke the seal and unfolded the pages, anticipating the memory of her mother's melodious voice in the neatly penned words:

Dearest Eliza,

Your father and I were so very glad to hear from you again. We miss you desperately but do understand your decision to remain in New York indefinitely. Our dear Phoebe has been alone far too long, and now that she is up in years, I know she must appreciate your company. I pray your presence will be a comfort and a blessing to her.

I hesitate to tell you this, daughter, but thought you should hear it from me rather than some other source. Melanie has come home, alone.

Eliza, caught completely off guard by the startling news, felt a chill run up her spine. Melanie, alone? What could have happened? Sympathy for her former best friend vied with the bitterness caused by the betrayal of their relationship. But even as her emotions warred within her, Eliza read on:

She refuses to talk to anyone and will not so much as set foot outside her room. She scarcely touches the lovely meals the housekeeper prepares for her, and her mother is beside herself with worry.

Melanie has taken no one into her confidence, so it is anyone's guess as to what occurred after she left town. I thought you should know about this, in the event you might chance to come for a visit.

Please take care of yourself, my darling, and give Phoebe our warm regards. Our prayers are ever with you.

With deepest love,
Mother

Barely able to draw breath, Eliza sank to her bed and let the crisp stationery flutter to the floor. She and the high-spirited Melanie had been bosom friends as far back as her memories of childhood reached. Together they had shared giggles and girlish secrets, tears, school years, and daydreams. And quite possibly the rift between them pained Melanie every bit as much as it did Eliza.

But, she reasoned, that did not alter the fact that Melanie had run off with Weston. If she had taken a butcher knife and cut out Eliza's heart, it could not have inflicted more pain.

Eliza filled her lungs and slowly let them deflate, knowing she should at the very least pray for the girl. And perhaps, in time, she would be able to do just that. But right now, Melanie Brown Elliot was one of two people in the world she could not bear to think about. All she wanted to do was rid her mind of all conscious thoughts and climb into bed.

"Here you are, Auntie. Your favorites." Eliza placed the bed tray before the older woman, then went to open the drapes.

"Thank you, dear. The coddled eggs look perfect. And you even remembered marmalade for my toast. Bless you."

With a thin smile in response to her aunt's cheerfulness, Eliza busied herself tidying the room. "Just ring the bell when you've finished, and I'll bring you your crocheting. Doctor Jenson said there's no reason why you shouldn't be permitted to do something that isn't strenuous." She turned to leave.

"Just a minute, child."

Pausing at the door, she swivelled to face her aunt.

"You look rather pale this morning. Did you not sleep well?"

"I'm fine," Eliza hedged, toying with a fold of her dark gray skirt. "I just have some things on my mind."

"Difficulties concerning the shop?"

She shook her head. "No, it's nothing for you to worry about."

"Well, should you need someone to talk to, you know where to find me." The old spark shone in Aunt Phoebe's eyes.

"Thank you. I'll remember that. Oh, I think I hear the bell. I'll be back to check on you in a little while."

Exiting the comfortable bedchamber, Eliza hastened to greet the day's first customer.

Phoebe nibbled a corner off a triangle of toast, then set the tray aside. During these days of lying in bed with nothing to do but sewing, the thought had come to her to put together a surprise for Eliza, one fashioned after the Epiphany tradition Cap had brought to their marriage from his Anglican background. For twelve nights following Christmas, Eliza would be given a different present. By the time she opened the last gift, she would possess a carved wooden box with twelve heirlooms, special items Phoebe had cherished throughout her own life.

So far she had only come up with six gifts. But on the spur of a moment, she'd remembered her grandmother's ornate pill box necklace. It would make a perfect addition to the other things collected thus far: a tiny silver hand mirror her father had given to her mother on their wedding day, four matching pewter napkin rings from her mother's hope chest, a gilt-edged picture frame, a set of crystal knife rests, a hand-painted silk fan Cap had purchased on his first voyage to the Orient, and an ornate-handled letter opener.

With a sly smile, Phoebe swung her legs over the side of the bed and maneuvered her feet into the warm knitted slippers next to it before padding to her dresser. Hopefully the pill box would be somewhere in the middle drawer. All she had to do was find it and sneak it into the wooden box hidden beneath her bed before Eliza returned and caught her up. That would leave a mere five articles to be added.

She could hardly wait for Christmas!

As Eliza straightened up the dwindling displays on the various shelves in the gift shop, the door opened. Her heart lurched as Micah stepped inside on a blast of chilly air.

"Good afternoon, Eliza. Thought I'd check in on that aunt of yours again."

"How nice. She always enjoys seeing a friendly face." Eliza purposely kept her tone breezy, hoping to recapture her poise and waylay the maddening blush that seemed to appear so easily in Micah's company despite her best intentions.

"Hope I won't be disturbing a nap or anything."

Eliza shook her head. "I'm quite sure she's awake. I took in a lunch tray a little while ago, and she didn't appear tired in the least."

"Good." He loosened his coat, flashing a jovial grin on his way past, and his confident footsteps took him down the hall.

She plucked the feather duster from its hook and flicked it over a porcelain doll and a pair of crystal candleholders, her movements carrying her before an oval wall mirror that was accented by a spray of dried flowers positioned above. Catching her reflection, Eliza realized the smile she had given Micah Richmond had yet to fade. With an exasperated huff, she schooled herself into line and attacked her chore with more discipline.

It wasn't long before she heard Micah returning.

He bent to pick up a crocheted coaster that must have fallen during her dusting and handed it to her. "Thank the Lord your aunt appears to be a little more perky each time I come by. Amazing resilience, that lady."

Eliza had to agree. "Of course, she knew she had to follow the doctor's instructions to the letter or face me, cracking the cat-o'-nine-tails over her back," she said facetiously, replacing the coaster on the stack of others.

A teasing light gleamed in his eyes, and for a fraction of a second, Eliza thought she saw them wander over her. "How true. The moment we met I saw right through you, to that mean streak that runs a mile wide."

Her soft laugh couldn't have been held in check no matter how much she might have wished it, and a similar, deeper one rumbled from his chest. Yet for some reason she sensed everything was not as it appeared. She hesitated about questioning him but gave in to her intuition. "Is there something wrong, Micah?"

His expression took a somber turn, and he shrugged. "I wasn't going to mention it, particularly to you. Perhaps I shouldn't even have come."

A jolt of alarm seized Eliza. "Whatever do you mean? Is my aunt not doing well after all?"

He held up a calming hand. "Please believe me; she truly does appear to be recovering quickly. No, I'm afraid my concerns lie in other directions just now."

Continuing to study his demeanor, Eliza drew her own conclusions as the memory of two heartbroken little girls huddled together on a miserable pallet surfaced in her mind. "Well, if you're hesitant to say anything to me about it, I must surmise it has something to do with the children. Am I right? Has something happened to them?"

Micah inhaled a long breath, then slowly expelled it. He rested an elbow on the shelf beside him, meeting her gaze. "It . . . uh . . . has more to do with the Garibaldis, actually."

"They've decided they cannot continue to look after Rosa and Gabriella."

An amazed smile spread across his lips. "That's one thing I admire about you, Eliza. You're very astute. I came here for the express purpose of assuring myself that Mrs. Harper is improving — definitely not intending to involve you in my problems."

"Quite gallant of you, I must say. However, if that *problem,* as you call it, concerns those poor little girls, then I'm already involved. I've felt deeply burdened for them since the day I first saw them. You might very well come out with it. I must know."

Micah pressed his lips into a grim line and stepped to the window, his back to her as he looked outside. His shoulders sagged. "The Garibaldis have made every effort to incorporate the Riccio girls into their household. Done their level best. But lacking the income the girls' parents brought in, it's nigh impossible for them to make ends meet. Mrs. Garibaldi as much as asked me to start making other arrangements for those little ones."

A heaviness settled over Eliza's chest. "But it's almost Christmas," she murmured. "Surely they can stay where they are until after Christmas."

"And then what?" Micah asked, turning to face her. "I've already contacted everyone I can think of, and all for naught. It's precisely the approaching holidays that make it next to impossible to find a haven for Rosa and Gabriella right now. To be perfectly honest, I haven't the slightest idea what I can do to help them."

"Well, we'll just have to think of something, then, won't we?"

"We?" A half-smile lit Micah's compelling features.

Not to be undaunted, Eliza only repeated herself with more conviction. "We."

"When you think of something," he said flatly, "be sure to let me know. I'm out of options at the moment. Even if I can't find a family who'll adopt them permanently, I need a place where they'll be looked after, a temporary shelter until a spot opens up for them. Our facility is filled to the hilt with other children in the same boat they are."

Eliza had surmised as much, but hearing the sad information again made the need seem even more acute. "I assume you've already made the matter public knowledge at church."

"Our church, Mrs. Wallace's church, and a raft of others."

"Well, then, we'll have to look elsewhere."

He chuckled, but without a hint of mirth. "No doubt you've a long list of places that fit the bill."

"Not yet. But I will." The strength of her certitude surprised even Eliza, yet she knew somehow that she would find a home for those girls, even if she had to build it herself!

Micah watched with fascination as it seemed as if the wheels inside Eliza's head turned like perfectly meshed gears inside a pocket watch. He really hadn't intended to dump this weighty matter on her slender shoulders. That had been the absolute last thing on his mind. He couldn't remember exactly how she'd managed to wangle the information out of him, but now that she had, it didn't seem quite so impossible. Nothing was changed. She knew even less people in the city than he did. But somehow he sensed the Lord would use her in this situation. He just didn't see how.

"Will you be calling on Anabelle this evening?" she asked out of the blue.

"Most likely. I go over there nearly every night. Her parents' sort of —"

"Splendid," she interrupted. "Then, would you please ask Ana if she can come over here tomorrow? Tell her I need her help."

"Whatever you say." Micah continued to stare, trying to decipher what was going on in that dark little head of hers, but at the moment he didn't have a clue. He cleared his throat. "Well, I'd best be going. I have some more calls to make this afternoon."

Tapping an index finger against her lips, she gave no indication she'd even heard him speak, but she nodded absently as she began pacing the floor.

"Uh, well, good day," he said, crossing to the door.

"Hm? Oh yes. I'll be praying, too. Something's bound to turn up. You'll see."

Slinging a glance over his shoulder, Micah chuckled under his breath and left. That young woman had come a long way from the timid, cowed soul he'd first met, and the change in her was utterly fascinating!

Whistling as he climbed aboard his buggy, he drove off.

CHAPTER 12

"It's now or never," Eliza muttered to herself. She'd paced the floor between the gift shop and her aunt's room so many times, trying to work up courage to broach the subject uppermost in her mind, she was surprised there was no obvious path worn in the carpet runner. But now that the shop was closed for the day and her constant prayers only served to strengthen her resolve, it seemed senseless to put the matter off any longer. She sloughed off her nerves and quietly entered the bedchamber.

An imperceptible snore drifted across the dimly lit room.

Eliza rolled her eyes and tiptoed out again, closing the door after her. Of course Aunt Phoebe would doze off at times, lying abed all day. But all that gathering of courage, for nothing. Oh well, it was her own fault for taking so long to make up her own mind.

The hearty smell of the pork roast Eliza

had started earlier permeated the house, making her stomach growl. Had she even had dinner? The day seemed little more than a blur. Going to the kitchen, she peeled potatoes and carrots and set them to boil. Then she took a lamp and headed for the stairs.

She'd been inside the spare room a dozen times over the last few days, getting replacement supplies or putting some unused object out of the way. She noticed that the pattern in the wallpaper had faded over the years, but the wainscoting was still in good shape. The room had been ever so pretty back when her family had stayed here on visits. But standing in the doorway now, the lamp held high, she envisioned it as something far more noble than a mere guest room. It could easily be transformed into a haven for a needy child, or even two. Two little girls. A hopeful smile tugged at her lips.

But how would she convince Aunt Phoebe?

Taking a step further inside the shadowed depths, Eliza imagined it housing a double bed with a colorful counterpane, a good-sized wardrobe, a rocking chair, and some bright curtains. Surely she could persuade Anabelle to help fix it up. And the two of them could sew some little dresses. . . . Each new plan gave birth to another, until Eliza feared her head would burst.

When Aunt Phoebe awakened a short while later, she appeared completely rested and more like her old self than she'd been for days. Eliza couldn't suppress the desire to compliment her. "You're looking wonderful, Auntie. How about coming to the parlor for supper? I'm sure Doc Jenson would approve if I helped you to the table and back afterward."

Some of the care lines vanished from the older woman's face. "Why, that's a splendid idea. I haven't had anything but these four walls to look at since Sunday. I'd dearly love a change of scenery."

"Then let me get your wrap and slippers." She snatched the flannel wrapper from where it lay draped over a chair back and helped her aunt into it, then supported her as she stepped one foot and then the other into the warm slippers.

They walked slowly up the hall, and reaching the parlor, Eliza seated her in a chair near the fire, then went to fill their plates with food. In no time at all they were enjoying the succulent pork with mashed potatoes and gravy and honeyed carrots.

"This is perfectly delightful," Aunt Phoebe

said, touching her napkin to the corners of her mouth when she finished. "I couldn't eat another bite."

"Not even a sliver of pie?" Eliza asked. "One of your regular customers, a Mrs. Knight, brought over a fresh apple crumb pie and asked me to pass along her good wishes for your recovery."

At this, the elderly countenance gentled. "Why, how very sweet of Mabel. I just might be able to down a small piece. With a cup of tea, if you don't mind. Maybe then you'll tell me what's on your mind."

In the process of rising to her feet, Eliza sank back down to her chair in surprise. "How did you know I wanted to talk to you about something?"

Her aunt smiled slyly. "When a person spends a good deal of her life dealing with the public, she becomes rather skilled at being able to read other folks."

Eliza shook her head in wonder. "I see. Well, I'll go get our dessert. Then we can talk."

Actually, she reasoned, it could be a good thing, her aunt's being so discerning. It saved her from having to think of a way to bring up the subject of the room.

As she poured the tea a short while later, Eliza retook her seat and sampled a bite of pie. She closed her eyes in delight.

"Mabel has a real way with pie, doesn't she?"

"It's excellent. I don't know when I've had better."

"So, what is it, child?" Aunt Phoebe took a cautious sip of the hot liquid and relaxed against the back of her chair in expectation. "Bad news from home?"

Eliza blanched. "I did receive some startling news from Mother, but this has nothing to do with that. It's a different matter entirely."

"Well, best you come out with it. That's the simplest."

Drawing a long, slow breath for fortification, Eliza plunged forth. "I hardly know where to start. You know about Micah's work and the frustrations he faces on a daily basis, trying to place orphaned children in a city that's already overcrowded."

"Yes, we've discussed the matter quite often."

"Well, until I actually made that visit to the tenements myself," Eliza said, "I hadn't the foggiest notion of the breadth of the problem. Now that I've been there and witnessed the sordid conditions, I feel almost guilty that we have so much, when others lack even the bare necessities."

"Which is precisely why I run the gift shop," her aunt reminded her. "So that I can help out in a tangible way."

"I know, Aunt Phoebe. Truly, I do. But don't you ever feel that it isn't enough? Don't you wish you could do more?"

"At my age? What more could I do, if I might ask?"

Eliza's pulse rate quickened, and her mouth went dry. She quickly gulped some tea and set down her cup. "I'm not asking you to do more, exactly. This is a project I would like to undertake on my own — with Anabelle's help, if she's willing."

Aunt Phoebe continued to stare but did not interrupt.

"It's the spare room," Eliza blurted. "I'd like to convert it into a child's room."

The older woman tucked her chin.

"Nothing permanent, mind you," Eliza quickly added. "But for those times when Micah's at his wit's end and needs a temporary shelter for one or two little children while he tries to find them a real home."

"But you don't know what you're suggesting! A child — children, here? At Harper House?" Her gaze making a swift circuit of the parlor shop, Aunt Phoebe seemed to center on all the breakable items, the shelves of fragile things that could meet their doom within a few seconds of a rambunctious child's entrance.

"I know what you're thinking," Eliza said placatingly. "But I really don't think a little girl would be much trouble. Or even two, at times. It would be just for a few hours, in some cases. Days, in others. With an assortment of playthings available for them to keep themselves occupied, they'd have no reason to venture down here and touch your things."

"Quite an interesting theory, I'd say," her aunt said without emotion. "Have you ever been responsible for little ones?"

"Not for an extended period of time, no. But I've been around enough of them to know that they will accept established boundaries when treated with respect and love and a firm hand."

Aunt Phoebe shut her eyes and rubbed the bridge of her nose under her eyeglasses in thought.

"And I don't foresee any problem with my plan. I think it's possible and worth a try, at the very least. Would you let me try, Auntie? For the sake of the children?"

She raised her eyelids and met Eliza's gaze. "Did he put you up to this? Micah?"

"No," Eliza said, shocked. "I never mentioned the subject to him at all, though I confess I've been considering my undertaking for several days now."

"I see." Her slight bosom rose and fell as her demeanor revealed troubled thoughts. "I must tell you, child, this whole notion of yours has caught me somewhat off balance."

Eliza didn't know how to respond. She remained silent.

"But I will pray about it —"

Blinding hope made Eliza smile. But the smile wilted as quickly as it had appeared once her aunt went on.

"That's the best I can promise. I know the need exists and is very serious. I also know I'm not physically able to deal with the noise and confusion or inconvenience of having little ones underfoot, but you are. For that matter, perhaps that's why the Lord brought you here in the first place. Not as an answer to my prayers, but to Micah Richmond's."

Eliza hadn't considered that possibility, but she had to give the suggestion merit. The ministry the young man was involved in was a very compassionate one, one that drew her in immediately and compelled her to do whatever she could to help.

"I'm quite tired now. Would you please help me back to my bed?"

"Of course, Auntie. And I won't bring up

the subject again until after you've had a chance to pray about it."

An almost imperceptible nod seemed all she could manage.

"So," Anabelle said brightly as she hung her cloak. "Micah says you wanted to see me."

Eliza nodded. "Come into the kitchen, and we'll have tea while I bring you up to date on a matter I'm considering." Linking her arm through her friend's she drew the girl along.

After a little more than a quarter hour had passed, Eliza realized she had been talking on and on with scarcely an interruption, and that a peculiar expression had drawn Anabelle's fine brows together in a frown. Her cheeks appeared nearly as white as the shawl collar on her gown. "You don't care for my scheme?"

"That's putting it rather mildly, but you did ask." Ana wagged her head in disbelief, her pompadour shifting ever so slightly with the motion.

"But, don't you see?" Eliza pressed on. "It's a way to help those who can't help themselves. As Pastor Norman said in his sermon, it's a way to serve God. A very noble way. Children are very dear to His heart."

"Yes, but one must look at the more practical side. Think of your sickly aunt in this houseful of lovely things having to endure the excessive racket children seem so fond of."

"But —"

"And that's another thing," she went on, tapping the bowl of her spoon on the table for emphasis. "They wouldn't even be children of . . . well, of class. They'd be riffraff, Eliza. Ragamuffins. Dirty, likely infested with lice or other such disgusting vermin. Perhaps even ill."

"But no less dear to the Lord," Eliza countered. "One's class is of little import here in America. We're all equal. And as far as dirt, that would wash away in a bath, and then we could provide the ragamuffins with some decent clothing."

Anabelle regarded her steadily, then raised her chin a notch. "Micah couldn't interest me in his plight, so he's latched on to you. He put you up to this, didn't he?"

Stunned by her friend's accusation, Eliza vehemently shook her head. "No. Aunt Phoebe asked me the same question last evening, and I assured her as I'm assuring you, this entire thing is my idea. Micah knows nothing of it. I haven't mentioned it to him at all. There'd be no reason to unless my aunt agrees to it."

Appearing somewhat mollified, Anabelle's features softened to their more natural beauty. "Forgive me, Eliza. I get quite upset when Micah suggests I involve myself in his calling. But I simply cannot do it. I loathe filth of any sort, bad smells, and places where diseases are rampant. Nothing would make me happier than for him to find some other line of employment."

"I'm sorry to say, I see little chance of that," Eliza admitted in all honesty. "He truly cares for those poor little ones, Ana. And the Lord reaches out to them through Micah. I do wish you'd go with him once, just to see how he talks to them, how he loves them. You'd feel differently, I'm sure."

"I doubt that." A shudder racked Anabelle's slim shoulders. "I'll never set foot in those hovels. I will pray for those people. I'll sew quilts for them and contribute funds. I'll even endure having my betrothed going among them when it's necessary. But that's as far as my constitution will allow."

Watching her friend's expressive face, Eliza knew she'd spoken truthfully. Not everyone possessed the fortitude required to work among the lowly masses. Anabelle had a good heart, but it was one that needed to be in an environment that was clean and sterile. Letting out a breath she hadn't known she'd been holding, she patted Ana's hand. "Well, would you still help me to fix up an appealing room, if Auntie decides in my favor?"

"I can't see why I shouldn't. It could be a lot of fun, really."

"And perhaps you might be prevailed upon to sew some dresses and nightclothes from time to time?"

Grudgingly, Anabelle acquiesced. "If necessary."

"That's all I ask," Eliza said. But inside, she pitied her friend. She was so wrapped up in fear of the unknown, she could never know the joy that came from helping others.

CHAPTER 13

Phoebe watched Eliza fussing about the room without ever making eye contact in her hurry to straighten things up. The girl was trying so hard to pretend that this morning was no different from any other. But the request she'd made the night before hung between them like yesterday's wash.

From the day of her arrival, Eliza had been like a ray of sunshine in the gloom of her solitary existence, and she had so quickly grown used to her niece's presence she could hardly remember what life had been like before. Eliza was a huge help around the place, quickly mastering the skills needed to keep the shop stocked with popular items. And she took it upon herself to do chores before they were mentioned. Yet the girl had not asked anything for herself. Not until now.

Studying her, she saw that Eliza looked particularly fetching this morning, having donned a chocolate-colored morning gown with a printed design in shades of rust and gray. Switching her gaze from her niece's lissome form to the nearly finished breakfast before her, she raised her cup and took a hearty sip of the freshly brewed tea.

"Can I do anything else for you, Aunt, before I open the shop?" Eliza asked, finally looking her way.

"No, dear, I'm quite fine, thank you. But I would like to say something first."

Eliza's expressive features fell a few notches in uncertainty. She approached the bed and stood there, nervously twisting the handle of the feather duster in her hands, eyes bright with hope, her heightened coloring revealing the fragility of her dream.

"I've been giving a good deal of thought to your proposal, Eliza, along with conferring with the Lord about the matter."

Eliza moistened her lips.

"And I can't believe I'm actually saying this, but . . . I'm willing to give you the opportunity to do what you feel you must."

Her niece let out a tiny gasp. "Truly? Oh, Auntie!" Bending over, Eliza threw her arms about her and kissed her cheek. "Oh, thank you. Thank you. Anabelle and I will start looking for things we'll need right away."

"Before you go too much out of your way,

check the attic. I did sell some of the furniture I wasn't using after Cap died, but I'm quite sure there's a sturdy bedstead, at least, and perhaps a few other items you might find handy."

"That's a wonderful idea. I'll go right up and see what's there. It'll give me a better idea of what's lacking."

"Indeed." She continued to regard her niece with a wary eye. "Of course, we may find out this whole scheme is impractical, you know. So I thought perhaps a trial run of, say, a month to six weeks. And, keep in mind, dear, you'll be taking on a lot. Should you decide to give up the plan later, I'll not fault you in any way."

Eliza's smile eclipsed the sun's brilliance. "I just can't thank you enough. I was afraid even to hope." She paused to draw breath, then continued in a rush, her words tumbling over themselves. "I realize it's going to cause some changes around here, but I promise to do my utmost to see that your life and your routine are affected as little as possible. You'll see."

"Yes, well, I assume we both will. In any event, you may take my tray now. And thank you for the lovely breakfast."

"You're ever so welcome. I'll be back to check on you soon." With the dazzling smile making her appear even younger than she was, she left the room.

Phoebe sank back against her pillows. "Dear Lord, I sure hope You know what You've gotten me into."

Eliza could hardly wait to get started on the new project. Working closely with Anabelle would be great fun — and not to be overlooked was the added bonus of keeping her own mind too busy to dwell on matters best ignored. With that thought, she headed for the enclosed staircase leading to the attic.

Not enough heat wafted from below to do much good in the steep-slanted top story of Harper House, she discovered upon ascending to its lofty heights. And in contrast to the warm sunshine, a brisk breeze whistled and howled around the structure's angles, adding an eerie quality to the venture. The cold made Eliza's teeth chatter as she stepped over a toppled dress form and picked her way through the dusty memorabilia of years gone by.

Arms crossed as she glanced around, Eliza debated going through any of the storage chests abutting one of the low walls. Undoubtedly they would contain outdated clothing, perhaps some seafaring mementos that once belonged to Uncle Amos. And the old lamp standing dejectedly at the end of the row was not suitable for a child, nor would any of the paintings be, she was sure. Her captain uncle's tastes had leaned toward dark stormy seas, with stalwart vessels tossing among the churning waves.

But then her gaze fell upon the bedstead Aunt Phoebe had mentioned, and she stepped nearer to examine it more closely. Even under the coating of dust she recognized the rich cherrywood bed which had once graced her aunt's other guest room. As her fingers lightly traced the carved design in the wood, it brought back pleasant memories. She saw that the headboard and footboard were propped against each other, with the side pieces stacked neatly on the floor in front of them. There didn't seem to be a mattress anywhere in sight, but it couldn't take more than a few days to arrange for one. During that time, the room could be made ready. And against the far wall, she noticed, stood the matching wardrobe. Together the set was a wondrous find!

Tossing a cursory glance around the remainder of the chilly area, she brushed her hands together and left for the stairs, decidedly elated over her good fortune.

"Well," Aunt Phoebe asked on her return, "did you come across anything you might be able to use?"

"Yes. As you said, the bedstead is there, along with the wardrobe. The two of them will be perfect."

She nodded. "Perhaps next time Micah comes by, we can prevail upon him to move those things down to the room for you."

"That would be marvelous. Well, I'd best wash the dust from my hands. It's time to open the shop."

It was all Eliza could do to keep her mind on business that afternoon, so taken was she in imagining a wallpaper pattern that would turn the dreary room into a charming haven and what type of yard goods to purchase for curtains. And she'd only just now thought of toys. At the very least there should be picture books and some dolls to cuddle, perhaps a miniature tea set.

It might do to have a ball and some toy soldiers as well, though at the moment it seemed more prudent to plan for girls. With the likelihood of the Riccio sisters not being able to stay where they were for much longer, Eliza wanted to let Micah know there'd be a place where they would be looked after until permanent arrangements could be made.

"I say," the rather portly matron dressed entirely in black spoke up as she compared two lengths of handmade lace Eliza had given her to peruse. "Which of these would you say might look better used to accent the front of a shirtwaist?" She looked from one to the other and back, then peered up at Eliza.

"If it were up to me, I'd use the one in your left hand. It's just a touch heavier and would stand more wear."

"That's just what I was thinking," the older woman said with a smile. "I'll take both."

"Excellent. Will that be all?"

"Yes, miss. This is all I needed to finish my Christmas shopping." Handing money to Eliza, along with her choices, she meandered among the remaining displays while her purchases were wrapped. "I thank you," she said then, and with parcel in hand, she left.

Eliza checked the mantel clock and sighed. Closing time at last. She hoped Anabelle would come by soon to hear about Aunt Phoebe's decision.

"That should about do it, I'd say." Micah set down his end of the wardrobe he and his friend Charles Sprocket had lugged down from the attic. "How many trips up and down those stairs did this enterprise entail, anyway?"

The wiry redhead wiped his forehead on his sleeve and narrowed his gray eyes to a wince. "Between what we toted up there and what we brought back down to this room, must've been a dozen at least."

On the edge of his vision, Micah saw Anabelle jab an elbow into Eliza's ribs. "Would you listen to those poor, soft, overworked fellows. I never heard such moaning and groaning in my life."

"Nor have I," she agreed as she and Ana began wiping down the wood cabinet inside and out. "Why, Aunt Phoebe was quite set on doing the entire chore herself until I convinced her some strong, handsome gentlemen would make short work of it." She slanted Anabelle a merry glance, and they both giggled.

Charles straightened to his full, unimpressive height and puffed out his chest, which only strengthened the nasal quality of his jesting voice. "Strong as a bull, eh?"

The lad's more-than-interested glances toward Mrs. Harper's alluring niece were not lost on Micah. Obviously his friend was looking forward to escorting her to this evening's sacred concert. "Don't forget handsome," Micah quipped, trying to keep the mood easygoing. "She said 'handsome,' too." But the wink he'd intended for Ana ended up heading in Eliza's direction instead. In their bustling about, the two had somehow changed places. He felt his neck growing warm.

"In any event," Eliza said more seriously, not letting on if she'd noticed his mistake, "we thank you for your trouble. It's been a huge help."

"Seems like an awful lot to go through in wintertime for a mere bedroom," Charles remarked.

Micah tilted his head back and forth. "Oh, I don't know. Mrs. Harper likes company. Must be more relatives coming for the holidays."

At his comment, Anabelle and Eliza traded sly smiles and returned to their chore with renewed fervor.

Whatever this pair was up to, he decided, they seemed to be gaining a lot of enjoyment out of it. He hadn't seen Ana so lively and bubbly in ages. As for Eliza, well, she'd been unaccountably effervescent since Dr. Jenson pronounced her aunt well two days ago. Still, what Anabelle had mentioned regarding a sad loneliness being evident in Eliza's dusky blue eyes now seemed so obvious, Micah wondered why he'd missed noticing it before. He only hoped his redheaded pal treated the gently bred young woman with the respect she deserved.

Beside him, Charles brushed some lingering dust from his trousers and vest, tugging the latter back into proper position. Then he arched his golden brows. "Well, hard work gives a man an appetite. I'm starving."

"Don't fret," Anabelle answered. "Eliza's aunt is planning to serve us a light supper before we leave for the program."

"And we seem to be finished here," Eliza added. "The food must be ready by now."

The fact that Micah's friend had come to lend a hand with the heavy furniture enabled Eliza to relax more than she normally would have in the presence of the virtual stranger. It also made it less awkward for her to agree to Anabelle's suggestion that they make a night of it, since one of the area's larger Presbyterian churches had scheduled a concert that evening.

By the time they arrived to enjoy the collection of hymns and carols rendered by organ, flute, and violin, she felt at ease, if not thrilled, at being in the company of the jovial bachelor. She wasn't quite ready to be escorted places by any young man but assured herself she could endure anything for a few hours. After all, she'd agreed to do

417

this for Anabelle's sake.

Charles, she discovered not long into the program, had what appeared to be a nervous habit, in that he sniffed quite often. It hadn't been obvious at Aunt Phoebe's, as he'd been in and out of the room so much. But here in the quietness of the sanctuary, the intermittent sniffing stood out rather blatantly. Trying not to let on that she noticed, Eliza pretended to be looking the other way whenever he wiped his nose on a wrinkled handkerchief from his pocket. She almost wished he'd just blow the silly thing and be done with it. But the comical mental picture of him honking like a foghorn made her giggle inwardly.

"Something the matter?" Anabelle whispered from the other side of her.

Eliza shook her head and forced her attention toward the front, but it took awhile for her to completely compose herself, until well into the musical numbers.

After the program, the foursome went to a nearby coffee-house called the Wooden Shoe. Each table was decorated in a Dutch motif with a red-and-white checked tablecloth and a vase containing red paper tulips, and Eliza noticed the menus were shaped like windmills. Only a few other tables were occupied when they entered, and those patrons gave them only casual glances as they passed.

Micah led their party to a quiet spot near the back of the establishment and seated Anabelle, while Charles pulled out Eliza's chair for her with exaggerated aplomb. "Your throne, milady."

"I thank you," she replied, elevating her eyebrows. His overt attentions merely encouraged her to maintain her distance from eager young bachelors in the future.

Within seconds, a waitress in Dutch attire took their orders for pie and coffee.

"That was a lovely concert," Anabelle remarked over their dessert. "They played some of my very favorites."

"And I noticed you paying particular interest to the woman at the organ," Eliza said.

"It's a habit of mine," she confessed.

"Well," Micah told her, "that young woman couldn't hold a candle to your talents, don't you agree, Eliza?" He flashed a warm smile.

Anabelle gave her no time to answer. She wrinkled her nose, her green eyes alight. "He always says the nicest things. Not always true, but nice, nonetheless."

Watching the interplay between them, Eliza wondered why they didn't sit closer to each other and why their little shows of affection seemed so few and far between. They almost gave the impression of being an old married couple rather than a man and woman deeply in love.

Well, it was no affair of hers, she told herself, and sampled another portion of her pie.

"Did you enjoy the ensemble's selection of musical numbers, Eliza?" Charles asked, his tone sincere.

"Yes, I thought it was a splendid program, especially the carol arrangements. I had a lovely time."

"Good. I was hoping perhaps you'd consider attending another similar concert with me two evenings hence."

She felt Micah's and Anabelle's eyes center on her. Eliza had told Ana before arranging this outing that she had no desire to begin keeping regular company with young men. Charles, it was true, had been the ultimate gentleman, and she really didn't want to encourage him. But neither did she wish to offend him. "Well, I —"

A shadow fell across their table as someone approached. "Why, Eliza!" a deep voice exclaimed. "What a surprise."

As her gaze swung up to that very familiar face, she felt all the color drain from her own. "W–Weston!" All but choking on the name, she sprang to her feet, toppling her chair in her haste. All thought vanished but one: escape.

Chapter 14

"Eliza! Wait!" Glaring at the intruder, who'd at least had the grace to step backward a pace, Micah jumped up and ran after her, barely acknowledging the astonished looks that passed between his fiancée and Charles Sprocket as he left them behind. He'd seen Eliza upset over her aunt's health, but never had he witnessed her turn white with shock and alarm as she'd done in this instance.

Nearing the door, he spied her warm cloak still hanging where they'd left their outerwear upon entering the restaurant. He plucked it from the hook on his way past and dashed out into the street.

Light snowflakes which had been floating and swirling on the night wind during the concert were now beginning to collect on the ground in a coating so thin it was almost transparent. But thankfully it was enough to indicate which direction Eliza had gone. In the flickering glow of the gaslights, he followed the small footprints around the next corner.

The sound of labored panting came from a darkened doorway of the second building, where he could see Eliza huddled in misery, pressing her hands to her cheeks, as if attempting to cool them.

She was turned slightly away, and at the sound of his footsteps, she let out a petrified scream. "Go away! Leave me alone!"

"Hey, it's all right," he crooned, stooping to draw her to her feet. "It's me. Micah."

She glanced beyond him, her eyes wide with fear. "D–don't make me go back there," she said between great gulps of air. "I don't want to face him."

"I'm not going to make you do anything you don't want to."

Compliant as a child, she allowed him to wrap her cloak about her shivering form. Then she began to cry.

Forgetting all but his concern for her, he pulled her close, cradling the back of her head as he rocked her in his arms. "Shh. You're safe now. No one's going to cause you harm. Come on, we'll see you home." Gently easing her away, he tucked her icy hand in the crook of his elbow and led her back to where they'd parked the buggy.

Anabelle and Charles exited the establishment as he was handing the still-distraught Eliza up into the upholstered backseat. He smiled with relief. "Sit with her, would you, Ana?" he asked quietly. "See what you can do."

She nodded, and when he helped her board, Anabelle took the spot next to Eliza, while the two men took the front seat. Draping an arm about Eliza, Ana hugged her close.

Until he had burst into her life again, Eliza had actually believed she was over the hurt and humiliation of being jilted by Weston Elliot. But the truth was that, for the most part, she had only suppressed her sadness and heartache. The few tears she'd cried in Aunt Phoebe's presence made her feel self-conscious, so she'd gathered the fragmented feelings together and pretended all was well. Yet running into her former betrothed here in New York was the last thing in the world she had ever expected.

Jostling homeward in Micah's buggy, Eliza felt her control gradually returning in the oppressive silence. But she knew her behavior in the Wooden Shoe had to have embarrassed her friends. Charles she cared little about, but what must Micah or Anabelle think of her? How would she ever hold her head up before them again?

Even as she pondered that heavy thought, she felt Ana give her an empathetic pat. Eliza raised her head and met her friend's concerned gaze. "I'm so very sorry. . . ." Her voice caught on a leftover sob. "I didn't mean to —"

Anabelle gave her an understanding smile. "Please; you mustn't apologize, Eliza. Whoever that cad was that he could upset you so, it most certainly is no fault of yours."

"But I spoiled the whole evening, and you must —"

"Pshaw! As I recall it, we were having the grandest of times up until that last moment. I'm just thankful you weren't alone."

So am I, Eliza vehemently agreed. *So am I.*

As it happened, Charles's house was the first they came to on the drive home. Upon reaching it, he hopped out. "Thanks, old man," he said with a smart salute to Micah and a reserved tip of the head toward Eliza and Anabelle. "Good evening, ladies. I rather enjoyed the concert. I trust you're feeling better, Eliza."

She nodded, but couldn't think of a suitable response. It was highly unlikely Charles Sprocket would ever venture within shouting distance of her again, she was certain of that. She just didn't care one way or the other right now.

When Micah at last pulled up before Harper House, he and Ana both alighted and helped Eliza down, then each took an arm to escort her up the walk.

"Thank you," she whispered. "But I can manage the rest of the way on my own. Truly."

"You're sure?" Anabelle prompted.

"Yes, perfectly. I'm fine . . . or will be, in time."

Ana continued to regard her. "Shall we postpone our shopping trip for a day or two?" she finally asked.

"No. Not at all. I'll be ready tomorrow at one, just as we planned. I promise." She added as much of a smile as she could manufacture.

"Well, watch your step," Micah urged. "The snow can be slick if you're not careful."

"I will; thank you." Eliza wanted to utter another heartfelt apology, but the kindness in their expressions would have been her undoing. She settled for something much simpler. "Good evening."

Her friends waited until she reached the door before driving off. Eliza waved and went inside. Finding the house quiet, she extinguished the downstairs lamps her aunt had left on for her, then trudged upstairs to give vent to the remainder of her anguish in private.

Awakening with the first streaks of dawn, Eliza snuggled deeper into the warmth of the blankets and quilts and once again thanked the Lord for getting her through the long night. Along with having emptied her soul of the last remnants of her tears, she had poured her heart out as well, ridding her being of the bitterness she'd been clinging to regarding Weston Elliot. It had taken that one glimpse of the man for her to realize the love she once felt for him was dead. He no longer had the power to hurt her.

With that final acceptance, a joyous peace flowed through her, filling all the secret corners inside. And now, by the grace of God, she knew she could face whatever lay ahead, be it the solitary life she'd found here with Aunt Phoebe or some other road of His choosing. All that mattered was that she be a vessel God could use to glorify His Son.

Gathering daylight had begun to creep between the folds of the window curtains, and Eliza pushed the covers aside so she could get up. She crossed to the washstand for the pitcher and basin and went downstairs for warm water.

Her aunt, always an early riser, was just coming from the kitchen with her own supply of water for her toilette.

"Good morning," they said in unison, then shared a smile as they parted company, each to prepare for the day.

When Eliza came down half an hour later, she found a breakfast of Aunt Phoebe's crepes and maple syrup waiting for her, a wonderful start for a busy morning.

By the time one o'clock arrived, and with it, Anabelle, Eliza was eager to go shopping.

"You're looking surprisingly well," her friend remarked as she stood waiting for Eliza to don her wrap.

Aunt Phoebe turned to Eliza, unspoken questions in her eyes.

"Not to worry, Auntie," she said, slipping into her coat and gloves. "I crossed paths last evening with an old memory, but I'm over it now. I'll tell you all about it later. Right now, we have lots to do. Come on, Ana."

But once outside, Anabelle was not so easily put off. "You're quite certain that everything is well, Eliza? After your distress of last evening, I felt compelled to pray for you when I got home."

Eliza stepped near enough to hug her. "Which is likely one of the reasons why I've come to terms with it, dear friend. Thank you, from the bottom of my heart." Reaching the coach, she accepted the driver's help in boarding and gave him a grateful nod.

"Micah, too, was quite troubled over the whole affair," Anabelle went on, taking the seat opposite her as Graham flicked the lap robe over their legs. "I've scarcely seen him in such a black mood."

Eliza couldn't suppress a guilty sigh. "I feel rather awful that he had to come to my aid, yet I appreciated the fact that he did. Weston's sudden appearance caught me off guard. I'd thought that part of my life was past. I'll apologize to Micah next time I see him for his having dashed from your side like that just to rescue me."

"It's not necessary, really." Anabelle averted her attention to the passing buildings, and for a length of time, neither of them spoke.

Eliza finally broke the silence. "Weston Elliot, the man who approached me at the restaurant, was once my fiancé."

Her companion's green eyes turned to Eliza.

"Yes," Eliza continued before she used up her nerve. "Shortly before our wedding was to take place, he ran off with my best friend." There. It was out. She'd actually said the words.

Anabelle's jaw dropped open. "You can't be serious. Why, no wonder it was a shock to see him again out of the blue."

With a nod of agreement, Eliza went on to confide the whole sordid affair. "So, as you might imagine," she said in conclusion, "I've been quite bitter at both of them for some time."

"And with good reason. Such nerve." Ana wagged her bonneted head.

"What's even more strange, however, is that I received word from my mother recently telling me that Melanie had returned home alone. She would speak to no one, but shut herself up in her old room. I didn't know what to make of it."

"Nor would I."

"In any event, last night I finally prostrated myself before God and turned over my misery and bitterness to Him. I didn't want to hold onto it for one more hour of my life. And He not only quite graciously took my burdens upon Himself like He promised, but He then filled me with the most incredible peace. I feel I can face anything now with Him beside me."

"Thank you, Eliza, for telling me all of

this. I understand quite a lot of things now."

The carriage came to a halt in front of Macy's department store, and Graham again assisted the girls. "I'll be back for you in two hours, miss, to see if you've finished or need to be taken elsewhere."

"That will be fine. Thank you." Smiling, Anabelle reached for Eliza's hand, and the two of them hurried toward the entrance.

Eliza had been inside some elegant stores in her life, but none compared to this one for the fashionably attired patrons bustling about or the variety of merchandise available on every floor. Her gaze lost itself in festive displays reminding her of the approaching holiday season, but she was quick to remind herself that Christmas was not the primary reason for this shopping excursion.

By the time the allotted two hours drew to a close, they both had their arms filled with packages. "We couldn't possibly have forgotten anything, could we?" Eliza asked hopefully.

"Not that I can think of," Ana replied. "If it weren't for the fact that we must wait for delivery of the mattress, we could have the room set up for occupancy by this evening. But in the unlikely event we've overlooked something else that's crucial, we'll just schedule another shopping venture. I haven't had this much fun in ever so long."

"Neither have I. Won't Aunt Phoebe be amazed at all the practical and nice things we found for that room? I can't wait to show her."

Exiting the huge doors to the street outside, they spotted Graham waiting for them, and in no time at all, they were back at Harper House.

"I'm afraid I can't stay longer today," Anabelle confessed as she and her driver helped Eliza take all the purchases inside, "but I'll be back tomorrow morning. Perhaps between the two of us, we'll be able to make some progress in the room."

"I'll look forward to it. Thanks ever so much for coming with me today. It was grand to have your help, Ana."

As Eliza hung her wrap and watched the Dumonts' coach pull away and turn homeward, she heard Aunt Phoebe's step approaching her from behind.

"You have a visitor, dear. A tall gentleman, waiting for you in the sitting room. I was busy with customers when he first arrived, so I'm afraid I didn't get his name."

Instinctively, Eliza knew who it was. Her calmness amazed her, but she breathed a prayer for strength.

"Shall I make tea?"

"No, thank you, Auntie. I would appreciate it if you would come with me as I speak to him however."

Though puzzled, Aunt Phoebe gave a consenting nod and moved to her side. "As you wish."

Eliza opened the French doors to the sitting room.

Weston got up immediately, dressed impeccably, as always. He'd grown a mustache, which somehow lengthened his face. "Eliza. Thank you for seeing me."

"Weston." She turned to her aunt. "Aunt Phoebe, this is Weston Elliot. I'm sure you've heard me mention his name."

"Yes." The older woman paled, yet remained nonplused as she glanced from the visitor to Eliza, then back again. "Mr. Elliot."

"Madam." He cleared his throat and sought Eliza's face. "Might we speak in private?"

"I think not. Whatever you have to say to me, you may say in front of my aunt." She motioned for the older woman to be seated, then took a chair near her. "Why have you come?"

A look of resignation crossed his chiseled features. Absently he toyed with the brim of his bowler, turning it around in his hands as his hazel eyes met hers.

"I hadn't planned to, actually, but when I happened to see you last night, I —" He glanced between them as if ill at ease, and his demeanor turned stony. "Confound it all, Eliza. I must speak to you alone."

Appalled that she had ever considered him handsome — or worse — compared him to a man as noble as Micah Richmond, Eliza hiked her chin. "I'm afraid that is not possible, Weston. You gave up that right some time ago. We have nothing further to discuss. I must ask you to leave now."

He studied her, as if expecting her to waver — as well she might have, in time past. When she did not, he expelled a huff of breath. "I'll go. For now. But not before I tell you what I came to say. I still love you, Eliza —"

Her incredulous gasp made no impression.

"And I shall be back. I want you to give us another chance."

Eliza turned to her aunt, her brows arched high. "Can you believe the man's gall, Auntie? Having cast me aside to dally with my bosom friend, he has now apparently done the same to Melanie, yet imagines I should take him back again, as if nothing untoward ever occurred between us."

Rising with measured dignity, he pursed his lips.

Was that anger she detected in that guarded expression?

"But I was a fool," came his placating explanation. "I see that now."

Even knowing what it cost a man like him to make that admission, Eliza held her ground. "Well so was I, Weston, the worst kind of fool. But I'll not make that mistake again. It is over between us, now and forever. I have no desire to rekindle the cold ashes of an old fire. And I do not wish ever to lay eyes upon you again in this lifetime."

As she spoke, she watched a mutinous gleam rise in his eyes.

"I suggest you go back to your wife. Melanie could still be vulnerable to those questionable charms of yours."

His mustache quirked to one side. "I have no wife. I never married Melanie."

Eliza's mouth gaped in shock. "Then you are without a doubt the most despicable man I've ever had the misfortune to know. Get out of my sight, Weston Elliot. And do not come back here again. Ever."

A muscle worked in his jaw as he stared at her long and hard. But with little more than a flicker of a glance at her companion, he slapped his gloves against his palm, plunked his hat atop his obstinate head, and stalked away.

More than the bell rattled as the front door slammed shut behind him.

Eliza and her aunt sat stunned.

"Well," the older woman finally said, giving Eliza's knee an approving pat. "I assume that was the 'memory' you mentioned earlier."

"One and the same."

She chuckled. "I was never more proud of you, my dear. You showed the snake a lot of backbone."

"It was a gift from the Lord. Last night."

"Odd, though," Aunt Phoebe remarked. "He reminded me vaguely of someone."

Eliza laughed aloud. "I thought the same thing once, myself. But believe me, Auntie, I was entirely mistaken."

With a nod of agreement, she looked directly into Eliza's eyes. "And are you truly all right now?"

Smiling, she stood to help the dear woman to her feet. "I feel a bit like someone who just survived a battle, but it's comforting to be on the side that won. Do you suppose a cup of tea might be in order now, for a celebration?"

"I do, indeed."

But despite her brave show of force, Eliza couldn't help feeling sad for the girl who'd once been her cherished friend and whose life now was ruined. Silently she asked the Lord to heal Melanie Brown and to restore her self-respect.

CHAPTER 15

"Well, that's the end of it," Eliza said, stepping back to admire the last length of wallpaper she'd hung in place, its design one of charming forest animals frolicking amid groves of trees. "And not bad, for someone who's previously only watched the process from a safe distance, I might add." She leveled a glance at Anabelle, seeking her approval.

Her friend, though decidedly less than keen on messing with gummy paste or sloppy brushes, had made a valiant attempt at lending a hand. She appeared almost as disheveled as Eliza felt. "I'd say it looks . . . sufficiently . . . childlike."

Sputtering into a giggle, Eliza turned her eyes heavenward. "Are you telling me it resembles the work of a child?"

"No, not at all." Ana pinkened delicately. "What I meant was it should appeal to one."

"Oh, well that's better. Then let's clean

up the rest of this clutter so we can go down for a bite of dinner. You must be just as hungry as I am, after all this hard work."

Already gathering remnants of discarded wall covering together in a somewhat neat pile, Anabelle straightened and assessed the room. "When the mattress is delivered and we make up the bed, it should be quite homey in here."

"Especially after I finish hemming the curtains and put them up," Eliza added. "I truly appreciate your help, Ana."

"I'm amazed we've been able to accomplish so much in only a few days."

"Well, I just hope it's soon enough." She swung dreamily around in a circle, her arms wide. "Oh, can't you just picture a little girl or two, coming here from a shabby hovel where people have been crowded together like cattle? Imagine how it'll feel to realize there'll be only one other person in this huge bed, in a clean room with pretty colors and lots of new playthings. . . ."

The honey blond tilted her head back and forth, her demeanor unreadable.

"Of course, I know this whole effort might be for naught," Eliza continued as she resumed tidying up. "It could turn out that there are suddenly enough beds at other shelters. Maybe there won't be a need for one more place, temporary or otherwise. But just knowing that if one arises, we do have a suitable room should make this all worthwhile. And won't it be fun seeing the expression on Micah's face when he finds out what we've done?"

"He's sure to be surprised. It's been hard not confessing why I've been spending so much time with you these past few days." A wistful smile lit Ana's features. "But here I've been, deriving pleasure from merely decorating a bedroom, while you've been thinking ahead to its occupants, to helping those he carries such a burden for. I . . . sometimes wish I could feel as strongly as he does about them. As strongly as you seem to."

Eliza knew the young woman had spoken candidly, and though she had almost as hard a time understanding how someone could *not* care about the hopeless predicament faced by so many immigrants, she did not feel it was her place to judge. "You do what you can in contributions and your sewing. Everything helps, believe me."

"Perhaps." She paused, as if trying to formulate her next comment. When she spoke again, her voice was subdued. "But I often wonder if I will ever truly be the wife Micah needs."

Setting aside the refuse she had gathered, Eliza crossed the room to give her an encouraging hug. "Don't be silly. You two have loved each other forever. And that's what's most important in a marriage."

"Is it?" Anabelle asked quietly, drawing away. "Then, why haven't we *been* married forever already? Most of our friends have made that commitment and are now in the throes of parenthood, raising broods of children. Micah and I, on the other hand, merely see each other every day — or almost every day. And instead of growing closer, we're almost —"

She waved a hand uselessly before her face. "Oh, never mind. I shouldn't bother you with our problems."

"That's what friends are for, is it not?" Eliza answered gently. "Personally, I feel your concerns are completely ungrounded, and that in time, you two will work out your differences and get married. See if you don't."

But Anabelle didn't seem overly comforted by Eliza's assurance. She just bent down and picked up some of the trash.

Making a hasty loop of the horse's reins at the hitching post in front of the Dumont house, Micah all but ran up the walk. He paused at the door to straighten his coat sleeves and catch his breath, then rapped.

In seconds, Anabelle swung the portal wide and stepped out of the way so he could enter. "We thought you weren't coming. We've already started without you."

"I'm truly sorry I'm late, sweetheart, but I'm afraid it couldn't be avoided." Removing his gloves, hat, and coat, he disposed of them on the hall tree.

"Let me guess," she challenged in syrupy tones, arms crossed as she eyed him with irritation. "Some destitute family needed groceries, and there's no one on Earth who can see they get some but you. Or yet another street urchin out in the cold, with no place to go until you happened by. Or —"

Clasping her upper arms, Micah looked directly into her eyes, the gray-green depths decidedly cooler than normal. He tempered the tone of his voice, not wanting to speak harshly to her, yet pronouncing the words slowly and distinctly. "It's what I do, Ana. I go where there's a need, wherever and whenever I must. You know that. You've always known it."

She pressed her lips into a thin line and stared for a few seconds before relenting. "Yes, I know. It's just — I get so tired of waiting for you, never knowing if you'll be on time, or late, or even come at all. And Mother and Papa are forever asking when they might start plans for the wedding, and . . ."

Drawing her close, Micah hugged her. "I understand, sweetheart, I really do. And I wish I could make things easier for you. I just don't know how."

"Yes, you do," she insisted, her cheek against his chest. "You could find some other employment. There are lots of other ways one can help people. In fact, Papa told me there's an opening at the bank for someone with your qualifications. You'd be able to arrange financial aid for the unfortunates."

"Ana, I —"

"Are you coming to the table, Daughter?" came her father's voice from the dining room.

"Yes, Papa. We'll be right there." Releasing a weary breath, she stepped out of Micah's embrace and took his arm. "Come on; we always set a place for you, regardless."

In the face of the false smile she'd plastered on, he hesitated.

She gave another tug, a trifle more playful this time.

He still didn't move. He could see she was in a mood, one that had been coming on for some time. Well, so was he, and he was getting rather tired of always defending his calling. "Now and then I wish you'd be just a little more understanding," he heard himself say, the words coming out before he could stop them. "I've had a beastly day today. Nothing worked out right, no matter what I tried. Everywhere I turn there's more need than I can alleviate —"

"Need, need, need," she wailed, rocking back on her heels, bright circles of color rising on her cheeks. "Honestly, between you and Eliza, I hear more than I can bear about poor people and homeless children and the miserable, huddled masses. Why don't you two put your heads together and come up with some grand plan or noble scheme that'll solve all the problems of mankind! Obviously she suits you more than I ever will."

"What?" Flabbergasted at the uncharacteristic outburst, Micah could only gape at her.

"Anabelle!" From the dining room a chair scraped back.

"Supper's getting cold," she muttered through clenched teeth.

"Well, I thank you for the invitation," he

said, rising anger throbbing through him with each beat of his heart, "but I find I have no appetite after all." Crossing to the hall tree, he put on his coat. "Good night."

"Oh Micah . . ." Her tone turned apologetic.

Past caring, and not even bothering to close the door after himself, Micah strode purposefully to his buggy, yanking the reins free on his way to the seat. He clucked his tongue and slapped the traces against the horse's back without so much as a backward glance.

In his room a short while later, he kneaded his jaw, forcing himself to relax those muscles. Now that he'd calmed down, he wasn't really angry with Anabelle so much as disappointed. And at the end of his patience. How could it be that despite all his efforts and a virtual mountain of fervent prayers, his fiancée was no closer to accepting his ministry, but in fact seemed to be drifting farther from it? Why couldn't she be more like —

Without permitting his wayward mind to complete the comparison, he sank to his knees. He was done in, mentally and physically, and knew he lacked whatever it took to deal with disillusionment right now. He needed a new supply of wisdom and strength . . . the kind he could obtain only from spending time with his Lord.

"Hm. I wonder why Anabelle hasn't come today?" Eliza mused, checking out the window for the dozenth time. The pale afternoon sun was well on its downward slide, lengthening the shadows of the hemlock trees.

Aunt Phoebe set down the crystal vase she'd been dusting and turned. "Well, it is quilting day. Perhaps she was needed at the sewing circle, for a change."

"I'm sure that must be it. I have rather been taking over her every spare moment lately. I just surmised that with the mattress due to be delivered this afternoon, she'd have wanted to be here to help me make up the bed with the lovely variegated green counterpane she helped pick out."

"I wouldn't worry about it, dear. No doubt she'll come by tomorrow."

Crossing to the chair to put the final stitches into a pair of soft green-and-white curtains, Eliza retook her seat. "I suppose you're right, Auntie." *But surely Ana would have mentioned something about having another engagement,* Eliza told herself.

Her unease multiplied a short time later, when she looked up from counting the

446

number of lace scarves remaining in one of the gift shop cabinets, to see Micah Richmond entering the room.

"Oh yes, the contribution," Aunt Phoebe said as he approached the counter.

"I know it's not my usual day, ladies," he said cheerily, "but I was in the neighborhood." He glanced around in curiosity. "Ana's not here?"

Eliza shook her head. "Her talents must have been needed at church. I've been monopolizing the poor girl far too much these days."

"Strange; I just came from there. When I stopped by to see if they'd finished any new quilts, everyone started hounding me with questions, wondering why she hasn't been coming lately."

Prickles of alarm skittered down Eliza's back. "Weren't you with her last night? Did she mention having other plans or anything?"

Tugging at his cravat, he cleared his throat. "I . . . uh . . . did go there for supper, actually. Couldn't stay long though. She didn't say much."

"How odd," Aunt Phoebe murmured. "Now I'm beginning to worry about the dear girl myself."

"Well, put your minds at ease, my friends,"

Micah said with assurance. "I'll call on her this evening and find out if anything's amiss. Perhaps she's had one of her headaches and wanted to rest at home."

"Of course," the older woman said, sounding somewhat encouraged.

"Be sure to give her our love," Eliza added. "And tell her we missed her smiling face around here."

"I'll do that." With a grin, he turned for the door.

"Wait, son. I've yet to give you my contribution," Aunt Phoebe said.

Halting, he swung around, chagrined. "Oh yes. I must be a touch overtired myself." Accepting the funds she held out to him, he left.

Eliza didn't know how long she continued to watch after him, but when she caught herself staring into nothingness, she sent a silent prayer aloft for Anabelle.

It took considerable courage for Micah to approach his fiancée's home that evening, considering his hasty and heated departure the previous night. But after so many people had asked about her during the day, he was concerned. Tying the horse at the rail, he strode up to the door and knocked.

Anabelle's mother answered the sum-

mons. "Oh. Micah. I wasn't expecting you."
Ever dignified and proper, every graying
brown hair on her queenly head in place,
there came no typical smile to soften the
timeless beauty of her face. But the familiar
countenance seemed no less friendly, despite a few added lines around her green
eyes — eyes that were lightly rimmed in red
at the moment.

"I wasn't coming for supper, Mother Dumont. I was wondering if I might speak with
Ana."

Nibbling the corner of her lip, she shifted
from one foot to the other, as if hesitating
to answer at first. "I'm afraid she isn't available just now."

"To anyone," he asked, "or just to me?"

Another slight hesitation. "She asked me
to give you something. Wait just a moment."
Withdrawing from the immediate vicinity of
the door, she returned directly, a sealed
envelope in her hand. "I hope this will
answer your questions. I —" A mist rose in
her eyes, and she closed them momentarily
while she swallowed. "Good evening,
Micah."

Ana's letter clutched in his hand, he
watched as the door closed gently in his
face, leaving him little choice but to go
home.

CHAPTER 16

Micah lingered on the Dumonts' doorstep for a long moment, debating whether to knock again and hope Anabelle would come to the door this time. Or if she didn't, perhaps her mother would go into a few more details. It was quite obvious the woman had been crying. What had upset her?

But considering the close relationship he had always enjoyed with Ana's parents, Mother Dumont wouldn't have hesitated to invite him inside — or at the very least, answer the question he'd put to her — unless something was very, very wrong.

Releasing a pent-up breath, he slid the letter she had given him into an inside pocket and walked back to his buggy. Then he took the shortest route back to Columbus Avenue and made quick work of stabling the horse and parking the buggy before going into his room.

The place was cool from being vacant and shut up all day, but the temperature didn't faze him as he tossed his coat and hat onto the arm of the sofa. More for light than heat, he lit the logs he routinely laid in the fireplace each morning, then lit the lamp next to his overstuffed chair and sank wearily to the seat. In seconds he had Ana's letter open:

My dearest Micah,

After the way I spoke to you when we were last together, I felt horrid. To think you and I would ever come to the place where we could actually say hurtful things to each other dealt me a crushing blow. Knowing you as I do, you must have felt the same.

Be that as it may, I cannot help but believe we were honest in expressing our innermost feelings. Perhaps more truthful than we have ever been before.

"Were we, Anabelle? We barely discussed anything. There wasn't time to really talk." Shifting in his chair, Micah focused again on the neatly penned missive:

But there were important things which I, for one, left unsaid. I will try to write

451

them as best I can now.

I think I have always loved you. Whether that fact can be attributed to the long-standing relationship shared by our parents, or perhaps even came to be because of it, I cannot be sure. Certainly knowing their grand expectations for us had to have played some part in our planning to marry one day.

Micah, despite himself, had to agree with that statement, at least to some extent. Yet there'd never been anyone else — for either of them. Didn't that prove something? Impatiently he looked back at the letter:

I doubt it is possible to completely analyze the deep affection I feel for you. You have been my best friend, my confidant, at times even a big brother, offering whatever I needed, always giving the best of yourself. You could give no less, for that is the kind of man you are.

I am, and have always been, very proud of you, Micah. It has been with great joy and wonder that I watched you turn from a freckle-faced lad who delighted in putting frogs in my pocket, to a handsome champion of the downtrodden. The Lord has blessed you with that kind of generous and unselfish nature, and in my heart I know He has wonderful things in store for you.

However, I have recently come to realize that those plans do not include me.

"You can't mean that, Ana. We've always planned to marry one day. There's no reason we couldn't. Or shouldn't. We'd be throwing away a lifetime of caring." Emitting a ragged breath, he read on:

Looking around at so many of our closest friends and their marriages, I cannot help but see that for a marriage to endure there must be a certain kind of harmony. And though you and I possess that in some ways, it is sadly lacking in the most important one. Try as I might, I cannot force myself to enter into that benevolent work you feel is your ministry.

"No, you're wrong. You just need time. Time, and maybe an opportunity to come with me on my calls, to see things with your own eyes. It would make a difference."

For that reason, I have decided to leave New York for an undetermined period.

Micah slammed a palm against the armrest of his chair. Where would she have gone?

I have petitioned my parents not to divulge my whereabouts. We need an opportunity to be apart from each other and seek the will of the Lord in regards to our future.

At this, he crumpled the pages in his hands and lay his head back, staring at the ceiling. A deep emptiness surged through him, one so profound he could hardly bring himself to read farther. But finally the need to know the rest made him unravel the letter and smooth out the wrinkles as best he could.

Meanwhile, I pray you will not cease your efforts concerning the immigrants for whom you carry such a heavy burden. I will think of you charging off to their rescue each morning. I draw great comfort from knowing that others, like Eliza, share that call. Through my friendship with her, I came as close as I ever could to actually entering into your ministry. Truly, her heart is as big as yours. The two of you would make a wonderful team. And should it grow beyond that, one day, I should hold no ill feelings against either of my two very dearest friends.

Please don't forget me, dearest Micah, for you will always be in my most fervent prayers.

With deepest love,
Anabelle

Utterly stunned, Micah could neither think nor pray. There'd never been a time in his life when Ana hadn't been there for him. True, they'd drifted somewhat apart when he began working with Child Placement, but he'd always envisioned their relationship eventually deepening to include that.

But this. This sounded so final, as if she had already thought about it and prayed about it and come to this irrevocable conclusion. She would go her way; he would go his. It wasn't supposed to happen like this.

Was it?

Morning dawned hours later than usual, Micah was sure of that. Not having slept at all during the longest night of his life, the first streaks of daylight found him still in his clothes in the upholstered chair. All too soon he'd have to leave for work.

455

Have to go about this day as if nothing unusual had occurred.

Have to get involved with other people's troubles and struggles with the same fervor he'd always shown.

His spirit was too heavy to pray. He'd tried, heaven knew he'd tried, but no words would come. And now as he sat listless and lifeless, he wondered how many days and nights would pass before he became accustomed to existing without the one person who'd made up almost the entire other half of his world.

Releasing all the air from his lungs in a whoosh, he dragged himself up and headed for his shaving brush and razor. And he hoped for all he was worth that there wouldn't be some huge problem to deal with today.

Eliza tucked the sheets around the mattress in the newly outfitted guest room, then added a blanket and counterpane before fluffing the pillows. She felt guilty that she hadn't waited for Anabelle, but there'd been no word of her friend as yet.

Moving to the wardrobe, she assessed its contents. Ana's parents, upon hearing of the venture, had contributed generously toward a variety of simple nightwear and everyday clothing and underthings to keep in store, plus several kinds and sizes of shoes for young children of either gender. But Eliza's first thoughts continued to center on the little Riccio girls, whose plight had inspired this action on her part. Somehow it seemed only right if they turned out to be the first occupants of this small haven.

She stepped to the doorway and swung a critical glance about. It was as ready as it ever would be.

It was nearing suppertime when Micah at last made an appearance. Something in the sag of his shoulders, the lack of the usual twinkle in his eye, signaled dire news. Eliza observed a peculiar tightness in his expression and new lines of strain, particularly around his mouth. It almost seemed an effort for him to smile.

Aunt Phoebe, obviously having drawn the same conclusions, spoke up first. "My. It would appear this has not been the best of days. Is something amiss?"

He drew his lips into a grim line. "I've had better."

"Well, sit right down, lad. We were just about to partake of supper, but there's plenty. If you've no other plans, perhaps you'd be interested in joining us, for a change — unless you're expected elsewhere."

His nod of acceptance seemed to indicate a slight improvement in spirit. "If you don't think you'll find me depressing company. As it turns out, I do happen to be on my own tonight."

"Not at all," she assured him. "It'll be a rare treat for my niece and me. We get weary of only having each other to look at across a table." Waving him to the nearest chair, she turned to Eliza. "Bring the man some tea, will you, dear? And I'll check on our meal."

Hurrying to do her aunt's bidding, Eliza couldn't help wondering why Micah wouldn't be supping with the Dumonts, as was his custom. Whatever the reason, though, it truly would be nice to have someone to talk to over supper besides her aged relative. She poured a cup of strong tea and took it to the parlor. "Do you take sugar? Cream?" she asked, handing him the drink.

Warmth returned to his eyes when he smiled. "Cream sometimes, but black will do. Thanks."

"Supper will be ready shortly. Just sit here and relax." At his nod, she returned to the kitchen.

Over succulent roast chicken and buttered

potatoes a little while later, Aunt Phoebe managed to keep the conversation centered around pleasantries while Micah gradually lost much of his somberness. And when at last he started appearing more himself, she finally broached the earlier topic. "So, you mentioned you were having a horrid day before you came to us."

He nodded grimly, but now, at least, with some of the old optimism.

"Bad news from the Garibaldis?" Eliza probed, her pulse quickening as she anticipated his surprised pleasure upon discovering her and Anabelle's secret awaiting upstairs.

"It's partly that, yes. I'm afraid it's as we feared. The couple finds it impossible to continue providing for their friends' orphaned daughters. They need to be relieved of the burden immediately. And I'm out of options. There's just no place to put them."

"Oh, but there is," Eliza blurted out.

He looked up, as if suddenly seeing her for the first time.

"It was a surprise. Anabelle and I have been working on it for days."

Some of the customary ruddiness in his complexion paled. He cleared his throat. "What do you mean?"

Eliza sought her aunt's approving nod and

took heart. "That guest room you and Charles carried furniture into — well — Aunt Phoebe has allowed me to furnish it to be used as a shelter for children. Whenever you find you have one or two little ones who have absolutely nowhere else to go, we can put them up, temporarily, until more permanent arrangements can be made."

"You're not joking?"

"Of course not, silly. And it would thrill me no end to be able to look after little Rosa and Gabriella while you find them a new home. However long it takes."

He shook his head in wonder. "I am speechless. Never in a million years would I have imagined something like this."

"Would you care to see it?"

Looking from Eliza to her aunt and back again, Micah blotted his mouth on his napkin and stood. "Lead the way, dear girl. Lead the way."

She smiled and impulsively snatched him by the hand, grabbing a lantern from the hallway on their way to the staircase. Then she all but raced up the steps with him in tow. Nibbling her lip in anticipation, she flung the door wide and gestured for him to enter. She held the lantern high.

"Look at this," he said in awe, stepping inside, his words carrying a tone of incredulity. He surveyed the new quarters momentarily, then turned to search her face. "And this was all your idea, I take it?"

Nodding, Eliza felt a blush warming her cheeks. "But Aunt Phoebe had some good suggestions, and of course, Anabelle helped me pick things out, plus did half the work. We could hardly keep from telling you! And her parents, the Dumonts, gave us money to buy some children's clothing. What do you think?"

"What do I think?" He scratched his head, still displaying overwhelming surprise. "I'm deeply touched, Eliza. More so than I can express. I felt on the verge of complete hopelessness when I arrived at your door this evening, yet now, I —" He turned to glance once more into the room, bracing a hand on the doorjamb as he took everything in.

Eliza, deeply moved at Micah's inability to express his feelings, stayed her tears. "I only wish Anabelle had come with you," she murmured. "It was as much her surprise as it was mine. She should have been in on your reaction, too."

Micah's back was to her at the moment, and she saw him stiffen, heard the ragged intake of breath. His palm slid down the wooden frame. "She . . . uh . . . is gone, Eliza."

"Gone?" she echoed, the pitch of her voice high in disbelief. "What do you mean, gone?"

"Just that." He turned, placing both hands on her shoulders as he looked straight into her eyes. "Anabelle has left New York — for good, apparently — and I haven't a clue where she is."

CHAPTER 17

Eliza gawked at Micah for a full minute, aghast. "You can't be serious! Anabelle, gone? How can that be possible? I don't believe it. I won't."

"Believe it or not, it's your choice," he said resignedly. "Nevertheless, she has left New York, for who knows where. Mother Dumont would give me no information, I can't think of any distant relatives. Nothing."

"And she led you to assume she won't be coming back?"

"Quite."

Becoming aware of a throbbing in her temples, Eliza drifted to the top landing and sank onto it, setting the lantern on the floor while she cupped her head. Then she looked back up at him, his features heavily shadowed in the subdued light. "But why? What possible reason could Ana have had for simply vanishing from us so suddenly? She never even hinted she was unhappy. Oh, this is all too much."

Micah eased down beside her and rested his elbows on his thighs, his hands dangling between his knees as he stared straight ahead. "I couldn't have put it better myself."

"But didn't she say anything to you? Give any warning at all?" It was so reminiscent of when Weston and Melanie disappeared out of the blue.

He shook his head.

Eyeing him, Eliza sensed he knew more than he was telling her. "And she left no word whatsoever?"

He winced. "A letter. Her mother gave it to me last night."

"Well at least that's something, is it not? What did Ana say? If you don't mind my asking of course."

"It's a long story, Eliza. I'm not sure I can go into it all just yet. I'm still having problems enough dealing with it as it is."

"Oh, do forgive me. I'm sure it must have been quite personal." She paused. "There wasn't . . . I mean, it wasn't . . . well, surely no other man was involved." The very idea made Eliza cringe.

"Not to my knowledge, no."

"That's comforting at least."

Micah gave a little huff. "Small comfort, I'd say."

"Of course. I'm sorry, Micah, really I am. This is just so unexpected. I can't quite figure out what to make of it. I can't even think."

He tilted his head and opened his mouth as if about to ask something, then closed it again.

"What is it?"

Studying his hand as he flexed and unflexed it, he finally turned to Eliza but then couldn't hold her gaze. "I don't suppose . . . that is, did she ever express any doubts to you . . . concerning our engagement?"

Eliza searched back in her memory, trying to dredge up every last word Anabelle had said during the times they'd been together. "I know she loves you very much and has done so most of her life. But she did wonder aloud, once, if she'd ever be the sort of wife you needed."

"That's what she wrote in the letter, too," he admitted miserably. "Utterly ridiculous, really — especially since her doubts seem connected primarily to my work. But any misgivings she might have had she should have discussed with me. And we could have worked them out together."

Eliza could only nod in agreement.

"Well," he said at length, "it seems neither of us has much light to shed on the situation. At least, not enough to make her action seem even remotely practical." He got up and offered a hand. "I do thank you for the listening ear, anyway. You're about the closest friend I've got at the moment."

Placing her fingers into his, Eliza shook her head as she rose, grasping the lantern on her way. "Considering what becomes of my 'best friends,' " she muttered dryly as they slowly descended, "I wouldn't count your association with me much of an asset."

He chuckled under his breath. "Nevertheless, we're all each other seems to have at the moment. And we may appreciate knowing there's one person with whom we feel free to unburden our souls."

Eliza found that statement oddly comforting.

"Speaking of burdens," he said as they reached the bottom, "might I assume your problem of the other evening has worked itself out?"

Another maddening blush did its best to appear. "Yes. After considerable prayer and submission to the Lord's will, the matter is ended. That particular man won't bother me again."

"Good. Ana and I prayed for you when we parted that night."

"Thank you. I —"

"Oh, there you two are," Aunt Phoebe said, breezing toward them. "I've cleared the table of the meal, made a pot of fresh coffee, and am about to serve dessert, if anyone's interested."

"Sounds good to me," Micah said pleasantly.

Eliza only smiled, and they gathered around the table once again.

"What did you think of the new guest room upstairs?" the older woman asked, slicing a generous wedge of chocolate cake and passing it to their guest.

"Most amazing. I had absolutely no idea the ladies had undertaken such a marvelous project. Eliza tells me you're in agreement to my bringing a child or two here on occasion, to be looked after temporarily?"

She nodded and served the next piece to Eliza. "I did have a few reservations about the matter, but my niece assures me she will manage the venture adequately."

"Well," Micah replied, "it would appear you'll be having your first young visitors tomorrow. I can't say for how long they'll need lodging, but I will be doing my utmost to find them a permanent family."

"We'll be ready," Eliza said. But the excitement she had expected to feel was tempered now with the sad news of Ana-

belle's absence.

Loading the meager bundle of his young charges' belongings into the buggy before heading back inside, Micah drew a fortifying breath and prayed for strength to get the children through yet another wrenching parting. Even before the Garibaldis' doorway came into view, he could hear wailing and sobbing echoing the length of the dreary hallway. A few curious heads peeked out of other apartments lining the corridor.

"Dere, dere, bambinos," the overwrought woman of the household crooned soothingly as he approached. "Nice'a Mr. Richmond, he finda you a new mama, new papa. Everyt'inga be better, eh?"

"N–no, no," Gabriella sobbed, clinging to her guardian's legs with the dogged strength of a six-year-old. "We s–staya here. Wit you."

Tiny Rosa, smothered protectively in a tangle of other dark-eyed children's arms, peered between them from a few feet away, her doe eyes huge with fear.

By now even the lady herself had to blot tears on her apron as she looked hopelessly to Micah, then patted the little girl's head. "It'a be better. You see. We come'a visit sometime."

"No, Mama," Vinnie whined, confusion

drawing his boyish eyebrows into a V above his nose as he huddled over Rosa. "Dey can have my food. Don'a make'a dem go. Please, no."

But in a show of sheer determination, she peeled Gabriella's thin arms from around herself and shoved her forcibly to Micah. "It'sa for da best. You see. Better nobody starve."

Trying his utmost to hang onto the distraught, weeping little girl even now twisting to get out of his clutches, Micah watched Mrs. Garibaldi extract the younger sister from her own children's embrace and deposit the toddler in his free arm. Then, somehow managing to corral her own little ones behind one deceptively strong arm and leg, she closed the door with her other hand, and the wailing on that side diminished by half.

Gabriella's, however, went up a few notches. "No! No! Don'a take us awa–a–y–y–y." Using all her energy now in a last desperate attempt to squirm free, she slipped low enough to give a mighty kick to her abductor's shin.

Micah saw stars as the searing pain shot up his entire leg but grasped the girls even harder, limping the remaining distance to the buggy.

To alleviate the damp chill of the day, he'd draped a quilt open on the seat beside his place. Depositing the children onto it, he held them in place while making swift work of wrapping the bulky lengths around the pair.

Gabriella, though still crying audibly, appeared to recognize her inevitable defeat. The sobs turned to coughs, and she went rigid, sitting stiff as a board while Micah tucked the free ends under her and her sister's slight weight. Rosa's bewilderment led only to whimpers as she huddled close to her sibling.

Fairly confident that he was winning, Micah gulped a huge breath and climbed aboard, clucking the horse into motion. He knew better than to count the victory prematurely, though, and sought assistance from the Lover of all children even as he pulled out onto the thoroughfare.

During the long drive to Harper House, he kept up a running dialogue in the quiet tones of a confidant. "I know you'll like the nice room where you'll be spending the night. Some of my real good friends have fixed it up especially for you. These ladies love children, but God never gave them any of their own, so they just help little ones whenever they can. They'll have plenty of good food and even some things for you to play with all the time you're there. I expect you to remember the manners your mama and Mrs. Garibaldi taught you and be on your best behavior."

Beside him, Gabriella hunched deeper into the confining folds of patchwork squares, leftover sobs still racking her spindly form. She stared miserably in the direction of her shrouded feet but didn't respond.

His own heart melting over their despair, Micah's prayers turned to petitions for Eliza and Mrs. Harper, that the Lord would provide wisdom, grace, and fortitude beyond all their expectations.

When they finally neared the wide panorama of the Hudson, its waves sparkling up ahead, he turned the bay toward Harper House, circling around to the back door. He felt Gabriella brace herself as he drew to a stop. "We're here, girls. Let me help you down."

As if all the spirit had drained out of her, the six-year-old offered no resistance when Micah unwrapped the quilt and set her and her sister onto the ground. Then, tucking their bundle under one arm, he took their hands on either side of him and led them up the walk.

A tapered finger parted the curtain, and Eliza met his gaze with a tentative smile before opening the door. She stooped down to the level of the little newcomers, but wisely maintained her distance since the pair had been sleeping the only time she'd been in their presence. "Well, who have we here?"

"This is Gabriella Riccio," he said, tipping his head first at one, then at the other, "and her sister, Rosa. Girls, I'd like you to meet Miss Eliza. She'll be looking after you for a while."

This time, the sad-eyed youngsters shrank imperceptibly back against Micah's legs, Rosa's inconsequential weight aggravating the knot which had already formed on his shin. He nudged them gently inside, two tiny hands tightening their grip on his.

"I hope those cookies are for us," he said brightly, nodding toward the kitchen table, where a heaping plate of cookies and sliced apples sat next to a pitcher of milk. "That ride made us pretty hungry." Bending over, he helped the two off with their threadbare coats.

Eliza smiled and hung the wraps on the wall pegs. "They sure are. Auntie Phoebe and I baked them while we were waiting for you."

The young faces brightened a measure.

As if suddenly hearing her name, the older woman entered the kitchen, beaming from ear to ear. "Well, well, well. I see our visitors have arrived."

"This is my aunt, children," Eliza said. "You may call her Auntie Phoebe or Mrs. Harper, whichever you wish."

But four yearning brown eyes were already devouring the treats in view.

"I'd say there are some hungry tummies around here," Micah piped in. "Come to the table, girls." He ushered them across the room, helping them onto chairs. Taking a seat next to Gabriella, while Eliza chose the one by Rosa, he bowed his head. "We thank You, dear Lord, for Miss Eliza and Aunt Phoebe's kindness in providing some good food and a nice place for Gabriella and Rosa to stay. Please bless them all. In Jesus' name, amen."

The children crossed themselves and centered their attention on the fruit and cookies, while Mrs. Harper brought glasses to the table and filled them with milk.

Picking up the plate, Eliza removed a cookie and slice of apple for herself, then offered some to Rosa.

When the youngster shyly met her gaze and warm smile, she hesitantly took one of each, immediately biting a chunk of apple, and Eliza passed the dish to Gabriella.

"I'm going to have two of each," came Micah's loud whisper and conspiratorial wink from her other side. "You may, too, if you like."

"Graci." She sighed and helped herself, but snatched another cookie and apple slice for her sister before relinquishing the plate.

"Did you see any pretty sights on the drive?" Eliza asked between bites. "There are so many lovely decorations up for Christmas."

Munching her cookie, Gabriella shook her head.

"Well, I sure did," Micah said pleasantly. "But I think what the girls would really like to see is the nice bed where they'll be sleeping later this evening."

"D–dis'a where you live'a too?" Gabriella asked him, her voice wavering.

"No, but I come by quite often to see my friends, so I'll be checking in on you and Rosa a lot."

That seemed to pacify her for the moment.

Micah took that as an encouraging sign. At least there wouldn't be another dreadful scene at bedtime — hopefully. He glanced at Eliza, awed by the love in those blue eyes as she gazed at the girls the Lord had sent her. *Too bad Anabelle could never find it within herself to be that way,* he thought with a bittersweet pang. But that was something he might as well accept.

Eliza looked up at him just then, nibbling her lower lip the way she did whenever she felt a little nervous. He grinned at her. The Lord knew what He was doing when He'd put thoughts of this undertaking into that pretty head. Micah had no doubt about that. And he knew somehow that it wouldn't take Gabriella and Rosa long to settle in.

Too bad it couldn't be forever.

CHAPTER 18

Eliza was extremely grateful that Micah hung around for a while, chatting casually with her and Aunt Phoebe, including the children now and then in the conversation. Soon enough, the older woman heard a summons to go attend the shop. And by the time the rest had finished the refreshments, Gabriella seemed a little more at ease, if not thrilled about her fate. Rosa had yet to utter a word, but stared intently at Eliza with childlike candor. Eliza wondered if the sprite even knew how to talk.

As she watched the somber expressions on the youngsters gradually softening, she ventured a suggestion. "Would you like to go upstairs and see your room?"

The older one slid a furtive glance toward Micah, as if looking for his approval . . . or perhaps wondering if this was when he, too, would go away, leaving her and her sister with these near strangers.

"I say," he answered, ruffling her dull, stringy curls, "that's a wonderful idea." Getting up, he swung Rosa up to perch on his shoulder and took Gabriella by the hand. "After you, Miss Eliza."

The children's looks of wonder at the rooms they passed on the way to the stairs were not lost on Eliza. She crossed her fingers as the small troupe marched up the steps and approached the guest room.

"Well, here we are, angels," Micah said, setting Rosa down and giving her a gentle nudge through the doorway.

"Iss everybody sleepa here?" Gabriella asked, rolling *r's* in her musical accent. She moved to touch the fluffy counterpane.

"Only you and Rosa," Eliza told her. "This is your bed. My room is just across the hall. I'll show it to you after a while."

"Da door," she said fearfully, "she will be closed?"

"No, sweetheart. We will leave it open, if that's what you'd rather."

During the exchange, her younger sister stuck to Micah like glue, until she spied two rag dolls occupying the rocking chair against the opposite wall. She swung her gaze up at the adults, then hesitantly inched toward the toys, as if expecting to be reprimanded at any moment.

Gabriella obviously knew better than to touch something so pretty. She just held her breath.

Eliza patted her shoulder. "Go right ahead, sweetheart. There's a dolly for each of you."

"For your very own," Micah added emphatically. "To keep."

The beginnings of a real smile tipped up the corners of her lips as she bolted toward the rocker and snatched up the one that wasn't presently being crushed in her sibling's arms. Both children sank to the floor cross-legged and cuddled their new treasures, Gabriella's eyes aglow as she chattered unreservedly to her baby in her mother tongue.

Watching their sweet exuberance, Eliza grew misty-eyed, wishing Rosa, too, would open up. She felt Micah's strong hand clamp onto her shoulder and give a light squeeze.

"So far, so good," he said for her ears alone.

She only nodded.

Micah filled his lungs and strode slowly over to join the girls. Squatting down between them, he drew them into a hug. "I would say these dollies are very happy to have two new friends to look after them and love them. Just like Miss Eliza and Auntie Phoebe want to love you and care for you."

The little ones gazed trustingly up at him.

"But, I'm afraid it's time for me to be going."

Gabriella's eyes welled. She swallowed in alarm. "You com'a back? See us?"

"I sure will, sweetheart. Bright and early tomorrow morning. We can eat breakfast together. Would you like that?"

"You take us backa home, den?"

He flicked an eloquent glance to Eliza, then looked again into the questioning brown eyes. "Sorry, pumpkin. You know Mrs. Garibaldi isn't able to take care of you anymore. So Miss Eliza is gonna do that for a while. But it'll be all right; you'll see."

She thought for a second, then gave him a brave nod.

"Meanwhile, you just stay right here as long as you like and have a grand time playing with your dolls."

"And I must go see if my aunt needs help with supper," Eliza added. "I'll come to get you when it's ready."

The little ones exchanged wary glances, but their grudging assent followed fairly quickly.

Eliza and Micah withdrew from the room and started downstairs again.

"Oh, I do hope they get by all right. There's a long night ahead," she said quietly, not wanting her uncertainties to spill over and affect the little ones.

Stopping as they reached the landing, Micah smiled gently. "They've had a pretty tough day. They should be tired early. You'll do fine, believe me. Children can sense a welcoming spirit. In no time at all, you'll have them both wrapped around your little finger."

"Do you really think so?"

"I know it for a fact. Besides, remember all the prayer that's gone into this venture. The Lord is even more concerned about those two tiny fallen sparrows than we are."

"I suppose. Ana was right; you do say the nicest things." But watching his eyes cloud over momentarily, she regretted mentioning her friend's name.

Emitting a weary breath, he finally gave her a half-smile, shrugging one shoulder as he did. "Well, it appears I'll see you tomorrow."

"Bright and early, wasn't it?" she added teasingly. "How do you like your eggs?"

"Hot."

She rather liked the mischievous sparkle in his eyes, but was sure the static current she felt so often in his presence was a product of her vivid imagination. "Thank you, Micah . . . for everything." With a last glance upstairs, she followed him to the kitchen and watched as he put on his coat and left. Then she let out the breath she'd been holding and went to start some water heating, hoping to persuade the girls to bathe before supper.

When she approached them and mentioned the idea, however, the mere suggestion made the pair skulk against one another and peer at her in disgust as they hugged their dolls tighter.

"We don'a wanna to," Gabriella said, her bottom lip making an appearance as she stubbornly hiked her chin.

"Oh," Eliza hedged, "what a shame. I was hoping you'd want to wear the pretty new nightgowns I bought you." She crossed nonchalantly to the wardrobe and pulled out the soft, long flannel shifts trimmed with ribbon and lace, holding them aloft as she pretended to admire them. "But I know you wouldn't want to spoil them by putting them on over your dirty hair. If you'd rather stay in your present things, that's fine." With an elaborate sigh, she folded the new purchases once more and started to put them back into the drawer.

Gabriella's inner war was almost palpable.

Her dark eyes made a once-over circuit of the soiled and patched dresses she and her little sister wore, both obvious hand-me-downs. She drew her lips inward and bit down on them in thought. A small grimace of defeat followed. "We go, eh?" she told her sister. "Take'a da batt." And dutifully, the pair hopped up, trailing behind Eliza as she led them to the bathroom.

From the way they stared at the water closet in passing, it was easy to tell they'd never seen that particular sort of porcelain wonder before, but they quickly became enthralled by Eliza's explanation of its function. And though wary, they even took cautious advantage of the thing. Anything to get the bath siege over and done with as quickly as possible.

Eliza tried not to show her alarm at the sight of their bony ribs and frail frames as she helped them climb into the clawfooted tub of warm water, but she soon had them washed. "My, you both have such curly hair," she said, soaping Gabriella's first. "So nice and thick, too. It'll be really pretty with the ribbons I bought to match your nightgowns."

"Dat'sa nice. We don' haffa da ribbons," the child admitted.

"Well, you do now. They'll look so lovely

against your shiny dark curls." Shielding the little girl's eyes with a folded washcloth, she dumped a pitcher of rinse water over her head to wash out the suds.

Gabriella sputtered and wrinkled her nose, but then giggled, which made tackling the same chore with Rosa a mite easier.

To Aunt Phoebe's amazement, two shiny, fragrant little girls appeared at the supper table that night, beribboned, abundant curls spilling over the shoulders of their pristine night shifts, feet clad in soft house slippers. Shy smiles were coming with more frequency. And not long into the meal, so did the yawns.

Seeing that their meager appetites had been sated, Eliza ushered her charges back upstairs, visiting the water closet en route to their bed. "It's been ages since I've had a chance to read a bedtime story to anybody," Eliza commented, turning down the quilts so they could climb in. "I think we'll have one every night you're here."

But before she even reached the midpoint in the account of Noah and the flood, both urchins nodded off. Gazing down at their sweet faces, so innocent in sleep, Eliza's heart crimped. She'd wanted them to hear it all, wanted them to say their prayers afterward, wished they could be part of a whole, happy family again. But all she could do was make it part of her own daily petitions. Putting out the lamp, she paused in the doorway just to look at them for a moment, then went downstairs.

Micah didn't know what to expect when he arrived at Harper House first thing in the morning. The whole place a wreck? Eliza and Mrs. Harper still in their nightclothes, frazzled and in shock, with dark circles under their eyes? A repeat of yesterday's wailing and flailing? Filling his lungs, he rapped on the back door.

"Oh, good morning," Eliza said brightly, admitting him into a kitchen whose enticing smells related the presence of bacon and toasting bread. He heard eggs sizzling in the pan Mrs. Harper was attending on the coal stove and returned the grin she tossed him over her shoulder.

"So, I see you two survived the night," he said casually, hanging his coat.

Eliza's light laughter floated toward him as she set the table for five.

He had to ask. "You had no difficulties whatsoever?"

"Oh, a little crying in the middle of the night, by Rosa," she admitted. "But I went into the room and rocked her for a while, and she settled back down again. By the way, have you ever heard her talk?" She gestured for him to be seated.

He crossed to the table and tugged out the end chair, lowering himself to it as he shook his head. "I believe she was getting to be quite the little chatterbox until her mama passed away. As far as I know, she hasn't spoken a word since, unless it's been to Gabriella out of anyone else's hearing."

"I wondered."

"Are the girls awake?"

"Those two early birds?" Mrs. Harper chimed in. "They've been skipping up and down the stairs since dawn, the new dollies under their arms. They traipse through here every now and then."

"But they've managed to keep out of mischief?"

Eliza set a cup and saucer before him, then put others out for her and her aunt. "It was part of yesterday's Grand Tour, after you left. I showed them through the whole house, but advised them not to set foot in the gift shop or bother any of Auntie's pretties. And they didn't seem to mind. They had dolls and picture books. They play rather happily in their own room most of the time."

"Well, well. That's good to hear." He took

a minute to digest that information while Eliza poured fresh coffee into his cup and passed him the sugar and creamer.

"I believe everything's ready," Aunt Phoebe announced. "Ring the bell, dear." At Micah's surprised expression, she smiled. "Much more pleasant than for us to holler the length of this big house, don't you think?"

No sooner did the tinkly sound fade, then the young charmers came running down the stairs and into the room.

"And who have we here?" he asked in surprise, taking in the brushed and gleaming hair, the dropped-waist dresses with sailor collars and broad sashes. White stockings covered their slim legs, ending in soft-soled house slippers.

Gabriella's eyes flared in delight, and she ran to hug him, little Rosa a mere step or two behind. "We haffa da new dress. Ribbons." Proudly she spun to display the maroon hair ornament that matched her burgundy dress, and her sister mimicked the action in her medium blue ensemble.

"And you look just beautiful." Acknowledging the contrast between the sorry condition they'd been in when he'd first brought them and the spotless, stylish — and smiling — young lasses he saw before

him, Micah had only the deepest appreciation for Eliza's rapport with the little ones.
Especially when Rosa gravitated to her for
help onto a kitchen chair whose low seat
had been boosted by the addition of pillows. What a change a loving home made.
For certainly this was no less than that.

Since Eliza was otherwise occupied at the
moment, he allowed his gaze to linger. Her
long hair, instead of being in its loosely
woven hair net, was tied at the nape of her
slender neck with a velvet ribbon . . . a
change he more than liked. Summery blue
eyes met his just then, and she smiled. And
he had to remind himself to breathe.

"Well, what do you think?" Eliza asked as
the youngsters scampered off to play after
the meal, leaving the adults to enjoy second
cups of coffee at their leisure.

"The word 'speechless' comes to mind,"
Micah said truthfully. "There's still a trace
of the old sadness in their eyes, but it's
wonderful to see them smiling again."

"Well, they're such dears," Aunt Phoebe
gushed. "When I think of how fearful I was
that children would cause nothing but
confusion and destruction, I see how foolish an old lady can be. This little pair seems
to delight in fairly quiet play. And they're

ever so obedient. I must credit their parents for that."

Micah nodded. "That was one thing I observed in my work in the tenements, actually. Even the youngsters living under such deprivation and woeful conditions are for the most part respectful toward adults and cheerful despite life's injustices."

"Yes," Eliza added. "I recall your telling me that many of the families in the tenements were quite well-off in the old country, with respected livelihoods."

"And they often manage to work their way back up to their old standard," he went on, "though it takes a fair amount of time and effort on their part."

"In any event, I truly enjoy looking after these darlings," Eliza said wistfully, "though I'm aware of the great responsibility I've taken on. I know I must endeavor not to allow the girls to become too attached to us, for their own good."

"But while they're here," Aunt Phoebe responded with a grin, "it's a delight to lavish just a bit of attention on them. They've been through so much. Christmas is just around the corner, and I can't help wanting to make it truly nice for them. It may be the first special one they've ever known."

Even as the older woman spoke, Eliza

could hear a statement Micah had made not so long ago. *"And then what?"* Three simple words, yet she couldn't help wondering what the Lord had in store for Gabriella and Rosa Riccio when the joy of Christmastime was past, and they had to settle for real life again, in whatever home or orphanage Micah could find for them.

CHAPTER 19

Eliza closed the Bible in her lap and met the little ones' fascinated gazes. "So you see, not only did the Lord take care of all of Joseph's problems in a wonderful way, as we read in last night's story, but He did the same for Ruth. She was no longer poor and lonely. Her faith in the God of her mother-in-law, Naomi, took her to a whole new land, and there God brought another man into her life. One who would love her and become her husband."

"It'sa hard not to feel'a sad when Mama and Papa go to da angels," Gabriella said, her eyes downcast.

"I know, sweetheart. Some things are very difficult for us to understand, especially when loved ones die, as your mama and papa did."

The small curly head nodded.

Sitting on the edge of the children's bed, Eliza leaned over and hugged them both.

"It hurts terribly to be left behind. That happened to me when the man who once promised to marry me just went away. I cried a lot, because I knew he didn't really love me after all. But when bad things happen to us, it doesn't ever mean God doesn't love us. He watches over everyone. He even sees when a little bird gets hurt and falls out of the sky. It makes Him sad when we are sad, and He wants to help us and make things better. Even when it feels like things hurt too much, we must learn to trust Him and wait for things to work out again."

"You mean, like'a for Rosa and'a me, God will bring to us da new mama and papa?" Her face scrunched up in question.

"What I'm saying," Eliza explained patiently, "is that God always does what's best for us, when the time is just right."

She turned her face up to Eliza's. "I hope He not'a work too fast, for da new mama. I like'a be wit you. Here. Dis house."

Her younger sister nodded in agreement.

Eliza felt a stinging behind her eyes, and it took a few seconds before she could speak past the huge lump in her throat. "I hope so too, kitten. I love you and Rosa very, very much. But if Mr. Micah finds someone who wants two sweet little girls to be part of their family, we'll all have to remember to trust

God. And try to be happy. Even if it's hard at first."

Seeing that her answer seemed to satisfy them, she gathered the girls into her arms and kissed their noses. "But right now I think it's time to say your prayers and go to sleep." Flipping the covers out of the way, she knelt beside the bed, and the two little ones joined her, one on either side, their hands steepled in prayer.

Wide awake as he lay in bed after yet another visit to Harper House, Micah's thoughts still remained there. He'd been stopping by every day since the Italian orphans had taken up temporary residence, and the improvement in their physical appearance was nothing in comparison to the changes in their outlook. He knew Eliza was doing her best to prepare the girls for yet another transition, hoping the next change would go more smoothly. And obviously it was working.

He could also see she was becoming more and more attached to the pair herself. Not uncommon for someone who looked after youngsters who'd been hurt by life's harsh realities. Who didn't wish for the ability to build a place big enough to take in all unwanted and destitute little ones and make everything right for them again?

Anabelle.

He exhaled a painful breath. For all her wonderful qualities, Ana hadn't found that desire, that compassion, within herself. Not that she'd ever kept it a secret. But somehow, that old disappointment didn't matter quite so much as it once had. Micah knew he would always carry a certain kind of love in his heart for his lifelong friend. But he knew she'd done the right thing, the valiant thing, in going away. That's what it had taken for him to see they'd never really been meant for each other. That, and some sleepless, prayer-filled nights. Slowly he'd reached the point of acceptance, the peace that comes from submitting to God's will.

He was still a bit numb inside, aware of an emptiness that would take awhile to fill completely, but he had the calm assurance that the Lord was in control and that "all things work together for good," just as the Bible promised in Romans 8:28.

Latching onto that precious hope, he turned over and closed his eyes, his thoughts drifting pleasantly to a slender, blue eyed angel who had two sweet little girls under her wings.

Christmas Eve arrived on Saturday, and

with it, Micah and his buggy, to pick everyone up for the traditional candlelight service at Faith Community Church. Eliza tried not to notice how his brown checked coat deepened the shade of his eyes, to say nothing of the blatant admiration in them when his gaze meandered to her and stayed for a timeless moment.

"Don't the girls look lovely?" she asked, averting her eyes before she blushed like a silly schoolgirl. She knelt to fasten Rosa's plush velvet cloak, then held the matching muff for the child to slide her hands into while her aunt saw to Gabriella's wrap and warm boots.

Removing his bowler, Micah tipped his head in a gallant gesture which included even Eliza's aunt. "I'll say this. I've never in my life seen a more beautiful group of young ladies all in one place. I'll be the envy of every man at church."

"Oh, pshaw! Everybody puts on their very best for the holiday services." With a cluck of her tongue, Aunt Phoebe took the six-year-old's hand and brushed past him on their way to the door. But not without giving a more-than-pleased grin.

Eliza couldn't help smiling herself.

"Well, that leaves the two of you for me to escort." Micah swept the little one up into the crook of an arm and offered his other elbow to Eliza. "May I?"

"We'd be most honored, sir." Though spoken in a teasing tone, she was all too aware that her insides were quivering like jelly as she took his arm. She hoped it wasn't obvious, but how could anyone notice anything other than the children's glowing eyes anyway? It had been difficult to keep them calm in the face of a special evening, only a prelude to the most wonderful day of the year.

Several inches of new snow had fallen during the afternoon, giving the girls a chance to bundle up and have a romp in the front yard. Now the runners of the sleigh swished over the packed ground cover, and bells on the harness jingled as the horse plodded toward the church, adding an even more festive air.

Once inside the brick building, the sudden warmth from the furnace, along with a multitude of flickering candles lining the front and sides of the sanctuary, stung their cheeks. Micah led the way to an empty pew, nodding in greeting to familiar folks along the way. He stepped aside for Aunt Phoebe, and Gabriella and Eliza filed in behind her. Setting Rosa next to Eliza, he took the aisle seat.

Quiet music from the organ already lent reverence to the occasion, and Eliza fought a twinge of sadness that Anabelle was not at the keys. Though capable enough, the pleasant-faced woman of middle years who had taken her place lacked Ana's natural flair and smooth touch. If Micah shared those sentiments, he did not let on, but Eliza noticed that he avoided looking directly at the big instrument.

She loosened the girls' cloaks, and the two settled back, hands folded in their laps, their attention centered on the large evergreen Christmas tree off to the side, decorated with shining ornaments and candles. It towered over a rough-hewn nativity scene, yet somehow didn't detract from it.

"Da baby Jesus," Gabriella whispered, pointing out the manger to Rosa, and her sibling craned her neck to see. It was the first time there had been extra objects displayed in the house of worship in the few times Eliza had brought them, and it made them both smile. Often, however, they'd stared in wonder at the empty wooden cross on the wall behind the pulpit.

Though the services contained far less ritual than the little pair were used to, they enjoyed the singing and would sit quietly to the end. Eliza knew they'd particularly like this special one, being mostly made up of carols and the reading of the Christmas story from the Gospel of Luke. It was her own favorite service of the year. This time it seemed all the more touching — whether it was merely having children around for the holidays or having Micah's strong baritone blending with her clear alto, she wasn't about to analyze.

When the program reached the conclusion, the little party bid the pastor and other church members good night, then headed for home.

"It'sa true? What da man say about da baby Jesus?" Gabriella asked along the way.

"Do you mean that He wasn't always a baby, but that He left heaven to become one just so He could die on the cross for us?" Eliza prompted.

She nodded.

"Yes, sweetheart. God loved us so very much that He sent His only Son to be a sacrifice for our sins. If we know Jesus as our Savior, we know we will go to be with Him when we die."

The tiny frown eased. "I like'a dat. It'sa nice."

Eliza put an arm about Gabriella's small form and hugged her. "Yes. It's very nice."

After reaching home and enjoying some

hot chocolate, the girls were tucked in for the night. The busy day had taken its toll. Smiling at the mention of surprises they'd find in the morning, they barely made it through the bedtime story before dropping off to sleep.

Eliza hurried downstairs where she found Micah and her aunt already well into trimming the tree he'd hidden behind the shed earlier that day and brought into the sitting room when she'd gone up with the little ones. The mere thought of the joy it would bring her charges elevated her own anticipation. "That looks ever so lovely," she breathed, assessing their work.

"And won't the little ones love it?" Aunt Phoebe asked, stepping back for an overall view. "Why don't you help Micah finish, while I start gathering the presents to go underneath?"

"*Start* gathering?" Micah echoed good-naturedly. "I hope you two aren't planning on spoiling a certain pair of orphans we all know and love."

"Wel–l–l," the older woman fudged, "they did need so much, you know. But we tried to bear the practical in mind."

"That's good to hear. We wouldn't want to make every Christmas from here on a letdown for them. Their new family might not be so well-off."

Eliza smothered a jolt of alarm. "Does that mean you've found someone willing to take them?" She nearly added "already," but caught herself in time.

As if he sensed her disquiet, he smiled gently and handed her a section of garland to drape around her side of the tree, then moved where he could take it again and continue on his end. "Nothing definite yet. As we all know, there's no shortage of homeless youngsters right now."

It wasn't much as far as reprieves went, but Eliza absorbed what little comfort she could from hearing she wouldn't have to bid Gabriella and Rosa good-bye just yet. Their presence had added so much to this big old house, and she truly hoped they could stay awhile longer. Even Aunt Phoebe appeared years younger and seemed far more energetic and cheerful than she'd been in ages. And with business certain to drop way down after Christmas, the dear woman would have time to spend reading to the girls and making them new treats or clothes.

"Wouldn't you agree?" Micah's voice penetrated her daydreams, and he handed her a brightly painted ornament to hang.

"Hm?" Not quite in her grasp, the shiny teardrop orb slipped to the floor, smashing into a million pieces. "Oh! How clumsy of me." She quickly sank down to gather the remains.

Micah knelt to help. "Tsk, tsk, tsk. Not paying attention, eh? Now you'll be in for it. This was probably a priceless family treasure, too, and now we'll have to mortgage our very souls to replace the thing."

The ridiculous taunt made her laugh. She'd never glimpsed such an embracing light in his eyes, and for a moment she lost herself in it, feeling suddenly warm and giddy and —

Something sharp cut into her palm. With a gasp she snatched her hand from where she'd inadvertently leaned on a fragment of the broken ball.

"Here, let me see," he said at once, taking her hand into his much larger ones. He unraveled the clenched fingers and carefully picked out the tiny shard of colored glass, then used his handkerchief to blot away the few drops of blood that had gathered.

By now more overcome by his tender ministrations than she was by the sting, Eliza watched him with fascination, noticing the play of firelight from the hearth over the lighter strands of his hair, the golden glow it cast upon the planes of his face. Sensations she'd thought had died with the betrayal of her dearest dreams now fluttered through her being, doing indescribable things to her insides.

"I think the patient will live," Micah murmured. Dipping his head as if for one more look, he pressed a light kiss into her palm, then closed her fingers over it. He met her gaze with a heart-stopping smile.

Something she could not name passed between them in that breathless instant, and for a few seconds she forgot how to breathe. "Th–thank you," was as much of a response as she could generate.

"All part of the service," came his own husky reply.

The soft tapping of Aunt Phoebe's shoes broke the spell as the older woman entered the room and set down an armful of colorfully wrapped gifts. "Oh, what's happened?"

"Nothing much," Eliza blurted a bit too quickly as she struggled to her feet, her face ablaze. "I . . . um . . . broke an ornament. I'm sorry."

Barely giving the shiny remnants more than a cursory glance, she peered from Eliza to Micah with a peculiar smile. "Not to worry. I've always had far too many of those baubles anyway. Well, keep up the good work." And with that, she turned back down the hall.

"I . . . think we're about finished. Don't you?" Eliza said brightly, purposely avoiding looking at Micah again as he put the star atop the tree.

He chuckled. "Yes . . . and no. But I do have to be going. It's getting late, and I must allow you to get whatever sleep you can before our little angels awaken in their roost."

Our. Eliza rather liked the sound of that. A lot. A whole lot. She swallowed. "W–will you come to breakfast?"

"Wouldn't miss it."

"Come as early as you like. We'll let the girls open a present or two beforehand and save the others until after. They'll probably want to wear something new to church."

He nodded. "Sounds good. See you in the morning then. Sleep well, Eliza. I'll find my own way out."

"Well, thanks again . . . for the help, and all."

A soft squeeze to her shoulder, and he strode for the kitchen. A minute more and the back door closed behind him.

Eliza sank to the nearest chair. She could hardly wait for the children to wake up tomorrow.

She could hardly wait for tomorrow — period.

CHAPTER 20

Somehow, Eliza managed to arise before the children awoke. She told herself it was because she didn't want to miss a second of their wonder upon seeing the sitting room decked out in all its Christmas glory, or the beautiful tree with the pretty packages awaiting them beneath it. Yet all the while, she knew it was more than that.

The memory of last night washed over her, bringing alive Micah's gentleness when he'd tended her cut, the quick wit he was beginning to display with amazing frequency. But surely some of the sensations she'd felt in his presence had to have been the product of her lively imagination. When he arrived shortly she would be much more in control, better able to conduct herself with propriety. Regardless, she was determined to look her very best. For the girls, she avowed.

Not long after she finished her toilette and

donned the emerald taffeta gown she'd saved especially for the holiday, she heard whispers and giggles drifting from the room across the hall. Eliza smiled to herself and tiptoed to their doorway. "Good morning, dearies. Merry Christmas."

Four tiny arms hugged her breath away as she bent to embrace them.

"Is'a time to get up'a now?" Gabriella asked in a small voice.

"It is time. Put on your slippers and let's go downstairs. I think I even smell breakfast — and here I thought we were the first ones awake. Isn't that silly?"

The girls giggled. Hopping out of bed, they did as told, then latched onto Eliza's hands.

The fragrant scent of the pine boughs which had been hung here and there about the first floor grew stronger as she and the girls descended the stairs. Partway down, Gabriella glimpsed the tree and some of the other decorations adorning the sitting room. She caught her breath. Wide-eyed, she tugged her fingers free and scampered the rest of the way, pausing just inside the doorway to stare.

Eliza and Rosa joined her within seconds, and the little ones beamed with delight when Micah and Aunt Phoebe also came from the kitchen. Eliza lowered her lashes.

"Is'a so . . . so . . ." Unable even to express herself in English, Gabriella grabbed Eliza and started pulling her closer to the lovely tree.

"Yes, it's ever so pretty," Eliza finished for her, warming under Micah's gaze. "And some of these nice presents are for you and Rosa."

Her chocolate-brown eyes widened. She stole a peek at her sister, and the two of them squealed.

"You may open one or two now, and after breakfast we'll all come back in here for the rest."

No other invitation was needed, as instantly the little ones chose tempting-looking packages and began tearing into them, Gabriella discovering a warm sweater and a coloring book with colored pencils; Rosa finding a new dress and a ball.

The length of time it took for them to put down the first items and take up the second touched Eliza deeply. For children who'd had so little, everything was appreciated.

A pancake breakfast followed, with the girls almost too animated to eat. But the adults prevailed upon them to finish their portions.

Returning to the sitting room afterward, a

pair of dainty little basket cradles Aunt Phoebe had fixed up for the girls' dollies were a great hit, as were new gloves and church dresses. They touched their new bounty with reverent fingers and hugged each one in turn. And Gabriella planted a huge kiss on Micah's cheek in thanks for the new picture books he'd brought.

"Oh, you're not quite finished yet," Eliza said, kneeling to reach below the bottommost branches of the tree for two more boxes. She held them out, and the girls happily came to get them.

Ripping into hers, Gabriella removed the lid and peered inside. "Ohhh." Her mouth dropped open as she pulled out some new, laced, high-top shoes for everyday and a pair with dainty buckles for Sundays. Then she caught her lower lip in her teeth and burst into tears.

Eliza flew to her side and stooped beside her. "But what is wrong, sweetheart? Don't you like them?"

At this, the little girl wailed even louder, throwing her arms around Eliza as she collapsed in wrenching sobs.

Eliza didn't know what to think and looked at Aunt Phoebe and Micah for answers, but they appeared as flabbergasted as she. There was nothing to do but wait it out. And when the weeping evolved into watery smiles, everyone was thoroughly confused.

"I . . . I . . . graci," Gabriella choked out at last as she eased from Eliza's embrace. "Da shoes, dey'sa new. Always'a we get old'a shoes, Rosa, me. Too big. Too small. First time'a new. Graci. Graci." And she crossed to hug Aunt Phoebe — the older woman unabashedly wiping her own cheeks — and Micah, who couldn't even speak.

Eliza, too, had been reduced to tears, but the short span provided a chance to dig out her handkerchief and recover a bit. And the sight of Rosa hobbling around in one of each of her new footwear provided some comic relief.

"Well," her aunt said at length, patting Micah's knee and smiling at Eliza. "I don't know about you two, but I almost don't care what we'll find in our packages."

"I couldn't have said it better myself," he replied. "Why don't we wait till later? I'd just as soon drink in the wonder of those young faces for a while." He averted his gaze to the children playing with their new toys.

"I'll go put on a fresh pot of coffee," the old woman offered. "It'll soon be time for church."

■ ■ ■ ■

The afternoon passed fairly quickly, and by the time it ended, all the grown-ups had entered into playacting with Gabriella and Rosa at one time or another. Aunt Phoebe pretended to be the dollies' grandmother and helped change and dress the babies; Micah read over and over to them from the books he'd brought, plus sat on the floor, too, with Rosa to roll her new ball back and forth; and Eliza rediscovered her love of coloring.

Finally, after partaking of a veritable feast the two women had prepared, the children actually asked if they could go to bed. "Go on," Aunt Phoebe told Eliza. "I'll clean up here." And a noticeable quiet settled over Harper House, one so still that Eliza's light steps could be heard on her return downstairs.

"My. What a day." She sank wearily into an overstuffed chair in the sitting room, where Micah was stoking up the fire in the hearth after adding some new logs.

He grinned over his shoulder. "I'll say. Longer than usual, too. I feel like I've been up forever."

"I think we all have. Thank you for coming to help make Christmas special for Gabriella and Rosa. And for the lovely necklace watch. It's simply exquisite."

"I hoped you'd like it. And I'll enjoy the devotional book and the new gloves from you. Thanks." Finished with his task, he brushed off his hands and took a chair across from Eliza.

"And wasn't my aunt's gift rather sweet? Imagine, that carved chest — which she alleges is only my first Epiphany gift."

"Yes, she's been in her element, coming up with surprises for the lot of us. She's recovered amazingly well from that last spell since the little ones have been here."

Eliza smiled. "She's doted on them every spare minute, and they get along wonderfully with Aunt Phoebe."

"Did I hear my name?" the silver-haired woman asked, drying her hands on a kitchen towel as she came into the room.

"Oh, we were just mentioning how well you've managed to cope with the girls' presence."

"Hmph. I daresay, I've done more than cope. It's been a downright pleasure to do for those two. They've got a lot of love to give. It's a crying shame they were left with nobody to give it to."

"Oh, now," Micah cajoled. "Looks to me

like they're not having any trouble at all passing their love around. In many ways, their sad loss has turned out to be a blessing."

"For us, perhaps. And I'm not at all in a hurry for you to plunk them in with another bunch of strangers, so you just take your time doing that, if you can." She gave a tired sigh. "Anyway, I was just finishing up in the kitchen and thought I'd see if there's anything you two wanted before I turn in. I've about walked these old feet off and need to put them up."

Eliza rose and went to hug her. "No, Auntie, you've done quite enough. If there's anything we want, I'm perfectly capable of seeing to it. You just have a good rest. Tomorrow's another day."

"Yes, dear lady," Micah added. "You've worked much harder than any of us deserved. Thank you for the hospitality — and the leather case for my papers. I'll put that to good use, believe me."

She looked from one of them to the other and smiled. "Well, good night, then. And merry Christmas."

Within seconds of the almost-inaudible click of her aunt's bedroom door latch, Eliza became aware of a sudden change in the atmosphere. The crackling of the fire was the only sound in the room. In the whole house, for that matter. She ventured a look in Micah's direction.

His gaze was centered on her, his expression unreadable.

She cleared her throat. "Would you care for some tea? Coffee?"

"Not especially, thanks."

Taking another tack to calm her growing nervousness, Eliza settled on a safe subject. "The girls had a truly delightful day today, far beyond what I'd even hoped."

Micah's eyes gentled with his smile. "Yes. Just watching them, witnessing their genuine thankfulness, was quite humbling, I must say. The rest of us, we take a lot for granted. They helped put things back into perspective for me."

"For me as well." She paused. "I . . . I don't know how I'll ever find strength to give them up when the time comes. I didn't mean to become so attached. In fact, I tried very hard not to. But now —"

"I know," he said gently. "I've been watching it happen. But you're only human, Eliza. How could a person open up her home to those less privileged, unless possessing of a heart easily touched by the need? And look at those two, for pity's sake. Those big doe eyes, the trust and vulnerability, the honesty.

It's a combination impossible to resist."

Neither spoke for a short span.

"You look very beautiful today," Micah said at length. "Is that a new gown? I don't believe I've seen it before."

"It's from my trou— I mean, yes. I've been saving it." Fighting a maddening blush, she gave a silent huff at her near blunder. She'd been so stupid — first for imagining she loved Weston and then for comparing him to Micah. Why, just looking at him, anyone could see Micah's face was not so long, his features were much more noble and expressive, his eyes — they were so much more compelling, so . . . *near.*

He had gotten up and now stood before her.

"Come here," he said, holding out his hand to her.

Eliza knew her knees couldn't possibly support her right now. She would collapse at his feet in a heap, and he'd have to pick her up. But as she placed her fingers in his, she felt his strength flow into her being, enabling her to stand.

"We almost missed a very important part of Christmas," he said, those hazel eyes challenging hers unmercifully.

Having no idea what he was talking about, Eliza nevertheless let him draw her toward the hallway.

But rather than leave the sitting room altogether, he stopped at the arch marking the entrance to it and smiled.

"What are you doing?" she asked, thoroughly confused now.

His gaze traveled upward.

Hers followed. And stopped directly above her head.

"Mistletoe!"

"A very important part of Christmas," he said again.

Every fiber of her being turned to liquid, and her heart raced as he turned her to face him.

"I've been waiting all day for this moment," he whispered. He was not teasing now, and his smile faded as his eyes searched hers, waiting for her reaction. Giving her time to pull away, if that's what she wanted.

What she wanted, she realized, was for this moment to be real. More than just a Christmas kiss. But dared she hope for that? Throwing caution to the wind, she leaned toward him ever so slightly, her lips parted.

With a smothered groan, Micah encircled her in his strong arms and lowered his head. His lips met hers in a kiss that was joyous, reverent, passionate, promising. And over too soon.

"Oh Micah," she whispered breathlessly, her cheek pressed to his chest, knowing he must feel her heart thundering against her ribs. As she could feel his.

He cupped the back of her head, rocking her for a moment in his arms. "I think I've known for some time that I was falling in love with you," he admitted. "But I tried to convince myself I was wrong. I don't want to be wrong anymore, Eliza."

She lifted her head and raised her lashes to look into those soulful eyes she loved.

"And I know you've been hurt before," he continued. "So I promise I won't rush you. But I'm asking for permission to court you, if you'll allow me to."

Her heart soared, but she wasn't about to interrupt. Not now. Not for anything.

"I don't have a lot to offer you right now, but I have plans and dreams I've never shared with anyone. Dreams I believe you could be a part of, if you'll only trust me."

Eliza felt a smile moving across her lips.

"Will you please say something?" he finally pleaded.

"For your information, Micah Richmond, I have quite a lot to say. That was quite a speech."

"It wasn't just a speech. I meant every word."

She placed a palm along his face, loving his warmth, loving the feel of him, almost beyond herself at God's goodness. She had gotten up this morning hoping the day would be one Gabriella and Rosa would always remember, never once entertaining the hope that it would be special for her, too. But Micah had made it so. Micah and Aunt Phoebe, and the girls, all together. And then came the heartfelt touches brought by little shoes and mistletoe. Her being could scarcely contain her happiness.

"I know you meant it, Micah," she said softly. "Your heart told me it was all true."

His face brightened as a hope-filled grin spread from ear to ear.

"So, yes, I will trust you. Because, yes, I love you, too. And it would be my great honor to hear more about all those dreams of yours."

"Well," he began, "my dearest dream has been to have someone I could share them with. So come with me, my love." He led her toward the sitting room once more. "I hardly know where to begin."

With her hand in his, Eliza felt supreme peace at last. A peace that brought with it a gentle conviction that God had already begun to work all things together for good . . . this was His time.

EPILOGUE

"Mama, Mama! Papa, he comes!" Rosa skipped up the steps of the big Richmond house and into the parlor, long curls askew from play, her arms golden brown from the summer sun. "He'sa bring a lady."

Moving to peer outside through the lace window shade, Eliza smiled with recognition and lumbered to the door with as much haste as possible, a hand on her rounded abdomen. She waited on the broad front porch for the buggy to draw to a stop.

Gabriella, who always ran ahead to latch on to the side and ride from the corner, hopped down from the vehicle's step and stood while Micah got out and gave a hand to his stylish blond passenger. A tall man of medium build alighted last and linked a proprietary elbow through the woman's before the small troupe came up the walk.

"Anabelle!" Eliza exclaimed as her friend, ever so fashionable in her leg-of-mutton-

sleeved gray jacket and matching skirt, swept up the steps.

"Eliza dear." She withdrew her arm and came to grab Eliza in a huge hug. "Ned and I are just now returning from our honeymoon in Europe. Micah happened along the quay as we were arranging transport —"

"And insisted they make their first stop here," Micah finished. Beside him, Gabriella smiled, appearing quite the young lady as she gazed from one adult to the other.

"Well, I'm so glad you did." Eliza stepped back to assess Ana's slender form. "You look simply marvelous!"

"And so do you." Anabelle patted Eliza's tummy with a smile and leaned close to whisper in her ear. "I think I might be joining the ranks of motherhood soon myself." But she put a finger to her lips before turning around. "You really must meet my husband. Ned?" She turned adoring eyes on him.

The finely attired young gentleman stepped forward, removing the bowler from his auburn head, silver-gray eyes obviously glowing with pride as they fastened on his wife. His reddish mustache quirked with a smile.

"Ned, love, I'd like you to meet my other dearest friend in the world, Eliza Richmond.

Eliza, my husband, Ned Fairbanks."

"It's an honor," he said pleasantly. "I've heard so much about you."

"Very pleased to meet you," Eliza said, offering a hand which he clasped warmly. "You both must be tired from traveling. I'll put on some tea."

"I'll help, Mama." Gabriella opened the door for them, while Micah took Ned on a tour of the grounds, Rosa tagging along with her papa.

"My," Ana gushed when they reached the kitchen. She took a chair and glanced casually about the tidy workroom, observing Gabriella's quiet movements as the child took cups down from the cupboard. "You've got a ready-made family."

"Yes. We've had our two sweet girls for a couple years now. Actually, they were the first residents in that guest room you helped me fix up at Aunt Phoebe's. Auntie's looking after an infant now, a little boy, while Micah finalizes matters for the family who will adopt him."

"You don't say. How interesting."

Eliza smiled. "But my heart went out to this pair from the start. We couldn't imagine being without them." She brushed one of Gabriella's silken curls behind the girl's shoulder and was rewarded with a tender smile.

"It's wonderful to know this grand old house is back in Micah's hands, too," Anabelle remarked. "So many memories. And now you and he will be making new ones."

Nodding as she poured their tea, Eliza met Ana's green eyes. "Are you as happy as you look, Anabelle?"

"I've never been more so," she answered honestly. "My Ned's a wonderful man, kind, thoughtful, and he is quite gifted musically. We're often invited to churches to perform on the organ and violin." She paused. "And I needn't ask if you and Micah are happy. I can see that for myself. I knew all along you'd be marvelous together."

"All the same, I know it took a lot of love for you to give him up," Eliza said. "I will always be grateful to you for that."

"I won't pretend it was easy, but I've not regretted it. The Lord had someone else in mind for me, my soul mate."

"And have you come back to the city for good now?"

Anabelle shook her head, her straw bonnet moving slightly with her movements. "Only for the next few months. Then Ned will take up a position teaching music at a school in Boston. But we'll be staying at

Mother's until then."

"Oh, well, we can get together for a while, at least."

"Yes. I doubt there's a greater blessing than friendship. I'm truly looking forward to renewing ours again."

"So am I."

The sound of clomping footsteps carried from the back porch.

"And here come those husbands of ours. Gabi, would you mind getting out a few more cups? We want our friends to tell us all about Europe and the wondrous sights they saw while they were there." But Eliza knew the most wonderful sight was the love between friends and family together at last.

ABOUT THE AUTHORS

Tracie Peterson, bestselling, award-winning author of over ninety fiction titles and three non-fiction books, lives and writes in Belgrade, Montana. As a Christian, wife, mother, writer, editor, and speaker (in that order), Tracie finds her slate quite full.

Published in magazines and Sunday school take-home papers, as well as a columnist for a Christian newspaper, Tracie now focuses her attention on novels. After signing her first contract with Barbour Publishing in 1992, her novel, *A Place to Belong,* appeared in 1993 and the rest is history. She has over twenty-six titles with Heartsong Presents' book club (many of which have been repackaged) and stories in six separate anthologies from Barbour. From Bethany House Publishing, Tracie has multiple historical three-book series as well as many stand-alone contemporary women's fiction stories and two non-fiction titles.

Other titles include two historical series co-written with Judith Pella, one historical series co-written with James Scott Bell, and multiple historical series co-written with Judith Miller.

Sally Laity has written both contemporary and historical novels, many of which have appeared on ECPA bestseller lists. She is a Romance Writers of America RITA finalist, a member of American Christian Fiction Writers, and has placed in the Inspirational Readers' Choice contest. Along with numerous romances and novellas for Barbour Publishing, she also coauthored with Dianna Crawford a three-book historical series for Barbour and a six-book series on the Revolutionary War for Tyndale House. She considers it a joy that the Lord can touch hearts through her stories. Her favorite pastimes include oil painting, quilting for her church's Prayer Quilt Ministry, and scrapbooking. She makes her home in beautiful central California with her husband of over fifty years, and loves that their four married children have made her a grandma and a great-grandma.